GW01167800

THE ALL SOULS' WAITING ROOM

By

Paki S. Wright

A Novel

© 2002 by Paki S. Wright. All rights reserved.

No part of this book may be reproduced, stored in a retrieval system, or transmitted by any means, electronic, mechanical, photocopying, recording, or otherwise, without written permission from the author.

ISBN: 0-7596-5618-5

This book is printed on acid free paper.

Cover Design: "What Makes It Go Round?" by Wm. Balfour Ker, Ms. Wright's paternal grandfather." *Life*. Jan. 3, 1907. Chicago, Time Inc. Used by permisson from: General Research Divison, The New York Public Library, Astor, Lenox and Tilden Foundations.

Excerpts from CHILDREN OF THE FUTURE: ON THE PREVENTION OF SEXUAL PATHOLOGY by William Reich, translated by Derek and Inge Jordan. Compilation and English translation © 1983 by Mary Boyd Higgins, Wilhelm Reich Infant Trust
Reprinted by permisson of Farrar, Straus & Giroux, LLC.

1stBooks – rev. 03/01/02

Author's Preface

In the early 1960's, when I was in my late teens, I thought I wanted to die. Although my background was belligerently bohemian, I was as far away from free love as a soul could get. In my youthful experience, real love was simply not to be found, free or otherwise, and so I tried to give up the ghost.

The All Souls' Waiting Room is about the decidedly different childhood that preceded my suicidal longings: I was to be kept free of repressive sexual and societal mores, largely through the child-rearing theories of the brilliant and persecuted psychoanalyst Wilhelm Reich.

In 1985, I visited Vienna, many years and many brands of therapy after my adolescent suicide attempts and while I was struggling to find a way of writing about my childhood. The checkered political history and oddly paradoxical charm of the old city, particularly Freud's flat at 19 Berggasse, made a visceral impression on me. Vienna is to psychoanalysis what Mecca is to Islam; anyone who was anyone in the pioneer days of the field had been there as a pilgrim. Jung had visited, Reich had spent many years as Freud's assistant at the Vienna Psychoanalytic Clinic. Since, almost at birth, I felt I had been laid on the altar of psychiatry—"Here, fix her! *Save* her!" —in Vienna I felt I had found a personal, cosmological home base.

Some time after my return, I had a half-waking dream of a dramatic scene. It seemed inspired, the answer to my creative problem. It was the scene that was the seed for this book:

In a celestial Viennese coffeehouse called Demel's, the shades of Sigmund S. Freud, C. G. Jung, and Wilhelm Reich sit around a round marble table. In front of each of them is a different kind of Sachertorte on a small plate.

The three dead psychoanalysts debate the merits of the Viennese chocolate cake, Demel's version versus the Hotel Sacher's. Jung, wearing a rumpled white linen suit, prefers the cake from Demel's. Freud, on the other hand, in three-piece gray wool, insists that the drier Hotel Sacher's torte is more elegant and besides, it is the original recipe and so by far the best. Reich, wearing a short white lab coat over dungarees and blue chambray work shirt, tells them they're both wrong, neither Demel's nor the Hotel Sacher's can compare to the sublime recipe of his mother's.

Schlomo (Freud's real middle name), Gus, and Willie, as they think of each other, proceed with their celestial taste-test.

Removing an ethereal cigar from his mouth, substituting a forkful of the Sacher's heady confection, Schlomo Freud chews thoughtfully. "Dreamy!" he exclaims. *"Wunderbar!"*

Gus Jung takes a bite of his Sachertorte, the one from Demel's. His small black eyes close briefly in pleasure. "Magic! Alchemy!" he declares.

Impatiently picking up his piece with his hand, Willie Reich takes several big bites at once. "Orgasmic!" he bellows. "And much better for you!"

Chapter One

December, 1962

Johnnine Hapgood came home from the miserable failure of her calculus final, sat down at her Formica-topped desk, and wrote a suicide note. This was after a last, one-for-the-road food binge, followed by self-induced vomiting.

"To Whom It May Concern," she began. She looked down at her little white dog, Moppie, busily playing with her little blue rubber ball. Pouncing, chasing, barking and wagging her tail, Moppie was trying to cheer Johnnine up, but nothing could.

> "I really feel like I've tried, but nothing I do turns out right, I don't seem to have the knack other people do. I think I'm defective, I go around feeling all shot through with arrows on the outside but on the inside I can't feel anything. If there was a place to go for a trade-in, I would. I need a thicker skin, elephant hide maybe. And a stretchier soul, something like Silly Putty. Otherwise the world hurts too much, everything bombs in a big way, I wish I could figure out why, but I guess I'm not smart enough and I just can't take a life of more of the same crapola..."

She crossed out the line 'I guess I'm not smart enough' and then thought of her ignominious incompletion of the calculus final. Which meant the loss of all her plans for the future, all her reasons for living. She put the line back in. Even though it tore at her pride, she refused to lie. Humiliation was familiar and well-deserved. She was a total and complete failure, a female putz.

Re-reading what she'd written, Johnnine thought hers was the worst suicide note she'd ever read. Just like she couldn't think of anything brilliant or redeeming to do with her life, she couldn't think of anything redeeming or brilliant to say. Shit, she thought despairingly, I can't even write a good suicide note. Then, without knowing why, she reached for her old diary, the one from junior high school. She rummaged through it until she found a poem she had written in eighth grade, or what would have been eighth grade except she had skipped it in a "Special Progress" program that smushed junior high school into two years:

> "The Man Who Killed Himself, 1958:
>
> > He's dead, my mother cries, keening.
> > Some boys found him this morning, in a rented car,

> He'd taken cyanide, his face was blue, she sobs.
> I look at her across the two feet of linoleum.
> But there is a yawning chasm, splitting the earth
>   between us as wide as a canyon.
> I suddenly know we always will be
>   a million miles apart.
> My mother's old lover,
> For whom she feels grief.
> The old hot night doctor
> Whose death brings me relief.
> Words of mourning are like dark stones
> Thrown down an empty well."

    Johnnine tore the poem out of the diary, stuck it behind her suicide note, and folded them up together. On the shag rug at her feet, Moppie was making a show of snapping her head back and throwing her rubber ball across the room so she could chase madly after it. Any other time, it would have made Johnnine laugh.

    Johnnine unfolded her note and added a postscript: "Please find Moppie a good home. Her AKC registered name is Flora Dora's Mopsy Topsy but it's not her fault, it was her breeder's idea."

    Johnnine put down extra food and water and some clean newspaper for Moppie to pee on. Johnnine hoped Moppie would whimper at her funeral, the way Lassie always did when anything sad happened. Then she straightened up, still holding a few pages of the *Village Voice*, realizing there might not *be* a funeral. Johnnine knew her mother's feelings about burial; along with a bewilderingly long list of other things, funerals and cemeteries were held in withering contempt. "Waste of space!" Dinah fumed. "The earth should be for the living, not rotting corpses!" Jesus, Johnnine thought, mom might have me cremated before she even told Duncan I was dead.

    She sat down at her desk and added a P. P. S: "Please let my father know, Duncan Cameron Kirk, he lives at 268 West 17th Street, top floor. CHelsea 3-8853."

    Johnnine imagined her father's look when he heard the news, the same blank, vacant, out-to-lunch look he'd worn at her high school graduation. Well, so he was out of it, so what, she thought, he couldn't help it. Nobody could help anything, which was also why she wanted to die. She knew exactly what her mother would do. Dinah would cry at first, then she'd drink, then she'd take some pills.

    Johnnine signed the note Sincerely, Forever, stuck the two pages in an envelope, and propped it up against the mirror over the bureau in her miniscule living room. She had a feeling she was forgetting a few things but when she saw herself in the mirror—round-faced, large-eyed, full-lipped—she got distracted, deciding she needed more Iridescent Ice lipstick. Just because she was killing herself didn't mean she didn't want to look good. She touched up her thick black eyeliner and brushed her long straight honey-blonde hair. Then she sat on the couch, opened the vial of barbiturates she'd swiped from her mother and a bottle of over-the-counter sleeping pills. Pouring them into her lap, she began swallowing handsful at a time, washing them down with a tumbler of the Ballantine's scotch Jerry had left on his last visit. She felt very, very shitty.

Moppie jumped up on the couch and started licking Johnnine's hand. Someone would be sure to want her, Johnnine thought, and then she felt like she was going to throw up. Quickly, she lit a Pall Mall and pulled the smoke inside her, which stopped the gag reflex. Then she felt dizzy, so she stubbed out the cigarette. She lay down full-length on the jade-green couch, the one she had bought from her neighbor Ginnie Lee for twenty bucks and which Ginnie said matched the color of her eyes. She made sure her black corduroy jumper came neatly down to her knees. She looked down at her nylon-encased toes. She sat up to put on her black fake-lizard high heels. Johnnine loved them and wanted to die with them on. She lay back down, crossed her arms over her chest, closed her eyes, and waited.

Her head started to dip and swirl and she hoped it wasn't going to be like a sick-drunk but then the whirling subsided and things started to feel dim, distant, almost peaceful. The unrelenting noise of the city outside began to fade. On the radio next door, Barbra Streisand was singing "Happy Days Are Here Again."

I look okay, she thought, it wouldn't be like finding someone's brains splattered all over the wallpaper. No drippy pools of coagulated blood or repellent bloated faces in her case. Just an artfully composed young woman who looked like an ancient Egyptian princess in her burial tomb, albeit (she loved the word) an Egyptian with blonde hair.

Some time passed, Johnnine was drifting off, when she heard a bell ring, it sounded far away. What was...? The phone, it was the phone! Damn, what if it was Jerry!? She knew she was kidding herself, he hadn't called in weeks.

The phone kept ringing, though it sounded like it was in the closet under a pillow. Johnnine roused herself to get up and answer it, but discovered she could not move a muscle. Exerting all her physical strength and mental will, she still couldn't move. Her body completely ignored her commands, which was scary. She kept struggling. Get up, damn it! This was ridiculous. Then she heard a loud resounding POP!—like the cork exploding out of a champagne bottle. Next thing she knew, she was looking down on herself from the ceiling.

She studied her former physical form with intense curiosity. Somehow, Johnnine wasn't surprised or even grief-stricken at the sight of her empty, motionless body: now this was interesting! She decided she did look like an Egyptian princess, a zaftig blonde Egyptian princess with her faithful little lapdog mourning beside her.

Johnnine heard the phone ringing but it didn't matter anymore. She took a last look around. The cockroaches in the kitchen and Moppie's tongue licking her lifeless hands were the only moving things in the tiny tenement apartment, for which new tenants were probably already lining up.

Her soul drifted out through the closed window, past the rusting metal fire escape, and hung in the air four stories above a busy, early-evening Bleecker Street. Johnnine looked down on the heads of people bustling in and out of the little Italian groceries, on their way home to dinner. The Christmas decorations wrapped around the lightpoles made them look like giant candy-canes stuck in the sidewalk; the rain had turned the oil on the street into puddles of rainbows. Johnnine was intrigued with her new perspective, but something made her feel she had to ascend. She loved New York, especially the Village, but it was time to go. She didn't know where her soul was taking her, but it couldn't be any worse than where she'd been.

Chapter Two

Johnnine's disembodied soul was closely watched as it ascended above the Earth. On a carpet of puffy, pewter-colored clouds, five angelic-looking cherubs jostled each other for a look through the eyepiece of an ornate brass telescope. As Johnnine's unborn confreres, the cherubs were far from pleased to see her soul wafting up towards the All Souls' Waiting Room like a lost balloon. She was sadly mistaken if she thought she could opt out of incarnation at will, just because she was miserably unhappy. The cherubim knew that if it were that easy, even the infinitely vast All Souls' Waiting Room—actually not a single room at all but a place of infinite expanse and titillating variety—would be Standing Room Only.

These particular All Souls' baby beings were dead-ringers for Michelangelo's cherubim. Wanting at some point to reincarnate, though there was definitely no mad rush, they knew that adult humans needed the bait of adorableness before they would put themselves on the hook of parenthood. Thus they were decked out with diamond gossamer wings, ruby-red lips and glowing skin of several beautiful Earthly shades. Strips of silky gauze covered their respective male and female genitalia, lest they offend the puritanical or excite the licentious, which groups made up a large portion of the population on Earth.

They made a pretty sight even as they grew very agitated, flying around first in one direction, then the other. They were quite upset about Johnnine's impending return. Normally they spoke in charming musical notes and phrases, but at this particular moment they tittered and chirruped in marked disharmony. They were in fact so upset they became discordant—until one of them thought to press the All Souls' alarm, on the base of the telescope.

A Klaxon went off. Instantly, an exquisitely adorable seraph appeared. Seraph A. was in charge of youthful attempts to jump off the Infernal Wheel. He had a cap of shining curls, rose-blushed cheeks, and a double set of wings that were his badge of office, which he had earned by having exceptional management abilities. Seraph A. shooed the discordant cherubs away long enough to peer through the marvelously powerful, highly-polished brass telescope sticking up through the celestial cloud.

As he homed in on Johnnine, the cherubs Fa, So, La, Ti, and Do sang the song of her soul. It was a quirky, plaintive tune. Seraph A. listened attentively as he watched Johnnine's free-floating ethereal essence—which was an unhealthy shade of gray and purple, like the color of bruised plums—billowing closer and closer.

There was very little time. Each case was of course different, but in Johnnine's, the seraph knew exactly where to go for help. He sped off to a peculiar part of the infinite All Souls' Waiting Room, one that had been fashioned into an exact replica of the city of Old Vienna.

With his double set of wings flying at double-speed, Seraph A. took a bead on the hard-to-miss black and gold pitched roof of the Stephansdom before veering off towards the highly ornate, marble and granite rock pile of the Hofburg Palace, with its higgly-piggly collection of Gothic, baroque, and Renaissance architectural styles.

Or rather, what *looked like* the ornate marble and granite Hofburg Palace with its higgly-piggly architectural styles. In the All Souls' Waiting Room version of Vienna, the buildings were of course not made of real stone but were constructed of their ethereal essence, whipped cream, or *schlag*, and got up to look like stone.

Taking a nose-dive down into the Heldenplatz, the Square of the Heroes, Seraph A. zoomed in through the imposing portals of the Hofburg Bibliothek or Library, where the Akashic Records were kept. He darted across the frescoed lobby to hover above the only desk in the cavernous space. A personage in a floor-length, dun-colored, cowl-hooded robe sat at the desk—the Akashic Recorder, overseer of the life stories of every soul who had ever taken a body.

"I see," the Recorder said after listening to the seraph's notes of alarm. His voice sounded like an echo of the ages, bouncing off the walls of a cave in the Pyrenees. "Just a mo—"

The Recorder wrote Johnnine's name down on a piece of what looked like fine parchment in a flowing, neo-Gothic script. He rolled it up and slipped it into a brass-capped pneumatic tube at his side, then patiently folded his hands together. His face could not be seen in the recesses of his hood and so he looked like a cross between a benevolent Benedictine monk and the Grim Reaper, but he was thinking that it was a thousand pities life on Earth drove so many young people to such desperate acts. He would have done things differently, but The Powers were in charge, not he, and they held that humans would sleepwalk through life unless they fell down a flight of stairs now and then. In The Powers' view, suffering was salubrious, the only way humans were brought to their real, i. e., spiritual senses. But the Recorder also knew there was such a thing as too much of a good thing.

Johnnine's soul scroll came back with the tube's characteristic *thwuff*. The Recorder scanned it quickly but thoroughly.

"Well," he said, "the bad news is she doesn't have any dead relatives up here. But the good news is she doesn't have a permit for a p. d.," which Seraph A. knew meant a premature departure. "So it's lights, camera, action time—"

Sitting on the edge of the Recorder's desk, where he sat resting his wings, Seraph A. warbled several delightful bars of Puccini.

"Yes, it does sound like a case for Xofia," the Recorder said. "But perhaps something more unusual as well. Will you go get her? I will inform the next-of-soul, who is in this case..." The Recorder scanned Johnnine's scroll. "Ah! How interesting. The psychoanalyst, Willie Reich—"

By this time, the five cherubs Fa, So, La, Ti and Do had caught up with their leader. When Seraph A. dashed out of the Bibliothek lobby, they formed a straggling V in his wake, like migrating geese. Above and due west of the Bibliothek, Seraph A. and the little band of cherubs streaked over the demesne of Viennese politicians, aptly named the Rathaus, and headed out the wide boulevard of Mariahilferstrasse to a former bordello, for a consult with the wisest entity they knew.

"*Darling*," Xofia was saying a few All Souls' minutes later, after Seraph A. had sung the sad song of Johnnine Hapgood. "*Angel*," Xofia purred in a thick, gravel-and-sorghum voice not unlike that of Earth's Tallulah Bankhead. "You know I'd love to help, it's just I don't see how. I mean, look where they've billeted me—"

Xofia flung her kimono-clad arm out in a languid semicircle, indicating the vulva-red four-poster bed and the tufted, labia-pink chaise longue on which she sat. Her face was indescribably lovely, her eyes bottomless. With her ash-colored hair billowing around her head like smoke, Xofia added, "I suppose it's fitting they'd stick me in a house of ill repute. Since my status is currently lower than a lizard's garter on Earth—"

Seraph A. tooted some clearly naysaying notes.

"Oh, all right, darling, if you think so!" Xofia acquiesced. "I suppose the girl's case comes under the All Souls' Freedom of Illumination Act?"

Seraph A. warbled that this was so.

"Then let's went," Xofia said, getting up.

Chapter Three

Johnnine, meanwhile, was quite enjoying her soul journey, serenely wafting she knew not where, although she did know it was away from pestilential Earth, and that made her happy. After a blissfully mindless interlude, she felt her soul bump up against something soft, something invisible yet distinctly There, because it impeded her progress. She thought she'd hit some sort of celestial ceiling, but in fact it was the floor of the All Souls' Waiting Room. She also thought she heard a bell ringing faintly, but decided that was impossible, she couldn't hear her phone this far away.

Then, without knowing how it happened, Johnnine suddenly found herself in an old-fashioned, foreign-looking apartment. Underneath prints and engravings of tombs and pyramids and the Sphinx, several dark mahogany, heavily-carved and uncomfortable-looking chairs stood against one of the walls. Glass display cabinets, crammed with ancient Egyptian and Greek artifacts and carved African masks, took up two more. Where was she, in some sort of museum?

Gingerly, she sat down on one of the straight-backed Biedermeier chairs, but it felt weird. When she touched it, it didn't feel like wood at all, more like...Jesus H. Christ, it felt like, so help her, it felt like ground sausage meat! She jumped up and backed away, accidentally bumping into one of the walls. But the wall, too, felt strange, spongy almost. What the hell was going on?

Just then the wildest-looking woman Johnnine had ever seen burst through the doorway.

"*Darling*! How *are* you?!" the woman exclaimed in a voice not unlike Tallulah Bankhead's, who happened to be one of Johnnine's favorite female celebrities.

Johnnine was speechless as she stared at the vision in front of her. Tall but neckless, clad in a red and white kimono and wearing wobbly-high red Wedgies, the woman waved an empty cigarette holder as she spoke, for emphasis. As if she needed it, Johnnine thought, still unable to speak.

"You probably have no idea what's happened to you, do you, pet?" Xofia asked gently. "Do sit down while I fill you in—"

The woman patted the chair next to her. "My name is Xofia, darling, and I am the ethereal essence of the feminine principle, the one which has been banished from Earth lo these many millennia—"

Johnnine sat down and looked at Xofia uncomprehendingly.

Xofia shook her head, her weightless hair drifting around her face, which looked both oddly familiar and intensely unknown.

"No, no, quite right, utterly superfluous information *au moment*, forgive me, I do run off sometimes..." Xofia put the empty cigarette holder to her lips and looked grave. "You tried to kill yourself, didn't you, darling? On Earth, I mean—"

"*Tried*??" Johnnine cried. "You mean I'm not dead yet?"

"Of course not, darling, and it's a good thing, too. You don't have a permit, do you?"

"A *permit*?"

"Yes, ducks, a permit, for a premature departure."

"You mean, like, a bathroom pass?" Johnnine asked sarcastically. "How was I supposed to know I needed one?"

Xofia smiled. "Well, sweet pea, you do, otherwise The Powers get rather *peeved*. You don't suppose they go to all the trouble of creation only to have things destroy themselves prematurely, do you?"

This had never occurred to Johnnine, who thought her body, her life, was hers to dispose of as she saw fit.

"So," Xofia continued, draping her kimono over her gorgeous Marlene Dietrich-like legs, adjusting the long red silk scarf around what should have been her throat except that she didn't have one, "now you get a Life Review, to see if you qualify—"

Johnnine tried not to be distracted by the way the features of Xofia's face seemed to change as she spoke. She thought she saw flashes of Eleanor Roosevelt, Marilyn Monroe, Rosa Parks, and other women she couldn't identify. Johnnine mobilized her mouth. "If I get a permit, then I can die?"

"Righty-oh, if you still choose—"

"What if I don't get one?"

"Then you'll be sent back, of course."

"To the way I *was*?"

"More or less. Although if there's been damage to the body, you'll have to live with it. Only one body per lifetime—"

"Shitpisscocksuck," Johnnine said, who was fond of obscenities even when she wasn't acidic with disappointment. Foul words exactly expressed her state of mind, plus they had the added advantage of driving her mother up the wall. "But I don't want to go back, I don't want to live, I want to die! *What do I have to do to get somebody to listen to me?*" she cried.

"There, there, poor darling," Xofia said, putting her hand on Johnnine's. More weirdness, Johnnine realized. Her fingers didn't feel like regular skin, they felt like hot feathers.

"You'll get a fair hearing, that's what we're here for," Xofia added.

"Yeah, sure," Johnnine said cynically. She was overwhelmed to find she wasn't dead. All she wanted and longed for was oblivion, a surcease of pain and emptiness, not some half-assed This Is Your Life. Gloomily, she asked, "Not that I really give a damn, but where *is* here, anyway?"

Xofia sat up smartly. "The All Souls' Waiting Room, of course, darling. The place all souls come back to in between lives, for re-routing, before the final, blessed jump off the Infernal Wheel."

Johnnine's interest was half-way spiked. "You mean the wheel of reincarnation?" Then her jaded self got the better of her. "What if I don't believe in it?"

"Well, maybe you'd better start, considering where you are," Xofia advised, tapping Johnnine's wrist with her cigarette holder. "Honestly, darling, some poor humans think there are no such things as souls, that they are nothing but unaccountable clusters of molecules spinning through a cold, black void, molecules that are *spit out*, as it were, once and once only! Imagine!"

Xofia's crowing laugh turned into a hacking cough. She glanced sideways at Johnnine as she hit her chest. "The Powers don't like it when I start sounding vengeful, though the Recorder knows it's hard not to be, the way I've been treated the last five thousand years—I've even been repeatedly ritualistically decapitated, my head severed from my body," Xofia simpered, touching the place where her neck should have been and which was now covered up by her scarf.

Johnnine had no idea what Xofia was talking about. "But where is *this*?" Johnnine asked, looking around the positively cuboid room stuffed with antiques. "It looks almost, like, real."

"We try for relevance, darling," Xofia explained, putting her own woes aside. "In view of your particular history, we thought this would be the most appropriate setting for your Life Review. We're in the Viennese section of the All Souls' Waiting Room, where souls like yours are brought, souls who've been brought up on the dogma of Psychiatry rather than the dogma of Religion. We expect this to be *quite* a busy place in the years ahead..."

Xofia glided across the room. Her face lit up with amusement. "—so where we are, darling, is in the flat of Professor Sigmund S. Freud."

"Freud!?" Johnnine was incensed. "But I didn't have anything to do with *Freud*." Of course, she thought, there's been a giant administrative screw up somewhere.

"Not in the flesh, darling, we know that, how could you? He died many years before you were born. But there is such a thing as coming under someone's sphere of influence—"

Standing in front of a tall and elegant display case, Xofia chuckled as she opened its glass doors. Or at least they *looked like* glass doors, Johnnine thought, but who knew, maybe they were solidified peppermint schnapps, and she and Xofia were uncooked pumpkin meat and the real name of where she was was Mondo Bizarro.

Xofia took out a small bust of blind Oedipus from the middle shelf and turned it over in her hand. "When Herr Doktor Freud found out he was going to be returned as a woman, you should have seen the carryings-on. He had a full-blown fit of hysterics."

Johnnine didn't get it, but then she was only eighteen, from the Earthyear 1962.

Laughing, Xofia replaced Oedipus and turned to face Johnnine. "But we digress. The psychoanalyst who did have a profound influence on you was trained by Freud, he even lived across the street, at 20 Berggasse, when he was Freud's chief assistant. We like to go back to the sources whenever possible."

"You mean Wilhelm Reich?" Johnnine asked apprehensively. Although Reich was not, strictly speaking, personally responsible for Johnnine's soul scars, his was not an acquaintance she was dying to renew.

"Of course, darling," Xofia said. Then she smiled. "Come look at Freud's famous old couch—"

Sulkily, Johnnine got up and crossed the room. Like she really gave a flying crap about the birthplace of psychoanalysis. As she looked into the small Victorian study, she saw Freud's desk, facing the most conspicuous object in the room, a tobacco-colored leather chaise covered in Oriental rugs. Johnnine's ethereal essence suddenly felt sick to its stomach; she staggered a little as she went back to her chair, or rather her ground-up sausage meat. She didn't even want to think what the couch would feel like.

"Then this—you mean I'm in the All Souls' Waiting Room, sitting in *Freud's* waiting room?"

"That's it, darling," Xofia smiled. "The Powers love a little laugh..."

Chapter Four

This was not Johnnine's idea of funny. Her tastes ran more to Mort Sahl and Lenny Bruce. She felt anxious and thought about trying to beat a retreat, but where was there to go from Mondo Bizarro? A commotion in the entryway startled her. So far, being half-way dead was proving far from restful.

A tall figure in a monk's robe emerged into Freud's waiting room, carrying what looked like a portable screen and a movie projector. Johnnine could barely discern burning eyes in the recesses of the cowled hood, but couldn't make out any other features.

"Who the hell is that?" Johnnine whispered to Xofia.

"The Akashic Recorder, darling," Xofia answered softly. "He only looks terrifying, actually he's quite a good egg once you get to know him." Johnnine thought it was funny how Xofia used so many of her mother's favorite expressions, like pet, ducks, and good egg. Otherwise, they could not have been more dissimilar. Dinah was short and stout, overwhelmingly intense. Xofia was tall, elegant, and ephemeral. Her mother's touch was like the bite of a steel saw blade, Xofia's was like sun-warmed wings. Still, were ultra-feminine creatures like Xofia to be trusted?

"—and these divine little creatures," she was saying, "are the cherubs, Fa, So, La, Ti, and Do."

Johnnine watched as the cherubim, each of whom seemed to be carrying a can of film, flew past them into Freud's study. If this was her dying dream, it was, like, *out there*.

Xofia laughed her water-plashing-in-a-fountain laugh as a blindingly radiant cherub, only with two sets of wings, flew in to the anteroom. "Darling," Xofia said, standing up and gesturing for Johnnine to do the same. "This is the child in question, Johnnine Hapgood Kirk—"

"I am not a child," Johnnine protested hotly. "I can vote, and drink, and drive!"

"I beg your pardon, but in terms of your soul-age, you are still in diapers. And as far as I'm concerned, no one should be allowed behind the wheel of an automotive vehicle, otherwise known as a killing machine, until they've passed a fear of dying test."

Johnnine smarted but stuck up for herself. Xofia was a bitch. "Could you also please get my name straight? It's Hapgood, not Kirk. Mom dropped my father's name when she left him."

"Did she, dear?" Xofia said archly. "How advanced of her—"

Xofia's tone reminded Johnnine of her mother until Seraph A. trilled a few bars and Xofia hissed at him. "I know, I know, but she tries my patience."

A short burst of an exceedingly beautiful melody, something like the overture from *Aida*, poured from the seraph's exquisite lips. Instantly, Johnnine and Xofia forgot their ruffled feelings.

"*Aprez-vous, darling*," Xofia said with what sounded like real fondness in her voice, ushering Johnnine into Freud's inner sanctum.

"Do I have to?" Johnnine asked glumly but obediently. Her ethereal spirits did not improve when she saw that Freud's oversized couch had been moved. It now faced a wall of bookshelves in front of which hung a large portable screen.

"What is this?" Johnnine asked. "We're going to watch a movie?"

"Of course, darling, your Akashic Record, only on film, milestones in the life of your soul. Soulstones, I call them."

Xofia smiled brightly at Johnnine.

Johnnine could not abide her ditzy self-satisfaction. "Are they like gallstones?"

"In your case, perhaps," Xofia shot back.

The sharp blast of a whistle blew from Seraph A's lips. His well-chosen notes soothed Xofia and Johnnine back to civility.

"Please, make yourself comfortable," the Recorder said to Johnnine, nodding at The Couch.

"Oh, God," Johnnine moaned, looking at it, forcibly reminded of her awful childhood therapy sessions with more than one Reichian analyst.

Xofia took pity on her. "While it's not a bed of roses, darling, it's hardly a bed of nails either. This will be over in what will seem like the blink of an eye—"

When, with extreme trepidation, Johnnine sat down on the Oriental-covered couch, a chorus of sleepy sighs punctuated by a few low-pitched screams were emitted. "What's this thing made of?" Johnnine asked nervously.

"Why, dreams, of course, darling. The dreams of many other unhappy souls—"

"Are you going to stay?" Johnnine also asked, which was the closest she could get to admitting she wanted Xofia's company.

Xofia beamed at her. "A team of wild asses couldn't drag me away."

The diminutive seraph flew up to the corner of the room. He perched on the ornate cornice, crossed his little legs and whistled what seemed to be commands at the cherubs, two of whom flew around the projector, threading the film, and two of whom futzed around with the screen. The fifth one—was it Fa or La? who could tell? and why, Johnnine wondered, did they look so damn familiar?—dimmed the lights.

The first flickering image came up on the screen.

Against an azure blue sea, in which were reflected humongous white clouds, words shimmered out of the water in sparkling gold: AKASHIC RECORDING STUDIOS PRESENTS: then a burst of light and a blast of corny music flooded

Johnnine's ethereal hearing and vision. The title came on. Painted in illuminated Gothic script, Johnnine almost groaned as she read "A Soul is Born."

She should have known. Instead of something à la Bergman, or even a 'fifties MGM musical, it looked like it was going to be amateur night. The hokey opening credits added insult to injury. Johnnine was a *New Yorker*, for Christ's sake, she wasn't from Podunk, Illinois. She *loved* movies, she was a sophisticated aficionado.

But the establishing shot, an aerial view of a snowy Central Park, wasn't bad. Then the camera glided down Fifth Avenue to Washington Square Arch and roamed around a pristine Washington Square, squarely setting the location in Greenwich Village. Johnnine felt herself warming to the film as it flitted through the winter streets. You could tell from people's clothes it was around 1940. New York in the early 'forties! Only her favorite time and place in the whole world, probably because she wasn't born yet. She went stiff with attention as the camera snuck inside a little bakery on Cornelia Street, Zampieri's, and she saw her father, with an unbelievable amount of hair on his head, rummaging through the bread on the day-old rack. Unimaginably young and handsome, he looked around as the bakery's front door bell tinkled. Johnnine felt the sharp hot pains of father-longing as she looked at him.

The Recorder's voice-of-the-ages voice broke the silence. "This scene shows the first meeting of Johnnine's future parents."

Dinah came through the door, a study in brown as she bustled up to the bakery counter. Johnnine was mesmerized by the sight of her mother as a svelte young knock-out; wearing a brown coat with dark sienna velvet collar and a matching hat sitting on masses of waving chestnut hair swept up from her face, Dinah had a noble nose, eyes the color of Hershey's chocolate and a full, fully mobile, almost ambulatory mouth.

Johnnine's father's jaw dropped slightly, rooted to the spot as he drank in Dinah's lush hourglass figure, the firm swell of breast and hip straining at the confines of her fitted coat.

"Duncan Cameron Kirk," the Recorder intoned in an overdub, "putative sperm, has just been bowled over by Dinah Hapgood, putative ovum."

The cherubim broke into a chorus of Bronx cheers. Even Xofia clapped animatedly. "What makes the world go 'round, darling," she explained to Johnnine in an aside.

On the screen, engaged in conversation with the Italian baker, Dinah's body gave off almost visible crackles and pops of sexual energy, overt signals of a receptive womb. Her rich, deep voice fairly quivered with humor and intense self-consciousness as she ordered a choco-mocha log roll. For a small dinner party her mother was giving, she explained to the baker, who took down her phone number so he could let her know when it was ready.

Johnnine knew this part, how her father had memorized Dinah's number as he made his way to the counter. He looked like iron filings in a magnet's tow.

The film seemed to go into slow-mo, while the cherubs gave out loud, lewd whistles and catcalls.

Dinah turned to look at Duncan—and here Johnnine might have been tempted to underscore with pinging cymbals and screaming violins—as the camera did a close-up on the questioning glint in Duncan's pale, Rasputin-blue eyes, a glint which held Johnnine's future.

Suddenly the film cut to a completely different scene, a bunch of flying babies buzzing around a huge telescope that looked like it was sitting on a cloud. Oh, they were cherubs, Johnnine realized, like Fa, So, and what's-his-face, only as the camera zoomed in for a close-up she had a shock of recognition. One of them elbowed the others away from the shiny brass eyepiece: holy shit, Johnnine realized, it's *me*!!

There was a jump-cut back to the scene on Earth, where her father was giving her mother a wolfish, hungry-male look. Dinah, neither coy nor virginal, returned a knowing, sensuous smile.

Then the screen showed a cherubic Johnnine back on the silvery celestial cloud. Hovering in mid-air with her eye glued to the telescope, at the moment her parents' eyes locked, an All Souls' ticket machine nearby dinged and spat out a number. For better or worse, unborn Johnnine tore it off.

Chapter Five

"Souls are promised bodies when a man and woman first look at each other with lovelust," the Recorder said. "Given the reproductive charge in her parents' first glance, Johnnine's fate was now sealed. I should add that while her first choice was Cary Grant and Katherine Hepburn, Johnnine was advised, like many other unborns, to take what she could get, what with the coming World War II shortages—"

Excusez-moi? Johnnine thought, her ethereal mind reeling. Was the guy in the ankle-length bathrobe suggesting she had *chosen* her parents?? "Hey, just a minute!" Johnnine interrupted. "Why would I pick a father who wasn't going to *be* a father?"

The Recorder and Xofia exchanged a meaningful look.

"Darling," Xofia said in a slithering-over-hot-stones tone. "There's a very complicated process of parental selection that only The Powers really understand, about who best matches up with whom for each life—"

Johnnine almost snorted in derision. Sure, she thought. She knew what that meant, it meant Xofia didn't have a clue. It was impossible that Johnnine would have picked Duncan and Dinah just from seeing them once in a bakery. Wasn't that a little too pig-in-a-pokish, even for Mondo Bizarro? Either that, Johnnine suddenly thought, or else picking your parents was like buying a new pair of shoes. They looked great in the store, all sexy and shiny, but after you wore them a while they got scuffed up, they got down at the heels and starting falling apart. By the time you went for another new pair, you looked at them sitting on the floor at the shoe salesman's feet and wondered how the hell you could ever have thought they looked so good in the first place.

"Roll it—" said the Recorder.

Fa, So, or what's-his-face doused the room lights. The film went into a montage of Johnnine's parents' five-year long, war-spanning, unmarried love affair. Johnnine was grateful the camera didn't follow them into bedrooms even though it did a good job of depicting two oversexed, bohemian neurotics who were quite mad for each other.

During the day, crisply professional, Dinah wore a white uniform and worked in the laboratory of a military hospital, looking through a microscope for parasites in soldiers' stool samples. Johnnine knew that Dinah loved her work, her boss had called her Goody Two Stools. Duncan the draft-deferred, up-and-coming artist, oil-painted society patrons onto canvas and did highly-skilled colorist's work at the Frick Museum, matching up the colors of the paintings with photographs for catalogues. At night, behind a beat-up old bamboo screen, they merged on a mattress on the floor of Duncan's then-studio, on the corner of Fifty-eighth and Lex.

The All Souls' Waiting Room

As the camera held on a tight shot of the bamboo screen, with blurred but rhythmic movements behind it, the Recorder spoke. "While Duncan Cameron Kirk loved to shake the tree, he did not necessarily want to be bombarded with fruit."

The film cut to a shot of Dinah on a kitchen table, her legs crooked over a bloody bolster pillow, her face a mask of pain as she bit down on a piece of rubber hosing.

"And so," The Recorder continued, "Dinah Hapgood denied entry visas to several intrepid, unticketed souls seeking to cross into corporeality, the same sort of beings who push ahead of others on lines. The future Johnnine, wisely, waited."

Johnnine had to look away. To him maybe they were 'unticketed souls' but to her they were unborn brothers and sisters. All the aching loneliness of being an only child welled up in her. But when she really thought about it, she was glad she didn't have any siblings; Dinah had only barely been capable of raising her, one or two more kids would have broken the camel's back. Plus she agreed with her mother's perfervid cry, "The world doesn't need unwanted children! Every baby a wanted baby!" But were those the only ones that got tickets?

The film showed shots of huge ocean liners sailing past the Statue of Liberty and into New York harbor, unloading a human tide on the docks, escapees from the European war. Johnnine recognized one of the emigres coming down the gangplank as a youthful-looking Wilhelm Reich before he got swallowed up in the crowd.

She'd only heard a hundred times how Duncan got out of the draft because of his genius IQ. More likely, Johnnine thought, the Army could tell he was half-crazoid and didn't *want* him running around with a gun in his hands. Duncan made good money for the first time in his life working as a draughtsman for the War Department, his finely-honed artist's skills commandeered to draw plans for armored tanks and heavy artillery. World War II also gave him his irrefutable argument to Dinah against a family: how could they bring a baby into a world gone mad?

By 1944, Duncan's studio shelves sagged under the weight of the books he bought with his war-gotten wages. The camera panned their spines; art books on Picasso, Sisley, Mondrian, tracts by the brothers Huxley, Bertrand Russell, the contraband novels of D. H. Lawrence. If Johnnine had heard Dinah say it once she'd heard it a thousand times, that no matter how broke they were, even if there wasn't money for food, Duncan always had money for books.

On a hot summer's day in 1944—you could tell it was hot because he was sweating even though he was wearing a short-sleeved shirt—Johnnine watched her father browsing absorbedly through an outdoor table in front of a used bookstore on Fourth Avenue. He picked up a dark blue hard-bound; the camera did a freeze-frame close-up on the cover, "The Function of the Orgasm", by Wilhelm Reich.

In the All Souls' Waiting Room, there was a knock on the doorjamb of Freud's ersatz office.

"Yes?" the Recorder called out. "Is that you, Willie?"

Room lights came up, the film screen went dark. Bizarre as everything had been up until then, Johnnine was still not prepared for the sight of a scowling, ethereal Wilhelm Reich storming into the room.

"*Jawohl*," he said, "I am instructed to be here, I am here." Stocky, energetic, and self-important, he wore his ubiquitous short white lab coat over dungarees and a lumberjack's shirt, his guerrilla scientist outfit. His thick white hair still looked as though he combed it, straight up, with an electric cattle prod.

Reich's steaming black-coffee eyes nailed Johnnine to the couch. He was intimidating as hell, no doubt about it, but his tone as he addressed her was curiously gentle.

"Yah, so, young one. We meet again, only we are at cross-purposes. I want to go back to Earth, you want to leave it—"

Johnnine swallowed but couldn't say anything; her vocal cords, in a classic demonstration of throat block, seemed to have seized up on her.

Chapter Six

Reich turned to the Recorder. "So—you wanted to see me? I am a busy man, my experiments—"

"You want a ticket to be," the Recorder answered calmly, "while our young woman here wants a permit *not* to be. But you both have unfinished business from your last life, including what we call 'uncancelled karma' together."

Reich grew belligerent. "I am a *scientist*! I do not believe in this mystical clap-trap!"

"The Laws do not disappear just because humans choose not to read them—" the Recorder said, unflappably.

"*Darling.*" Xofia put in her oar. "Johnnine needs you. You're the next-of-soul, all her next-of-kin have been sent back—for parental re-training, I might add." Here Xofia looked over at Johnnine and actually winked.

Johnnine couldn't believe any of what was going on was going on. If she was dreaming this up, she was bent as a pretzel.

"Just relax, darling, pull up a chair," Xofia oozed at Reich, her voice particularly appealing. "It's a *movie*, everyone likes movies. You like movies, don't you, darling?"

"Yah, I do, when I have the time—" Reich looked a lot less bellicose under Xofia's attention.

"We only have Eternity..." Xofia teased.

"But I don't want to spend it here! There is too much to do on Earth!"

Instead of giving him a rejoinder, Xofia smiled and patted the chair next to her. To Johnnine's amazement, Reich took it. He was buying it! This was when Johnnine realized Xofia was a great artist. To be able to turn Reich's growling mastiff into a truculent puppy...

"Did you see 'The Invasion of the Body Snatchers'?" Reich asked conversationally, apparently soothed by Xofia's proximity. "*That* was a great movie! So true, too—the dead-eyed aliens of course symbols for the emotional plague that is destroying the world..."

"Interesting interpretation, darling," Xofia said as the room went dark. "We'll talk, later—"

Johnnine had been raised in a circle of worshipful analysts, patients, and followers of Wilhelm Reich. Finding out that Reich did something as mundane as go to the movies was like finding out God went to the bathroom.

The Akashic film picked up the billowing silver cloud at the edge of the All Souls' Waiting Room. Unborn Johnnine was hanging out with her cherub pals, clustered around a baize-covered card table, drinking beer and smoking, their gossamer wings at rest. When the camera moseyed in for a medium shot of the assembled angelic faces, you could see that their game was blackjack, that the beer was Eternal Return, and the name on the packs of cigarettes was Bright Sparks. Periodically, Johnnine would leave her little cloud-seat and buzz over to the telescope. Peering through it, she returned to the card game looking disgusted.

"Johnnine's parents were trying not to slip up again," the Recorder explained, "which meant Johnnine had rather a long wait for conception."

Suddenly switching to fast-forward, the screen showed colorful blobs and blurs as the Recorder over-dubbed. "Here we skip over a period of conflict between Johnnine's parents, the details of which are not all that relevant except to say a real rift was forming. Dinah's biological clock was ticking. She wanted a child, Duncan did not. In his uneasiness, Duncan sought out the company of other women, which in turn made Dinah feel compelled to move in with her mother. There were passionate fights, there were passionate make-ups. Finally, one night in early 1945, Johnnine got the signal she'd been waiting for—"

On the screen, just as Johnnine was putting a slam together, a deafening Klaxon went off. AWAUUGGHH! AWAUUGGHH! AWAUUGGHH! Highly excited, all the cherubs dropped their cards and flew straight up in the air while unborn Johnnine darted straight to the telescope. Peering through it, she turned to her peers with a lascivious grin, which looked odd on her innocent and adorable face. Giving them the All Souls' gestural equivalent of a thumbs-up—a circle of two fingers and a pointer of another—she flew to the edge of the cloud. Whereupon she abruptly stalled, her little wings beating frantically, but in reverse.

"The moment of truth," the Recorder intoned over the wailing Klaxon. "Like most returning souls, Johnnine was trying to assure herself it wouldn't be so bad this time. She knew Earth was the only place to learn what she needed to learn but she also knew it was a rough and dirty sandbox—"

Finally, unborn Johnnine gamely turned and waved at her confreres for the last time. Then she squeezed her eyes shut, held her nose, and jumped off the edge of the cloud. The screen showed a whirring maelstrom of light and color. There was a loud and liquid PLOP!—and then a dim but clear pin-point glow surrounded by murky, sloshing fluids.

In the All Souls' Waiting Room, the camera cut to a discreet shot of the climactic faces of Duncan and Dinah, eschewing any nudity, which was a good thing, Johnnine thought, otherwise it would have been too vomitoso.

"Because of another fight after Johnnine's inception, Dinah made up her mind to leave Duncan—but *without* telling him she was taking a rapidly-dividing blastocyst with her. The film resumes a few months later, in late spring of 1945—"

In a soft May twilight, Duncan could be seen sitting on the bottom step of a stoop on St. Luke's Place, where Johnnine knew her grandmother Esther had had an apartment. Reading a book as always, this one "Character Analysis" by

Wilhelm Reich, Duncan looked up as Dinah approached. She was carrying two shopping bags on either side of an unmistakably fecund belly. The streetlamps twinked on, lighting the silver-green gingko trees that lined the street.

"I knew you were avoiding me for a reason." Duncan pushed his hat back off his forehead. His dark hair was quite thin on top. "November?" he said.

Dinah's tone was defensive, protective. "You can't change my mind, I'm going to have this baby with or without you."

Duncan sighed. "All right, Dinah. But we'll have to get married—"

Dinah's laugh was slightly derisive. "What on earth for?"

"To give the baby a name."

"It will have *my* name. Hapgood."

"You know what I mean, society's not as progressive as we are, you'll be ostracized—"

Dinah laughed outright. "You know I don't give a damn about society's approval. The war's almost over, things are different now—my Lord, it's 1945! I can earn a living and take care of a baby. We don't need anything else."

"Not even a father?"

The shadow of a doubt passed over Dinah's features, which had lost their girlish softness in the intervening five years. Wasn't she going to mention the other women? Johnnine wondered. And wasn't her father even going to pay lip service to wanting her?

Jump-cut to a no-frills civil wedding ceremony in Manhattan's City Hall, attended only by Dinah's stunning, cruelly capricious mother and a lesbian sculptress friend of Duncan's. Standing up in front of the judge, Duncan looked surprisingly hail and hearty, while Dinah looked pretty, plump, and nervous as hell. Based on their expressions, Johnnine would have sworn that if anyone was having regrets, it was her mother.

Johnnine knew the story behind the next bit of film, of her mother and father serenely canoeing along on the river upstream from Niagara Falls. Duncan had gotten a defense job nearby. They'd taken a bungalow for an extended honeymoon; with Johnnine in *in utero* attendance, the film showed her parents as scrapping, but basically congenial.

"As a not-quite embodied spirit," the Recorder narrated, "Johnnine now had several months of free ingress and egress, meaning she could go back and forth between the All Souls' Waiting Room and Dinah's womb. Most baby beings 'try out' a set of parents, rather like humans try out automobiles. The same principle applies, that you shouldn't take possession until you've had a test-drive..."

Chapter Seven

Johnnine watched herself sloshing around in the amniotic sac, the incandescence of her soul changing from a candle's glow to a small campfire. Her mother's womb was a lively place, particularly when her parents made love. In her weightless condition, Johnnine quite enjoyed the intra-uterine blanket toss.

Dinah talked to her, addressing her as babushka, which had a nice sound to it. Dinah didn't realize it was Yiddish for head scarf. Johnnine did not take offense. So her mother-to-be wasn't a linguist, who cared? Dinah had a vigorously healthy body and a ribald sense of humor, she would do. Her father was harder to get to know, but Johnnine found he grew intrigued whenever she took a constitutional. Duncan would put his hand on Dinah's mounded stomach and Johnnine would give back a good swift kick. All in all, gestation wasn't too boring, there were plenty of things to do, though after being in the dark so long Johnnine was definitely looking forward to the Great White Way.

She began to harbor hopes that being born wouldn't be too big a drag. Even though she knew things were far from perfect between Duncan and Dinah, maybe her arrival would fuse them into some sort, however *fakockteh*, of a family. And so finally, on a snowy night in mid-November, Johnnine communicated to her mother, via the umbilical telegraph wire, that it was high time they were introduced. Dinah's obliging pelvis went into heavy labor and within hours everyone was piling into a cab for a thrilling, white-knuckle ride to the hospital.

Cut to a shot of Duncan pacing the two-tone green corridors. The jerky motion of the film—hadn't anyone in Mondo Bizarro heard of a fluid-head tripod? Johnnine wondered irritatedly, or were they trying for *cinema verité*?—showed doctors and nurses and other distraught-looking fathers-to-be squeaking past him on the waxy linoleum. Duncan slumped into a chair, his clothes as rumpled as his face, and picked up a book. He tried unsuccessfully to read, sucking on an unlit pipe and looking up every time someone's steps came close. The screen bloomed with a close-up of the cover, "Sexual Revolution" by Wilhelm Reich.

Johnnine's soul was in turmoil as she lay on Freud's ersatz couch in the All Souls' Waiting Room. Watching her father was like looking at a glamorous, irresistibly fascinating stranger, someone she very much wanted in her life who never would be. Thirstily, she drank him in, all the details of his trim, well-shaped physique, his natural, easy movements. She tried to match the anxious and worried expression on his face with the neglect and indifference he had shown her after she was born. Nothing jibed. In these shots, he looked like a normal, out-of-his-mind, about-to-be father.

All too soon he was gone, and the next scene was of the labor room where Dinah toiled to give birth, only Johnnine couldn't believe it wasn't a scene out of Dickens. The walls were dark and all the hospital's medical equipment looked antiquated. There were screams and moans and groans and blood everywhere. Johnnine knew she'd been born in a Salvation Army hospital because it was the cheapest her parents could find, but the place looked like a throwback to the Dark Ages.

A harried woman doctor at the end of the delivery table yelled at Dinah. "Harder, push harder, Mrs. Kirk!"

In some kind of weirdo empathy, Johnnine's ethereal body instantly felt it was being throttled, her mounting excitement mingled with stark terror that she wouldn't be able to make the dicey transition from spirit to substantiality.

Off-screen, as if on cue, other women shrieked, wailed, and cursed in their birth agonies. When the camera locked on Dinah, Johnnine almost didn't recognize her. Her powerhouse mother was barely able to raise her head, face and hair were drenched with sweat, her facial muscles contorting in the effort to expel her baby.

"Come on, Mrs. Kirk, I don't have all day!" the woman doctor abjured.

"Neither—do—*I*!" Dinah slurred, but with some vestige of her usual personality.

'Doped to the gills' was how Dinah always disparagingly described Johnnine's birth. Johnnine saw and simultaneously felt the final push down the birth canal, lubricated by a rush of bloody fluids. Crushing pelvic contractions moved her along the birth canal ridge by engorged ridge. It was a hellish, hellishly bumpy ride, the most terrifying journey imaginable. When she finally sensed light at the end of the vaginal tunnel, Johnnine's sensitive hearing was overwhelmed by a swelling, frightening roar of sound outside her mother's quaking body.

As she felt the doctor's hands clamp like a vise on her still-slippery limbs, Johnnine's first physical sensations were of cacophonous noise, freezing cold air, and blinding light. She was turned upside-down and given a resounding slap on the buttocks. Johnnine let out a gusty cry of pain, an immediate protest, an act which introduced her to her amazing new vocal cords and the giddiness of breathing. Her umbilical cord was cut quickly and unceremoniously, she was whisked away from her sobbing, semiconscious mother. Nurses swaddled her in heavy, rough blankets, stuck a rubber suction tube down her throat, and squirted caustic silver nitrate drops in her eyes. The scene closed on a close-up of Johnnine's alternately stunned and squalling infant face.

In the All Souls' Waiting Room, Johnnine felt the slap on her bottom and the bitter sting in her ethereal eyes as the cherubs turned the room lights up and stopped the projector.

Reich's enraged voice filled the room. "Did you see that?? How the mother was drugged, how the newborn was treated like a reviled little *rat*? Such birth practices were created by evil men, by sadists! Is it any wonder humanity's such a murderous mess when this is how we treat our *babies*? *Alley cats* are better at giving birth!!"

Johnnine could now fully understand why her mother had become a natural childbirth midwife, her birthing of Johnnine had been a chilling experience. She could also understand why some unborns, like Fa, So, and what's-his-face, chose to stay in the Waiting Room. Earth looked grimola in comparison.

"I devoted the last years of my life to giving women an alternative to such barbarism," Reich eulogized. "In the early 'fifties, *before* anyone else, I was the only one offering home births to my women patients. No drugs, no episiotomies, no infant genital mutilation, and most especially no separation of the mother and her newborn, the most essential thing of all!"

"Yes, but darling—"Xofia amended Reich's tirade, swiveling her charming but neckless head to look at him. "Did you serve champagne?"

Reich was nonplussed for an instant before he broke into a surprising smile. "*Jawohl...*"

"Good, then let's have some—such a primitive scene puts me in dire need of what you would call oral compensation..."

Xofia addressed Seraph A., silently but intently whittling a stick up on his cornice. "*Darling*, be an angel and send out for supplies, will you?"

Seraph A. blew a few piercing notes. Two of his minions immediately flew out of the room.

What was this? Johnnine thought. Flying gofers? "Mondo Bizarro," she said under her breath.

"What was that, young woman? Something to say?" the Recorder asked.

Johnnine's ethereal tongue suddenly felt frozen, stuck to the roof of her mouth. If part of the deal for a permit to die was talking to these guys, particularly Reich, maybe she'd be better off alive. Not that she was afraid of him exactly, it was just that...there was so much more of him than her, as if there were several souls instead of one packed into his dauntingly sturdy frame. Johnnine shook her head.

The Recorder spoke. "I should add at this juncture that The Powers do not wax mealy-mouthed about the joys of becoming Earth-born. Sometimes there is very little joy about it at all, humans all too often taking the path of cruelty and ignorance if left to their own devices. Many newborns take one look at their new parents and take desperate action—lights, please."

The film held on a shot of infant Johnnine in her wood-slatted hospital crib, vacantly staring off into space.

"Parents think of this as the infants' wide-eyed gaze of wonder, but in fact it's a look of profound spiritual stupefaction."

Johnnine next saw her baby soul peeling away from her body. Beating it back to the Waiting Room, Johnnine's flight took her straight to the All Souls' Complaint Department.

"Leaving the world of the spirit and re-entering that of the body is often a rude reawakening..." the Recorder said.

Baby Johnnine angrily confronted an official-looking cherub wearing a long white English judge's wig, and gave forth with some very nasty notes, first haranguing and then clearly begging the implacable, wig-wearing cherub.

"Here our young soul is asking for a reprieve," the Akashic Recorder continued. "Part of the initiation process of infancy, seemingly callous but equally necessary, is readjustment to the quixotic world of three dimensions—"

Johnnine was turned away from the All Souls' Complaint Department, neither too good nor too brave to be allowed to die young. She sobbed her way all the way back to her Salvation Army crib. When she rejoined her body, her bleary-eyed father and berouged grandmother were tapping intrusively on the large glass pane between them.

"—beginning with the newborn's life being dependent on inscrutable and usually highly unstable strangers. This realization, in addition to the extreme physical frustration of being a knowledgeable soul in a virtually useless body, is what causes infants' frequent and lengthy crying jags."

On-screen, baby Johnnine howled inconsolably in her swaddled and isolated state, a perfect picture of pure misery.

Freeze-frame, as the cherubs flew back in with Xofia's Dom Elysee champagne and Dark Star cigarillos. Quickly popping the cork, Xofia poured herself a glass and took several swigs. "My deepest sympathy, darling," she said to Johnnine. "Being a baby's a shit deal and everyone knows it."

"Then why isn't it changed?" Reich demanded. "May I smoke?"

"Of course, darling," Xofia smiled, handing him her pack.

"Can I have one too, please?" Johnnine asked, emboldened by Xofia's sympathy.

"Don't be silly, darling!" Xofia chided. "You're not dead yet."

Chapter Eight

Johnnine smarted at Xofia's comment. It sure as hell wasn't *her* fault she wasn't dead yet, it was this bunch of weirdo old farts who were holding things up.

"I repeat my question," Reich said, exhaling a spume of what looked like satisfying smoke. "If everyone knows it's a faulty system, why then isn't it changed?"

"Humans really aren't very bright, darling," Xofia said in a confidential tone, as if Reich might not believe her. "They run around calling themselves geniuses because they build bridges or skyscrapers, when they don't even know how to raise a happy child!"

Reich warmed visibly at Xofia's remark. "A woman after my own mind," he said, his black-brown eyes flashing.

"No, darling," Xofia said, smiling brilliantly at him. "A woman after *my* own mind—"

The Recorder broke in. "The Powers take the view that things work perfectly well the way they are. The Laws apply to everyone equally. There is no such thing as favoritism."

Xofia winked at Reich. "Yes, *but*—the trick with The Laws is that not everyone is equally good at interpreting them..."

"Let's get back," the Recorder said.

The All Souls' flick flared up with a coming-home-from-the-hospital scene. Johnnine had never seen herself and her parents as a family before, had never had the experience of having a matched set of mom and dad. It almost broke her heart to see them getting out of a big yellow Checker cab on the corner of Seventeenth Street and Eighth Avenue, Johnnine, invisible in her mother's arms, inside a mound of baby bunting. Duncan crossed the slush-covered sidewalk and opened the door of a small, down-at-the-heels Chelsea apartment building. The bar next door wafted out a few strains of Nat King Cole. "ChestNUTS roasting on an open fire, Jack Frost NIPping at your nose..."

They looked so young, so handsome, as Duncan led the way up the dimly-lit, corkscrew stairs, carrying Dinah's cardboard hospital suitcase. The only sound was the grind of New York grit under the soles of their shoes. Johnnine could almost smell the old building again, familiar from her few but vividly-remembered childhood pilgrimages to her father's apartment. Cheap perfume from the white Russian hooker on the first floor, sour milk from the empty glass bottles on the second, in front of the crazed Hungarian musicologist's apartment. The top, fourth floor smelled like Duncan: turpentine, pencil shavings, and pipe tobacco, heavily overlaid with male sweat. Duncan didn't believe in wasting time on too much bathing. Cleanliness, to his way of thinking, was next to anal-compulsiveness.

Dinah stopped below the last flight to catch her breath. "This," she said in her richly inflected voice, "is going to be hell on wheels every day."

Duncan bounded athletically up the stairs, taking two at a time. "Be good for you," he said over his shoulder. "Get you back in shape for intercourse in no time—"

Johnnine cringed, wanting to sink into the couch. Didn't they ever think about anything else?

"Excellent, healthy genitality!" Reich bellowed from his chair.

Oh, *God*, Johnnine thought. Grown-ups were *gross*.

Dinah leaned against the door frame of what was clearly Duncan's studio. The nearly-finished oil portrait of a beautiful, dark-haired woman rested on an easel.

"Who's she?" Dinah did not succeed in keeping jealousy out of her voice. Johnnine slept soundly in her arms.

"This month's food and rent," Duncan answered breezily. His voice trailed after him from the next room. "She's rich, bored, sexually frustrated, and she thinks I'm brilliant—here, I put the crib in the kitchen, by the stove."

Dinah walked up close to the painting, examining it minutely. Then she vehemently stuck out her tongue before wheeling around and following Duncan into the kitchen.

Johnnine's crib had been painted the colors of a Tahitian sunset, and it made Dinah smile. She lay Johnnine down and peeled away layers of blankets and clothing. Duncan blew on his hands and lit the burners on the gas stove to heat the freezing room. His newborn daughter mewed at being woken up.

Duncan and Dinah leaned over the crib, admiring their pink-skinned child as she worked up to a good cry. "She's beautiful," Dinah said reverently. "Good strong lungs, too!"

"I think my genes dominated, except for the slope of her forehead..."

"She does not have a slope!" Dinah said sharply. She returned to her scrutiny of her infant. "I don't see any body armor, do you?"

"Don't be obsessive, Dinah, she's not even a week old."

"Reich said armor could start in the womb—"

"That's if the mother doesn't want the baby. Not the case with you two—"

"No," Dinah smiled, studying her squalling baby with loving eyes. "No, it certainly wasn't. I never wanted anything so much in my life..."

"Aren't you going to pick her up?"

"In a minute. Crying's good for her, lets her get rid of her anger."

"How angry could she be at five days old?" Duncan asked. "Remember Mead's study, the way the native women carried their babies everywhere?"

Dinah laughed, taking off her coat. "This isn't Samoa, and she needs to cry. It'll keep her chest from getting blocked, help the flow of her orgone energy..."

Dinah hung up her coat on a nail in the back of the kitchen door. She rolled up her sleeves as she advanced towards the crib.

The screen went black, lights came up.

"I will not stand for character assassination!" Reich spouted angrily. "I am not responsible for the mother's behavior—or the world's wilful misinterpretation of my work!"

"No one is accusing you, Willie," the Recorder said. "You aren't back in court, you needn't defend yourself."

Seraph A. trilled a few bars of Straus' *Blue Danube Waltz*. Reich's ire instantly disappeared.

"Young woman?" the Recorder said to Johnnine. "Any comments?"

"I—I'm cold," was all Johnnine could say.

Reich's expression gentled as he looked at Johnnine. "Her soul's contracted—"

"Can't imagine why," Xofia clucked, pulling one of the rugs on Freud's couch over Johnnine's ethereal, suddenly bluish legs. "Two breathtakingly-unprepared parents, leering down at their newborn like cats at a canary. Gives me the heebie-jeebies every time..." Sitting back down, Xofia quickly quaffed a glass of Dom Elysee. "If I hadn't been banished—"

"We know, Xofia, we know," the Recorder said, a little wearily.

"Can I have some chocolate cake?" Johnnine suddenly asked. The deprivations of her infant scene set up a strong craving for something good, something delicious, to fill the aching void.

"Of course, darling!" Xofia said. "You can have almost anything you want—"

"No, make it a Devil Dog. Can I have a Devil Dog, or maybe two?"

"And what, pray tell, is a Devil Dog?"

"It's devil's food cake, shaped like a hot dog bun, only with a layer of whipped cream in the middle," Johnnine explained, her enthusiasm clearing her throat block. "I used to spend my allowances on Devil Dogs—and Little Lulu comic books."

"She's regressing," Reich said. "To be expected, under the circumstances—"

"You may have to settle for a Limbo Dog," Xofia said sardonically, looking up at Seraph A., who was still whittling up in the corner of the room. "Darling? Can we oblige?"

The seraph blew a few commanding notes from between his perfect, puckered lips. Ti and Do buzzed out of Freud's office before the other three cherubs doused the lights and started up the projector. Johnnine wondered if the little flying Kewpie-dolls were the same things as guardian angels. She half-believed in their existence from the time she hadn't gone right home from junior high school—something she always did otherwise—on the one afternoon her apartment was robbed and vandalized. Johnnine was forced to wonder why on that day of all others, the only time she'd ever done so, she had asked a classmate if she could go home with her. She had been forced to conclude that there was some sort of beneficent Providence looking after her. Was that the same as Fa, So, and what's-his-face?

Chapter Nine

Meanwhile, in the commodious kitchen of the All Souls' Hotel Sacher on Philharmonikerstrasse, amid the copper pots and porcelain sinks of the facsimile of Vienna's famous, four-star restaurant, the gofer-cherubs Ti and Do were re-sculpting a Sachertorte. Backing up in the air, hovering over their handiwork, Ti sounded a sudden sharp note of displeasure and flew at the cake wielding his pastry knife, denuding it of its outer chocolate icing.

Simultaneously, Ti and Do yodeled a G chord of approval and slapped opposite palms together. Then they picked up the platter and flew into the Sacher's oak-panelled bar, stopping just long enough for a few fortifying snifters of schnapps.

Ti and Do flew right by an old soul sitting contentedly alone in the Hotel Sacher's dining room. In a three-piece gray wool suit, the ethereal essence of Sigmund Schlomo Freud sat at a pink-linened table, enjoying his first decent cigar and *kaffee mit schlag* in what seemed like ages.

He was remembering a dream, very vivid, palpably *real*, in which he'd been trapped in the body of a young woman. Schlomo shuddered. In a mood of desperate despondency, he—as a she—had stepped off a curb into a busy street. At the very same moment, the harried driver of a city bus, wishing intensely he was closer to retirement, barreled straight at her.

There was a sudden powerful, mechanized pummeling of Schlomo's female body, followed by an explosion like the shattering of a small star. Next thing he knew, Schlomo was back in his favorite restaurant, sipping his favorite jackhammer-strong Viennese *kaffee*, smoking a Cuban cigar, and reflecting on his dream, a perfect example of his theory of wish-fulfillment.

But he was bemused to see two bewinged angels fly by, tipsily holding onto a large silver plate between them. Clearly, then, he was still dreaming. Curious and amused, Freud downed his coffee, left the paisley-papered dining room and stepped out onto an empty Philharmonikerstrasse. From under the rich maroon canopy over the entrance, he saw the figments of his imagination—such transparent symbols of his own Eros principle—dart up Augustinerstrasse. Purely out of scientific curiosity, and because he had no patients waiting, he set out to follow them.

The motley assembled crew in Freud's crowded office was watching Duncan paint his partially-nude patroness. Ursula Strong was posed provocatively on a divan, draped in a gypsy-colored scarf that left her right breast uncovered. The large canvas in front of Duncan showed a recumbent woman's body. But the head bore little resemblance to Ursula's.

"...we should celebrate! What would you like to do?" she asked Duncan merrily.

"What...?" Duncan answered. "Don't talk so much—"
"Duncan!"
"What?!" With quick brush strokes he began to fill in the facial features.
"It isn't every day a man is set free. We need to honor your divorce. My treat. Somewhere special, like the Rainbow Grill? Or dark and bohemian, Chumley's, maybe?"

Duncan's voice was gruff. "I don't want to go anywhere—"
"Don't be anti-social, Duncan."

The face under Duncan's hand was looking more and more like Dinah. "I'm not interested in going out, or being seen with you. I'm an artist, not a paid escort."

Ursula's eyes began to tear. "You are heartless, too, did you know that? An egomaniacal, ruthlessly self-centered paint dauber!"

Duncan scowled as he turned the facial features on the portrait into a Picassoesque abstract with two mouths, four eyes and three noses. The scene dimmed. Johnnine was caught between feeling a vague pity for her father and a second-hand, slimy sort of triumph at her father's treatment of Ursula.

But before she could dwell on it, she saw her baby self sitting on a beach blanket, propped up like a moist and sagging sack of groceries between her mother and her grandmother. Dinah, still a shapely size 12, was watching the waves as she peeled a banana and handed pieces to Johnnine. Dinah's mother, Esther Hapgood, was a strikingly beautiful middle-aged woman whose heavy chestnut chignon was only beginning to show traces of gray. The three Hapgood women, fully-dressed, faced a sinking sun and a surf-crashing, undulating ocean.

"I know what she needs," Esther said, unceremoniously laying her eleven-month old granddaughter on her back, stripping her of her corduroy jumper and cumbersome wad of diapers. "Salt water's just the thing for diaper rash."

"Don't, Mother," Dinah protested, though her voice was more timid, less sure of itself, than with other people. "She won't like it, it won't feel good."

Esther was used to not listening to her daughter and continued her undressing of Johnnine. "Immaterial whether she likes it or not. The important thing is that it will be good *for* her—"

In a flowered housedress and matronly brown leather shoes that contrasted sharply with her smart figure and trim ankles, Esther marched herself and Johnnine down to the water's edge. The autumnal beach was largely deserted. Johnnine gasped and spluttered as her grandmother plunked her on the wet sand and the ocean's cold froth hit her raw, red, bare bottom. She began to cry, looking to her grandmother for help or sympathy.

Esther gave her neither. She pulled a small, morocco-bound book out of her pocket and held it up as she read aloud, a few feet away from the tide's reach. "Cast the bantling on the rocks," Esther read, from Emerson's *Self-Reliance*.

"Suckle her with the she-wolf's teat. Wintered with the hawk and fox, Power and speed be hands and feet."

Johnnine stared at her grandmother as the water foamed over her link-sausage legs.

Esther lowered the book and addressed her naked infant granddaughter with complete seriousness. "I may not be here much longer, Johnnine, so as my first and only grandchild, I will tell you something now you must remember. Put yourself in touch with the internal ocean and do not go begging water from the urns of others. Particularly the urn of your mother, of whom your grandfather and I, in our youthful folly and ignorance, made an unholy mess."

The sun behind Johnnine was just about to set, its rays illumining her red-blonde baby fuzz into a flaming halo. Johnnine made a sour pickle face as she sucked on a chubby, salty fist and gawped up at her earnest grandmother.

"Emerson says 'we lie in the lap of Immense Intelligence' and I believe him, though you wouldn't know it to look at most of us. It won't be easy, Johnnine Hapgood Kirk, or Kirk Hapgood, or Lord knows what name your mother will take a fancy to next. You must accept the place Divine Providence has found for you. Though half the time it will feel like punishment."

A wavelet surged up and doused them both with sea spray. Johnnine's shoulders jerked up to her chin. Her rounded baby belly became suddenly concave as she gasped at the cold water. Esther scooped up her dripping grandchild and kissed her briskly on the forehead. Then she plopped her sidesaddle on her hip and strode back to the blanket.

Johnnine supposed it was a good thing her grandmother had given her this *al fresco*, transcendentalist baptism since she hadn't gotten any other. While Esther put her fervent faith in Emmet Fox and Ralph Waldo, her daughter Dinah was as anti-religious as anyone could get. In life-long rebellion against her preacher-grandfather, whose aim was to "scorch me with hellfire and brimstone if I ever so much as touched myself."

Sadly, Johnnine didn't remember her grandmother. Though she could sorely have used an ally, Esther had given up the ghost by the time Johnnine was two.

Chapter Ten

The All Souls' screen showed Dinah in the kitchen of the Lower East Side tenement apartment, doing dishes at the sink. On the kitchen table, the camera panned over the remains of a half-eaten chocolate cake. A single small candle, unlit, stood at an angle. One-year old Johnnine and a friend of Dinah's, fortyish Tillie Lindstrom, sat in the steaming bathtub next to the sink. Tillie applied a washcloth to Johnnine's chocolate-smeared face. Then she leaned back in the tub and sighed. "There's a great deal to be said for domesticity," Tillie said, luxuriating in the hot water.

"Especially if someone else does the cooking," Dinah said.

Tillie laughed. "Yes, that helps."

A studious, introspective look stole over Johnnine's face. She scrunched up her facial muscles until she looked like a head of cabbage with two eyes, staring unseeingly at Tillie.

Tillie sat up with a jolt, splashing water over the edge. "Dinah! She's shit in the tub!"

Dinah looked into the tub and turned off the faucet. "My Lord, Till, it's not going to bite you, and it's bowel movement, not shit."

Tillie was busily flicking water at the floating turd. "Well, would you please get whatever you want to call it out of the tub?"

Dinah hung up her dishtowel. "Keep your shirt on, we don't want her to think there's anything wrong with having a b. m. Don't look so horrified—"

"Right. You're right..." Tillie carefully recomposed her face, wiping off her look of dismay, exchanging it for a not entirely genuine benign smile, both at Johnnine and the turd.

Johnnine's head swiveled back and forth between her mother and her "aunt," logging their interchange with innocent, wide-eyed, rapt attention.

Tillie added in a low voice between clenched teeth, "Does it have to be a *lengthy* lesson in loving our feces or can I get out now?"

Dinah leaned over the tub, matter-of-factly scooped up the small brown offending article and beamed at her infant daughter. "Look, Johnnine! This is what we do with b. m.'s—"

Dinah crossed to the old-fashioned, closet-like bathroom off the kitchen and deposited the turd in the toilet bowl. As she pulled the flush chain hanging from the wooden box over the seat, Dinah sang, "Remember when we took the train to my mother's? Toot, toot! All aboard! We are going bye-bye..."

A mesmerized Johnnine blinked at the sudden cascade of watery noise. After washing her hands, Dinah came back to the tub with a towel, lifted Johnnine out and vigorously rubbed her dry. Tillie also stood up. The water sheeted off her tall, womanly figure. "Will it be too traumatic if I I let the water out?"

Dinah chuckled as Tillie reached for a towel. "Don't be sarcastic. You know how important toilet training is."

Dinah carried a pink, buffed and polished Johnnine back to the toilet. She pulled down her own undies, hiked up her skirt, and sat on the back of the seat. She placed a naked Johnnine just in front of her on the toilet. When Dinah began to pee, Johnnine leaned over to watch her mother's golden stream fall into the bowl.

Tillie laughed warmly as she got dressed. "Darling Dinah, you are something new under the sun—"

"*Well*," Dinah said, a little testily. "Fathers teach sons how to aim, mothers need to show daughters where to squat." To Johnnine, she said, "*You* decide when you want to use the toilet, ducklet. I don't care when you start, it's entirely up to you. I just want you to know it's here."

Johnnine looked questioningly up at her mother as Dinah smiled at her. "Tinkle, tinkle, little star, now we're going bye-bye." Dinah pulled the flush chain and everyone blinked.

The All Souls' screen went to black.

"Enchanting!" Reich said heatedly. "The mother was applying my principle of self-regulation, letting the *child* determine when it is ready. Do you have any idea how much healthier the world would be if children weren't dictated to about their own bodily functions?!"

The tipsy cherubs, Ti and Do, flew into the room carrying the cake platter, elliptically circling a small table until finally they managed to land it safely. Johnnine's attention was riveted on the covered platter as though it were the cure for what ailed her.

A moment later, everyone in Freud's office was astounded when a small dapper man of middle years stepped through the doorway. "*Was macht Sie*!?" he demanded proprietarily.

"Herr Professor!" Reich exclaimed, standing up.

"Willie??" Freud answered. "What the *blazes* are you doing here?"

"We could ask the same," Xofia purred. She shot a look at the Akashic Recorder. "Is this a scheduled arrival?"

"I'm not sure," the Recorder said. "We'd have to check the Records."

"And who, may I ask, are you?" Freud's tone was slightly imperious as he addressed Xofia. "What is that screen doing there? And what is this girl doing on my couch? *What is going on here*?"

Ti and Do flew around in slightly inebriated circles, the wings of one grazing those of the other. Reich, Freud, Xofia and The Recorder all began talking and gesticulating at once, no one was listening to anyone else. Just when Johnnine was certain chaos was about to break out, Seraph A. blew several notes that sounded like the opening bars of the William Tell Overture. The cherubs instantly sobered up and shot back to their seats on the room's moulding, the small assembly became becalmed.

"Darling," Xofia soothed, getting up and gliding close to Freud's ethereal essence. Her loosely-tied kimono revealed an appealing amount of cleavage. "My name is Xofia, the essence of the long-banished and much-maligned feminine principle? I can't *tell* you how thrilled and delighted I am to meet you. *Finally*, I might add—" Xofia extended her hand.

Johnnine clearly saw Seraph A., up in the corner, withdraw a hollow tube from between his gossamer wings. Inserting a dart, he put his perfect lips around the end and aimed at the itchy gray wool ethereal essence of Sigmund Freud, landing it squarely in the heart zone. Johnnine wasn't sure she'd seen what she thought she'd seen. Except that Freud's hostile demeanor vanished as completely as did the dart.

"Call me Schlomo," he insisted, warmly grasping Xofia's hand and brushing it with his lips.

"So gal*lant*!" she murmured.

Reich bristled like a porcupine. Seraph A. whistled melodically, pouring musical oil on the turbulent waters. Reich sat back down and nonchalantly lit a Bright Spark.

"Why don't you take our distinguished drop-in somewhere and explain the situation to him?" the Recorder said to Xofia. "Somewhere you won't be disturbed—like the *Bibliothek*? We'll carry on until you get back."

Xofia winked and nodded at the Recorder. "Let's go somewhere private, Schlomo, somewhere we can be alone."

"You mean just the two of us?"

Xofia nodded and gently ushered a smitten Schlomo out the door.

Johnnine got up to try the remodeled Sachertorte, breaking off and tasting a piece. Glumly, she sat back down on The Couch. "Jesus, what hope is there for my immortal soul if you guys can't even make a decent Devil Dog?" She picked up Xofia's pack of Dark Star cigarillos, flipped one out and lit up. Then she poured herself a glass of Dom Elysee champagne. "While the cat's away," she said a little flippantly.

Neither Reich nor the Recorder said anything while she sipped and puffed. But either due to her disembodied state or the specific qualities of All Souls' tobacco and alcohol, Johnnine instantly felt crappy. She put out the cigarillo in the champagne. "Tastes like puppy piss and singed rabbit hair..."

"A good sign," the Recorder said. "You have to be thoroughly dead to appreciate their taste. Since that's all they're good for anyway. Are we ready?"

Johnnine groaned, closed her eyes, and put her hand on her stomach. "*Oy.* I suppose—"

Reich turned around in his chair to address Johnnine in his earnest, I-am-a-doctor tone. "Breathe deeply," he advised. "Don't hold your chest so tightly, soften your belly muscles—"

Johnnine was greatly relieved when Willie's attention was drawn back to the film. The first shot entranced him. "Oh, look, it's me!" He turned to face the screen.

Cracking an eye open, Johnnine saw a much younger Wilhelm Reich standing at the front of a half-filled lecture room. At the rear, a door opened cautiously and a contrite-looking Dinah made her way to a seat. Reich, wearing his short white lab coat over tan chino pants, ignored the late arrival. His eyes burned like chunks of bituminous coal as he spoke extemporaneously, one hand jammed into the pocket of his lab coat. His Austrian accent was thick, but his English was excellent.

"...and the birth of my own son has given me much opportunity to study infant sexual development on a daily basis. Peter's has been a natural unfolding, unhindered by parents who are terrified of their own sexual energy. His upbringing is what I would wish for all children—he has the freedom to explore and take pleasure from his own genitals, the purpose being to keep the child from becoming armored in the first puberty, between three and six."

Reich stopped to take a sip of water. "At my research center in Forest Hills, I have brought together a group of interested laypeople, as well as educators and physicians, to study orgone energy in the infant—so that we may discover what a healthy, unarmored child is like. We can study pathology for a thousand years, but it will not lead us to a definition of health...

"Many of you know how strongly I feel that the only way to produce unsadistic, non-neurotic adults is to begin with a healthy birthing process. We must build a new orientation of life, one based on the newborn child, and we must realize our proper function.

"As parents, we are no more than transmission belts from an evil past to an eventually better future. Should our children adapt to war, or the tyranny of the emotional plague? I say NO.

"We cannot hope to build independent human characters if education is left to the politicians. Since we have proved unfit to build our own present, we have no right to tell our children how to build their future. All we can do is be honest, tell them where and how we failed. *And* do everything possible to give them the biological vigor they need to build a new and better world—for themselves. Thank you."

The medium-sized audience applauded loudly and enthusiastically. The camera showed Dinah's round, intelligent face beatifically fixed on Reich as he stepped off the podium to talk to a cluster of front-row supporters.

Dinah was still clapping energetically as she turned to the man next to her. "A wonderful speaker, isn't he?"

Johnnine felt even sicker to her stomach when she saw the large and troubling face of her guardian, Daniel Pahlser, fill the screen. "Yah, he certainly is that—" Pahlser said, also clapping demonstrably.

Chapter Eleven

On their way to the Bibliothek, past the twin wedding-cake spires of the neo-Gothic Votivkirche, past Schottenring and down the narrower Herrengasse, Xofia gave Schlomo much the same rap she had given Johnnine. Only Schlomo was less inclined to believe her.

"A permit to die?" he said contemptuously. He had taken his ivory-handled walking stick from the foyer of the flat and now waved it in the air. "Bah! Reincarnation is a refuge for weak minds, as bad as Religion, for those who can't accept the permanence of death."

"Then what's your rationale for being here?" Xofia teased. "I have an inkling you do not consider yourself cerebrally inferior."

Schlomo looked a little smug. "I am dreaming. Rather amusingly, I may say. Tell me—I feel inexplicably compelled to ask—you look so familiar, have we met before?"

Xofia laughed her water-plashing-in-a-fountain laugh. "Not exactly, Herr Professor," she said, leading him up the *schlag* steps to the Hofburg's vast library. "Although it's not been for lack of trying on my part." The motto over the portal read, "Abandon All Ignorance All Ye Who Enter Here."

"I insist that you call me Schlomo," he said, stamping his walking stick lightly on the ground.

"I personally prefer 'darling'," Xofia purred.

"Oh, well, that's good, too—" Schlomo capitulated.

They walked into the enormous vaulted lobby. "This is where the Akashic Records are kept," Xofia said, sweeping a kimonoed arm about. The gesture showed off her long-legged, hourglass figure. "Would you like to know where your wife is now?"

"Martha?" Schlomo asked, looking over his shoulder guiltily.

"I'll show you how to find out." Xofia sat down at the desk. She wrote Schlomo's wife's name on a piece of parchment and slipped it into the pneumatic tube. A moment later it came back and she handed a soul scroll to Schlomo. While he unrolled it and began to read—"Ha!" he said, "She turned into an army captain!"—Xofia slipped Schlomo's name into the tube. When *it* came back, she quickly scanned to the end of his last life.

"Whose is that?" Schlomo's sharp eyes looked over at her.

"Yours, darling," Xofia said, not taking her eyes off the illuminated Gothic script.

"Let me see—" Schlomo moved behind her.

"Won't do any good, ducks."

Schlomo squinted, stepped closer and then away. "But I can't make it out!"

"Of course not, darling. No one can read their own soul scroll. It wouldn't be kosher." Xofia finished reading the last paragraph, about the end of Schlomo's last life. "Borderline," she said out loud.

"What is?"

"Whether or not you should be here. You may need your own Life Review. Look, darling, I've got to dash, I have some imbuing of the will-to-live to do, but do stay and amuse yourself. Under the Freedom of Illumination Act, you can read up on anyone's soul history, learn as much as you like about anyone. Willie Reich, for instance."

"Pish!" Schlomo said aggravatedly. "I already know all about Willie, you forget he was my assistant for eight years —I had hopes for him, until he became *meshugge*!" His expression changed from disdain to lechery. "I think you need to tell me your most intimate fantasies—"

Xofia parried with an evasive move. "I understand Adler's back on Earth...building powerboats."

"Feh! The man always was an idiot—tell me, how's your sex life?"

"Darling. Johnnine's case is my top priority at the moment. While you are certifiably dead, her life hangs in the balance. We'll talk later, I *promise*. I must fly—" Xofia made a graceful exit.

Schlomo saw Xofia as a blonde *shiksa* showgirl with teeth like pearls, legs like a can-can dancer's, and boobies like ripe winter melons. Then he was appalled at himself. Where were these lecherous thoughts coming from? Still, he had never felt so bereft in all his lives as when she glided out of the lobby. Almost as though he had lost half his own soul.

When Xofia breathlessly returned to Freud's quarters on Berggasse, she told the Recorder Schlomo's case was too close to call, it would have to be taken up by the Life Review Board. Luckily, this was out of her jurisdiction. She could not promise even The Powers to be objective in his case. "Did I miss anything juicy?" She poured herself a libation of Dom Elysee.

Johnnine snorted derisively, uncrossing and recrossing her legs, studying her beloved fake lizard black high heels, which happily had made the transition to the Waiting Room with her. Probably she loved them so much because they made Dinah apoplectic. "Only a fight between my mother and Tillie. Tillie hinted maybe Mom wasn't doing something right in raising me, so Mom threw Tillie out. My mother is not into being critiqued."

"Delicious! What was the fight about?" Xofia asked over the rim of her glass.

"Breast-feeding." Johnnine shrugged. "I bit Mom's breast and drew a little blood. Mom cried and told Tillie I was being plaguey. Tillie tried to calm her down and said maybe it was because I didn't want to be on the tit anymore, that maybe Mom was forcing the issue for her own reasons. That's what it looked like to me, but what do I know? I guess it's plaguey to grow teeth. Anyway, Mom got really mad and told Tillie to split."

"Oh *good*. I love a good catfight, can we rerun it?"

"NO!" Johnnine shouted. "Enough already! Why can't we just fast-forward to the end? I don't *care* about the past, the only good thing about the past is that it's *over!*" Johnnine choked on her own words, tears spilled down her cheek. "History bores the living shit out of me..."

"Vox Americana," Xofia said sardonically to The Reporter, at the same time handing Johnnine another hankie. "Darling," she continued smoothly, changing her tone. "Are you peckish? How long since you ate?"

"I'm *starving*, if you want to know—" Johnnine said petulantly.

"Why didn't you say so?" Xofia appealed to Seraph A. "Darling, would you?"

Seraph A. dipped down off the cornice, hung prettily in place like a hummingbird and burst into a few bars from the wedding feast of *La Cenerentola*.

"Something simpler would probably suffice—" Xofia answered. The little seraph flew away.

Johnnine felt dimly gratified that the seraph as well as two of the cherubs were off on food-finding missions: Johnnine had not spurned her mother's breast because she didn't like to eat. Weaning herself was a move toward independence from an overbearing mother. Maybe it was a symbolic episode: her baby teeth had drawn first blood in the battle that was to come.

The next segment of the film showed Dinah in a sparsely-furnished, white-painted room, on an analyst's couch, naked under a sheet that covered only her torso.

Daniel Pahlser sat on a low stool next to her. He was such a large man that even sitting down he seemed to tower over his patient. "...yes, and how did you *feel* about your mother dying?" Pahlser asked.

Dinah's face was a constricted mask of pain. She spoke haltingly, as though with great effort. Tears squeezed out of the sides of her tightly-shut eyes. "I was...Mother was on her deathbed for three months, I couldn't...stand it anymore, I had...nothing left...but then, when she died, I almost, almost fell off a subway platform...I realized I had no family, no one, no one in the world who cared about me..."

"And how does your body feel now?" Pahlser had a slight Bronx accent.

"It feels very tight, here, in the chest." Dinah raised a heavy arm and touched herself on the sternum. Her large, loose breasts shifted under the white sheet.

Pahlser got up and placed his enormous hands on Dinah's chest, pushing down as he spoke. "I want you to think about your mother, all your feelings for her. How did you really feel about her?"

The All Souls' Waiting Room

Dinah exhaled under Pahlser's hand pressure. "I was mad about her, everyone was. Mother was beautiful, charming, witty. She could be quite risqué when she got a certain little wicked gleam in her eye—"

"Yah," Pahlser said seriously, applying more downward pressure to Dinah's chest.

Dinah struggled for breath, erupting into explosive, raging sobs, her words coming out in staccato bursts in between Pahlser's downward thrusts. "I *hated* her—she never let me—touch her!—She never—held me in her arms!" Dinah cried uncontrollably as Pahlser continued pushing down on her torso.

He didn't say anything for a minute. "Now I want you to kick the couch with your heels and fists, kick it *hard*."

Dinah opened her eyes wide, as though double-checking his instructions.

"As hard as you can—" Pahlser repeated. "And I want you to yell out loud while you kick. No one will hear you, the office is sound-proofed. Come on! Let me hear your feelings about your mother, from *here*!" Pahlser touched Dinah's solar plexus.

Unchecked screaming and thrashing followed for several minutes. Finally, Dinah's well-padded limbs stopped moving and her sobs turned to sniffles and heaving whimpers. Her face, however, looked softer.

"You see now why you were depressed?"

"I wasn't being honest with myself," Dinah said in a raspy voice. She reached for a tissue and blew her nose loudly.

"Yah," Pahlser said, his word for yes sounding exactly like Reich's. "*And* you felt guilty. One night you wished your sick mother dead and the next morning she *was* dead!"

"Yes!" Dinah said excitedly, her deep brown eyes flashing at him. "I felt like a murderer, I thought I killed her, that it was my fault she died!"

Pahlser nodded gravely.

Dinah's eyes shone with gratitude. "Thank you, doctor. I can't, I couldn't begin to tell you...I feel so much better..."

Pahlser's wide, loose-lipped mouth, which reminded Johnnine of the wavy edges of a giant clam shell, stretched taut across his clean-shaven face. His close-set, gray eyes peered down his broad bony nose as he smiled at Dinah.

Next, the camera caught Johnnine, at age three, standing near the bottom landing of a winding wooden staircase. She looked very pretty in a lilac pique summer dress, her fair blonde hair falling to her shoulders. Dinah stood near her, perspiration beading her forehead and upper lip. Dinah patted her face with a handkerchief as footsteps were heard above them.

Camera panned up the stairs and held on Wilhelm Reich. Sunlight streamed in through a small window in the stairwell behind him and bounced off his white lab coat and shock of white hair. He was surrounded by a haze of cigarette smoke and appeared part of a luminous cloud. "Miss Hapgood," Reich said, politely shaking Dinah's hand. "And your daughter?" He gave Johnnine a brilliantly warm smile. She gaped up at him.

Dinah's returning smile was strained but proud. "Yes. This is Johnnine."

Johnnine was clearly awe-struck, her eyes were wide and her mouth was slightly open.

"It appears I've made an impression," Reich laughed softly, bending at the knees to be on eye level with her. "How do you do?" he said. Johnnine smiled broadly and put out her hand. Reich laughed a smoker's congested laugh and shook hands with her. Then he stood up. "Come please, my office is through here—"

Reich led the way through a dining room, its counters and large table crowded with laboratory equipment. In a corner were several small wire-mesh cages stacked on top of each other, each containing a single white rat.

"Look, Mom!" Johnnine pointed.

"You know not to put your fingers near them?" Reich admonished over his shoulder.

Johnnine nodded gravely, clasping her pointer finger protectively. "They might bite me..."

A small pantry had been turned into an office off the dining room. Reich took a seat behind his overflowing desk. "Please, sit. Excuse the mess, we are converting a room in the basement into more lab space, which is where you would be working. If we agree—"

Dinah held onto her purse tightly, perching on the edge of her chair. She was dressed in a white uniform and thick-soled white duty shoes. Her figure had gone from a pleasingly-plump size 12 to a stocky 16. "Dr. Reich," she said, giving it the German pronunciation, *ryesshh*, "I have to be honest, I'm not sure I would work out in this job. For one thing, I hadn't realized how long it took to get here from Manhattan."

"But you could move, could you not? Forest Hills is a pleasant part of the city. We like our people close by in any case, there is always extra work."

"I—" Dinah said awkwardly, looking down, "when I heard you needed a laboratory assistant I thought I should at least talk to you about it. But I suppose I'm here mostly because I wanted to meet you."

"Well," Reich said. "Thank you for your honesty." A thin stream of cigarette smoke flowed out his nostrils.

"You see, your work is very important to me. I'm trying to raise Johnnine as a self-regulated child, but I am alone, I have no partner."

"Her father?"

"He is...disinterested."

Reich glanced at Johnnine, who was watching the rats in the next room as she leaned against her mother. "She is a lovely girl, I commend you on your success so far."

"Thank you. It's not easy, as you know. There aren't many people who agree with what you're—what we're trying to do."

Reich dragged on his cigarette and smiled. "Yah, I know. So we must show them."

"I have friends who are also interested in your work. We get together and talk about how to raise our children orgonomically."

"*Brav!*"

"Would you consider looking at Johnnine? I'm concerned about her early body armor. I've heard you started an Orgone Infant Research Center, is that something—"

Loud men's voices in the dining room interrupted Dinah. The 6'5" frame of Daniel Pahlser loomed in the doorway. "Excuse me, Dr. Reich, may I see you?" Pahlser and Dinah acknowledged each other with a smiling nod.

Reich lit a fresh cigarette from the dying butt of his last. "Dr. Pahlser is heavily involved with the O. I. R. C., but I don't see any particular need—" Reich transferred his cigarette to his left hand and gently laid the other on Johnnine's head, who looked unembarassedly up at him. He studied her closely but fondly. Johnnine did not look away. "Her eyes are not blocked, she has a lovely soft, full mouth, her face is full of life and expression. Whatever you are doing, Miss Hapgood, I would say keep it up. Now you must please excuse me."

Pahlser's piercing gray eyes flicked back and forth between Johnnine and Dinah as Reich showed them out. Reich came upon a dark-haired younger man in the hallway. "What is the matter, Katzman? I heard you and Pahlser arguing."

Dr. Nathan Katzman, Reich's assistant, was younger, shorter, and smaller than either Reich or Pahlser, but he had a stubborn, quiet authority. His red, bee-stung lips were dry and his dark eyes were restive under Reich's disapproval. "I was telling him you were busy." He looked angrily at Pahlser.

Impatiently, Pahlser broke his news. "Two U. S. Food and Drug Administration agents paid a call on Tripp and Cooke this morning." Pahlser wore a gray gabardine flight suit that matched his fringe of grizzled hair. He darted a challenging look at Katzman, but when he spoke to Reich his tone was one of urgent persuasion.

"Yah, *gut*!? Then they are finally doing their job, getting testimony for the investigation." Reich was brisk.

"No," Pahlser said heavily. "They wanted lists of patients in orgone therapy, patients who used the accumulator."

Reich's face flushed bright red. "Zo! This they know they cannot have! Why do they ask? It is an outrage!"

Katzman said, "They're only government hatchet men, just doing their job."

"Yah," Reich answered heatedly. "Like good Nazis, they just 'do their job'. I know these little men well, they are the same as the ones in Europe. But do not forget, our work has friends in high places!"

Katzman looked uncomfortable and Pahlser pressed his argument. "We need to warn the patients, and the other therapists. They should know that any questions put by the F. D. A. are hostile."

Reich exploded. "I will not stoop to scare tactics! That is the government's way, not mine! You do not fight the emotional plague on its own level, it will defeat you every time!"

"Forewarned is forearmed, Reich," Pahlser said, flushing.

"The forewarning I want to make to the world is about the current planetary emergency. We are under siege by the emotional plague. I will not concern myself with hoodlums in government! They cannot dilute the energy of truth, the energy of orgone—go back to work, Pahlser. You will feel better—"

A small boy came running down the hall, blasting away with a toy gun. "Bam bam bam!"

Reich caught him up in his arms. "Peter, we do not shoot at our guests!"

"But I want to, papa!"

Reich smoothed back the boy's thick brown hair. "Ah, *liebchen*...where is your mother?"

Peter Reich pointed one of his guns upstairs. "Bam bam bam bam bam!"

"Shall we go see her?"

Peter nodded but didn't look at his white-haired father. Reich gently cupped the boy's chin and turned his head towards him. "Peter. Give me your eyes."

A profoundly loving look passed from father to son. Peter's body softened visibly. He put his arms around Reich's neck and kissed his father's cheek. Daniel Pahlser's expression, watching the exchange, was like a starving man at a banquet.

"I'll have Tripp and Cooke call you," Pahlser said.

With Peter clinging to him, Reich watched Pahlser out the door.

Katzman waited until the door closed behind him. "I don't trust him, Reich, he's a zealot. I get this funny feeling in my gut about him—"

"Yah? You think perhaps he is destructive?"

"Yes. And I wonder why you want the fox in the chicken coop."

"Because I understand foxes," Reich said, turning up the stairs, carrying Peter in his arms. "And if there is anyone who can save him, it is me—"

Several weeks later, the film picked up again in the anteroom of Daniel Pahlser's office. Dinah, fully dressed, was being escorted out. "Should I make another appointment?"

"I don't think you need one, Hapgood. The last few sessions were very productive, I think we got to the core of the problem. Reich doesn't believe in lengthy therapy, it isn't necessary if you get directly at the body armor. Not depressed anymore, are you?"

Dinah smiled gratefully. "No, not at all. You mean, we're done?"

"Yah, unless something comes up. But I don't think it will."

"I have to thank you from the bottom of my heart. I can't tell you what treatment's done for me. I feel...years lighter, pounds younger." Dinah smiled at her own words, glowing as she looked up at him.

"Yah, good," Pahlser said earnestly. "Remember about breathing deeply and keeping your throat clear."

At the door, doctor and patient stood and faced each other. Inhaling deeply, they bent their knees slightly, expanded their chests, and uttered a loud, back-of-the-throat HA-RUMM at each other in parting. Dinah looked self-conscious but determined to follow her new regime no matter how foolish it made her feel. Her smile at Pahlser was gay before she turned towards the staircase.

In the All Souls' Waiting Room, Schlomo's shrill voice broke the stillness. The lights came up. "*Ha!*" he laughed. "The woman thinks she's cured of her mother complex! And all she had to do was kick a couch! *Haha*!!" There was a slightly hysterical edge to his laughter.

"Schlomo! What are you doing back here?" Xofia asked.

"I was an *innovator*!" Willie boomed at Schlomo, standing up, his eyes narrowed, his face on fire. "Before me there was only talk, talk, and more talk! You do not get at the root of neurosis through the *head*. You get at it through the *body*!"

The two former psychoanalysts advanced towards each other menacingly, nostrils flaring.

Xofia was between them in a flash. "Schlomo, you have to leave—"

"*Ferkockteh* heretic!" Schlomo shouted at Willie.

"Armored old anal-retentive!" Willie yelled back.

Seraph A. dive-bombed off his cornice. From his porcelain-perfect lips poured the bullfight chorus from *Carmen*. Instantly, the would-be combatants were becalmed.

"Schlomo, you mustn't pop up like this, it's disruptive—" Xofia said.

"*Disruptive*? This is *my* office!"

"Not until you've gotten clearance," she rejoined.

"Xofia!" Schlomo pleaded, taking a different tack. "I *miss* you. I can't live without you, I'm yours, body and mind..."

"What about your soul?"

"Don't ask for that, I'm not sure it exists—"

"Schlomo." Xofia was not unsympathetic but she was also stern. "I'm going to quote you a song lyric: I cried, for you. Now it's your turn, to cry over me—" Then she looked up at Seraph A. "Darling? Would you do the honors?"

Seraph A. whistled a brain-rattling chord. The cherubs Fa, So, and La picked Schlomo up by the elbows and lifted him off the ground. Schlomo protested violently. "Unhand me, you little pissants! You are mere figments of my imagination! I made you and I can break you!" At another whistled blast from

Seraph A., the cherubs forcibly ejected Schlomo out of his office. "I know what the A. stands for—" he shouted at the seraph, who was back up in his corner, serenely whittling a dart. "*Anteros*, the *destroyer* of love!"

"Wrong, darling!" Xofia called after him. "'A.' is for Aloysius, which means famous warrior! He goes into battle to save young souls!"

Johnnine still didn't have a clue what the old farts were talking about half the time, but she loved broad farce as much as anyone else. Her mother's therapy had been upsetting to witness, but Johnnine knew it would probably appear to fall under the farcical category to the uninitiated. She herself was so used to Reichian weirdness it didn't look weird to her. When you grow up in a land of three-eyed people, it's the two-eyed who look strange, she thought. Which was a large part of why she was in the All Souls' Waiting Room. She couldn't handle being a three-eyed freak in a two-eyed world.

The Recorder's cavernous, rock-of-ages voice startled all of them. "May we return to the business at hand? Even The Powers don't like waiting Forever."

Chapter Twelve

While the film took a moment to rev up again, Johnnine took the opportunity to stuff her face. The cherubs' idea of nourishing fare corresponded exactly with her own: under the silver dome were two plates, one containing creamed corn, butter-soaked mashed potatoes, and sweet and sour beets, some of her favorite childhood dishes. The food didn't taste anywhere near as sublime as it did at Horn & Hardart's, but how could it? She wasn't in New York, she was in Mondo Bizarro, a place where the shades of Sigmund Freud and Wilhelm Reich verbally abused each other. And were stopped by snatches of operatic arias whistled by a dart-blowing midget in silk diapers. So she shouldn't have been surprised by the cherubs' second attempt at a Devil Dog, a chocolate torte stripped of its icing and sculpted into a bust of Lassie. "Jesus H. Christ," Johnnine groaned. "The Powers of Creation here, and they can't duplicate the recipe for a snack cake."

"Darling," Xofia chided, in what Johnnine was coming to recognize as her axiom-giving voice. "Eat the bird in your hand instead of pining for the two that are beating around the bush. And be grateful about it. Now hush."

The room lights went out and the Akashic film came up.

In Dinah's white-walled Lower East Side living room, a single bed covered with pillows and a chenille bedspread did double duty as a couch. Steam heat hissed and clanked from the ancient radiator in the corner. Dinah, dressed in a vivid aqua long house robe, sat on the couch with a drink in her hand. The underfurnished room was made colorful with home-made paintings tacked to the walls, some of Johnnine's, some of Dinah's.

"...worried about her," she was saying to Daniel Pahlser, who sat on an orange crate across from her, also drinking. "Since I started back to work, her nursery school teacher says she's been constipated a lot."

"Hmmm," Pahlser said thoughtfully. "Of course it goes without saying that you know not to spank her, that contracts the anus severely—"

Dinah looked shocked. "Never! Good God. No, I slap her across the face when she needs it, it's much more honest..."

Pahlser nodded his approval and took another sip of his drink.

Dinah smiled. "I made a vow to myself when she was born. She could do anything she wanted to me, crawl on me, chew on me, I didn't care if she threw up on me, just so long as there was physical contact—"

"And she toilet-trained herself, you say?" Pahlser's face was highly-colored, pink with drinking. He and Dinah looked well-oiled as they sipped their amber-colored Manhattans.

"Oh, yes. I've never had a minute's trouble with her that way. Johnnine, come in here for a minute, ducklet—"

Four-year old Johnnine came into the room, carrying a small yellow Mexican rocking chair. She was a beautiful child. Honey-blonde hair framed a strikingly alert face with enormous, almond-shaped blue-green eyes and a fully-formed, sensuous mouth. Johnnine put the chair down, facing them, and sat in it.

Dinah laughed. "You see what I mean about her own definite and distinct personality? Johnnine, this is Daniel Pahlser. He's a doctor, and he wants to talk to you."

Johnnine scrutinized Pahlser carefully. "I don't want to," she said clearly, then took her rocker to the other side of the room.

Dinah's laugh was one of nervous embarrassment. "I know. I'll play some music. She loves this song..." Dinah put a record on the Victrola. Johnnine's head swiveled toward the record-player as a razzy trumpet intro filled the room.

"*You smile...and the angels sing...the sweetest love song that the world has ever heard...*"

Pahlser took off his huge leather shoes, revealing stockinged feet as big as egg cartons. He crossed to Johnnine and made a formal, condescending bow. "May I have this dance, please?"

Johnnine shook her head.

"Johnnine." The unspoken command in Dinah's voice carried over the music. Johnnine looked at her mother and tightened her mouth. Pahlser took her hand and placed her small bare feet on his arched insteps. Beginning slowly, he built up speed until he was exuberantly whirling her around the room, whooping and singing out loud as he hung onto her tightly. Johnnine looked worried, like a baby monkey tethered to a dancing bear.

Dinah beamed at them as she finished her highball. Camera did a close-up on Pahlser, laughing uproariously, his huge face red and sweaty. In contrast, Johnnine was grave, her expression withdrawn, while Pahlser's eyes glittered with wild abandon. In the All Souls' Waiting Room, Johnnine felt sorry for herself, forced to carouse with a man she had from the beginning mistrusted. She hadn't liked the way he looked at her and paid too much attention to her, his forced, unnatural laugh.

Next was an episode Johnnine remembered all too well, her first therapy session with a Reichian analyst. She and her mother entered a doctor's waiting room and took off their coats. The door to the inner sanctum opened and an acne-faced young man emerged, followed by Doctor Ernesto Febrillo, a handsome, olive-skinned Spaniard, his dark-haired matinee-idol looks set off by a starched white linen shirt, open at the neck and rolled up at the sleeves.

He greeted Dinah and Johnnine in his heavily-accented English. "An' how are joo today?" he asked, smiling at Johnnine. She did not smile back.

Dinah answered. "I'm fine, but I think she has a block, doctor. In her chest—"

Febrillo's gaze swung to Johnnine. She didn't speak but she did return his look. "Jes? She does seem a li'l wi'draw—jore a pretty girl, Johnnina."

"John-*neen*," she corrected him distinctly.

Dinah looked down on her daughter but continued to talk as if she weren't there. "All she thinks about is herself and getting her own way, doctor. She's very selfish. She just bucks me on everything I tell her to do. Pahlser recommended, I mean, I thought maybe you could do something with her..."

"Jes, I talk-ed to him this morning—will joo come with me now, Johnneen? I wan' to talk to joo for a few minutes. OK?"

Johnnine did not move.

Dinah said, "Go on, Johnnine."

Without looking at her mother, she pushed off the couch and followed Febrillo into his office. There was a modern black leather chaise against one wall, an old wooden desk, and a single chair in the middle of the room.

"Come an' sit on my lap, pliss, Johnneen—"

Johnnine hesitated, looking around the Spartan room.

"Jore mother would li' joo to sit on my lap, Johnneen."

Gingerly, she walked to his side. Febrillo lifted her onto his thighs. "Johnneen, 'ow do joo fill today?"

"I'm not sick."

Febrillo smiled. "Do joo ever fill sad sometimes?"

Johnnine shrugged.

"Think...remember the last time joo fel' sad?"

Johnnine shrugged again but then almost imperceptibly nodded.

"Do joo remember why joo cried?"

Johnnine abruptly raised and lowered her shoulders, followed by a slight shake of her head.

"Do joo ever think abou' jore father?"

Johnnine shook her head.

"Look me in the eyes, pliss, Johnneen...Jes."

Febrillo tilted her face towards him. Johnnine did not squirm or move away. Instead, she regarded him with a cool and guarded look.

Febrillo reached into his pants pocket and took out a faded pink, flannel phallus. "Do joo know what this iss?"

Johnnine looked at it and shook her head.

"What does it look like to joo?"

Johnnine stared at the stuffed rag, then away.

"Look at me, pliss, Johnneen. Joo know that women have baginas and men have, what?"

Johnnine proudly rattled off her precocious knowledge. "Penises."

"Jes, that's ri'...now I wan joo to bite thiss penis for me—"

Johnnine looked at Febrillo directly this time, clearly alarmed.

"Jes, iss all ri', we're playin' a game. I wan' joo to bite it as if joo were *angry* at it—"

Johnnine shot a desperate look at the door.

"Jore mother is still here. She'll be waitin' for joo when we're done." Febrillo dangled the fake penis in front of Johnnine's face. "It's all ri', Johnnine, bite it now, pliss, as if joo were *rilly rilly angry*—open your mou'..."

Camera did a close-up of Johnnine's unhappy face as Febrillo held the padded, substitute phallus in front of her. Her eyes welled with panicky tears as Febrillo continued to encourage her.

In the All Souls' Waiting Room, Johnnine felt like screaming, "Kick him! Kick the creepy bastard where the sun doesn't shine and run for your life!" Then she starting crying, remembering the terror of that session, when she had realized the people in control of her life were mad.

Jump-cut to Johnnine and Febrillo coming out of his office. Stiffly, formally, like a guest at a funeral service, Dinah rose to greet them. Johnnine's face showed the aftermath of tears but she did not look at her mother or Febrillo as they talked over her head.

Dinah's voice was deep and grateful as she shook Febrillo's hand. "Thank you, doctor. She needed to cry."

Cut to Johnnine abjectly following Dinah up the steps of their apartment building. As Dinah fished in her purse for the door keys, four-year old Johnnine suddenly looked up at her. "Do you love me, Mom?"

Dinah appeared to consider the question carefully. "I don't love you the way I did when you were a baby. You don't need me as much."

The metal door shut behind them with a heavy, hollow thud. The screen went black.

As the lights came up in the All Souls' Waiting Room, Johnnine was crying hysterically. Suddenly she turned on her side and threw up all the food she had just eaten, coughing and choking and fighting for breath, feeling like she was really dying this time. Oh, God, why didn't they just let her go, why did they want to keep her alive? Just so they could torture her some more?

Xofia was at Johnnine's side, holding her head and patting her back. "There, there, pet—"

Willie ran his hands through his thicket of hair. His face had a desperate look. "Your mother was being honest!" he said. "Expressing true feelings is the only basis for good parent-child relations. If she had been phony, you would have known it! Truth is always better than dishonesty, no matter how painful..."

The cherubs clustered around Johnnine, humming a soothing bit of Brahms as they cheerfully and effortlessly cleaned her up.

Willie paced back and forth. "Febrillo's technique was much too heavy-handed—but it is better to break through the armor at any cost! The price for repressing sadness is becoming dead to joy, dead to sexual feeling, dead to *life*!"

Johnnine continued to retch over the side of The Couch. Ti and Do held the silver food cover upside down for her.

"There is no hope for an armored world," Reich inveighed. "It is armor that enables man to murder his fellow man!"

"Willie," Xofia said sternly. "Get the hell down off your soapbox and HELP US CLEAN UP THIS MESS..."

He appeared offended. "I am a scientist! I do not clean up messes!"

Xofia was far from calm and collected. "You helped make this one!"

Seraph A. again worked his musical magic, in an amazingly soft voice this time, burbling a few bars of Wagner's *Rheingold*, restoring equanimity if not amity.

Johnnine had thrown up everything she had eaten and lay on her back catching her breath and crying softly. She felt totally empty, in body and soul.

"Anything to say, young woman?" the Recorder asked.

Johnnine looked blank.

"You'll feel better if you talk," Xofia urged, handing her a glass of bubbly.

Johnnine looked at her uncertainly, taking a sip of the terrible stuff to wet her parched mouth. "I remember...I remember when I came out of Febrillo's office I knew I had more problems than I went in with..." She frowned and looked at her hands. "I couldn't understand what everybody thought was so wrong with me—I mean, left to myself I was pretty happy. Was that my crime?" Johnnine's angry tears gathered force. "Why didn't they fix themselves and leave me alone?"

Xofia held one of her hands. Johnnine was surprised when Reich took her other one. His hand was warm and amazingly soft, almost like baby's skin. "I am very, very sorry for the sins that were committed in my name."

Johnnine looked up at Reich, whose burning black eyes were full of remorse. She couldn't seem to answer him, there were too many memories in the way. She had a sudden, intense craving for a chocolate egg cream. "Do you think I could have...?" But the thought of what the cute little klutzes of Mondo Bizarro would come up with made her feel sick again. "No, nothing, forget it," she said.

And then it was movie time again.

In a large, high-ceilinged basement room, criss-crossed with silver-painted, asbestos-wrapped overhead pipes, rows of wooden chairs faced a simple raised platform. At a table on the platform, Wilhelm Reich sat smoking and making notes.

A few feet away on the platform, on separate folding chairs, were Dinah and Johnnine. Dinah, wearing her white duty uniform and clutching a brown purse in her lap, looked scared as several dozen people began filing into the improvised meeting room. Some people were dressed casually, others wore white lab coats. Johnnine slowly kicked her legs back and forth until Ernesto Febrillo and Daniel Pahlser took seats in the front row. Then she stiffened and looked everywhere but at them.

Reich raised a hand for quiet. "Welcome. For the benefit of our new guests, I will begin by restating the purposes of the Orgone Infant Research Center. The basic aim of the O.I.R.C. is to reach the naturally-given plasmatic bioenergetic functions of the infant, through the following steps—

"First, prenatal care of healthy, pregnant mothers, encouraging regular orgasmic release, periodic exams, et cetera. If the surrounding environment is clean enough, free of deadly orgone, then regular use of the orgone accumulator...

"Second, careful supervision of the delivery and first few days and weeks of a newborn's life, trying to find out what the newborn feels and how it experiences its first weeks of life outside the uterus.

"Third, prevention of armoring during the first five or six years of life. And fourth, the study and recording of the further development of these children until well after the *second* puberty, usually between 12 and 14."

Reich paused to look around the room at his audience. "Let mother and child simply enjoy each other and orgonotic contact—my phrase for the positive flow of orgone energy—will develop spontaneously. Health consists not in the total absence of sickness but in the ability of the organism to *overcome* sickness and emerge basically unhurt..."

Camera panned to Dinah, who was looking more and more uneasy. Johnnine stared up at the ceiling pipes.

The highly-charged, highly-animated face of Wilhelm Reich filled the screen in a tight close-up, his eyes blazing. "Every worker in this field should know that in handling children orgonomically we are participating in the most radical revolution in human life ever attempted. *Nothing but the child and its life interests counts*, they alone will provide the answer to the mess of the world.

"Make no mistake, however. This effort will meet with intense anxiety, even brutal hatred. Suppression of the life force is everywhere around us. Terrific obstacles will be encountered—*because no human character structure molded during the last several thousand years is free from this hatred toward the living.* I want no one under false illusions!"

Reich paused dramatically. The camera panned over the now-sombre faces of the audience riveted on him. "I want now to introduce Dinah Hapgood and her daughter Johnnine, who is 4 1/2. Miss Hapgood, would you tell us about your daughter's development so far?"

Dinah cleared her throat loudly in the proscribed Reichian manner, sweating and supremely uncomfortable. She had a clear, strong, almost theatrical voice. "Yes, Dr. Reich..." She looked down at her lap as if gathering her thoughts and then looked up and out at the audience resolutely. "I nursed Johnnine until she was ten months old and highly enjoyed it, often allowing myself to come to orgasm. I toilet-trained her by sitting her on the seat in front of me when I had to urinate. She had no difficulty going from diapers to using the john and does not wet the bed. Johnnine knows the proper names for the male and female genitals. I don't use euphemisms and I don't allow people to speak to her in baby-talk, I feel it's demeaning to children's intelligence. I address her as an adult and so she has an excellent command of the language. She fully understands what sexual intercourse is and where children come from. I have told her about masturbation, which of course she has my full permission to do..."

Camera panned to the audience reaction. Some people shifted in their seats, others looked away, some took notes. Many looked uncomfortable, some showed a good deal of emotional distancing, as if the subject were distasteful to them. Pahlser showed an obvious heightened interest in Johnnine. Johnnine concentrated intently on fidgeting with the hem of her dress.

Dinah continued with her deadly serious recitation. "I don't believe Johnnine has actually seen sexual intercourse as I've been without a partner for some time now, but she may have heard me crying out when I masturbate—" Dinah looked at Reich, as if for approval.

He nodded at her. "Thank you," Reich said. "We would like to observe Johnnine's body armor now. Johnnine, would you come here to me?" He held out his arms as encouragement.

Slowly, Johnnine got off her chair and approached him.

When she stood quietly in front of him, he asked, "Will you take off your dress for us?"

Johnnine looked out at the coolly critical, note-taking audience and back at him. "No, I don't want to."

Reich smiled, fully and warmly reassuring her. "It's all right, Johnnine, you don't have to. You may go back to your chair..."

Johnnine went back to stand by her mother, leaning against Dinah's arm.

"Remember we must have the child's permission, otherwise we are simply being bullies. Miss Hapgood, would you and your daughter please wait outside for a few minutes?"

Self-conscious but trying not to show it, Dinah got up, took Johnnine's hand, and stepped down off the stage. When Johnnine got to the edge, she held onto her mother and took a big jump, which made several of the people in front laugh. Camera panned to show Pahlser avidly following them out with his eyes. The rest of the audience averted their gaze as Dinah softly shut the door behind her.

Reich was angry. "Does anyone have a comment on what just happened? I want you all to take note of the fact that the child had agreed to undress prior to the meeting."

People from the audience began speaking.

"There was too much emphasis on the mother, she used her sexuality belligerently, as if she were throwing down a gauntlet—"

"The child shouldn't have heard what the mother said, it could end up being very harmful to her."

"It's cold in here and these seats are too damn hard!"

There was a minor ripple of laughter at the last comment.

Reich did not smile as he gestured for silence. "You are right about it being cold, the atmosphere changed perceptibly as Miss Hapgood spoke, but no, I will tell you what just happened. In spite of our training and our work, the emotional plague is still strong enough in us that we feel dangerously threatened by someone as sexually vital and open as this particular mother. In spite of all her handicaps, she has the courage to raise her child free of society's sexual pathology. I wish I could say the same for us. Until we overcome our own plaguey-ness, we are not ready to work with anyone else's children. This meeting of the O.I.R.C. is at an end!"

Reich clapped shut his notebook, got up and stormed off the stage. His followers looked like chastened children as they watched him exit.

In the All Souls' Waiting Room, Johnnine was in anguish. If her mother was a heroine—and Johnnine had grown up believing this to be true—someone who had done everything possible to raise a happy, healthy child, and Johnnine still didn't want to live, that meant Johnnine really was a hopelessly screwed-up, ungrateful little bitch and everything that had happened to her was her own fault. This thought did not appreciably increase her desire to live.

Xofia approached it from another angle as she spoke to Willie. "Can you perhaps see now what the presence of Febrillo and Pahlser might have done to taint the atmosphere?"

"Yah," Willie said, sadly running his hands through his hair. "I can see many things I could not see then..."

Chapter Thirteen

"The mother was defensive and high-strung," Willie continued, lighting a Dark Star cigarillo. "But I found that understandable in view of her difficult situation as a single working mother. She followed her own life-affirming instincts rather than the so-called 'common wisdom,' which included forced toilet training and vigorous repression of the child's natural sexual curiosity..." He exhaled a white veil of smoke, glancing at the color print of the rock-cut temple of Abu Simbel hanging over The Couch. Schlomo had been an inveterate collector of Egyptiana whereas Willie was more interested in living bodies. "Dinah Hapgood was an extremely courageous, necessarily aggressive woman, a pioneer in one of the most important experiments in the history of the human race. She was also a very lonely person who was desperate to belong to a group of like-thinkers. Unfortunately," Willie eulogized, "that was the last meeting of the O.I.R.C. I remember writing it up just before I moved to Orgonon, my research facility in Maine—"

Johnnine felt defensive. Was he saying she was responsible for the demise of the Orgone Infant Research Center? "Did it ever occur to you I just might not have wanted to take my clothes off in front of fifty strangers?"

Reich stared at her as if surprised she had vocal cords.

"*Bravo*, darling!" Xofia applauded.

"But there was nothing prurient about it." Willie's tone was one of mild reproof. "I would not have tolerated—"

"One of his better traits," Xofia stage-whispered to Johnnine, pouring herself another glass from her bottomless bottle of champagne. "Lights, darling?" she called up to the seraph as she sat down again. The room plunged into darkness.

The film's next scene showed a sway-backed, spavined old moving truck as it caromed down East 21st Street off Lexington. The tracks of the Third Avenue El were visible in the background, the thunderous racket of the elevated subway regularly shattering the calm of the otherwise peaceful neighborhood. The ancient green truck with its peeling sign, the Flying Ferragamo Brothers, heaved to a stop in front of a fancy apartment building with shallow marble steps and cast-iron lamps cemented into the curved balustrade.

The Ferragamo brothers stood out in Johnnine's memory of her childhood with the two-dimensional vividness of cartoon characters. Piling out of the cab, she saw hefty, bossy Giuseppe, then Luigi, the slow-witted beast of burden, and last Salvatore, dark and sleek, a young man with the look of a spoiled pet ferret. The brothers began arguing loudly in Italian the minute they began unloading.

The next shot showed the interior of an apartment as Giuseppe and Salvatore struggled down a long hall with a cumbersome ticked mattress. Dinah came out of a small kitchen with a dishtowel in hand and a scarf over her hair. A voluminous tent dress could not disguise her bulk.

"Where you want this, lady?" Giuseppe asked. "Feels like it's got rocks in it—"

"It better not," Dinah said saucily. "I have big plans for that mattress..."

"Ooh, jeez, lady." Giuseppe ducked as though hit with a flying brick. "Not in fronta Salvatore here, he's still a unmarried man."

"*Giuseppe*—" Salvatore whined.

Dinah and Giuseppe laughed. Dinah pointed to one of the bedroom doors open off the square living room. "In there, please, Mr. Ferragamo."

Gray-haired Luigi lumbered into the room, sweating copiously. Mute and uncomplaining, he panted where he stood, slightly bent over. Strapped to his back was a large box, made out of chipboard, about five feet high and three feet square. With only dim comprehension, he looked around for his brother.

Dinah pointed to a corner but Luigi was clearly waiting for orders from his real master. "Mr. Ferragamo, could you come help your brother, please?" Dinah asked. Giuseppe and Salvatore emerged from the bedroom and undid the canvas straps tied around Luigi's broad back.

"*Madon*, one hell of a big box thing, weighs a ton here—" Salvatore moaned for effect, though he did no more than lower the wardrobe-sized box to the floor. "What the hell is it?"

"Salvatore!" Giuseppe slapped his brother on the back. "Jeez! Don' be so dam' nosy!"

Dinah smiled. "It's an orgone accumulator. Invented by Dr. Wilhelm Reich."

"Orgo *wha'*?" Salvatore asked, looking inside through the small square opening cut in the front door. The interior was lined with fine steel mesh and had a simple shelf seat about two feet off the ground.

Daniel Pahlser came into the room carrying a beautiful old Chinese cloisonne table lamp. Johnnine followed close behind, hoisting her little yellow rocker. "Orgone energy accumulator," Pahlser said in a tone of helpful authority. "It's designed to intensify the positive effects of cosmic orgone, the energy that's in the air around us..."

"Yeah? But what's it for?" Salvatore asked while Luigi and Giuseppe stared uncomprehendingly at the unpainted chipboard box.

Pahlser's smile was patiently patronizing. "Increased skin contact with orgone energy makes the body feel warm and tingly. Eventually, the patient gets healthier and finds his orgonomic potential..."

"You mean—sick people sit in there and think they get better?"

Pahlser's smile was a little strained. "They do get better."

Giuseppe looked at Salvatore. Salvatore looked at Giuseppe. They shrugged and began rocking the accumulator into the corner of the living room Dinah had pointed to. "You say so, doc. Sitting in a box sounds pretty *fazoolle* to me—"

Pushing Luigi before them, the Ferragamos filed down the hall, Giuseppe circling a finger near his temple.

Later that day, Dinah, Pahlser, and Johnnine walked into a White Rose Bar and Grill on Third Avenue, still wearing their moving clothes. A large cloth banner draped across the front said "Air Cooled" and showed a polar bear sitting on an ice cube. Inside, the bar was dark, full of blue-collar working men in sweat-stained clothes. Booths and tables along one wall paralleled a long row of steam tables. Pahlser, Dinah, and Johnnine pushed plastic food trays along a grooved counter. Johnnine came up to a heavily-muscled, tattooed forearm wearing a cook's apron and holding a ladle. She gave her order clearly and distinctly. "Mashed potatoes and gravy, and pissgetti. Please!"

The next shot was of Johnnine in a dark green leatherette booth, happily fixated on her plate, a white mountain of mashed potatoes with a craterful of brown gravy surrounded by a low-lying forest of spaghetti.

Dinah and Pahlser were eating, drinking, and talking shop.

"...she's due in six weeks. Will that give you enough time to get your certificate? Not that Reich gives a damn about the license," Pahlser was saying to Dinah, "but we need to go through the motions for the Board of Health."

"Yah, I think so..." Dinah sipped rye from a shot glass and chased it with a swallow of beer. She laughed as she applied herself to her roast beef blue plate special. "I wonder what the lab will say when I tell them I'm quitting to become a Reichian midwife—"

Johnnine raised her glass of ginger ale laced with red grenadine syrup, peering at her mother and Pahlser through the distortions of the bubbles and ice cubes. She giggled at the way they looked, like reflections in a fun-house mirror.

"And what's so funny, young lady?" Pahlser asked, trying to sound jocular.

Johnnine frowned and blew loud bubbles through her straw.

"Johnnine, don't play with your drink!" Dinah hissed.

"I'm not!" Johnnine raised her voice in protest.

Dinah's eyes darted around the bar nervously. "Keep your voice down! You know what good table manners are. I won't have you embarrassing me in public."

Johnnine looked at the rough-hewn men in the nearby booths, none of whom took any notice of them.

Dinah downed her boilermaker and abruptly broke out in a wide smile. "Pahlser and I have..." She looked down demurely before giving Pahlser a glowing smile. "Now that we're living together, we've made something called a will, it says if anything happens to me, he'll be...he'll take care of you. Pahlser's your legal guardian now."

Johnnine looked carefully at Pahlser and then at her mother. "I thought we didn't like legal. *Legal-shmegal ahbee gezint,*" she parroted.

"That's only for marriage," Dinah said impatiently. "People don't need a piece of paper to live together. This is different."

Johnnine's eyes showed a mix of hope and fear as she turned them on Pahlser. "Are you my father now?"

"Well," Pahlser's large wavy lips split his broad face in a fitful smile. "Sort of—"

Johnnine addressed her mother. "Did Duncan get dead?"

"No, he's not dead, he's just not interested in you. But Pahlser—"

"Are you going away?" Johnnine asked her mother.

Dinah laughed heartily. "Not in the foreseeable future."

"OK," Johnnine said, returning her attention to her food.

Dinah raised her eyebrows at Pahlser. "So much for that little item."

"Are you going to sleep in the same bed?" Johnnine asked suddenly.

"Yes..." Dinah answered steadily, bracing for the next question.

"How come I can't see Brian any more?"

Dinah was caught off guard by Johnnine's change of tack.

Pahlser's brow furrowed. "A little understandable jealousy here," he said in an aside to Dinah. "Brian's too blocked for you, Johnnine, his parents are very repressed Catholics. You need healthier playmates—"

"But I like Brian, he's nice. He kissed me!"

Dinah and Pahlser exchanged an uncertain look. "How now brown cow?" Dinah whispered.

Johnnine glared at them.

"Don't tighten your mouth, Johnnine," Dinah instructed when she looked back at her.

"And lower your shoulders, don't clench your body—" Pahlser added.

Johnnine's glance held a measure of defiance before she looked away.

"Look at us when we talk to you," Dinah said sharply. "You know how important eye contact is—"

Johnnine's large grey-green eyes looked up at her mother, her expression a scrubbed and careful blank.

The scene faded out. In the All Souls' Waiting Room, Johnnine supposed such tactics helped keep her from getting into bad habits of expression and body language, though she still didn't like the act of instruction one bit.

The next scene showed Johnnine at the same age, on a beach with a freckle-faced, red-headed Brian Kelly. A long shot showed Dinah and Pahlser a good distance away, strolling bare-footed along the surf's edge behind darting lines of tiny, rushing sandpipers.

The camera zoomed in on Dinah as she looked back at the children. "Do you think they've had genital contact yet?"

Pahlser shielded his eyes from the sun with his hand as he turned around to look at them. "I'm not sure Brian knows he has genitals. At least he wouldn't if his parents had anything to say about it..."

"Daniel!" Dinah laughed.

Brian and Johnnine were playing house, using beach flotsam and jetsam as props, outlining the shape of a house in the sand.

"Let's play house," Johnnine suggested.

"Okay. I'm the daddy and you're the mommy." Brian picked up an empty beer bottle and staggered through the driftwood door. Swaying on his feet, he yelled, "I'm home!" before he knocked Johnnine down and climbed on top of her.

Johnnine tried to get out from under him, rolling to the side, but Brian rolled with her. She laughed in his face. "Are you going to do it to me?"

"Do what?" Brian said in a deep, gruff voice, impersonating an adult.

"You know—intercourse."

"Inner*what*?" His puzzled voice became that of a five year-old's.

"Don't you *know*?" Johnnine was disgusted. "First your penis gets big like a hot dog and then you put it in me—"

"Where? In your belly-button?" Brian convulsed with laughter.

"No, in my *vagina*, dummy!" Johnnine said heatedly.

A middle-aged man walking his dog on the beach stopped to ogle them. "And just what are you two naughty children up to?"

Johnnine and Brian, heavily coated with sand, lay with their arms around each other, staring innocently up at the intrusive stranger. They looked like pieces of white-meat chicken coated with batter, ready for the frying pan.

In the All Souls' Waiting Room, Johnnine remembered her amorous feelings for Brian and her frustration that he did not, or could not, return them. Her sexually precocious upbringing doomed her to being outside both the adult world which she could not understand, and the world of other children, who could not understand her, too young for one, too old for the other.

The film cut to the interior of a late-forties Plymouth, Dinah in the front seat, Pahlser driving. Johnnine and Brian bounced up and down on the back seat. A huge blue-and-orange Howard Johnson's 31 Flavors sign became visible off the highway.

"Pistachio ice cream!" Johnnine said excitedly.

"Ood-shay ee-way op-stay?" Dinah asked Pahlser in pig Latin.

"Es-yay!" Johnnine shouted.

Pahlser and Dinah laughed. The car took the next exit and turned into the Ho Jo parking lot.

Johnnine sat forward on the edge of the seat as Pahlser steered into a slot. "Pahlser, Brian doesn't know how, so will you show me how to have intercourse?"

The car slammed to a stop as Pahlser hit the brakes. He and Dinah turned their heads and stared at each other.

Dinah looked pale. "Dear Dod, what do we do now?" she whispered.

The screen dimmed as Johnnine looked intently from one to the other of the adults' faces while Brian jumped up and down and demanded a double vanilla ice cream cone.

In the All Souls' Waiting Room, Johnnine felt sick again.

Willie felt a speech coming on. "The child is in the throes of first pubescence, what Freud called 'polymorphous perversity,' but which is not at all perverse, merely a normal instinct to duplicate what she sees going on around her. In a healthy world, her little boyfriend would have known what she was talking about, they would have had some playful, pleasurable genital contact, and life would have gone on..."

Christ, Johnnine thought, maybe Reich was right, maybe if Brian had known what to do it would have prevented the disaster with Pahlser. Out loud, she embellished. "You mean that maybe the reason I'm in Mondo Bizarro is for want of a little early sex education?"

Chapter Fourteen

"The child does have a droll sense of humor," the Recorder intoned. "It may just be her saving grace—"

In the next shot, Johnnine was one of a small pod of children leaving a kindergarten classroom. Hitting the street, they flew off in different directions like the spurs of a dandelion. Johnnine remembered the pretty pink-and-brown pique dress she was wearing. She watched herself reflected in storefront windows as she walked the two blocks home under the rumbling shadows of the El, its high overhead tracks and trestles cutting the street into geometric patterns, dark spider-like shapes that had always frightened her.

Johnnine opened her apartment door with a key on a long string around her neck. As she came down the hall, Dinah called from the living room. "Johnnine? Come here, please."

"Just a minute, Mom, I have to go b.m..." Johnnine turned into the bathroom, pulled down her pants and quickly hunched down on the toilet, her face turning beet red.

Cut to Dinah in the living room, smoking and holding a highball in her hand. She was crying, pacing back and forth, looking distraught. After the sound of the toilet flushing, Johnnine came into the living room, putting her Hopalong Cassidy metal lunchbox on the low-slung, Danish modern couch. The orgone accumulator stood like a mute, Cyclopean sentinel in the corner.

"Pahlser wants to see you, in the bedroom."

"What's the matter? Why are you crying, Mom?"

"I'm not crying," Dinah said, brushing tears from her puffy cheeks. "Go on, he's waiting." Dinah upended her glass and moved into the kitchen for a refill.

Johnnine watched her mother leave the room before she opened the bedroom door. Pahlser was sitting up in bed, naked under a white sheet. Everything in the room was stark white, the walls, the sheets, the drawn window shades.

"Close the door, Johnnine," Pahlser said in a low voice.

"Did you get poison ivy bumps again?" Johnnine asked.

"No, I'm not sick. Close the door. I want you to take off your clothes and get into bed with me."

Johnnine's eyes widened while her face whitened a shade. "Are you going to show me what you do to Mommy?"

Pahlser's face was deadly serious. "Yah. Take your clothes off, Johnnine."

Johnnine shut the door and lifted her dress off nervously. She moved slowly to the side of the bed where Pahlser pulled down her panties and lifted her on top of him. He turned back the sheet to reveal his huge, semi-erect penis. Johnnine's eyes darted to his groin and then immediately looked away.

"I want you to sit on my penis, just the outside, feel what it feels like," Pahlser said, his tone one of professional detachment. "Here, touch it, feel it." He took Johnnine's hand and began stroking himself with it. "Does it feel good to you? It feels good to me."

Johnnine let him manipulate her hand but did not initiate any movement of her own. Wide-eyed, she appeared frozen, a child-sized marionette.

Pahlser was by now fully erect. "Here, rub your vagina on it." His voice had become husky. He positioned her so that she was sitting astride him. Holding the tip of his penis with one hand, Pahlser caressed Johnnine with the other. "Up and down. Rub up and down on it."

Johnnine did not move or say anything. Pahlser held her just below her waist and began sliding her back and forth. White-faced and immobile, she stared at the wall above Pahlser's head.

"Johnnine, look at me." Johnnine shifted her gaze, but Pahlser's eyes were now closed to her fear. "Yah, good. Oh, it feels good, doesn't it? Don't you want to feel it inside you?"

Pahlser's face was red and his movements became jerky as he tried to insert the head of his engorged penis into Johnnine, but it was too large.

Johnnine held her arms away from her sides, her hands curling into tiny fists, but she didn't speak, or move, or look at him.

Pahlser lay back with his eyes glazed. "Just feel it then, rub up and down on it...yeah—" Pahlser wrapped her hand over the tip of his penis and closed his eyes. "Oh, yes! I can feel the excitement in my penis! Can you feel it, Johnnine? Feel it!"

Pahlser's pelvic movements became intensely rhythmic. Her small body stiff and rigid, Johnnine rode Pahlser's body as though he were a bucking bronco, her face and eyes expressionless, empty with shock.

Pahlser's eyes squeezed shut and his body seemed to contort. "Yah! Oh, *God*!!!"

The All Souls' screen blacked out to the sound of Johnnine's tormented howl, ripped from her throat after years of being buried inside her. She was too traumatized to speak, but the flood of tears and wails of pain felt like a fresh razor cut, as though what she had just seen had just happened. Her whole life been buried in that room, in that bed with Pahlser, while her mother paced and cried outside.

Willie's bellow drowned out Johnnine's crying. "*NEIN!*" he shouted at the screen. "Nein, nein, nein!" Without looking at her or Xofia, Willie half-staggered out of the room. Seraph A. sang three abrupt notes as a signal and Ti and Do flew out after him. Then the seraph joined Xofia in ministering to Johnnine, who was curled up on The Couch in the fetal position, clutching her stomach and sobbing.

The All Souls' Waiting Room

Willie almost fell down the stairs of Schlomo's building. Stumbling up to the corner of Berggasse, not seeing his surroundings, he swung his large white head from side to side. Ti and Do fluttered close in around his ears, twittering like noisy sparrows, until he turned to the left and struck off past the Votivkirche. Ti remained in place as his path-prodder while Do zoomed ahead, vanishing out of sight around the stone *schlag* corner of the Universitat. The cherubs directed Willie's steps towards the Hofburg, into the Heldenplatz, the Square of Heroes, like goading a bull into the bullring.

At the same precise moment, Fa and So were herding a furious Schlomo Freud down the steps of the Bibliothek into the Square. "Leave me *alone!*" He swatted angrily at the cherubs. Already beside himself with irritation, Schlomo's mood was not improved at the sight of Willie being teased across the square towards him. Except that Willie had lost his air of defiance. He looked, in fact, like a broken man. "Willie! *Mein Gott, was machst Sie?*"

Willie's black earth eyes were dulled, devoid of answers.

"Come, tell me—" Schlomo suggested, leading Willie by the arm towards the Reitschule.

Xofia soothed Johnnine with a gentle, feathery touch. "Tears are healing, darling—"

Johnnine sobbed softly into a handkerchief. She had tried her whole life not to think about what had happened that day, but whatever else the All Souls' Waiting Room was about, it was not about forgetting. "I remember knowing then that my mother had to hate me, that she wanted to punish me. The only way I could go on living was to turn my heart to stone, pretend I didn't care, that I wasn't there in the room with Pahlser, that I was really somewhere else, a million miles away." Johnnine's glance idly registered the contents of one of Schlomo's glass display cases, full of the artifacts of ancient civilizations. Her eye was taken by a small carved stone Janus head.

"You *were* a million miles away, or at least your soul was," Xofia said.

"No riddles right now, okay?" Johnnine's voice was still shaky.

Xofia's smile was like sunlight after a storm. "Okay. You banished a big part of your soul from your body, the part that felt scared and betrayed and unloved, unprotected. Suicide is sometimes a last gasp effort to re-unite the banished bits of the soul. The good news is that here your soul bits are all re-assembled. The bad news is you have to learn to feel the pain of your past."

Johnnine still did not see the light. "*Non capice,*" she mumbled, falling back on two of her five words of street Italian.

"You don't suppose something as marvelous as life comes without a price tag, do you, darling? You may still be too young to understand, but that's why you need to go back. The chick can't possibly know as much as the hen."

Barnyard Confucianism we get now. Great, Johnnine thought, stung by the 'too young to understand' line, which she'd heard all her life. "What's the goddam point?" Johnnine said out loud.

"We'll get into that when the film's over," Xofia purred. "Want anything before we get started again?"

"A pint of hemlock, or a quart of scotch, on the rocks."

Xofia laughed. "How about a pot of chamomile tea?"

"*Tea*?" Johnnine snorted. "I don't drink tea, for Christ's sake." God, the people in Mondo Bizarro were just too obtuse for words.

"Bad for your health or something?"

"No, worse. Bad for my image."

Schlomo and Willie sat at a round marble table in Demel's, a famous old Viennese coffeehouse with apple-green walls, gilt-framed mirrors and sparkling chandeliers. Over cups of *kaffee mit schlag*, kept full by the attentive cherubs, Schlomo heard the story of Daniel Pahlser's transgression and Dinah Hapgood's collaboration.

"Sickening, but hardly surprising," Schlomo said when Willie had finished.

"What do you mean?" Willie challenged. His demeanor around his former mentor swung from reverence to bellicosity.

"A case of repetition syndrome on the mother's part, since she was also molested at an early age, creating the unconscious, irrefutable need to recreate the situation for her daughter...your analyst was a willing player in the piece, a player with his own perverted agenda. One could say, my dear Willie, that you chose some of your disciples neither too wisely nor too well."

Downcast, Willie looked into his coffee cup. "You are right."

Schlomo pressed his advantage. "And of course you know why you sabotaged yourself—"

"I did not sabotage myself!" Willie disputed. "The world was not ready for my breakthroughs in sexual theory. The emotional plague came after me!"

Schlomo dismissed this answer. "Are you of a mind to go back to the beginning?" Schlomo was conscious of time on his hands and not much, since Xofia would not have him, to do with it. The Akashic Records were diverting, but he'd read up on everyone he was even vaguely interested in, including the *mishugayes* goy relatives of the unfortunate young girl in his office: Schlomo was nothing if not a quick study.

"You mean here, now?" Willie looked apprehensively around the fussily-decorated coffeehouse.

"Certainly, why not? Perhaps I was wrong in refusing to analyze you all those years ago," Schlomo said, putting several curlicued, wrought-iron chairs next to each other. "In that sense, I may even be partly responsible for the problem at hand. Maybe it is time to make amends—"

The All Souls' Waiting Room

Schlomo snapped a tablecloth open and draped it over four chairs, like a magician transforming several objects into one. The cherubs made a pillow out of table napkins.

"Please, Willie—" Schlomo gestured, "make yourself comfortable."

Willie watched these preparations with fascinated interest, but did not make a move once they were completed. The five cherubs flew to support Willie's stocky limbs and heavy head and quickly and efficiently air-lifted the former psychoanalyst, currently the reluctant analysand, into a horizontal position before laying him gently prone on the improvised couch.

Schlomo sat at a table behind Willie's head and pulled a notebook and pen out of his breast pocket. "Wouldn't it be ironic," he said, also taking a cigar out of his morocco cigar case and biting off one end, "if one had to die to truly finish analysis?"

Chapter Fifteen

"You can watch for half an hour a day and no more. Reich says they give off radiation, so if I see you sitting closer than six feet away, out the damned thing goes. And afterwards I want you to sit in the accumulator for half an hour...we'll sing happy birthday a little later," Dinah said as she clicked on a new black-and-white Zenith console television.

A very subdued five-year old Johnnine sat on a straight-backed chair in the living room, holding a plate of chocolate cake and peach ice cream on her lap. Her party dress and paper party hat contrasted sharply with her somber air as she stared at the screen. Johnnine remembered her fifth birthday. There had been no other children, just the new television set. By then she had begun living in a diminished, withdrawn state, behind a barricade of thorns deep inside her. Her policy for survival was to shut out her mother's presence as much as possible. She didn't understand why, all she knew was that Dinah was now her enemy, a powerful and capricious one whose authority had to be placated.

"Yah, Mom," Johnnine said tonelessly, automatically, mesmerized by the television images. A big man in a fringed shirt with a phony-cheerful voice yelled at a wooden puppet as if it were hard of hearing.

Disgusted, Dinah bustled out of the room. "I don't know why you want to watch such crap anyway."

From the TV, Buffalo Bob coerced the peanut gallery. "Okay, kids! *What time is it?*"

The kids in the TV audience were allowed, even encouraged to scream. Johnnine whispered along with them. "IT'S HOWDY DOODY TIME!"

From the All Souls' Waiting Room, Johnnine watched herself as a lonely five-year old, staring at the other children on the TV. She remembered longing to know what kinds of lives they led, thinking they all had to be rich and live on Park Avenue because they looked so squeaky clean, so well-dressed. The girls had mothers who knew how to set their hair so it came out in pretty, soft curls. The handsome, wholesome-looking boys wore white shirts and *bow-ties*! Johnnine thought they were the luckiest children in the world, shining like stars far above her.

The next scene in Johnnine's Akashic film showed one of her rare get-togethers with her father, a visit to the Met. Once in a while, Johnnine would ask her mother to call him on the phone. Duncan's response was invariably the same. "Johnnine?" he would ask when she came on the line, sleepily, hazily, as if trying to remember her. Then he would tell her how busy he was. He did not acknowledge her birthday or Christmas with cards or presents, but he wasn't unpleasant to her. If she asked to see him, he usually agreed. Johnnine grew up thinking this was the norm for paternal behavior.

The All Souls' Waiting Room

Still five years old, Johnnine entered the grand marble foyer of the Metropolitan Museum with her father. Shaking a sprinkling of light snow off their coats, they checked them at the front coat-check counter. Duncan kept his brown, wide-brimmed hat on, probably out of vanity about his premature baldness. He looked very handsome wearing it.

Johnnine appeared happy to be with her father. She held his hand and took a few skip steps. He smiled down at her briefly but was more intent on their cultural mission. On their way to the palatial central staircase, Johnnine's feelings overflowed. She broke away from him and twirled around several times in the middle of the huge marble space. "See how my new dress goes out when I spin around?"

He reached for her hand. "We're not here to play, Johnnine."

Johnnine stopped twirling. "I wanted to see the elephants in the zoo."

"We're going to see some paintings instead."

Johnnine excitedly put the two interests together. "Show me how to draw an elephant, I *love* elephants."

Duncan led her up the wide, elegant staircase, divided in half by red velvet ropes and heavy brass stanchions. "No one can teach anyone else to draw, Johnnine, it's something people either know how to do or they don't. An artist has to put down what he sees in his head. If I drew it for you, it wouldn't be your picture. Do you get what I'm saying?"

In the All Souls' Waiting Room, Johnnine thought this response rather miserly when all she had wanted was two circles for a head and a body, four legs and a trunk.

Looking a little sullen, five-year old Johnnine followed her father into a suite of beautiful, well-lit galleries. Duncan, never Daddy, swept his arm around the room, which was aflame with the colors of Impressionism. "Do you see? These painters painted what they saw in their heads, even though no one else saw things in the same way. It's like I'm doing with my work. They were trying to show transitory visual impressions, directly from nature, and they achieved luminosity by the use of broken color. Do you get it?"

The camera took Duncan's point of view, looking down at Johnnine, miniaturized as though she were on the wrong end of a telescope. Johnnine looked up at her incomprehensible father with her mouth slightly agape. Very slowly, she nodded.

"Good!" Duncan said. He pointed out other paintings, becoming increasingly energized while Johnnine lagged behind. His unbuttoned old tweed jacket flapped open in his self-created wind as he tore from room to room. He stopped in front of a wildly colorful canvas. "Now *he's* essentially an expressionist, because his work is characterized by a bold distortion of forms and vibrant color, get it?"

Johnnine nodded. "Can I sit down now?"

Duncan's cheeks had spots of color, his pale blue eyes gave off sparks. "Not yet, there's so much more. Show me when we come to one you really like, we'll analyze it together..."

Johnnine dragged along until they came to a room with a bench. She sat down and pointed to the painting opposite. "That one," she said. "I like that one."

"Really!" Duncan enthused. "Now you're cooking with gas! This one has a sophisticated use of linear perspective, very sharp of you to notice..." The scene faded out as he continued his lecture.

Later that same day, Duncan and Johnnine were in Central Park standing at the base of a five-story high rocky crag. Little piles of blackened snow in its crevices lay waiting forlornly for spring. On the frozen lake behind them, intrepid ice-skaters glided by.

"...Weatherman's Hill," Duncan was saying, "so called because they take the temperature here every day, for the New York Weather Bureau. See the building on top?"

The camera took Johnnine's perspective as she looked up and squinted into the frozen white winter sun. The square, unadorned red brick building appeared miles above them.

"Doesn't it give you any ideas?" Duncan prompted.

Johnnine turned her gaze to her father. "Can we get a hot chocolate?"

Duncan blithely evaded her. "Did I ever tell you, when I was at the Art Institute, how I used to climb the outsides of buildings?"

Johnnine was amazed. "Didn't they have stairs then?"

"No," Duncan frowned. "You don't understand. I did it for the *fun*, the challenge of it..."

"Hot chocolate's fun," Johnnine quipped. "Even Mom and Pahlser let me have some."

"Later, later." Duncan was jamming his hat on his head, craning his neck to look up at the steep rocky challenge of Weatherman's Hill. "First we're going to climb!"

Johnnine looked up at the sheer bare slab of dark gray rock and back at her father incredulously.

Duncan glanced down at her. "You can do it, it's easy! Watch me—" He leapt onto the base of the rock and began scampering up. Half-way up, he stopped and turned to yell down at her. "Come on!" He turned and resumed his mad goat climb, his steps nimble and sure-footed on thick rubber soles.

"I can't!" Johnnine cried, tears of panic in her eyes. "Duncan, I can't! It's too high!" But Duncan was already out of earshot and Johnnine knew better than to harbor hopes of rescue from passersby. Gingerly, miserably, she began picking her way up the freezing rock face, her patent leather Mary Janes slipping, her fingers red with cold. She began crying, plastering herself to the rock.

Duncan called down to her from the top. "I'm not coming to get you, Johnnine. Come on, you can do it!"

Without hope, Johnnine kept climbing, her face looking unhappier the higher she got. She found footholds in cracks and crevices and handholds wherever there was enough horizontal space for a patch of snow. As she pulled herself over the top, she looked as though she'd been through a small war: her navy dress coat was filthy and missing several brass buttons, her shoes were scuffed, her face was dirty and streaked with tears. Scared, raw, still snuffling, she scoured her father with lost eyes.

Duncan was brushing off his own knee-length winter coat with his hat, as pleased as though they had conquered Mt. Everest. "See, you didn't need my help. You did it all by yourself!"

Johnnine did not look at her father as they trudged out of the park. The trees were bare and the ground was littered with unappealing clumps of sooty late-winter snow. They walked side by side but she did not reach for his hand. The screen went black.

"While I certainly don't subscribe to his methods, your father was trying to teach you a valuable lesson," Xofia pointed out.

"Yeah, that he was completely *non compos mentis...*" Johnnine said bitterly. Seeing the Central Park episode, which she had managed to forget, clinched it. Now she knew beyond the shadow of a doubt that there was no hope, her mental and emotional problems were genetic. Killing herself would simply insure that she was kept out of a straitjacket.

Seraph A. sang a few bars of a sad refrain.

"'What child does not have cause to weep over its parents'?" Xofia interpreted. "You have yet to figure out why you picked them, I take it?"

Johnnine fairly snorted. "What a crock! Why the hell would I want to give myself shit, shit, and more shit? Unless maybe I was crazy *before* I was born?" Johnnine slapped her thigh. "Yup, that must be it—"

Xofia ignored Johnnine's theatrics. "Your admittedly idiosyncratic parents also gave you character, creativity, and enthusiasm. Not to mention beauty and brains, if you ever use them. These are not minor blessings, darling."

"Please." Johnnine held up a hand. "Spare me a lecture on my many blessings."

"You won't get anywhere feeling sorry for yourself."

"I'm not trying to feel sorry for myself! I just want to die, goddamit! Only you shitheads won't let me!" What *was* it with grown-ups? If she tried to just live, mind her own business and be happy, they wouldn't let her. If she wanted to get it over with and die, still no go!!

Seraph A. suddenly broke out with the melody of "Flow Gently Sweet Afton," an old folk song Dinah used to sing her to sleep with. The familiar notes short-circuited Johnnine's recriminations and reminded her of her babyhood, when she hadn't had to share her mother with Pahlser or a bottle of rye. The song even helped her remember a Christmas party her father had taken her to. It had been a disaster, of course—Johnnine remembered yelling when the fat stranger with the fake white beard grabbed her—but he had at least taken her to one, once upon a time.

Xofia showed off her incisive mind-reading talents. "There were a few other positive influences, darling. It wasn't all shit, shit, and more shit, as you so eloquently put it—"

The Akashic film now did an artsy winter time segue. Shot from the inside of a moving car, pristine, snow-covered fields flashed by under a full moon, black trees edging a narrow dirt road.

Dinah was at the wheel of a late-forties model Plymouth sedan. Dark and sultry Harriet Millar sat next to her in the passenger seat while her daughter Alix and Johnnine slept under a leopard-spotted car blanket in back. Dinah pulled up a little hill and turned off the road into a plowed parking area. There was a small old farmhouse nearby. "Okay, kids, we're here!"

"Wow, Goody, this is beautiful!" Harriet gushed. An outdoor light from the house threw a gleaming cone of gold over the snow.

They listened to the deep quiet of the country for a moment. "Yah, the place has a lot of serenity for me—c'mon, kids, up and at 'em! Johnnine! Alix!" Dinah got out of the car, leaving her door open and inhaling deeply. Her boots crunched on the pure white, powdery ground.

"God, Mom, shut the door, it's *cold*!" Johnnine said crankily.

"Don't say 'God'," Dinah corrected.

"Come on, honey, wake up—" Harriet gently shook Alix's arm. "We're here—"

"Where's *here*?" Alix said, one eye half open, one eye stuck shut.

"Up country!" Dinah enthused in her booming, hail-fellow-well-met voice. "Honey Hill Road, North Valley, Otsego County, New York State. Get out and look at this night sky!"

Harriet was the only one to do as she was told, clutching her coat and scarf tightly around her. "Brrr, colder than a witches'..."

"Look up there!" Dinah was ecstatic as she craned her head backwards. "Cassiopeia, Orion's belt—you can't see them like this in the city."

"C'mon, Alix." Johnnine's tone was petulant. "We gotta look at some dumb *stars...*"

The girls piled out of the car and stood unsteadily by their mothers.

"See—there's the Big Dipper, you can always find it by finding the North Star—"

"I want to go inside," Johnnine whined. "The stars are shivering, just like us." She turned and saw the house for the first time, an out-of-plumb, pitch-roofed, tiny old wood-frame with peeling white paint and dark green shutters.

The All Souls' Waiting Room

There was an enormous denuded maple tree in the front yard. "Mom! Whose house is that?"

"Ours." Dinah's smile, in the moonlight, was very proud. "It needs work, it's over a hundred years old, but once I saw it, I couldn't resist..."

"You mean we're gonna live here?" Johnnine's eyes went wide.

"No, it's just for weekends and summers."

"Do I get my own room?" Johnnine was excited as they shuffled through the calendar-pretty scene, along a shoveled path from the parking area to the front door. A line of pine trees in the front yard cast long blue shadows on the snow.

"You have the whole top floor to yourself—since you seem to want to be alone so much..."

"I *do*? Come on, Alix—" Johnnine raced to the door.

"Boots off, everybody!" Dinah commanded cheerfully as they walked through a lean-to shed attached to the side of the house.

"Oh, thank God. It's warm inside," Harriet sighed, opening the door into a small, low-ceilinged kitchen.

"We found a wonderful man to do the care-taking..."

"You're not supposed to say 'God,' Harriet," Johnnine repeated solemnly. The proportions of the house were diminutive and cozy, almost child-sized. She looked around at the comfortably used, country farm furnishings, a white enamel table in the middle of the kitchen, an old Mother Hubbard cupboard in one corner. "Where's the upstairs, Mom?"

Dinah cracked open a door between the pantry and the bathroom, revealing narrow wooden stairs as steep as a ladder. "Up here, ducklet."

"How'd we get it?" Johnnine had to take giant steps to mount the high-rise stairs.

"Pahlser and I bought it together," Dinah answered, raising her voice. She didn't see Johnnine stop in mid-flight. Dinah continued conversationally to Harriet, "I call it our little hidey-hole—ooh, Pink Stink, a sweet retreat—"

"Is Pahlser coming?" Harriet asked casually as she unpacked groceries.

"Yah, he's driving down from Orgonon later tonight..."

Johnnine reached the top of the stairs with suddenly much slower steps. Alix had already run ahead into the main room and run back to her. "There's beds and everything! You're a lucky bitch, Johnnine—"

Johnnine's face was pale as she turned the corner into the low-ceilinged room. A double dormer window looked out on the front yard's huge old maple tree and snow-covered hills beyond. There were three old single beds and two small oak dressers shoved up against the walls. The ceiling came down low in the corners and the room was papered with a faded design of a little girl and a Scottie dog.

In the All Souls' Waiting Room, Johnnine felt the twin emotions of dread and nostalgia, her remembered fear of another 'session' with Pahlser, mingled with her love of the little farmhouse. Why did the good and the bad have to be so mixed up together all the time?

Seraph A. burbled a few soothing chords from "La Cenerentola" before the film cranked up again.

Chapter Sixteen

"But the whole room is blue!" Daniel Pahlser was saying in an urgent voice to Wilhelm Reich. They were standing in a large, square, metal-lined room at Orgonon and the camera panned around showing several tall orgone energy accumulators, six feet high by four feet wide. A far wall seemed to glow from some undefined light source.

"Yah. The orgone intensified when it reacted with the nuclear material—" Reich said. "I've been airing it out for a week, but there's still a lot of deadly orgone, you can tell from the pronounced odor."

Pahlser's face went suddenly chalk white and he swayed on his feet. "I think I'm—I feel sick..."

"Quickly." Reich led Pahlser through the lab. "Outside."

Pahlser rushed through the building and vomited into the snow just in front of the lab's door. The camera showed the barracks-like student lab with its long empty work tables and microscopes. A blackboard was filled with a chart, three separate columns meant to be read from left to right as well as up and down. It was headed "ORGONOMY IS A BODY OF KNOWLEDGE WHICH DEALS WITH THE BASIC LAWS OF NATURE:

GOOD	EVIL	Ethics
GOD	DEVIL	Religion
LIFE	DEATH	Biology
ORGONE (OR)	NUCLEAR (NR)	Physics
COSMIC ENERGY	COSMIC ENERGY	Astrophysics, Cosmology
before MATTER	*after* MATTER	

The scene shifted to Reich's Observatory. A fortress-like construction of river stone and concrete positioned on the crest of a hill, it commanded a sweeping view of wooded, snow-clad rolling hills and overlooked a small frozen lake.

The windows were wide open in Reich's ground floor study. Daniel Pahlser, pale and sweaty, was stretched out on a cot. Reich sat next to him. Both men were warmly dressed for the outdoors, attesting to the freezing temperature in the room. Reich's hair was stirred by the wind coming in through the windows. His manner was solicitous but purposeful. "...I am immunized to the poisoned atmosphere by now, whereas this was your first exposure—you needn't have come, I told you it might affect you."

Pahlser's voice was weak. "You needed the medical emergency instructions, and I wanted to be here. I feel so...cut off from the work in New York. Seeing patients isn't the same as doing orgone research..."

"Yah," Reich nodded, holding his hands together in front of him. "There is so much to do. I feel the pressure of time closing in on me."

Pahlser turned his head to look at Reich. "I want to be of more use to you, Dr. Reich."

Reich smiled. "You are bringing healthy newborns into the world. There is no more useful thing you could be doing." His attention shifted to the Geiger counter at his feet.

Pahlser sought Reich's face. "Hapgood and I delivered our third baby last week."

Reich looked up at Pahlser warmly. "*Brav.* All went well?"

Pahlser nodded. "Wonderfully well. The mother was scrubbing floors an hour before birth—she said she felt a sudden 'burst of energy'. She stayed quite happily conscious through the delivery. We just reminded her to keep breathing and focusing."

"Excellent!" Reich sat back, beaming. "You see? If we simply let nature do her work without always rushing in to 'fix things'—"

"There was something else I wanted to tell you. About Hapgood's daughter, Johnnine. She's five, in her first puberty...she's made several pronounced sexual invitations to me and I've started showing her what intercourse is, so she can—"

Reich sat up straight in his chair, his expression changing from pleasure to one of alarm. "What do you mean?"

"Oh, not with her mother, but in line with an honest and direct answer to Johnnine's sexual curiosity. I did a session with her in bed, so she could begin to understand her feelings. She called it 'what you do to mommy', obviously feeling displacement..."

Reich was incredulous. His face colored, his eyes flashed. "Pahlser, what are you saying?"

Pahlser became confused, less sure of himself. He looked away for a moment before forcing his eyes back to Reich. "There was no penetration, but I think the genital contact helped her see what—"

Reich bolted up from the chair, his face turning bright red. "This is a deadly violation of your role! I can't believe what you are telling me. You must stop seeing patients immediately!"

"But it didn't seem to throw her off, she hasn't shown—"

Reich gripped the back of the chair, his fingers turning white. "We cannot discuss it now. This is obviously a major blind spot of yours, a deadly dangerous one. I have to take background readings around the lab, but I want you to call Cooke tonight. You need to get into treatment immediately. Tell your patients you are suspended from giving orgone therapy for three months. And never touch the child in a sexual way again!" He picked the chair up off the floor and slammed it down with a resounding thud. He left the room, angry and disturbed, bundled up in his heavy wool red and black lumberjack's jacket.

His face gray and pinched, Pahlser looked after him dejectedly as the winter winds seemed to gather momentum, howling balefully through the room.

In the All Souls' Waiting Room, Johnnine wanted to cry. So Reich didn't approve of what Pahlser had done. Why didn't anyone think to tell *her*? What a difference it would have made if someone, anyone, had said Pahlser made a hideous, a horrible mistake, but that it wouldn't happen again, that they were *sorry*. She could have lived with that. But it was never talked about openly. What she couldn't live with was the way the session with Pahlser had twisted everything in her life into an ugly knot, destroyed her relationship with her mother, killed her ability to trust anyone, made her hate herself.

Just as she hadn't been told directly about Reich and Pahlser, Johnnine also hadn't told about the Oranur experiment. But she remembered the feeling of vague, disjointed fear at the time. Johnnine had picked up that Oranur was something to do with seeing if orgone energy could overcome the effects of nuclear fallout. Again, the grownups didn't talk to her about it, but she could tell from their constricted faces that 'the accident' had been a serious one. She had wondered why things had gone wrong at Orgonon and why they were so close-mouthed. Why did they look so afraid—and what did it mean for her?

The scene in Reich's study faded out on a close-up of Pahlser's dejected face and came up on him again, in the next episode, as he slowly opened the kitchen door at the country farmhouse. Dinah was sitting at the big white enamel table, drinking and smoking, reading a paperback. A long, sticky filament of fly paper left over from the summer and embedded with long-dead flies hung from the low ceiling.

Pahlser took off his coat tiredly and hung it on the back of the door. The ceiling was only inches higher than his head. "Roads were icy all the way from Rangeley..."

"Have a drink, it'll warm you up."

"Is Johnnine asleep?"

"Yah, she's in bed upstairs."

"I'll just go tuck her in," Pahlser said, opening the warped and narrow little door to the second story.

Dinah's dark brown eyes flashed a look of deep hurt before she nodded and poured more rye whiskey into her shot glass.

With the covers pulled up to her chin, Johnnine's eyes were wide open as she heard Pahlser's footsteps creaking up the steep wooden stairs. When he reached the top step, Johnnine turned her head quickly to the wall and squeezed her eyes shut, pretending to be asleep, her body rigid with fear.

Bending over, Pahlser stood by her bed and gently stroked her hair. Johnnine appeared wooden under his touch, holding her breath until he turned and quietly left the room.

In the All Souls' Waiting Room, Johnnine remembered the terror she had felt when Pahlser came into the room that night and the enormous, almost giddy sense of relief when he left. His caresses had made her feel sick to her stomach, but as she watched him in the film, even though she hated the way he showed it, she could tell that he had really loved her.

Back in the New York apartment, camera showed Johnnine walking into the small kitchen. The album from the Broadway show "South Pacific" blared from the new record player in the living room. Dinah, at the sink, hummed along with the record, breaking into her plangent singing voice to accompany Ezio Pinza's maudlin show-stopper, "Some Enchanted Evening."

"...*you-will-see-a-STRANGER, across-a-CROWDED-room, and-somehow-you'll-know, you'll-suddenly-know...*"

Johnnine sang along with her mother. "...*once-you-have-found-her, never-let-her-go, once-you-have-found-her, never-let-her-go, or-all-through-your-life, you-will-live-all-ALONE...*"

The record ended. Standing near her mother by the stove, Johnnine was fascinated by strong but very different objects of interest. On the stove, a pot of simmering soup, and on the sink's counter, two small wire cages, each containing a pink-eyed white rat. "Another pregnancy test, huh, Mom."

Dinah dusted her hands with talcum powder and pulled on rubber surgical gloves. "Yes, a very special one this time." She poured ether on a rag and opened a glass jar.

Johnnine pinched her nose. "Peeyew, that stuff *stinks*!"

"Not *stink*. *Odoriferous*." Dinah opened a cage and expertly slipped her hand around the rat's body. Holding it carefully, she dropped it into the jar with the ether-soaked rag.

"Yah, odoriferous," Johnnine repeated, her eyes glued to the rat, who scratched at the sides of the jar before falling back unconscious, showing its tiny, rodent overbite. Johnnine looked back and forth between the limp, doomed rat and her mother's steady brown eyes, Dinah's dispassionate expression. Dinah slid the animal out of the jar with professional aplomb and used a small scalpel to make a quick, deep cut down the middle of the rat's belly. Its body parted bloodlessly, like a piece of soft white bread, revealing a viewing slit into its glistening insides.

Dinah read the tiny pink and yellow entrails intently. A strange smile played over her face. She repeated the procedure with the other rat and gave the same smile. She left the kitchen whistling along to the tune of *"Bali-Hai."* Dinah was an expert whistler.

The All Souls' Waiting Room

Johnnine sat down at the kitchen table as the toilet flushed in the bathroom. Dinah was clearly in a cheerful mood when she bustled back into the kitchen. She pulled off her gloves and washed her hands at the sink. Then she laid out two soup bowls on the table. Taking the pot off the stove, she began ladling it out. "Ready for lunch?"

"Yah." Johnnine sniffed deeply. "Cream of mushmaroom!"

Dinah's smile was distant. "Yah. How would you like a baby brother or sister?"

Johnnine's eyes held greedily on the steaming soup. She crowded close to her bowl. "I don't know," she said guardedly. "Who's the daddy?"

"Pahlser..."

"No!" Johnnine frowned and shouted, slapping her hand on the built-in table and rising onto her knees on the bench seat. Startled, Dinah jumped and dropped the pot, which hit the side of the table. Johnnine screamed as the boiling soup sloshed into her lap and ran down her legs.

"Pants OFF!" Dinah yelled, grabbing her off the seat. While Johnnine cried and hopped around and shrieked, Dinah struggled to pull down her sopping dungarees. "Don't fight me!" she yelled at Johnnine, who calmed down long enough for her mother to get the pants down around her ankles. The sight of her splotchy red thigh made Johnnine cry more violently.

Dinah frowned. "Stop over-reacting, it doesn't hurt that much."

Johnnine stared down at herself, awash in tears. "Yes, it does!"

Dinah turned to the refrigerator and took something out. "Here." She began applying a stick of butter to the scalded skin.

Johnnine's face convulsed in pain, anger, and revenge. She yelled as loud as she could. "Yes, it does, it *hurts*!! Ow! Ow, ow, OW! OW, *OW*!"

Dinah slapped her once, hard, across the face. "Stop it! You're hysterical!" Her eyes were hard as stones.

Johnnine's screams turned to muffled whimpers. "Owwie, owwie, oww—" she murmured.

Dinah ran the melting butter up and down the scalded thigh. "Go sit in the accumulator, that'll make it feel better." She blotted Johnnine's skin with a paper towel and stood up.

Johnnine's face looked like the remains of a small firecracker that has burst and gone out. "I don't want a brother or sister if Pahlser's the daddy!" Johnnine was hobbled by her dungarees around her ankles as she shuffled and sobbed out of the kitchen.

Dinah looked after her with a mixture of sorrow, amusement, and pity.

"And I don't want Pahlser to touch me anymore. You tell him, Mom," Johnnine cried as she left the room. "Okay, Mom?"

The camera did a close-up of Dinah, her face as shocked and disbelieving as Johnnine's after Dinah had slapped her. She stood stock-still for a minute, staring at the empty rat cages. Then she opened a cupboard and took out a fifth of Seagram's.

In the living room, a bare-bottomed Johnnine was still crying as she opened the door of the orgone accumulator, its outside panels the color of cooked Wheatena. Once inside, she turned around to sit down. The scene faded out on a close-up of her face, staring forlornly out of the little window cut in the front.

Little Orgone Annie, Johnnine thought to herself in the All Souls' Waiting Room. My mother expected me to be happy she was pregnant with Pahlser's kid and I actually expected her to feel sorry for me. She shifted her weight on The Couch, which gave off a low susurration of sympathy.

Seraph A. hit the room lights.

"What's the deal with love, anyway?" Johnnine asked in a loud, bitter voice. "You only get the kind you don't want, right? Pretty fucked system, if you ask me."

Xofia addressed The Recorder as she poured herself a glass of ethereal bubbly. "The child has a heavy load."

"As do all souls..."

Seraph A. broke into a chorus of "Old Man River."

Chapter Seventeen

Over at Demel's coffeehouse, the ethereal essence of Schlomo Freud sat impatiently behind the prone figure of Willie Reich. Schlomo's pen was poised in readiness over his notebook, he had his professional, psychoanalyzing demeanor in place, but he could barely contain himself—or believe he had invented anything so achingly, tortuously boring. Not for the patient—people loved nothing better than talking about themselves—but for the analyst. Schlomo crossed and uncrossed his legs restively, entertaining treacherous thoughts of using Reichian, hands-on therapy, beginning with boxing Willie's ears. Only just barely, he restrained himself.

"Yah, and then what happened?" Schlomo repeated quite automatically, even though he already knew Willie's traumatic young history. His reluctant patient was being led up to the terrible events of his early adolescence, the events that had led to Willie's parents' death, in whose early demise Willie played a pivotal role. Schlomo reminded himself to have compassion.

Willie lay supine on his row of chairs. He looked neither comfortable nor un-, he was totally absorbed in the retelling of his youth. "I had enormous vigor for a child of that age. My sexual curiosity was satisfied by Gretchen, our beautiful young parlor maid. I was fully orgasmic by the time I was 12."

Yah, of course, Schlomo thought. Willie's braggadocio undoubtedly meant the exact opposite, that he had lusted after and never achieved coitus with the desirable Gretchen. More than likely as well that Gretchen was a mental substitute for Willie's unacceptable incestuous urges towards his mother. The same young mother who betrayed him by taking Willie's tutor, Nils, as her lover. Well, Willie had had his revenge, although Schlomo knew Willie would not really have wanted her dead, except in moments of infantile rage.

"Yah, and how did you feel about Nils?"

"Oh, I revered him. He was a man of wide learning, a great intellect, a wonderful mind..."

Oh yes? Schlomo thought, making a note. Was this before or after Willie found him shtupping his mama?

Johnnine felt bombarded with new insight she wasn't sure she wanted, insight about the damaged people who had raised her. Insight made things more complicated. Things like life.

She furrowed her brow, staring at but not seeing the prints of ancient archaeological sites on Schlomo's wall, his crowded bookshelves, display cabinets crammed with ancient artifacts. "What I *need* are some simple, easy answers to living."

Xofia was leafing through Schlomo's well-worn copy of the Egyptian "Book of the Dead." "Brace yourself, darling: there aren't any. We have a special, a separate Waiting Room for fundamentalists, where everything is either black or white—walls, floors, furniture, everything. But that's hardly the way things are. And such myopia is hardly all you're capable of," she added, patting Johnnine's arm with her warm, feathery touch. "I detect great possibilities for you—"

Yeah, Johnnine thought, the possibility of scaling new lows, hitherto undiscovered. She held out her hand hopefully. "Can I have some champagne?"

Xofia handed her her glass but Johnnine's face screwed up after a sip. "Still tastes like puppy piss..."

"A good sign," The Recorder intoned. "Let's continue—"

Seraph A. cut the lights. They were back at the movies. The palsied green moving truck of the Flying Ferragamos shimmied down Bleecker Street, turned onto Grove and stopped in front of a gray apartment building with a bright red enamel door. Daniel Pahlser, wearing his gabardine flight suit, waited in the doorway. He looked tired.

The truck pulled to the curb and Giuseppe jumped out. "Hey, doc, you wan' us to take the box thing up first?"

"Yah, I do—"

Giuseppe snapped his fingers at Luigi and Salvatore, who were opening the rear of the truck. Salvatore wrestled the cumbersome orgone accumulator to the edge of the truck bed. Positioning their luckless brother as though he were an inanimate object, Giuseppe and Salvatore strapped the unwieldy box to Luigi's back.

Pahlser held the building's door open. "Third floor, I'll show you which apartment..."

A little later, on Bleecker Street, the Ferragamo truck barreled past numerous small Italian grocery stores, the front windows hung with huge netted balls of cheese and waxy pigs' heads with dead, disconcerting, milky-blue eyes. The truck turned right on Carmine Street, past an imposing church on the corner, Our Lady of Pompeii. Three-quarters of the way down the street, the truck screeched to a halt.

"She sure moves a lot," Salvatore said as Giuseppe jumped down from the cab.

"Shut uppa your face, she's a good customer. Come on, just the stoop and one flight, she's onna first floor—"

They looked up at a narrow, grimy, four-story brick building overlaid with a fire escape. Dinah's bulky outline could be seen hanging white Venetian blinds in the front room's windows.

Salvatore groaned as he peeled himself off the cab's seat. Giuseppe hit his brother on the head with the heel of his hand. "Thank the Virgin there's no piano!"

The All Souls' Waiting Room

Dinah stood at the top of the stairs as the Ferragamos trudged up towards her. Giuseppe carried the mattress while Luigi toiled behind with a bureau on his back. "Where you want these, lady?"

"Front room, please, Mr. Ferragamo."

The men turned left at the landing and bumped their way down the narrow outside hallway. "Jesus, lady, whatcha need such a big bed for, you gonna take in boarders?"

"Unfortunately, Mr. Ferragamo, I sleep alone now—"

Giuseppe grunted as he maneuvered the clumsy mattress through the door. "I'll tell Salvatore, he's still single."

Dinah laughed, too heartily. "Well, so am I! Again, or should I say still..."

Behind her, the apartment was strung out in a floor-through of long, skinny rooms, all floored with the same fake-brick linoleum. At the back, next to a galley-like kitchen with high orange cabinets, was a square bedroom with a view of the back yard.

Johnnine stood listlessly at one of the tall windows in her new room, looking at the mountain ash tree growing out of the garbage-strewn concrete below. Clotheslines criss-crossed the open space like a giant game of cat's cradle.

Several months later, on a sub-freezing, mid-winter night, Johnnine and Dinah were ice-skating on a tiny frozen pond up country. An enormous, lemony full moon had just come up over the mountain ridge behind them and lit the sky like a black noon. There was not a whisper of wind. With an expert cut-and-glide motion, Dinah skated with her hands clasped behind her back, her short, rotund figure surprisingly graceful on the ice. The rhythmical swaying of her knee-length brown skirt kept perfect 3/4 waltz time as she hummed the Blue Danube to herself.

Johnnine wobbled around one end of the pond alone, trying to keep her ankles straight. She would get herself going, fall down, get up and try again, much too preoccupied to notice her mother silently crying.

"It's not fair," Johnnine said, highly annoyed. "You can do it and I can't..."

Dinah's voice was throaty and sad. "I've had a lot more practice, Johnnine, I told you. I used to skate to school and back, three miles each way."

Johnnine was peevish. "I don't get to have fun on *my* way to school."

"It wasn't always fun. Sometimes, if it got dark on the way home, I could hear wolves howling in the woods by the side of the canal—"

"What's a canal?"

"Irrigation canals, to water the fields in summer. Grandfather Sheppard farmed almost fifty acres..."

"You already told me about it." Johnnine wobbled away, cutting her mother off. Then she wobbled back. "No wolves around here, right, Mom?"

Dinah skated smoothly over to a log on the side of the pond, coming to an elegant half-circle stop before she sat down. She took out a flask from a pocket of her tan Army surplus bomber jacket. Tears leaked from her eyes. Dinah wiped them with a handkerchief and raised the flask to her mouth. "Cold enough to freeze your oonka-voonk tonight...here's to a Happy New Year!" Her mother looked more peaceful after her drink.

"Can I have some?" Johnnine asked.

"You won't like it, ducklet."

Johnnine flailed her arms and stuck her tongue out in a concentrated effort to get across the ice without falling down. She couldn't manage an executed stop and more or less crashed into her mother, whose large body offered a soft berth. Johnnine took the bottle from her mother. After swallowing, she shuddered and made an awful face. "Yucchh! Why do you like it so much?"

Dinah waxed poetic. "Ah, because it makes my insides lovely and warm and it helps me to forget things."

"Why do you want to forget stuff?"

Dinah smiled at Johnnine indulgently, but her eyes were now filled with tears. "You know we're all the family we've got, Johnnine. It's just you and me now, we don't have anybody except each other—"

Johnnine did not look happy with this news. "What about Pahlser? Is he still my guardian?"

"Yah. There isn't, there wasn't anyone else, in case anything happened to me. But since we don't live together anymore..." Dinah's voice trailed off. She took another swig from the flask.

Instead of being touched, Johnnine became angry. She scowled and shivered. "It's too freezing. I want to go back."

"Okay by me." Dinah began whistling "On Top of Old Smoky" as she untied their skate laces. Johnnine looked around the icy pond, the skeletal trees, the lonely country road. The full moon, now much higher and smaller over the mountain, had turned bone-white, a bitter cold spotlight in an ink-black sky, shining down on the only two moving figures in the frozen landscape.

In the All Souls' Waiting Room, Johnnine remembered the desolate feeling of that New Year's Eve, the burning cold, the overbearing brightness of the moon, the way her mother's whistled notes seemed to hang in the frigid, windless air like joints in a frozen meat locker. What she saw now was how they had been feeling completely different things. Her mother was sad about Pahlser, while Johnnine was angry that her mother was sad.

Chapter Eighteen

"Starting about here," The Recorder said in his deeply resonant voice, "we cut back and forth between Johnnine's life and Willie's, the latter having had such a formative effect on the former...and it bears to keep in mind that these are the Earth years of the 1950's, not exactly a time of riotously free expression—"

The All Souls' screen showed a fiftyish Wilhelm Reich alone at his massive wooden desk in the Orgonon observatory office. Everything in the room was large-scale and modern, from the Scandinavian rya rug to the molded gray fiberglass Eames chair he sat in. He held a Stenograph microphone in one hand and a filter cigarette in the other. From over his hefty shoulders, camera showed the view out the large window in front of him, the Maine landscape in late fall foliage.

"...sense of time passing too quickly while there is yet so much to do," Reich dictated. His high energy and robust vitality showed traces of weariness. "Work on 'The Murder of Christ' is going well and fluently. I am writing directly from my core and not from my intellectually-armored self. The world will not like my book, because it is the truth. I want to convey Jesus as the highest example of unarmored life, what it could be like for man if he were truly to take the path of orgonomy. It is armored life which seeks to betray unarmored, the emotionally-plagued who betray those who offer liberation to the human race. Saint Paul was to Christ what Stalin was to Marx, the rigid betrayer of the original truth..."

Reich paused to take a deep, lung-filling drag of his cigarette. Successive emotions surged over his full, highly-colored face like waves. A deepening furrow creased his forehead.

"...paragraph...F. D. A. agents have now questioned several of my analysts and patients in New York about their use of the accumulator. It is beginning to feel like Norway, persecution by the armored of anything that threatens their strangle-hold on joyful, free, unashamed life. Paragraph. Not only do we need to break through the deadly encasing armor of civilized man, we *must* harness atmospheric orgone for the present planetary emergency. Man's use of nuclear energy in his death-revering, armored state is like giving children matches and then locking them in an arsenal."

Reich put out his cigarette and immediately lit another, frowning as he spoke into the Stenograph. "New paragraph...I have noticed a disturbing stillness of the landscape since the Oranur experiment. It is as if the land has become biologically dead. There is no birdsong, no wind, no sign of animal life. The leaves on the trees have lost their lustre. New paragraph. Oranur has left me with the inescapable conclusion that radioactivity irritates natural cosmic orgone and changes it into *deadly* orgone energy, DOR, not the other way around as I had hoped. This is very disturbing as it means..."

Reich suddenly stood up abruptly, convulsed with pain. Pressing his chest with his fists, he gasped for breath. His ruddy face lost all color. He turned and staggered toward the couch. Falling to his knees before he reached it, he passed out on the carpet of his office. Camera faded out on the burning cigarette in the glass ashtray.

In the All Souls' Waiting Room, Johnnine keenly felt Reich's pain, physical and moral. She was very confused about how she felt about him. She knew that a lot of people considered him crazy, but as far as she could tell the world was not a fit judge of what was sane or insane. *Hadn't* the world gone off the deep end with nuclear power? Did anyone know how to cure its effects? When Reich talked about his 'planetary emergency,' wasn't he talking about the insanity of the whole world choosing the path of death over the path of life? How, then, could he be dismissed as irrelevant?

The scene dissolved into an exterior shot of Johnnine's old elementary school. The camera panned up the outside of the large red brick P. S. 8 on King Street, past the American flag drooping from its horizontal pole just below the principal's office and into a second-story window. The walls of Johnnine's first-grade classroom were covered with cut-outs of brown construction-paper turkeys and red and gold maple leaves. Johnnine sat close to the front, her head one of the few blonde ones in the room. There was plump-cheeked, pretty Mrs. Antonelli taking attendance, the Italian names rolling off her tongue with native ease, while Johnnine's got read as a question. "DiGiacomo, Angela...Ferari, Eduardo ...Giannini, Roberto...Hapgood, Johnnine?...Lapelli, Vincente... Maldonado, Alma-Maria Therese..."

Mrs. Antonelli's large black eyes flitted back and forth between the children's silently-raised hands and the attendance sheet. A stern older woman appeared in the doorway and gestured to Mrs. Antonelli. "Hands behind backs, children," Mrs. Antonelli said. She half-closed the door behind her as she spoke to the principal's secretary.

A boy from the back of the room rushed up the aisle and planted a kiss on Johnnine's cheek. The class exhaled a collective astonished sigh. "*Ooohhh, Vinnie!*" Mrs. Antonelli quickly cracked the door to glare at them. Smiling mischievously, Vinnie Lapelli resumed his seat and the scene dissolved.

After school that day, Vinnie bounced along beside Johnnine, proudly carrying her books. He was olive-skinned and lively, his walk more of a self-confident strut. "Know why I kissed ya?"

Johnnine shook her head. She appeared uncertain of herself and more than a little puzzled by him.

"'Cause you're the prettiest girl in the first grade an' I want we should go togedda. I kiss ya, it means you're mine."

Johnnine stared at him as they turned down Bedford, whose old tenement buildings seemed to lean over the street in a conspiracy to block out the sun.

Vinnie danced around her as they passed a group of teenage boys in black leather jackets hanging out in front of a candy store on the corner. They jostled each other and feinted with their fists, combed their hair back into d.a.'s, or duck's ass hairdos, and casually but frequently spit on the sidewalk. One of the boys began whistling, cat-calling, and making lewd gestures at Johnnine and Vinnie. "First comes *love*, then comes *marriage*, then comes Vinnie pushing a *baby* carriage..."

"Ahh, shut up, Frankie—" Six-year old Vinnie didn't seem at all frightened. This impressed Johnnine, who was.

"Whatsa matta, little Vinnie? Don' wan us to say nothin' in fronta your new *girl*friend?" Frankie repeated his hand gesture. The other boys howled and shoved each other.

Vinnie and Johnnine turned the corner onto Carmine. The fitful November sun added to the forlorn look of the wide, two-way street, where dusty, empty storefronts alternated with tenements. "Who are *they*?" Johnnine asked.

Vinnie shrugged and spit, though he did it off the curb and not on the sidewalk. "My brudda's gang."

Johnnine's hair blew around her face. She pulled back a strand that covered her mouth. "What were they doing with their hands?"

"Ahh, just bein' stoopid," Vinnie said, shifting Johnnine's book bag to his other shoulder. "Makin' the sign for...for you know, what dogs do in the street."

Johnnine was amazed. "Sexual intercourse?"

"Nah, what's dat? Wanna come over to my house? We got a new TV. I'll walk ya home afta, and no funny business, I swear!"

Vinnie lived on Carmine Street, too, close to the triangular-shaped little park on the corner of Sixth Avenue where old men sat around smoking and playing checkers or bocci ball. His building was directly across from the squat, pigeon-streaked, menacing white marble edifice of Our Lady of Pompeii Catholic Church.

In the All Souls' Waiting Room, Johnnine remembered being mystified by the rites of Catholicism seen from afar. Churches were places into which it seemed only people wearing black were allowed, nuns and priests in long black gowns and thick-waisted old Italian women in black dresses. The only times there were any signs of life were when they hung banners for a bazaar or bingo nights. Our Lady of Pompeii had a hushed, funereal gloom that made Johnnine walk on the opposite side of the street. She almost laughed at her childhood fears, remembering how she had thought of it as a giant stone toad that could at any moment shoot out a long, sticky tongue and suck her inside its sepulchral gloom like a luckless fly.

Vinnie led Johnnine into his dark and narrow building, like her own except even darker and narrower. Up two flights of stairs he flung open the door and shouted. "Hey, ma! It's me. I got someone wit me—"

A large woman in a severe black dress, her black hair scraped back into a face-lifting bun, emerged from a doorway, wiping her hands on an apron. Speaking rapid Italian to her son, she smiled at Johnnine.

"Dis is my ma. She don't speak no English. She says hello, nice to meetcha. Come on—"

With a wide-eyed, awestruck expression, Johnnine followed Vinnie down the hallway. She saw quick glimpses of tiny rooms crammed with overstuffed furniture. Lace doilies and fancy glass candy dishes, all empty, graced every available surface.

The closet-sized living room was painted a glossy, dark olive-green. Vinnie switched on a new console television set and jumped up on a faded red mohair sofa barely four feet opposite, the size of the TV dwarfing everything else in the room. Johnnine stood in the doorway, transfixed. She was unable to take her eyes off the grimly realistic crucifix on the wall over the TV: a tortured Jesus, writhing in His death agony, from whose open wounds glistening blood appeared to drip.

Vinnie stared at the TV, Johnnine at the crucified Christ. Vinnie's mother carried in a tray with two glasses of milk and a plate of lady fingers. Vinnie did not acknowledge his mother as she put the tray on a table near his hand, wordlessly staring at the TV and reaching for the milk and cookies.

Mrs. Lapelli smiled warmly again at Johnnine, who gaped at her hostess as if she had just met a new and different species. "God, Vinnie, your mom is *nice*," she whispered with feeling, sitting down next to him and helping herself to the cookies.

Johnnine found the room much more fascinating than the TV. On one wall was a candle-lit triptych of Mary and the infant Jesus, draped with a wooden rosary; on another, a glossy magazine picture of an old bearded man surrounded by a choir of angels blowing long golden horns, and on another, the pathetically-burdened Christ traversing the Stations of the Cross.

"Do you go to church?" Johnnine asked Vinnie.

Vinnie turned and stared at her. "Whaddya mean? A course! Don't you?"

Johnnine blushed and looked at the TV set.

"Mom, can I watch television?"

Later that same day, Johnnine let herself in to the noisy front room of her apartment. Several grown-ups were making a racket with their sawing and hammering. Johnnine looked around at her mother's white walls and saw mirrors, a blow-up of two lovers lying in the grass with their arms around each other from "The Family of Man," and a large red, blue and yellow abstract Calder mobile twisting in the hot air drafts over the steam radiator. In the middle of the spacious living room, a group of boisterous adults were putting together layers of glass wool, fine steel mesh, and pre-cut panels of chipboard, building orgone accumulators.

The All Souls' Waiting Room

"Mom!" Johnnine repeated, shouting over the industrious din. "Can I watch TV?"

Dinah looked up from the sawhorse where she was working and noticed Johnnine for the first time. "In the middle of the day? You most certainly cannot! If you need something to do, go read one of your books."

Johnnine turned away and pouted through the apartment towards the back, passing by various baby-holding pens containing various babies. She slammed the door of her room behind her. Sitting in her little yellow rocker by the window, she stared out at the denuded mountain ash tree in the back yard before she picked up her first-grade reader. "*See Dick. See Jane. See Dick run. See Jane run. Run, Dick, run. Run, run, run...*" Johnnine yelled the words out loud at the top of her voice.

The Akashic film scene seemed to flare up into a sunburst before turning black. What the...? Johnnine wondered, as the seraph turned the room lights on, warbling some sweet notes which Xofia duly interpreted.

"A small technical delay, not a portent—"

The Recorder and Seraph A. converged on the projector. After splicing out a small hunk of damaged film, they threaded it up and got it going again. It showed Johnnine, in her room, writing something in a black-and-white marbleized notebook, before it broke again.

Damn, Johnnine thought, annoyed that the film was fucking up on something she *wanted* to see, though she remembered the incident vividly. It was the first time she had written a poem, a little two-line thing about snowflakes. She recalled looking at her wobbly inch-high letters scrawled in pencil and feeling as though she were present at a miracle.

"It is a miracle," Xofia said softly, once again displaying her unnerving mind-reading ability. "All creativity is miraculous."

"What?" Johnnine asked, her attention still riveted to the scene. It had been the first time she made the connection between her outer reality, in which soft fat snowflakes were tumbling slowly past her window, and her inner, which was her reaction to the action. The very act of being able to describe something seemed momentous, revelatory, earth-stopping. And then to *read* —to watch letters turn into words, things that had meaning, that made little popping sounds in your brain!! Gadzooks, she was getting all goopy and mushy inside.

"You see," Xofia pointed out. "There are some things you love about living."

But just then, as if to contrast Xofia's encouraging words, a scene started up that reminded Johnnine of the miseries of childhood. She was still too young to appreciate such events as character-building.

Johnnine and Alix Millar, dark and slim to Johnnine's fair and rounded, stood watching the noisy tumult of hop-scotching, marble-shooting kids as a phalanx of older boys swaggered over to them. The biggest and oldest boy was a sixth-grader with eyes like the pigs' heads in the grocery stores, even though his were brown. "Youse know who I am, right? *Evvybuddy* knows Mousey Tanucci. I hear youse two got funny names, so me an' da boys wanned ta ax ya. What are ya?" Mousey was two feet taller than the girls, pudgy and threatening.

His interrogation flustered Johnnine. Her face turned red and she looked scared. "I—I'm, we're girls."

Disgusted, Mousey dismissed her answer. "I ain't blind, am I? I *mean*, what *are* ya?"

Johnnine looked quickly at Alix, who raised her thin shoulders up to her ears. Both of the girls were bewildered and frightened. "Americans!" Johnnine burst out. "We're Americans!"

The boys behind Mousey snickered into their hands. *"Evvybuddy's* Amerrican!" Mousey said irritably. "I MEAN, ARE YA CATLICK OR AIN'T YA?"

Alix and Johnnine looked at each other, dumfounded. "I don't know," Johnnine said to Mousey. "I don't think so, but I'm not sure—"

Mousey pushed the girls roughly against the brick wall. "Whaddya mean ya doan *know*?" His silent lieutenants crowded around them. Looking over his shoulder first, Mousey raised his fist. "Well, youse betta find out, uddawise you'll get one of dese in ya face!"

The after-lunch bell clanged. Yard monitors blew ear-splitting silver whistles for class line-up. Teachers testily segregated the laughing, overheated girls and boys into separate lines.

Mousey shook his fist under their noses one last time. "If youse two ain't Catlick, we wanna know what!"

At the end of the day, Johnnine and Alix came flying out of the wide school doors. They were small bobbing components of the onslaught of children to which King Street, with its neat little brownstones and geranium-filled window boxes, was subjected twice a day. The girls ran straight to Johnnine's apartment. Red-faced and out of breath, they charged up the stairs and rushed down the hall to the kitchen, the apartment's nerve center. Dinah was dragging on a filter-tipped Viceroy and swigging coffee while she jiggled a bawling, six-month old baby on her overflowing hip. From a bottle of baby food she fed another one that was slumped over the messy tray of a high chair.

Alix panted patiently behind Johnnine, catching her breath. Johnnine had to raise her voice over the rumble and slosh of the washer/dryer and the wails of the complaining baby. "Mom, Mom! This big kid named Mousey Tanucci is gonna beat us up if we don't tell him what we are. I gotta know! Are we Catlick?"

The tow-headed baby in the high chair suddenly vomited. Dinah swabbed at the mess with a diaper she had draped over her shoulder. "If you mean Catholic, you most definitely are not."

Johnnine was annoyed. "Then what *am* I?"

The All Souls' Waiting Room

"I suppose..." Dinah said as she rinsed the diaper in the sink. "—considering your grandparents, you could say Presbyterian..."

"Pressbee—??" Johnnine faltered.

"Presbyterian."

"How come you never told me before?"

Dinah shrugged. "It never came up. I don't believe in organized religion."

"Pressbetearian," Johnnine repeated to her mother, who nodded. The girls clattered at full speed down the hall.

Dinah threw the soiled diaper into a pile in the corner, muttering into her coffee cup, "If anything..."

Alix and Johnnine tore around the corner of Carmine, past the carapace of Our Lady of Pompeii. Racing down Bleecker Street, they turned right onto crooked little Cornelia, its undernourished-looking old brick buildings sagging against each other like exhausted rush-hour commuters.

The sound of a piano and several people singing got louder as they bolted up the uneven, grime-encrusted stairs. Alix flung open the door to her father's apartment, which looked as though it had been recently bombed. Walls were stripped down to bare studs, the floor revealed successive layers of old linoleum, a naked light bulb swung from the ceiling in the breeze from the broken windows. There was almost no furniture except for the beat-up upright piano in the middle of the empty living room. Jake was pounding out a song with Delia and Steve, all of them in multicolored paint-spattered work clothes. The kids' loud entrance didn't keep them from finishing their silky-smooth, jazz rendition of a Gershwin standard. "*...summertime, and-the-livin'-is-easy. Fish-are-jumpin', and-the- cotton-is-high. Man, your-big-daddy's-rich, And-your-ma, she's-good-lookin'. So-hush, little-baby, don'-you-cry...*"

Johnnine clapped politely but Alix had not lost her worried look. "Daddy, what religion are we?"

"*Religion?*" Jake turned his head towards the panting girls. His hands remained on the piano keys. He rolled his large, green-gray, pop eyes. "Oh, man—who wants to know?"

"Some big fat slob kid at school."

"Well, you tell the big fat slob kid you're half-Jewish and half-Protestant. And if he doesn't dig it, he better come see me. Okay, half-note? Hey." Jake reached into his a pocket of his overalls, which looked as though they'd been designed by Jackson Pollock. "Here's a dime, go have a ball. We got paid this morning."

"But don't spend it all in one place," Steve joshed, polishing his horn-rimmed glasses.

Alix looked disappointedly at Johnnine. "Thanks, dad. See ya later."

"...alligator!" Jake called cheerily after them. He turned back to Steve and Delia, but Delia short-circuited him. It was as if the children had never put in an appearance. The group went right back to its former business without a ripple. "I know," Delia said, passing a bottle of beer to Steve. "'One more time, I think we almost got it'..."

Alix and Johnnine slowly made their way past the little pie-slice park near Sheridan Square. A fancy wrought-iron fence protected its trees and minute patches of grass from the riffraff. Exclusive little shops and old, glass-canopied apartment houses facing the tiny, For Residents Only park had the air of quiet, unassuming sophistication.

Johnnine and Alix went into the candy and cigar store on the corner of Seventh Avenue and Christopher Street and came out with their cheeks bulging with jawbreakers. They walked along Seventh Avenue with their eyes glued to the sidewalk, carefully avoiding stepping on the cracks.

Alix slurped in the candy juice, licking the corners of her mouth with a purpley-blue tongue. "Mousey's gonna *kill* us."

Johnnine was also dispirited. "*Pressbetearian*. GOD." Her full lips were turning orange as the jawbreaker clacked against her teeth.

Alix spit her jawbreaker into her hand, a small, gangrenous golf ball. "*Half-Jewish, half-Protestant!*" she despaired. "I don't get it. What's the big deal about being Catholic, anyway? All they do is wear crosses and put ashes on their head—"

Johnnine rolled her jawbreaker to the other side of her mouth, where it popped out her cheek like a sudden blistering toothache. "I know whah!" Her lips could not quite come together. "Les's mape up our ohn beligion, someffing Mousey never *her* of—"

Alix stopped in her tracks. "Yeah! But what??" Alix palmed her jawbreaker back into her blue mouth.

The girls stood on the corner of Seventh Avenue and Perry Street, below a huge red, white, and blue oval Esso sign painted on the unwindowed, blind side of a four-story brick building. Johnnine spoke rapidly around her jawbreaker. "Then we'll boff be the fame ffing and Moufey won' be able to bea' uff upp if ffere's two of uff an' we're the ffame..."

"*Yeth!*" Alix enthused, pale blue spittle flying. She wiped her mouth with the back of her hand. "Buh whattle we *caw* it?"

They were making each other laugh. Johnnine looked up at the Esso sign with her eyes shining. "How abow...if we puh Mom and Effo togeffah...nah Momeffo, buh how abow—how abow *Mome?*"

Alix sharply sucked in her candy-colored saliva. "Buh whah abow a *croff*—?"

Johnnine's face lit up and she grabbed Alix's hand. "I goh a idea—c'mon!"

The girls ran back down Seventh Avenue holding hands, their dresses flying out in back of them, giggling as they sliced through clots of indifferent pedestrians.

The next day at school, Alix and Johnnine were sitting in their seats, one row apart. Both girls sported large, conspicuous brass paper clips hung from string around their necks, spread slightly open so that the ends formed a small X, and leaving green smudges on their skin.

While Alma-Maria Therese Maldonado haltingly read out loud the dull doings of Dick and Jane, a fire engine came screaming down King Street. Johnnine and Alix beamed at each other, delighted with their luck.

First Mrs. Antonelli crossed herself reverently as the fire truck clanged and wailed past the school. The Italian-Catholic kids, virtually the whole class, piously followed suit. Smiling broadly, Alix and Johnnine tapped first their right and then their left elbows, made a sweeping motion over their heads and ended with their hands pressed together in an attitude of prayer: their obeisant movements followed the shape of their Mome crosses. Mrs. Antonelli looked puzzled but didn't say anything as the recess bell serrated the air.

Mousey and his pint-sized henchmen were waiting by the head of the stairs. Before he could speak, Alix and Johnnine lifted their twisted brass paper clips to their lips. "You better leave us alone, Mousey," Johnnine warned. "Our religion is Mome, we're Momessians. And Alix's father's gang'll beat the crap out of you if you bother us again."

Like two young convent novitiates, the girls glided haughtily down the stairs, prissy and inviolate. Alix turned around to stick her tongue out at the boys, who looked to their leader for a response. "What da hell she say? Mo-messy-whaa?"

The scene faded out on Mousey's pasty-cheeked face.

In the All Souls' Waiting Room, Johnnine could not suppress a smile. She'd had the unexpected satisfaction, just a year ago, of catching sight of a grown-up Mousey. Obese and going prematurely bald, he was parking cars in a mid-town garage as Johnnine walked past. He'd gotten his just reward for being a bigoted bully. Yeah, but what about me? Johnnine suddenly thought. Is being dead *my* just reward for being an over-sensitive mess? Is that all I get, all I deserve? One lousy eighteen years and then lights out?

The film switched to a luxuriantly green Orgonon. The Maine countryside was in high summer growth as a late-model gray sedan pulled to a stop in front of a dirt driveway. "This is it," the driver said to his passenger. The other man, who wore a flat-topped straw boater and a seersucker suit, got out and unhooked the heavy chain. A large, red-lettered NO TRESPASSING sign hung from the middle links.

Cut to the same battleship-gray Ford in front of Orgonon's long, low student lab building, surrounded by trees and verdant grass. The driver got out. He was dark and jowly and wore a gray serge summer suit, white shirt and non-descript striped tie. Both he and his passenger stood for a moment looking at the unoccupied laboratory.

"Place looks deserted."

"Wouldn't hurt to check..."

They opened the unlocked door and peered inside. "Jeez, what a stink!" the driver said, whipping a handkerchief over his nose. "I wonder if this is where they hold the orgies?"

"I don't know, but there's one of his boxes."

They entered and crossed to an orgone accumulator in the corner, standing as tall as they were, square and dun-colored. On the floor next to it rested a Geiger-Müller counter.

"Look at this, for Pete's sake. Now what the hell would he use one of these for?"

"Probably to see how hot people get after they come out of the box. I hear people actually take their clothes off!" He shook his head as he scanned the half-empty lab. "All my years with the Bureau, it's still hard to believe what people fall for."

"Yeah, I know. Let's get out of here, this smell's making me queasy—"

The film cut to the front hall of the Observatory. Dr. Katzman, who looked unhealthy, his face gray and drawn, was standing in front of the men.

The dark one flashed a badge. "Timothy Wurton, Dr. Katzman, FBI—and this is Dr. Clement from the Food and Drug Administration. We'd like to see Dr. Reich, if you'd tell him we're here."

"Dr. Reich does not see uninvited callers. He is very busy at present." Katzman could barely contain his hostility.

"Yeah, well," Wurton drawled laconically, "he'll see us. We're here on official U.S. government business, Dr. Katzman..."

Reich erupted from an upstairs room and stormed down the stairs. His barrel-chested body, his eyes, even his thick white hair seemed ablaze with outrage. "Officials who do not honor No Trespassing signs, I see," he said angrily. "My work is not to be interrupted at your whim, gentlemen!"

Wurton pushed his hat back on his forehead. "Only need a few minutes of your time, Dr. Reich, we just drove up from D. C.—"

Dr. Clement adjusted his bow-tie as Reich glowered at them and led them into his ground-floor office. Nathan Katzman watched him close the door with a worried look.

Inside the study, Reich stood facing the two men with his hands jammed into the pockets of his lab coat, his black eyes like flashing jet. "Yah, so, you have a warrant for this invasion of my privacy?"

Wurton put a thin-lipped smile on his professionally unexpressive face. "Nothing like that, Dr. Reich. I just had a few questions and the good doctor here wanted to come up and meet you personally, that's all."

Reich's temper was near the boiling point. "Proceed, then, but quickly. I have many more important things that need my attention—"

Wurton flipped open a small notebook. "Our files show that you were once affiliated with the Communists, Dr. Reich. Now we know you renounced your ties with the Russkies before the war, but we have to ask you if you know of anyone in this country who is now or who has ever been a member of the Communist Party—"

"Whatever I have been or am now is none of your business!" Reich exploded, his pent-up fury unleashed. "You are both dupes of the Red Fascists, agents of the Plague!" His face had turned sclerotic with rage. "I do not inform on anyone—especially for hoodlums in government!"

Wurton and Clement looked at each other with raised eyebrows. "As a naturalized citizen of our free democracy, don't you think it's your duty to help clear out the Communists trying to destroy us from the inside?"

"No, it is not! It is *your* duty to run a government without inventing things to control the masses by means of terror! Now you will either arrest me or leave my property at once!"

Wurton held up a hand. "Nobody's here to make any arrests, Dr. Reich—"

"Then be so good as to go, NOW!!" he bellowed.

Dr. Clement and Agent Wurton left the Observatory office with compressed mouths. In the car going back down the driveway, Wurton said to Clement, "Just like the Chief said, completely looney tunes."

"...confirms what I suspected. Too bad our department had to waste taxpayer's money checking his experiments. I knew he was a quack even before we started."

"Guys like that shouldn't be running around loose," Wurton said, watching the road as he simultaneously shook a cigarette out of a crumpled pack.

"He won't be for long." Clement's arm rested on the back of the bench seat as he looked straight ahead.

Chapter Nineteen

In the All Souls' Waiting Room, as the scene blacked out on the faces of Agent Wurton and Dr. Clement, Johnnine felt a chill all through her ethereal body. Implacable forces were preparing to crush her mother's merry little band of hard-drinking, free-loving Reichians, and, by extension, Johnnine. Had the gathering storm of government persecution been the reason for Dinah's increasing rages? Xofia, The Recorder, and Seraph A. were unusually silent, though Xofia did splash more Dom Elysee into her glass. A fitting commentary, Johnnine thought.

The next scene opened on Johnnine skipping along next to her mother on their way to the Leroy Street public swimming pool. At six-and-a-half, Johnnine was startlingly pretty. Huge almond-shaped green eyes and a surprisingly full mouth took up most of her lively round face. She ran up the wide stone steps at the pool's entrance two at a time, her swimsuit and towel rolled up and tucked under her arm.

Johnnine only came up to the waist of the straw-haired matron, who stood in the doorway of the women's changing room like a surly dragon in front of a cave, clouds of steam wafting behind her. A cloth badge on her starched white uniform identified her as belonging to the New York City Parks Department. Bored and indifferent, equally hostile to everyone, she tore their tickets in half, handed them damp elastic bracelets with small brass keys attached, and nodded at a long double row of khaki green metal lockers. They found an empty changing booth, marble-sided and wooden-seated.

Johnnine sniffed the moist billowing air as she peeled off her shorts and polka-dot halter top. "Smells like the Chinese laundry, huh, Mom?"

Dinah pulled her sleeveless tent dress over her head, pressing her lips together so she wouldn't smear her lipstick. Her full-figure, Lane Bryant bra molded her large breasts into the shape of twin torpedoes, ready to be launched. "It's disinfectant. They think it kills germs—"

"What are germs?" Johnnine wriggled into a green tank suit and pulled on a yellow rubber bathing cap edged with three-dimensional rubber daisies.

"Some people think germs are what make people sick. But what really makes people sick is being mad at someone and keeping the anger inside..." Dinah stepped into an outsized floral bathing suit, zipped up the back, and took Johnnine's hand as they stashed their clothes in a locker and began making their way to the exit.

The matron barked commands from her post at the door. "*Hi*-jeen, ladies, *hi*-jeen! Hot showers before you get in the pool! Keep your bathing caps on or you will be told to leave! Use the foot disinfectant trough on your way out—we don't wanna pass foot fungus around!"

Dinah and Johnnine took showers with their bathing caps and swimsuits on. "She must be a angry woman, huh, Mom?"

They left the changing room and padded past the large empty indoor pool, used only in winter, towards the raucous melee of the outdoors. They stood in the colossal open entryway to the Olympic-sized pool, squinting against the blinding, mirror-like flashes of sunlight reflecting off the water. The pool was chaotic, clogged with people. Loud yells and laughs from wet, rushing young bodies, nerve-jangling blasts from lifeguard's whistles, boys like flying fish diving into the water over the heads of imperturbable older swimmers. High chain link fences and concrete slab walls surrounded the pool, which held hundreds of people and children. There was little room to walk between the tightly-packed sunbathers on the dirty pebbled concrete. Johnnine noticed a select group of young grown-ups in revealing swimsuits sitting against one of the walls. They smoked forbidden smuggled cigarettes, chatted, joked, and flirted.

Johnnine's look of somewhat frightened interest in her surroundings changed to a small frown as Pahlser materialized out of the crowd.

His flesh was firmly-muscled but deadly pale above maroon wool swim trunks. She did not offer her hand but he took it proprietarily. "It's less crowded on the other side."

"This is a madhouse!" Dinah exclaimed, stepping distastefully over tanned and oiled sunbathers.

Johnnine disengaged her hand from Pahlser's as they rounded the far, shallow end of the pool. "I can walk by *myself*—"

"Do you want me to teach you how to swim?" he asked her.

Johnnine looked at the children flailing the water around her, then at her mother. Grimacing, trying to retain her dignity, Dinah was slowly easing her bulk into the water of the shallow end. Johnnine nodded at Pahlser, who had put on a flesh-colored racer's swim cap and black-rimmed goggles. Pahlser slid into the pool, standing in the water up to his waist, and held out his long white arms. Hesitantly, Johnnine lowered herself off the side near her mother.

Dinah pinched her nose and suddenly dunked herself under the water. A muffled noise and thick rush of air bubbles churned the sun-shot, aquamarine liquid all around her, the full skirt of her swimsuit billowing under the surface. "Put your head underwater and scream," Dinah directed. "It's good therapy." Without looking at Pahlser or Johnnine, Dinah pushed off down the side of the pool in a sidestroke interrupted by the many other swimmers in her way.

"Here," Pahlser said to Johnnine. "The first thing you've got to do is learn to kick like mad—"

Johnnine shouted after her mother. "I don't feel like screaming!"

Dinah couldn't hear her.

The scene faded out on Johnnine gingerly letting Pahlser hold her horizontally on the surface of the water. It faded back up on her happily dog-paddling around the shallow end, under her own steam. The sun was no longer high overhead, the pool was less crowded, the high walls were casting shadows on the water.

A skinny, shivering, brown-skinned little girl bounced up and down in the water next to Johnnine. "Can you open your eyes underwater?"

"Sure, watch." Johnnine pinched her nose, jumped up above the surface, and let herself sink like a stone, pulling her legs up to her chest. Bumping gently on the concrete bottom, she opened her eyes to a forest of rubbery white legs.

Dinah and Pahlser sat glumly on the tiled lip of the pool nearby. Their serious, quiet absorption contrasted vividly with the playful turbulence around them. Dinah's calves were giantised by the water as she listened to Pahlser and slowly kicked them back and forth.

"...it's done something to him, he hasn't been the same since Oranur." Pahlser looked sad.

"But, Daniel, neither have you—"

Pahlser's heavy sigh almost broke into a sob. "I feel so helpless." His swimming goggles hung around his neck, the flesh-colored cap made him look bald.

Dinah glanced at him quickly, then tentatively touched his hand. "You know I would do anything to help—"

Pahlser nodded, staring at the water which was churning with overactive children and tired parents.

Two feet away, Johnnine shot straight up out of the water like a sleek baby seal, laughing and spluttering. "I can hold my breath underwater!" she boasted to Pahlser and her mother as she paddled towards them. They greeted her accomplishment with morose faces, as if she hadn't spoken.

"Time to go home, Johnnine," Dinah said.

Johnnine's happy expression immediately changed to one of resentment. "I don't want to. We just got here!"

"Your lips are blue. It's time to leave," Dinah repeated.

"NO!" Johnnine said, pushing off from the edge. But Dinah caught her before she could swim away and slapped her, once, hard, across the face. "When I say it's time to leave, it's time to leave!"

Johnnine cried bitterly as Dinah pulled her from the pool. She was not the only child to be yanked screaming from the water. No one in the overcrowded pool gave them a second glance as they rounded the shallow end. Johnnine's cries gained intensity the closer they got to the exit. Just before they reached the doors, Johnnine wrenched herself free of her mother's hands, planted her feet, and screamed as loud as she could, her tightened face and body a fierce concentration of howling protest. Her piercing yells ricocheted off the huge iron doors.

Dinah clenched her jaw as her hands closed into fists. "*Stop it!*"

The All Souls' Waiting Room

Pahlser quickly stepped between them and grabbed the door handle. "See," he said to Dinah, making light of it. "She did feel like screaming after all."

Dinah shot Johnnine a withering look. Johnnine stuck her tongue out at her mother and then made a dash for the women's changing rooms.

"It's good for her to express herself," Pahlser added in front of the men's doorway.

"Not in public, it's not —" Dinah's expression was grim.

"Where else could she get such gratifying results? See you outside." He pulled the cap off his head before he disappeared through the door.

Dinah's tightened mouth softened a bit. Her bare feet slapped the wet blue and green tile as she made her way to the women's changing rooms. The screen went dim.

In the All Souls' Waiting Room, Johnnine reflected angrily that while she wasn't allowed to express herself in public, Dinah also did not encourage self-expression at home. The only thing that her mother approved of or thought was funny was when Johnnine mimicked the people they knew. She had the ability to copy the way Pahlser and other people walked so exactly that Dinah roared with laughter. The pool scene left her with another disturbing feeling. It was weird, disconcerting, to see Pahlser playing the part of intermediary, acting as a buffer between Johnnine and her mother. Hadn't he been the main problem between them? Was there anything but irony in her life?

The scene at the Leroy Street pool dissolved into one at Lake Belvedere, a large natural lake several miles from the house up country. I get it, Johnnine thought. Water theme time.

The lake was fringed by large Scotch pines, birches, elms, and maples. A small group of adults and several young children were relaxing on an open square of grass at the lake's edge. Johnnine was swimming towards a warped wooden raft some fifty feet away when she suddenly gave out a ringing yell. "Something's biting me!" she shrieked. She turned around and paddled frantically towards shore.

Dinah lolled largely in a lawn chair, a highball glass in one hand and a paperback in the other. Lily Neary was on a blanket with naked, eleven-month old Noelle. Sy Minnowitz inexpertly fly-cast from the shore, his hook getting snagged in the cattails as often as it landed in the water.

Dinah looked up for a second. "Don't get hysterical, there's nothing out there, Johnnine—"

Johnnine's screams echoed out over the lake. A flock of ducks lifted off the water. "Yes, there is! There's a monster under the water, and he's trying to get me, just like on the Buster Brown Show!" She stumbled up the muddy slope and threw herself down on the blanket near Lily Neary, crying, examining her legs for tooth marks.

"What Buster Brown Show?" Neary asked in her thrillingly low, beautifully-modulated actress' voice. She ran her slender, nervous hands back and forth over Noelle's pearly bare skin, which made the baby gurgle and kick her legs with pleasure. Neary had woven wildflowers into crowns and necklaces for the other children, who were also diaperless, so that they all looked like little nature sprites as they crawled and toddled around on the grass.

Johnnine was swallowing down her sobs. "The one where a little boy is a pearl diver, and his mother gets drowned by a *octopus* and he has to go down under the water and kill it!" Johnnine covered her eyes.

Neary rubbed Johnnine's back. "Well, but, you know what? You're much luckier than he was. There aren't any octopuses here. In fact, what you felt was probably a water baby."

"A water baby?" Johnnine stopped crying and twisted her head around to look at Neary. She also wore a garland of daisies and tiger lilies but it looked incongruous above her long, seamed face framed with her long, untamed, gray-streaked hair. "You mean like in my water baby story?"

"Yah. You know how they like to play tricks. But they're not trying to hurt you."

"God, I'd like to see one some time!" Johnnine's voice was filled with longing.

"Don't say 'God', Johnnine," Dinah spouted mechanically from her chair, turning a page of her Agatha Christie.

"Keep your eyes open and maybe you just might." Neary's large, softly expressive brown eyes allowed for the possibility of magic.

"Pink-stink!" Dinah said, loud enough so Sy could hear her. "An adventurous youngster—"

"*Wild child*," Sy threw back, reeling in another soggy cattail. "Here's one for you: the best place to be on a commuter train..."

"But that's not a two-word definition," Dinah complained.

"*Bar car*!" Neary clapped. "Good one, darling."

"Speaking of b-a-r." Dinah spelled the word and hauled herself out of the collapsible canvas chair. "Who feels like potato chips and something cold to drink?"

"Me, me, me!" Johnnine jumped to her feet. "Rozenheimer's! Yay!"

"Well, that makes one country heard from—" Dinah smiled tartly.

"Second the motion," Sy shouted, picking up his bait can. "I'm not catching anything but weeds anyway."

"*Someone's-in-the-kitchen-with-DINAH, someone's-in-the-kitchen-I-know-ow-ow-ow, someone's-in-the-kitchen-with-DINAH, strummin'-on-the-old-banjo. And-he-said, Fee-fie, fiddley-I-oh, fee-fie, fiddley-I-oh-oh-oh-oh, fee-fie, fiddley-I-oh, strummin' on the old banjo, banjo...*"

The All Souls' Waiting Room

The scene segued into a shot of a packed two-door sedan, clipping along a country road past apple orchards, towering green rows of corn, and dairy farms. Dinah was driving and leading the group in song, her booming voice dominating all the others.

Outside the small farming town of Cherry Valley, the light blue Plymouth pulled up in front of a cracked stucco country tavern next to a dusty weeping willow. The front screen door of Rozenheimer's Bar and Grill had a large tear in it, the neon beer signs in the window had burned-out long ago, the Miss Rheingolds on the faded posters were probably grandmothers.

"Howdy, folks, howdy! Come on in and roll your socks down, as my pa used to say—" Mr. Rozenheimer was memorable-looking, with a high, hard, enormous beer belly, like several watermelons stuffed in his abdomen. He had crazily-crossed, tiny black eyes, and a large wart on the end of his nose. "Sit yourselves down. Got a bunch of babies there, I see. You folks run a baby farm or something?" He tossed round cardboard coasters down the bar.

Johnnine looked at the rows of Wise potato chips on either side of the fly-specked mirror behind the bar. Large jars of pickled eggs, beef jerky, and bowls of beer nuts and pretzels also drew her greedy attention.

"Three vodka tonics, please, Mr. Rozenheimer," Dinah said, nodding at Sy and Neary.

Rozenheimer purposely misunderstood. "Oh-ho, tying one on today, I see—" He poured the drinks as he winked at Johnnine. "And what'll you have, young lady?"

"Squirt, please."

"Squirt? You want a *Squirt*?" Rozenheimer put the vodka-tonics in front of the adults. "Why, I thought *you* were the only little squirt around here—"

Johnnine blushed and firmly repeated her order. "I want a Squirt. And some potato chips. Please!"

Dinah took a cigarette out of her purse.

With a practiced flair, Rozenheimer lit a match by striking it across his teeth. "Good-looking women shouldn't ever have to light their own smokes—"

"Flattery, Mr. Rozenheimer," Dinah said, leaning toward the flame, "will get you everywhere."

"Everywhere?" He made his crossed eyes carom around like billiard balls after a bad break. "Hooeee, best offer I've had all day..."

Johnnine pursed her lips in disgust and slipped off the high, cracked leather bar stool. "Can I play the jukebox, Mom?"

"Here, dearie." Rozenheimer flipped her a red dime. "Just don't play 'Melancholy Baby'..." He winked again, this time at Neary.

"You're a big winker, Mr. Rozenheimer," Neary said. "And I detect a bit of the showman in you as well—"

"Ah, well, this is my little thee-ate-er and I like to see people smile. One thing I can't stand is a maudlin drunk, or a mean one, and the worst is when they're mean *and* maudlin—"

"Like Dad," Dinah said, finishing her drink. "Charming as hell when he was sober, talk the birds out of the trees, but when he'd had a few—another, please, Mr. Rozenheimer."

"Thirsty, eh?" With the vodka in one hand and the tonic in the other, Rozenheimer lifted his arms high up so the two streams blended together in a perfect arc. The screen door slammed. "Dammit, Owen," Rozenheimer said at a grimy-faced boy, "you almost threw my aim off."

Owen came inside carrying a cardboard box. "Got them pups you wanted to see. Fresh weaned."

"Puppies?!" Johnnine skipped towards the boy. "Ooh, let me see?"

Johnnine picked up a squirming ball of black and white fur, nuzzling it close. "They smell so *good*." The puppy began earnestly licking her cheek and excitedly biting her nose. Johnnine giggled and held her face to one side. "Oh, Mom, can I have this one? See how much she likes me already—"

Dinah looked down at the puppies gravely. "Are they for sale, Mr. Rozenheimer?"

"Ask Owen. I'm taking one for a watch dog."

"They're a cross between a Collie bitch and a cocker spaniel." Owen spoke proudly.

"They're awfully cute, Goody." Neary peered into the box. "Just what you need, too," she added drily.

"Listen, Mom!" Johnnine jumped up and down, sensing a sale. "They're even playing the right song!"

"*...the-one-with-the-waggly-tail. I-must-have-that-doggy-in-the-window, I-do-hope-that-doggy's-for-sale*," Patti Page's syrupy voice crooned from the purple, red, and green Wurlitzer in the corner.

"Only if it's a female, I won't have a male lifting his leg around the house. Here, let me see..." She took the handful of wriggling puppy from Johnnine and turned it over. "Okay, you win." Then, to Owen, "Will you take two dollars?"

Owen's dirty face creased into a broken-toothed smile. "You kin have 'em all for five—"

Johnnine happily cradled the puppy in her arms.

"She's your responsibility, Johnnine," Dinah admonished. "You'll have to feed her and walk her by yourself. I've got enough to do." She fished two bills out of her purse.

"I'll take good care of her. Won't I, puppy puppy?" She kissed the top of the puppy's head, who responded by frantically, desperately, licking the inside of Johnnine's ear.

"We better get the kids back to the house," Sy put in, changing the baby in his arms to his other side. "Stevie here's trying to get milk out of my finger."

"But we have to get some dog food," Johnnine piped up. "And she needs a leash and a collar, too!"

"Oy vey gefilte-fish." Dinah rolled her eyes at Mr. Rozenheimer, pushing herself off the bar stool. She broke into her deep melodic voice on her way to the door. *"That's-where-my-money-goes, to-buy-my-baby-clothes—"*

The group slammed the screen door three times on their way out. The screen went blank.

In the All Souls' Waiting Room, the sight of Spot as a puppy made Johnnine's eyes fill with tears. "I loved her so much. I don't think I've ever been as happy as when we first got her. She was the best thing in my life. At least at first—"

"What do you mean?" Xofia asked.

Johnnine looked away. "Mom gave her away. She said Spotty got neurotic after her first litter...we kept one of her puppies, but it wasn't the same. Then we had to give *her* away, too. We ended up having about ten different dogs. After Spotty there was Taffy, then Copper, then Cleo-patter—one for almost every year. It got so I didn't care too much when they had to go..."

Xofia and The Recorder exchanged a glance.

Johnnine cried out with feeling. "How come seeing Spotty makes me almost sadder than watching my parents?"

"She gave you unconditional love, darling," Xofia intoned. "What everyone wants and no one gives..."

Something in Johnnine pulled back. She hardened up again. "You're not going to give me that dumb line about d-o-g spelling God backwards, are you?"

"I don't have to. You've already got it."

Damn, Johnnine thought. How was it that one way or another, Xofia always managed to have the last word?

Chapter Twenty

"Spotty, don't do that!" Johnnine laughed, pulling a dirty sock out of the pot-bellied puppy's mouth. Spot waddled around the lawn on short fat legs, sniffing and mouthing baby toys, dandelions, random twigs and spikes of grass. Johnnine followed her movements with happy, proprietary eyes. She was kept busy by having to be buffer between the children, who wanted to pull her tail, and Spotty, who wanted to chew on their toes.

Johnnine was just putting Spot in an empty playpen when an unfamiliar car, a long and shiny black LaSalle hearse, pulled into the parking area beyond the white picket fence. Johnnine was amazed to see Alix jump out while Pahlser and the Balikovskys, Monte and Karna, got out on the other side. The Balikovskys were patients of Pahlser's and parents of ten-month old Julie.

"What're you doing here?" Johnnine asked Alix as she ran towards her.

Alix flapped her arms with excitement. "Surprise, surprise! I asked my Mom to ask your Mom if I could come for a visit and Pahlser picked me up at my house in his new station wagon!"

The girls turned to look at the imposing LaSalle hearse, a gigantic, midnight-dark beetle come to rest next to the house. The adults swarmed around it, opening doors, unloading. Wearing his gray gabardine flight suit, Pahlser pulled luggage and groceries out of the gray-padded interior. Dinah and Sy Minnowitz came out of the house. Sy was carrying his daughter Noelle, Dinah held Julie Balikovsky. They both stood and stared, speechless.

Monte put down his overnight bag and reached for his brown-haired, diapered daughter. "Quite a vehicle, huh?" he said to Dinah. "We got a lot of sympathetic looks on the Thruway." Monte's loud laugh was an aural assault, combining the effects of a honk and a snort. He was round-shouldered with long arms and mischievous reddish-brown eyes. Thick plackets of arm and chest hair gave him an energetic, simian appeal.

Pahlser brought up the luggage-bearing rear.

"Daniel—a hearse?" Dinah asked incredulously.

"Yah!" Pahlser looked fondly over his shoulder at the elongated black thing on the grass. "I got a great buy on it. Top of the line Cadillac engine, they build those things to last—it's only got forty thousand miles on it, should go another hundred. We'll paint it, I brought the paint up with us. Dark green—"

Dinah shook her head. "Well, come on in and have a drink. I guess I'll get used to the idea eventually. What about my Plymouth, do we have to sell it? I love that car," she said to Pahlser. "More to the point, can I give it up for a hearse?" Dinah hesitated on the doorstep of the house, looking back at the hearse apprehensively.

"I'll take the Plymouth when I leave tonight and leave you the LaSalle. I have to be in Rangeley tomorrow morning, I'm helping Reich with the cloud-buster experiments. This way you'll have something big enough to haul everybody around—"

"All the warm bodies, you mean?" Sy quipped as they filed into the house.

"Sy!" Dinah remonstrated. "No ghoulish puns. Please!"

"Right." Sy agreed, jostling Noelle in his arms, planting a wet kiss on his daughter's rosy cheek. "No more more-bid puns, get it?"

Standing next to the playpen that held Spotty, Johnnine and Alix watched the adults disappear inside. "See my new puppy?" Johnnine asked. In a very pedantic voice she explained, "I have to be the only one to hold her, 'kay?, 'cause she's only used to me. But she'll lick your face if you want her to—" Johnnine leaned over, picked Spot up and handed her to Alix.

"Oh, she's so *cute*! Are you lucky! Mom won't even let me have a kitten."

Johnnine smiled and took Spotty back, cuddling her. Spot by now had left her mistress' bare arms, hands, and cheeks alive with small pink welts from needle-sharp puppy teeth.

A rust-colored pick-up truck hove into view past the front yard's bushy young pines and venerable old maple, crunching onto the gravel and parking parallel to the hearse. An old man in denim overalls and faded visor cap got out of the truck and slammed the door. "Well, I'll be a goddam sumbitch," he said, staring at the LaSalle through round wire-rimmed glasses. "Goddam crazy New Yorkers!"

Laughing to himself, shaking his head, the old man stomped sturdily for the house. He was more than a bit bow-legged. "Hell of a nice day, ain't it, young 'uns?" He smiled and touched his hand to his cap.

Johnnine brightened. "Sure as hell is, Mr. Briggs!"

Briggs laughed, a smoky, vehement bray, and continued past them into the house.

"Who's he?" Alix asked. She was holding up first one of her legs, then the other, trying to keep steady on one at a time, like a stork.

"Sam Briggs, our caretaker." Johnnine's eyes glowed as she looked after him. "He curses *all* the time and he likes kids a lot. Come on, I want to show him my puppy."

"Okay," Alix agreed, letting down a leg. "But afterward let's get an ice cream."

"Ice cream?! There's no stores up here, this is the country!"

"We passed one in town, I saw it—"

"South Valley's a *mile* down the road!"

"Oh." Alix looked very disappointed. Jadedly, sulkily, she scanned the lush green, hilly countryside, bursting with summer birdsong, plant and insect life. "Well, what else is there to *do* around here?" she whined.

Johnnine nodded at the sagging old barn across the road, abandoned and unused. "Wanna see the bird's nest in the barn over there?"

The prospect failed to excite Alix. She pouted. "I'd rather get a Fudgsicle..."

The film cut to the interior of the farmhouse. Sam Briggs sat at the head of the kitchen table, a drink in front of him, his cap pushed back off his forehead. A deep crease across his brow marked a facial Mason-Dixon line. Below, his skin was leathery tan, above, fish-belly white. Pahlser, Dinah, Sy, and Monte were a captive audience.

Briggs' pale, round blue eyes twinkled and sparked as he held court. His small round glasses fogged up when he laughed, which was often. When he took them off to wipe them on his thin flannel check shirt, his weathered, craggy face looked defenseless, just-born. "...never heard such a crazy goddam thing in my life! A hearse?—for a goddam *passenger* car? I allas knew you city people was out of your minds, but this takes the goddam cake!" He laughed and coughed a little and took another swig of his whiskey.

Pahlser reverentially refilled Briggs' shot glass. "We were hoping you'd give us a hand re-painting it..."

"Me? Nawh, wouldn't go near the damn thing! But I'll tell you what you need to do first. You need to get about a mile and a half of sandpaper. You're talkin' about some sumbitch job there, gettin' that finish off—worse'n a time I had to haul them goddam electric line poles down over by Oneonta and put 'em up in a thunderstorm!"

Briggs laid his enormous hands on the table. "That's when I got my goddam hands all lobstered up—" His fists were the size of canned hams, the skin a scaly red crazy-quilt of lines like deep razor cuts. "Weren't anywhere near as big as this before the goddam lightning—"

Johnnine and Alix had crept into the kitchen, standing silently behind Briggs' chair. Wide-eyed, Johnnine peered around the edge. "You mean you were hit by *lightning*?"

"Pshawh. Couple a times! Ain't nothin' to it—" He winked at the grown-ups around the table, who were in thrall to this latter-day Paul Bunyan. "Whatcha got there, miss?"

Johnnine showed Briggs her puppy. "I just got her! I named her Spot because she's black and white and fluffy like Dick and Jane's dog."

Briggs gave the dog a quick going-over, proficiently inspecting Spot's teeth, eyes, ears, even her anus. "Well, she won't be very big, but she's healthy, got good conformation." The puppy fit into the palm of one of his huge, boiled-looking hands. "Real soft, too, ain't she?" He smiled warmly at Johnnine as he handed Spot back.

"Yah, she is!" Johnnine said happily, holding Spotty to her chest. She appeared to consider something for a moment. "Do you have any grandchildren, Mr. Briggs?"

The All Souls' Waiting Room

Briggs expertly rolled a cigarette between two fingers. Everyone's eyes were glued to his deft, almost unconscious manual operation. "Me? Nawh! Mostly on account I ain't never had any kids!" He laughed, lightly licked the paper, and lit his cigarette.

"Then would you adopt me?" Johnnine's expression was one of earnest beseechment. She moved closer to him, forgetting the other adults in the room. "Could you be my grandfather?"

Some of the grownups around the table laughed. Briggs just smiled at her. "Can't do that, miss, it's too late fer me, I'm all done in—"

"Hardly," Pahlser demurred. "We know the way you work around here."

"Go outside and play now," Dinah said. "We've got to talk to Briggs about the new well—"

"Can we go to town and get a Fudgsicle?" Alix asked.

"It's a *mile*, I already told you!" Johnnine snapped.

"You mean to tell me you can't walk one little old mile?" Briggs feigned incredulity. "What the hell you got them there legs for then?"

Johnnine reddened under his rough teasing.

"That's a good idea," Dinah seconded. "It'll give you two something to do. Here's a quarter. And take Spotless Cleaners there with you."

"Her name is *Spot*." Johnnine scowled as she took the coin from her mother.

"I'm just *kidding* you," Dinah demurred. "Don't take everything so *seriously*."

In the farmhouse kitchen, Johnnine jangled Spotty's leash, while Pahlser redirected the conversation. "I've been meaning to ask you, Briggs. Your talent with the dowsing rod shows you have strong natural instincts. You're what Reich would call an unarmored man. You watch the skies a lot, don't you? For weather indications?"

Briggs laughed. "Well you sure as hell can't trust them weather fellas on the radio. They wouldn't know an east wind from a loud fart. Oh, excuse me, missus—" He ducked his head in Dinah's direction.

"Have you ever seen a UFO?" Pahlser persisted.

"A what?"

"An unidentified flying object." Pahlser was leaning forward in his chair.

"You mean a flying saucer? Hawh!" Briggs guffawed. "Now I know you folks is loco."

"Actually, there's quite a bit of convincing evidence," Sy Minnowitz broke in enthusiastically. "A book by a man named Donald Keyhoe, for instance."

"He's an ex-Army major," Monte added, his eyes lighting up. "Collected a lot of very substantial testimony, even photographs..."

"Stop it, Johnnine, you're being annoying." Dinah clamped her hand over Spotty's leash to stop it from making noise. "Go outside."

"I don't want to..." Johnnine said firmly.

The others ignored them.

"Reich's seen UFO's up at Orgonon." Pahlser said and then frowned at his glass. "He says they're coming into our atmosphere in greater and greater numbers because of our development of nuclear energy." He raised his head to look at Briggs. "In any case, I thought you should keep your eyes peeled, you may see more up here in the country. There's a lot less DOR—deadly orgone energy..."

"Less whatsit, doc?" Briggs asked.

"Go *on*," Dinah hissed at the girls. Johnnine made a face but left the room. She closed the kitchen door and stepped down into the adjoining lean-to shed, clipping the leash to Spot's red collar.

"Do you have any more money?" Alix asked in a conspiratorial whisper.

"No." Johnnine looked disgruntled after her interaction with her mother. "Why?"

"After we buy our Fudgsicle, I'll show you how to get some candy, for free!"

"Yah?" Johnnine's interest was peaked. "The general store has a lot. They even have wax lips and sugar dots on paper!"

"And red licorice?" Alix's eyes dilated with desire.

"Yah," Johnnine joined in with her own candy lust. "and root beer lollipops and licorice moustaches..."

"Great! Come on!"

The All Souls' Waiting Room

Chapter Twenty-one

In the All Souls' Waiting Room, Johnnine nearly fell off The Couch when all five cherubs burst into the room like air-borne cavalry, accompanying themselves with blasts of notes like blaring trumpets. "Jesus H. Christ!" Johnnine exhorted, her hand on her heart.

"Darlings," Xofia growled at the noisome cherubim. "A *tad* too bugle-boyish—"

The cherubs were unrepentant. Fluttering their shell-pink wings, they deftly lowered a large pewter tray onto a claw-legged oak table near Schlomo's desk. Twittering at Seraph A. and Xofia, they were clearly imparting information.

Curious, Johnnine followed Xofia to the table where she peeked under the cover of a fancy crystal cake dish. "What is it?"

"Sachertorte, darling." Xofia nodded at the chocolate-covered confection as she poured herself a cup of coffee from an elegant coffee service and added generous dollops of heavy whipped cream. "And this is *kaffee mit schlag*, from Demel's, where our five little angels say things are progressing nicely..."

"What things?" Johnnine asked with only part of her attention, most of it concentrated on cutting herself a large slice of the delicately-layered torte.

"Willie's final analysis." Xofia sipped her coffee with her pinkie sticking up in the air. "Mmm, divine. How's the cake, darling?"

"Nah bah." Johnnine spoke with her mouth full, testing the limits of eating etiquette in Mondo Bizarro. "Buh nah as gooh as a Devil Dog."

Xofia, as usual, did not reprimand her. Johnnine was amazed. Was there no end to the woman's tolerance?

"Try the java," Xofia urged.

Johnnine swallowed her bulging mouthful of Sachertorte. The viscous black coffee was too bitter for her, even with its toupee of abused cream. She wrinkled her nose. "Tastes like India ink topped off with white Scuff-Kote."

"A good sign, Xofia," The Recorder intoned, getting up from his chair. "If it tasted good, it means she would be closer to a permanent departure."

All five radiantly adorable cherubs were clustered around the table, eating Sachertorte and slurping *kaffee* heaped with mounds of *schlag*. Seraph A. flew down from his molded cornice into their midst, chittering loudly. Finally, sheepishly, one of the cherubs produced a bottle of beer from between his wings. The seraph took the bottle—its label read Eternal Return—and with a little chirrup of reprimand zoomed back to his perch.

The Recorder was helping himself to *kaffee* without *schlag*. "I think we should get back to business." His deep voice sounded like the distant tolling of bass church bells.

"You always say that," Johnnine said, no longer quite so intimidated by him. She had not yet been able to make out any facial features behind his cowl, but then she was not sure she wanted to. If the price for ignorance was bliss, the price for knowledge could easily be the heebie-jeebies.

The Recorder shrugged, taking his *kaffee* back to his seat at Schlomo's desk. "Part of my job description."

Seraph A. warbled a set of whistled instructions. Ti and Do flew out the door of Freud's facsimilar office, their fluffy pink wings beating limply and unenthusiastically. In contrast, Fa, So, and La settled like happy baby birds on wall sconce, mantelpiece, and gaslight fixture respectively, primping and preening and looking pleased.

"What's going on?" Johnnine asked Xofia. "Banishment?"

Xofia seated herself in the tufted armchair next to The Couch, elegantly draping her cherry-blossom kimono over her long legs. Pouring the coffee, she had looked like Greer Garson in "Mrs. Miniver." Before that, Rosalind Russell in "Front Page." At the moment she was looking like herself again, which was to say a visual palimpsest of all the women Johnnine had ever admired, from Jane Austen to Zora Thurston, with Pearl Bailey and Tallulah Bankhead thrown in for added zest.

"No, darling, changing of the guard. Ti and Do have to go back to Demel's to stay caught up with Willie and Schlomo. They're downhearted because our famous analysts are not, apparently, as entertaining as our little group. Fa, So, and La stay here with us..."

"Yah, but why?"

"So everyone will know as much as everyone else, darling—"

Johnnine reflected that in Mondo Bizarro this was either saying a lot or very, very little. The lights went off and the film struck up again. Here we go loopdeloo, here we go loopdelah, she thought. Her choice of phrase was not necessarily a commentary on the static exterior shot of Orgonon that filled the screen.

In the early evening of a darkly-clouded summer's day, a thinner, older-looking Wilhelm Reich came out of the Observatory wearing his ubiquitous short white lab coat over dungarees and work shirt. His face was weary but hopeful as he looked up and scanned the sky, which seemed to press heavily down on the earth. He walked to a platform near the cement-collared well behind the Observatory. All the surrounding trees were in full leaf but they were bestilled in the windless twilight. There was not a breath of air. On the platform was something that at first glance looked like an artillery gun. Johnnine knew it was Reich's cloud-buster.

Reich climbed into a tractor seat on the platform, threw a long-handled lever, and swiveled the turret, mounted on which was a double row of hollow steel pipes. The theory behind the cloud-buster was that it could draw off negative atmospheric energy and dissipate it in water, in the same way that a lightning rod drew atmospheric electricity through heavy wires and dissipated the excess charge into the ground.

Reich aimed the bank of pipes at the center of the purply-brown, oppressive sky, the color of rotting eggplant. He turned the turret to the left. Flexible metal conduit cables, attached to the ends of the pipes, noisily rasped the lip of the well into which they were sunk.

Reich shouted at the sky. "*Komm heran*, all right now! *Die Erde hat Not deiner Tränen*! The earth has need of your tears!"

He pushed and pulled on different levers and gears in the cockpit and rotated the battery of pipes. It described a counter-clockwise circle of about ten feet in diameter. He worked the cloud-buster in a continuous circular motion for several minutes, still aiming the device at the middle of the ominous sky. A towering, dark cumulus cloud mass was moving across Reich's field of vision. "*Ja, gut! Noch mehr Wind*! Yes, good! More wind!"

There was a tentative, strobe-like flicker of lightning on the horizon, then a bone-rattling clap of thunder. The sky became full of swirling motion and visibly crackling energy as wind currents spun boiling clouds towards and away from each other, an improvised ballet of thermodynamics.

Reich cried out ecstatically as he felt the first drops of rain on his face. "Yah, cry! Weep for us!" His voice skimmed above the rising wind.

The black-shrouded sky was tearing apart. Above and behind it gleamed the luminous, dark blue satin of star-strewn space. The rain, at first a hesitant spatter, quickly gathered enough force to become a drench. Reich was soaked to the skin in the downpour. His uplifted, pock-marked face looked beatific as he shouted. "Yah, good! *More*! THE EARTH NEEDS YOUR TEARS!!!" He spread his arms wide, opening them to the freshening wind.

Reich beamed into the driving rain like a proud warrior, a conjuring wizard of the cosmos. The camera panned upward to a patch of clear, moonlit night sky, then faded to black.

Meanwhile, on the other side of the Viennese section of the All Souls' Waiting Room, Schlomo had led Willie up to this exact point in time, his early cloud-busting experiments. "And you believe you made it rain," Schlomo said without any inflection in his voice.

"Don't patronize me. Of course I did! One does not imagine being wet through like that!"

No, Schlomo thought, but one does not necessarily produce the rain, either. Willie's madness was oddly touching, his scientific pursuits were so clearly rooted in his troubled psyche's need for peace. "And this machine was for—?" Schlomo prompted.

"I told you," Reich said irritably, getting up on one elbow to scowl at his interlocutor. "And do me the courtesy of remembering that every advance in science has been at first vehemently denounced. Most especially including your own theories..."

Difficult as it was to do, Schlomo held his tongue.

A disgruntled Willie lay back down and re-settled himself on the uncomfortable ersatz couch. "The cloud-buster was designed to break up deadly orgone, what I called DOR clouds. I made rain to make the atmosphere life-supporting again. You and I are both aware of the therapeutic effects of deep crying. So—just as deeply-felt, freely-flowing tears soften a hardened, armored heart, so a good soaking rain softens the parched earth..." Willie's brow was creased in annoyance at his former mentor.

Schlomo adroitly changed topics, taking his cue from Willie himself. "And what is it you remember most vividly about your mother's death, Willie?"

Willie turned his head away, but not before Schlomo caught the glint of tears in his eyes. "...*grausig*—" Willie said, his voice full of unforgotten, unforgettable pain, "—it was horrible, her face, her beautiful young face, unimaginable agony—" Willie's sobs cracked through the ethereal air of Demel's coffee shop.

Schlomo was quiet, letting his patient cry. Willie's *mutter* had chosen a hideously painful way to die. Had she swallowed the caustic household cleaner as self-punishment for her infidelity? To punish Willie for telling his father? Or as final retaliation against her jealous, domineering husband? Whatever the reason for her slow and tortuous method of suicide, her son had grown up with an enormous psychological need to repent for the childhood betrayal of his mother. Willie had always needed to do things on a grand scale, Schlomo thought. Save humanity from its self-destructiveness, find a cancer cure, change the weather, discover the biophysical source of libido energy. But he had not completed the inner work on his own terrible psychic wounds. And so he invented a "cloud-busting" machine. If Willie could not himself grieve, Schlomo thought, then it was imperative that the heavens should weep for him.

Chapter Twenty-two

"*Buono notte!*"

"Good evening, Aldo," Dinah said merrily. "The usual, please—"

The film showed the dim interior of a bar in Greenwich Village. Johnnine remembered the Leroy Street Tavern for its odor, stale beer and cigarette smoke overlaid by heavy disinfectant. The floor was an immensity of tiny white octagonal tiles sprinkled with clots of dampened sawdust. The long, polished wooden bar looked as though it stretched into infinity and the little red table lamps were kept low so that the daytime seemed like night.

Dinah was usually the only woman in the place, Johnnine almost always the only child. The Italian bartenders were unfailingly cordial. Dinah's female presence perked the place up. She had a ribald sense of humor, she tipped well, and she never got sloppy drunk. Dinah carefully instructed Johnnine in two bits of bar etiquette: one, that a lady never spilled her drink. And two, if she had to pass out, she did so outside.

Aldo put a vodka-tonic in front of Dinah as she took a seat at the bar. Johnnine climbed up next to her mother and asked for a Shirley Temple.

A young man with curly black hair falling into his eyes spoke to Dinah. "I buy you two lovely ladies a drink?" His grey eyes were clouded and he was hunched around his glass as if protecting it.

Johnnine peered around her mother to look at him.

"I don't see why not." Dinah turned towards him, favoring him with her deep and full-toned voice. "As long as there are no strings attached."

He held up a naysaying hand.

Dinah smiled. "Then thank you."

The young man smiled back, revealing two missing front teeth and the fact that he was far from sober. He nodded at Johnnine. "You like to play the jukebox, kid?"

"If I can play Nat King Cole," Johnnine said pertly.

"Here's a quarter. Have a ball," he said to Johnnine, who jumped down from her bar stool. To Dinah, he added, "Cute kid. Your little sister, right?"

Dinah laughed and shook a cigarette out of her pack. Like a quick-draw artist of the Old West, the young man instantly produced a flaming Zippo lighter from the pocket of his leather jacket.

Johnnine ran to the jukebox and was happily poring over the titles while the young man whispered in her mother's ear. At first Dinah was amusedly attentive, then she pulled away. Just as the dulcet tones of Nat King Cole came on—"*There-was-a-boy, A-very-strange-enchanted-boy*"—Dinah downed her drink and picked up her purse. "Come on, Johnnine, we have to go."

"But I didn't get to hear my songs!" Johnnine complained, not moving from where she stood.

"It's late, you need to get to bed." Dinah stubbed out her cigarette. "I've had my birthday eve drink." She nodded at the young man. "Now it's time to leave."

"Speaking of bed," the young man asked, slurring his words slightly. "Where do you live?"

Dinah's round brown eyes flashed provocatively. "Around the corner." Her only touch of makeup was a slash of strong red lipstick. She feigned disapproval as her full mouth took on a prissy shape. "But not tonight, you're too drunk. We'll see each other again, I come here regularly. Thank you for the drink, and good night, Mr.—?"

"Call me Johnny. Johnny Ace."

Dinah's manner was flirtatiously formal as she extended a plump hand. "Well, then, good night, Mr. Ace." The young man's returning handshake was nowhere near as firm or energetic as Dinah's. "My name is Miss Hapgood, and this is my daughter, Johnnine."

Johnnine frowned at being named to a stranger. Dinah shooed Johnnine towards the door and sailed regally out of the bar, her head held high.

Johnny Ace called after her. "You say *miss*? Hey, I'll be right over!"

Dinah did not turn around or answer him. To the bartender, Johnny Ace said, "You know where she lives, right, Aldo? Fix me up with some black coffee—"

Scene faded out on Ace's sodden, boyish face and came up again the next morning. "Wake up, ducklet, it's late. I overslept..." Dinah, still in her long flannel nightgown, called to Johnnine from the doorway, which she almost filled with her fertility-goddess figure.

Johnnine's eyes fluttered open and she yawned. She shared her pillow with Spotty's small black-and-white head.

A man's voice groaned from the kitchen. "God, I need some coffee—"

Johnnine got dressed quickly, yanking a dress over her head. She grabbed her plaid school bag and hurried into the kitchen. Johnny Ace sat at the narrow kitchen counter, holding his head in his hands, nursing a palpable hangover.

Johnnine gawked at him. "What's the matter with you?"

Dinah distracted her by handing her a quarter. "Go get some breakfast at Mike's. Hurry up or you'll be late—"

"But I need to walk Spotty." Johnnine pulled on a sweater.

"I'll put more newspaper down. She'll be okay."

With a last darting look at Johnny Ace, who smiled weakly, painedly, at her, Johnnine raced down the long hall, her unbrushed hair flying out behind her.

In the All Souls' Waiting Room, Johnnine remembered Johnny Ace as well as her mother's bars. While she couldn't remember ever liking any of the men her mother brought home, she did remember the bars with some fondness. She was paid attention to—drunks were sentimental about children, other people's at any rate, and could be generous with jukebox dimes—and her mother was at least distracted for awhile. Besides that, she got to eat potato chips and drink soda, things she wasn't allowed to do at home. In the war zone of Johnnine's childhood, bars stood out as a sort of peaceful sanctuary.

The next shot showed her running south on Sixth Avenue. She was chewing a large, salt-sprinkled soft pretzel and her jaws were working as fast as her legs. When she turned the corner of King Street, she saw the street in front of her school deserted, devoid of other children. She bolted down the block.

Cut to Johnnine creeping up on the door of her second-grade classroom. Red-cheeked and panting, she held her breath and listened to the teacher taking attendance. The door creaked on its hinges as Johnnine tried to sneak unnoticed into the classroom.

"Johnnine!" Miss Laputo said sternly. "You're very late, do you have a good excuse?"

Johnnine warily approached her teacher's desk. Miss Laputo had bushy dark red hair and eyeglasses with upwardly-curved, rhinestone-edged fins.

Johnnine nodded, swallowing. "Yes, Miss Laputo—"

"Well, we're waiting," she said, her pen poised over the attendance sheet. "What is it?"

"My mother—" Johnnine took a deep breath, "—my mother had a baby."

Miss Laputo's black olive eyes grew larger. "This morning??"

"Yes."

"And that's why you're late?"

Johnnine moved closer to Miss Laputo's desk, warming to her story. "Yah, I—I wanted to see what it would be—"

Miss Laputo broke into a believing smile. "Well! And what did you have, a little brother or a sister?"

"A...a sister—"

"How nice! What did your parents name her?"

Johnnine paused for a fraction of a moment. "Tallulah."

Miss Laputo was taken back. "Tallulah?"

Johnnine nodded solemnly. "After Tallulah Bankhead—on the radio? She has this really deep voice and she's really *funny*."

"Yes, well—take your seat, dear. I'm sure we're all very happy for you. Say congratulations, class..."

The class raggedly, half-heartedly repeated the word. Blushing profusely, Johnnine did not look at anyone as she found her desk. The scene in the schoolroom dissolved into one of her entering her room at home, later that same day.

"Hi, girl!" Johnnine flung open the door. Torn and soiled sheets of newspaper were spread over the linoleum in wildly messy disarray. Spot yipped and yelped and wriggled her greeting, unmindful of where she stepped. Johnnine threw down her book bag and carefully picked up the puppy. She rolled up the pissed-on, shat-on newspaper. Johnnine put Spot on the bed, laughing at the way the round-bellied puppy lost her balance on the mattress. "You look like a drunken bum, you know that?"

She reached for a pink-and-blue spotted piggy bank on her desk. Coins fell onto the green corduroy bedspread as she turned it over. Johnnine spoke to Spotty in a high voice, drumming up enthusiasm as she pocketed the change. "Wanna go out now? Do you?"

Spotty ran around in excited circles on the bed as Johnnine took her leash and collar from the doorknob. The four-month old puppy jumped off the bed and bounded haphazardly down the hall. Laughing, Johnnine tripped over her as Spotty ran back and forth between the door and her mistress. When she leaned down to buckle on Spotty's collar, she heard Dinah crying and talking. Johnnine changed direction and followed the sound of her mother's voice to the front room of the railroad apartment.

Dinah sat on a low leather ottoman, a cigarette and a Kleenex in the same hand, crying into the phone receiver. "Yah, I know she is, but I can't stand this kind of spite. She knows how much my birthday means to me, there's no excuse for her forgetting..."

Dinah did not look at Johnnine until Spot whimpered in impatience at being on the leash. Then she gave Johnnine a cold, hard look. In response, Johnnine nervously picked Spotty up and nuzzled her silky ears.

Dinah looked away but kept talking into the phone. "Will you see her, please, Daniel? She needs a session, she's gone badly off—yah, I will, 'bye." Dinah hung up and turned to Johnnine with eyes like wet agate. She got up heavily and reached for a Kleenex box.

"Happy birthday, mom," Johnnine said anxiously. "I just came home to get the money for your present. Where's Mr. Ace, did he leave?"

"That's none of your business," she said in a tight low voice. She blew her nose. "And you're lying. You deliberately forgot. You wanted to hurt me. You need to see Pahlser right away, find out what's making you so spiteful—"

Johnnine colored deeply. A confused look shot over her face. "I didn't forget! Except maybe this morning I did, but then I thought I'd get you a sussprise." Johnnine used one of their special words to try and soften her mother's anger. "Double peach sugar cone. *Breyer's* peach, your favorite. Honest!"

Dinah glared at Johnnine. "*Stop lying*! You're a spiteful, selfish little bitch! Pahlser's waiting to give you a treatment. I want you to get over there, right now!"

Johnnine almost choked on her words. "I'm not lying! I'm telling the truth! And I don't want to see Pahlser!"

Dinah screamed in fury, advancing on Johnnine. "You're too plaguey to talk to! Put Spot back in your room. She can damn well wait!" Johnnine saw a pint of vodka next to the phone. Backing up, shaking, she turned and fled from the room.

Cut to Johnnine threading her way through crowds of preoccupied shoppers bustling in and out of the little Italian groceries on Bleecker Street. She brushed angry, desolate tears from her face. It had not occurred to her not to go. Dinah's word was law. She had no thought or hope of escape.

Johnnine crossed Seventh Avenue, streaming with cars, trucks and taxis. In the middle of Grove Street, she opened the Chinese-red enamel door of Pahlser's gray stucco building. Woodenly, she climbed two flights of dusty stairs.

Pahlser opened his door when she rang the bell. He looked sad and serious as he peered down at her from his great height. "Come in, Johnnine."

Johnnine followed him slowly down the hall to his office, a square, high-ceilinged corner room with two walls of tall windows, two of built-in bookshelves. She stood in the middle of the carpet looking sullen, withdrawn, and forlorn.

With a grave manner, Pahlser took the chair behind his desk. "So. Hapgood says you forgot her birthday..."

"I didn't forget," Johnnine said resentfully. "I just came home to get my money for her present, but she didn't believe me. It was supposed to be a sussprise."

"Did you wish her happy birthday this morning?"

Johnnine lowered her eyes. "I forgot. There was a man there."

"You know how important birthdays are to Hapgood, don't you?"

Johnnine met Pahlser's intrusive gaze and then glanced away.

"Look at me, Johnnine."

Johnnine looked at him, defiantly at first. Pahlser held her gaze with a sorrowful, earnest expression. Johnnine tried not to cry by swallowing repeatedly, holding her chest high and hard.

Pahlser sighed and stood up. "You know what you need to do. Take your clothes off and lie down on the couch," he said matter-of-factly.

She glanced at the white sheet draped over the leather chaise. Near the head of the couch, six small hollow pipes were stuck through a wooden rack. Conduit cable snaked from the rack into a large plastic bucket filled with water. Johnnine stood immobile.

"Johnnine, did you hear me? You need to take your clothes off," he repeated. "I want to use the medical DOR-buster on you." Sensing her reluctance, he added, "All it does is take away emotional plague."

Johnnine moved to a chair in the corner. Keeping her rigid back towards Pahlser, she inched her dress over her head and turned around.

"Undershirt and panties, too, you know that—"

Johnnine turned crimson as she awkwardly removed her underclothes. Her eyes sprang tears as she crossed to the couch but her face was lifeless. She lay stiffly on her back and stared at the high white ceiling looking quite small on the long white sheet.

Pahlser moved the rack of pipes closer to the couch. "The buster will help you cry, break up your armor—"

Johnnine shivered as Pahlser pointed the pipes at her naked body. He began moving them up and down between her groin and her head, keeping them about twelve inches away from her skin. "I want you to look at me as I do this, Johnnine. It's not cold in here, you're just very contracted. Just let the feelings come through."

Johnnine looked at Pahlser with terrified, forsaken eyes. Then she screwed her eyes tightly shut as Pahlser began pressing down on her chest. Broken sobs were unwillingly torn from her.

"Yah, good," Pahlser said, "let it all out." He looked distraught and unhappy himself, like a doctor who knew the cure would be as painful as the disease.

The screen in the All Souls' Waiting Room went blank. There was a heavy silence before Johnnine could be heard crying. When the lights came up, she turned her face to the wall. She didn't want them to see her tears. She knew how to play a tough, cynical teenager, had learned how to use alcohol and food and cigarettes and pills to keep from feeling much of anything. But seeing herself as a powerless seven-year old overwhelmed her. "All the kids in the world should kill themselves all at once," Johnnine said furiously. "In mass protest against the sick grown-ups who pretend to know how to raise them."

Xofia looked stricken—and as angry as a crusading Carrie Nation. Her eyes threw off sparks and her nostrils fairly smoked. Johnnine was crumpled up on The Couch. "Come here, darling," Xofia said, sitting next to her. Johnnine felt Xofia's arms around her, soft but strong, warm, and comforting. She had never felt anything so good in her life, which made her cry harder. Xofia just held her, quietly and patiently. Seraph A. whistled a lullaby, very softly.

"Things get pretty foul on Earth," Xofia soothed, rocking her gently back and forth. "But that's not *all* there is down there. You're here to retrieve your lost feelings—and then you need to go back, to feel them on Earth."

Johnnine's voice came out muffled from inside Xofia's encircling arms. "I don't *want* to go back!" She sat up, peeved and sulky. "What is the goddam point?"

Xofia shrugged, which looked strange on a person with no neck. "Only The Powers know for sure. Maybe there isn't any. But one thing I do know is that along with life goes a mandate for love. You know the song, 'love makes the world go 'round'—" She handed Johnnine a tissue.

"No." Johnnine blew her nose noisily. "They don't play it in New York..."

A low laugh rumbled in Xofia's throat. "No, maybe not. Still, you need to think about what you love on Earth."

"There isn't anyone, don't you get it? That's why I'm here, for Christ's sake!"

Xofia was unflappable. "I don't only mean people, *anything*—"

Johnnine looked petulant, her lips pouty. She raised her eyes. "Are we gonna play animal, mineral, or vegetable now?"

Xofia was silent but her fiery expression spoke volumes.

"Okay, okay! I love...books...and trees...and most especially," she added, trying to outdo her sarcasm, "my favorite things in the world, the best things on the planet, bar none, are Little Lulu comics and Devil Dogs."

"Good," Xofia smiled. "A good beginning. Keep those things in mind—"

"Why," Johnnine said tauntingly, "is there gonna be a quiz?"

Xofia threw up her hands in exasperation. "Will you never realize how you stab yourself with your own tongue?"

"Xofia," The Recorder cautioned from the corner. "No instructions, the child has to figure things out for herself—"

Johnnine slapped The Couch in anger and vexation. It gave back a little 'ooff.' *"Why am I expected to figure things out when nobody else can, for Christ's sake?"*

"We all have our destinies, darling. Yours is a very rich one."

"Yeah, sure! Rich in doodookaka!"

Chapter Twenty-three

"I'm afraid we have to cut you off," The Recorder intoned as the lights dimmed and the film cranked up. "Not that we wouldn't ordinarily love to listen to you rant."

"I *wasn't* ranting," Johnnine protested.

Seraph A. belted out a few pitiful bars of *O Sole Mio*.

Johnnine felt a sudden irrefutable urge to be quiet. "Okay, I'll be good..."

"*Bene.*" The Recorder's voice was approving.

Johnnine got her first taste of the rewards of eating crow. It wasn't *that* bad, she thought.

The lights went off completely and there she was again on the screen, still seven, caroming out of another of Dinah's favorite taverns, the run-down, workingman's White Rose on Sixth Avenue near the Waverly Theatre. Johnnine ran out of the bar to free Spotty, who waited impatiently on the sidewalk, her leash looped around a No Parking sign. "Hi, baby girl, did you miss me?" The dog pulled at the leash, making it harder to untie.

Dinah followed her daughter onto the street. Her walk was well-oiled, there was a sated smile on her flushed face. "That was the best venison stew I've ever had..."

"'Damn good, missus,' Briggs would say, huh, Mom?" Johnnine finally untied Spot. The puppy leaped up to lick her face.

Dinah laughed, forgetting to correct Johnnine's swearing. "Yah, he would. I wish he could try it sometime..." She frowned. "Other things I wish he'd try, too—" Dinah's jovial mood threatened to darken.

Johnnine anxiously diverted her thoughts. "We could bring him some, couldn't we? When we go up country again?"

With an older-, wiser-than-thou smile, Dinah said, "We'll see, ducklet, we'll see..."

They walked south on Sixth Avenue, heading into the wind. Passersby had red noses and wind-blown hair, testaments to the nippy November weather. On the corner of Carmine, where the wind was gusting, Dinah stopped in her tracks to peer up at the overcast sky. Even though her pile-lined coat was unbuttoned, she was warm from internal anti-freeze. "Looks like snow..."

Spotty pulled Johnnine over to another dog tied to the leg of a table set up on the sidewalk. Eagerly wagging her tail, Spotty tried hard to make friends with an indifferent, disdainful Scottish terrier. There was another table five feet away. Behind each of the tables huddled a person wrapped in heavy blankets. Looking miserable but dedicated, they were selling presidential campaign buttons. The Scottie was tied to the Eisenhower table. Johnnine fingered an "I Like Ike" button.

Dinah finished her thorough inspection of the sky. When she saw where her daughter was standing, in what camp she was in danger of drifting into, she grabbed Johnnine by the sleeve and pulled her over to the Stevenson table. *"This one's our candidate—"*

Johnnine looked wistfully over at the rows of red, white, and blue Eisenhower buttons. "But I like that one better, there's an elephant—"

"Eisenhower isn't the man we want in office!"

"He's not?" Johnnine squinted up at her mother.

"No, silly goose, we're Democrats!" Dinah laughed at Johnnine's ignorance. "God help us if the Republicans get into power..."

Dinah nodded at the stalwart Stevenson for President campaign worker, nearly invisible in her cocoon of blankets, and bought two round celluloid pins picturing a balding, smiling Adlai above the Democrat's mascot.

Dinah attached the button to the collar of Johnnine's blue duffle coat. "We want a donkey to win?" Johnnine asked as she was summarily pinned to the Democratic party. Scene faded out on Johnnine's face.

"And it is as of this moment official, ladies and gentlemen. Governor Stevenson has just formally conceded, General Dwight D. Eisenhower is now President-elect of the United States. The next voice you hear will be that of our newly-elected Vice President, Richard M. Nixon..."

Wearing a thick wool sweater, Reich's assistant Nathan Katzman sat at a desk near the radio. He looked glum as he turned it off.

Wilhelm Reich kneeled in front of a huge stone fireplace, feeding wood into an already-blazing fire. "This is good news, Katzman!" Reich said, the heat of the flames reddening his full cheeks. "I am very happy with Eisenhower. He is a genital character, a warm human being who will understand and help the cause of orgonomy..."

Katzman spoke softly but distinctly. "I don't think so, Dr. Reich."

"You don't agree?" Reich looked healthy, ruddy-faced and vigorous, but he sounded confused.

Katzman shook his head. "American politics are not as simple as they seem, or as benign. Eisenhower's a Republican. The Republicans' first order of business is business, not the good of the people—"

"Ah, but Eisenhower is not a politician. He's a good man, he will protect me from my enemies. You will see—" Reich went back to tending the fire. Katzman frowned and left the room.

Johnnine sat quietly reading in the child-sized orgone accumulator, about four feet high and three feet wide, which stood in the corner of her room. Through the small square opening in the front panel of chipboard, she could be seen sitting fully-clothed, smiling as she leafed through a comic book. In the All

Souls' Waiting Room, Johnnine's associations to being in the accumulator were pleasant. She'd spent a half-hour a day in one the whole time she was in elementary school, often doing her homework there. It was quiet, warm, and peaceful, a place where Dinah never bothered her.

Johnnine jumped when she heard several loud, repeated knocks on the front door. Spotty started barking. Johnnine quickly opened the accumulator door, leaving her Little Lulu on the wooden bench seat, trying to catch Spot before she ran down the hall. She stopped in the doorway of her room, when she heard someone call out her mother's name.

"Dinah Hapgood?" A man spoke from the outside hallway. His voice was raised over the din of Spot's frenzied barking. "U. S. Food and Drug Administration, Washington, D. C. We'd like to talk to you—"

Dinah stood motionless, frozen in front of the washer/dryer as the man knocked and then pounded. She stared at the door like a rabbit in its burrow with the fox at the entrance.

"Miss Hapgood, we need to talk to you—!" the man called again.

Johnnine sidled the few feet from her doorway to her mother. "What's the—" she said, before her mother clapped a hand over her mouth.

"Shut up!" Dinah hissed in a panicked whisper. "I don't want them to know we're here—"

The harrowing sounds of the heavy door-pounding combined with Spot's insistent, high-pitched barking echoed up and down the narrow, tunnel-like hall. Dinah's fear infected Johnnine, who now stared at the front door in terror.

"We only need a few minutes of your time, Miss Hapgood. We'd like to talk to you about your association with Wilhelm Reich. If not now, we'll have to come back—"

Dinah said, "The bastards," under her breath. She glared at Johnnine to stay put, then stole quietly down the hall towards the front door, stealthily throwing the dead-bolt. There was a tell-tale click.

"All right, we know you're in there now. We'd advise you to cooperate with us, Miss Hapgood. For your own good as well as our investigation. We'll be back—"

Spot scrabbled at the door, yapping loudly. Dinah looked angry and scared as she came back down the hall. She was dragging Spot by the collar.

"Mom, don't, she can't breath," Johnnine whispered worriedly.

"Well, neither can I." Dinah threw the dog into Johnnine's room and shut the door. Visibly shaken, Dinah poured herself a double shot of vodka and lit a cigarette. Spot kept on barking.

Johnnine whispered anxiously. "Who was that, Mom? What do they want?"

"Government agents." Dinah frowned, also keeping her voice low though it was no longer necessary. "Men who are after Dr. Reich and the accumulator—"

"What's wrong with accumulators?"

Dinah's eyes flashed. "Nothing's wrong with them! Stop asking questions, you're too young to understand—"

Spot's barking had not lost any of its urgency. Darkly rolling up a newspaper into a long bat, Dinah brushed past Johnnine with her lips pressed into a hard straight line. "Shut up, you stupid little bitch! *Shut up!*" Dinah screamed as she burst into Johnnine's room. There was the sound of hard thwacks followed by Spot's loud yelps.

Johnnine rushed into her room after her mother. "Don't hit her, Mom, don't! I'll make her be good! Please, Mom!"

In the All Souls' Waiting Room, Johnnine had the same sick feeling watching the scene as she had had in real life, a watery loosening of her bowels, a gut-wrench of terror at Dinah's uncontrollably violent rages. Her mother looked so ugly when she was hitting Spotty, cold, murderous, and unreachable. Or when she was in fear, like when the agents pounded on the door. Johnnine now understood why she jumped at loud noises, why a sudden knock on the door always made her heart explode in her chest. What the scene reminded her of most was the movie of Anne Frank's diary, with the Gestapo stomping around downstairs and the Jewish families in the attic holding their breath.

The screen went black over the sounds of Johnnine crying and pleading, Dinah yelling in rage, and Spot howling.

"Aren't we ever going to see something that doesn't reinforce the child's decision to commit hara-kiri?" Xofia asked.

Seraph A. whistled a spunky, happy tune. Was Johnnine imagining it or did it sound exactly like "Zippity Doo Dah?" Gagola, she thought. However the little seraph did it, the oppressive, clammy atmosphere in Freud's office brightened considerably as a new scene lit up the screen. While she liked the effect, Johnnine wondered why he consistently picked tunes without a hint of hip—why couldn't he sing something, for instance, by Oscar & Hammerstein, Cole Porter, or her all-time favorite, George Gershwin?

"*'I'll-build-a-stairway-to-para-dise, With-a-new-step-every-day/I'm-gonna-get-there-at-any-price, stand-aside-I'm-on-my-way'*—fantabulous movie, huh, Mom?"

"Yah, ducklet, it was." Dinah pushed open one of the glass doors of the thickly-carpeted lobby of the Loew's Sheridan on the corner of Greenwich Avenue. In the early winter twilight outside, the large marquee read "An American in Paris." Dinah sighed lasciviously. "Gene Kelly in tight pants is a sight for sore eyes."

Johnnine looked enchanted and bemused as she danced around her mother's cumbersome figure.

Dinah stopped at a metal pushcart to buy a bag of roasted chestnuts. They munched the sweet, steaming nutmeats as they made their way down Greenwich toward the Women's House of Corrections. Aside from the prison, the street was gaily lit and decorated for Christmas.

"I loved the music! and the guy who played the piano, with the droopy eyes, he was so *funny*..." Johnnine looked radiant, transported.

"Oscar Levant. Yah, he was wonderful."

"The piano is the bestest instrument—" Johnnine skipped ahead of her mother, turned around and flung out her arms. "*I-got-rhythm! I-got-music! I-got-my-gal, who-could-ask-for-anything-more...*"

Whistles, jeers, and catcalls from the tall red brick building across Greenwich Avenue cut short Johnnine's playful, impromptu performance. Women's voices drifted down to the street, along with pieces of paper wrapped around small weights.

"Hey, sweetie, call my boyfriend for me, will ya? Here's the number!"

"Yeah, mine too. Tell him I'm horny as hell—"

"*We* got rhythm too, doll-face, only they locked us up for ours!"

There was a chorus of rude laughter from the throats of many women. Johnnine stopped singing and looked up at the building's high barred windows.

Dinah kept up her brisk walking pace. "Right opposite the Women's House of Correction is probably not a good place to emote in public, ducklet, especially something suggestive—"

"What are they doing in there?" Johnnine looked over her shoulder at the imposing building where bare arms waved at them from between bars.

"They're in jail. A lot of them are prostitutes..."

"What's that?"

"A woman who sells her body for money."

"They sell their *bodies*?" Johnnine was incredulous. "How can they do that? What for?"

Dinah reached for Johnnine's hand as they came to a corner, watching the traffic as she spoke. "For sexual intercourse, with poor sick men who can't find release with open, loving women like me. There aren't enough of us to go around."

Johnnine thought for a moment as they walked along. "So then they're kind of like nurses?"

On the corner of Sixth Avenue, they stood and waited for the light to change. "Well...not exactly," Dinah said. "You'll understand when you're older."

Johnnine frowned and persisted. "But I want to know *now*."

Dinah resorted to distraction tactics, pointing to the Nedick's on the corner of West Eighth Street. "How about a hot dog?"

"*Okay!*" Johnnine enthused gluttonously, pulling Dinah across the street as the light turned green. "And french fries and an orange drink?"

"How about a root beer float instead?"

"YAH!!"

Dinah opened the steamed-up glass door to the enclosed hot dog stand. In her rich, mellifluous voice, she addressed the small, tired man wearing a white paper hat behind the counter. "Two kosher, please—on toasted buns—"

"We always toast the buns, lady," the man said boredly, spearing two franks off the roller-grill.

"Do you?" Dinah sounded fascinated, as though this were a gem of information. "I didn't know that. I shall remember in future..."

The man gave Dinah a mildly quizzical look as he put the hot dogs on the counter and the scene faded out.

The street lamps had come on when Dinah and Johnnine left Nedick's. On the corner of Waverly Place, Dinah grabbed Johnnine's hand and turned left towards Washington Square. "I want to check on the Berman baby—"

"Is she the new one?"

"Yah," Dinah smiled, but not at Johnnine. "A week old today."

"What's her name?" Johnnine asked, disengaging her hand and skipping alongside her mother.

"Barbara. Although they've started calling her Babs."

A uniformed, older doorman let them in to a chandeliered, black-and-white marble-tiled lobby with potted palms in the corners. It was a grand old building with an old-fashioned frosted glass canopy over the entrance, gilded mirrors and vases of flowers on marble tables inside.

Johnnine absorbed the opulent surroundings with eyes that had grown larger. "This looks just like the movie, Mom!"

"Third floor, please," Dinah said to an elderly black elevator man. He wore a neat maroon uniform with gold braid epaulets and a round flat hat. Johnnine stared at him with her mouth slightly open.

"Want to push the button?" he asked Johnnine as he pulled the inner folding metal lattice door across.

Johnnine smiled and nodded. The elevator man took her hand and firmly pushed the "3" button with Johnnine's index finger. He smiled at Dinah, who beamed back at him, then proudly, proprietarily, down at Johnnine.

An apartment door opened as they got off on the third floor. A young man with thinning, wheat-colored hair had tortoise-shell glasses pushed on top of his forehead. He looked harried. A baby could be heard crying in the recesses of the apartment.

"Hapgood, thank God! Babs is in a snit, she won't stop crying, we can't figure out what she wants—"

"Probably that you stop calling her Babs," Dinah quipped, then bustled brusquely off down the hall.

Berman chuckled. "Your mother's quite a character, isn't she? Hello, it's Johnnine, isn't it? I'm Phil Berman. Come in."

Johnnine followed him down the hall to a large and luxurious living room, warmly lit with several silk-shaded lamps. "Make yourself at home. I'll be right back. Babies are so *demanding*!" Berman crossed his eyes in fake exasperation. Johnnine laughed.

The main feature of the room was a black Steinway baby grand. Béla Bartók sheet music was scattered on the matching piano bench. Floor-to-ceiling bookcases, crammed with hard-cover books, lined one wall. The thick wool carpet was cream-colored and a glossy panne velvet couch was the color of sautéed mushrooms. Several small Oriental rugs were islands of jewel-toned brilliance under glass-topped tables. A porcelain vase of fat gold chrysanthemums stood on a lace throw on one end of the piano.

Johnnine was drawn to a lamp with a carved white jade elephant finial. She was tracing its outline with her finger when Berman returned. He was round-faced and comfortable-looking, dressed in a pink oxford shirt and dark flannel slacks that were a little tight at the waist.

Berman smiled at her conspiratorially, looking furtively over his shoulder and putting his finger to his lips. "Do you like Mallomars?" he whispered.

"Mallomars? I *love* Mallomars, almost as much as Devil Dogs!"

"Ooh, those are good, too," he said appreciatively. "Come on, I'm supposed to be on a diet, but..."

Johnnine followed him into a fancy, gleaming kitchen, avidly watching his every move. He put out heavy cut-crystal Baccarat glasses and a carton of milk. Then he opened a folding step stool to reach a box of cookies on the highest shelf in the tall cupboard. "My secret hiding place—don't tell on me, now!"

"Cross my heart and hope to die," Johnnine swore solemnly.

"Probably don't need to go *that* far..." Berman opened the box and Johnnine helped herself. Berman popped a whole Mallomar into his mouth and gave her a fiendish, chocolate monster grin, wiggling his eyebrows.

Johnnine giggled.

Berman smiled as he chewed and swallowed his cookie. "Yumm..." His light blue eyes were kindly behind his glasses. "Do you ever watch Captain Kangaroo?"

"Yah, when Mom lets me..." Johnnine was nibbling her cookie around the edges slowly, trying to make it last.

"Would you like to meet him and Mr. Green Jeans?"

"Sure!"

"I'll take you, then. Next week maybe." He made another cookie disappear.

"How can you?" Johnnine asked.

"I work on the show, I'm the makeup man..." Berman wolfed down two more Mallomars.

"Mr. Green Jeans wears *makeup*?" Johnnine was aghast. Berman laughed.

The All Souls' Waiting Room

Dinah shouted authoritatively from the bedroom. "Berman! You should be here for this—"

Berman swallowed so fast he almost choked. "Coming!" he shouted, before downing half a glass of milk.

"*BERMAN*!" Dinah yelled.

"I love this, *I just love it*," Berman said to no one in particular as he flew from the room, smacking his lips.

In a small TV studio makeup room, the actors who played Captain Kangaroo and Mr. Green Jeans sat side-by-side in barber chairs facing garishly-lit large mirrors. They were draped in long white bibs as big as sheets. Phil Berman and Monte Balikovsky daubed their faces with thick, orangey pan-cake, darkened their eyebrows, and powdered their chins.

Johnnine stood watching quietly and unobtrusively in a corner of the tiny, cluttered room. Berman pulled a grizzled wig from a bodiless head mannikin on the counter and positioned it on the actor's head. The instant transformation from nondescript, middle-aged man into famous children's TV star made Johnnine blink.

"See if this fits any better, Bob—"

"Ummm," Captain Kangaroo said to his reflection in the mirror, pulling and patting the wig into place until he was satisfied with the way it looked.

"*Ta da*!" Monte exclaimed, looking over at him. "Presenting the all new and improved Captain Kangaroo—"

The Captain's smile was perfunctory. "Who looks exactly like the old one...finished, Phil?"

"Almost, just one more bobby pin—"

Mr. Green Jeans got out of his barber chair. Monte whipped off his bib and brushed off his overalls. "Bet you never knew Captain Kangaroo used bobby pins," Green Jeans smiled at Johnnine.

Johnnine blushed hot pink as Mr. Green Jeans walked by her. She didn't say a word. Captain Kangaroo's bib was removed and he was revealed in his mouse-colored costume.

"Nice meeting you, I hope you like the show..." Captain Kangaroo said as he passed Johnnine on his way out.

"Johnnine," Berman prompted, putting away his skin brushes and sponges and pencils.

"Johnnine," Captain Kangaroo repeated dutifully before he vanished out the door. Johnnine gawped after him, wordless, star-struck.

"Want to see the set?" Berman asked her.

Johnnine turned back to Berman and nodded.

"Who's on today?" Monte asked Berman, shaking out Mr. Green Jeans' bib and folding it up.

"Well, the pony was yesterday, so that means a dog today."

Monte let loose with his demented laugh, like rampaging pigs and geese raiding a still.

"...actually," Berman said, "it *is* a dog, network's doing a plug for the Lassie show—"

Johnnine came out of the corner with her eyes lit up. "Lassie?? The real Lassie? I *love* Lassie, I have all the Albert Payson Terhune books, she's my most favoritest dog in the world. After Spotty," she added loyally.

"Johnnine," Berman said carefully, "I hate to be the one to have to tell you this, but there actually a bunch of Lassies."

"There are?" She looked confused.

"Yah." Berman was almost apologetic. "They use different ones for different scenes. One dog does the whining, another one digs, and another does the pulling-the-blanket-off-the-bed bit. I think the trainer said there were seven all together."

"Oh," Johnnine said blankly, digesting this news for a moment. "Can I go to the john?"

"Sure, the door's right opposite."

When Johnnine was gone, Monte snapped shut his makeup kit. "So how come you're playing Uncle Philly?"

"I'm not playing anything. She's a bright cute kid who happens to be fatherless."

"I wouldn't worry about her with a mother like Hapgood."

"Would you want Hapgood for your mother?"

"Are you kidding?" Balikovsky snorted. "Her balls are bigger than mine. Well, see ya tomorrow, *unka Phil...*"

"Oh, shut up," Berman said good-naturedly.

Berman was closing up the briefcase containing his tools of the trade when Johnnine came back in. "So—do you want to meet Lassie even though there's more than one of her?"

"Yah, I think I better," Johnnine said seriously. "I'm going to be a veterinarian when I grow up."

"A veterinarian?"

"Yah. So I can help sick dogs get better."

Berman led her out of the room. "What about being a doctor, helping people?"

Johnnine frowned. "Dogs are nicer than people. Besides, grown-up people can't be helped. They're too armored—"

Berman carefully controlled his amusement as they emerged into the studio. Casually but smartly clothed in a tan safari jacket with lots of pockets, he held Johnnine's hand. She was dressed up for the occasion in a pretty blue dress and shiny new oxblood Buster Browns.

The All Souls' Waiting Room

They walked through a vast, dark cavern dotted with large cameras like slow-moving, one-eyed robots. The floor was littered with serpentine coils of television cable held in place with silver gaffer's tape. Near the show's brightly-lit main set, Captain Kangaroo's gingerbready house and garden, Berman introduced Johnnine to Lassie's male handler. Lassie, or one of the clones thereof, sat stoically by his side, waiting to go on. The handler gave the beautiful, perfectly-groomed Collie the command to 'shake hands.' The dog offered her paw to Johnnine like a queen to a royal subject. In a glowing close-up, camera showed Johnnine holding it, smiling with delight, as the scene faded slowly to black.

Chapter Twenty-four

"So you see, darling," Xofia said, underlining the obvious, "it wasn't all blackness."

Johnnine didn't say anything. She had adored Phil Berman and his light-hearted glamorous world, a sparkling counterpoint to her mother's dark and gloomy Reichian forest. But at the same time, Johnnine wondered why she was forced to starve in a dungeon while just around the corner was a banquet and masked ball that she couldn't get to because she was chained to the wall.

So the Bermans helped, and then again they didn't. Johnnine didn't see that much of them in any case, they had their own growing family, she was an afterthought. Still, even Berman's occasional kindnesses stood out in her childhood like a slick new coffee table book in a bin full of torn, used paperbacks. When he became makeup man for the "What's My Line?" show, he sometimes took her along to meet the writers, actors, musicians, and athletes who turned up as guest celebrities.

Lily Neary had also been kind. Johnnine remembered Neary's theatrical readings of "Grimm's Fairy Tales," "Winnie the Pooh," and all the beautifully-illustrated stories in "East of the Sun, West of the Moon." Neary would change her voice to fit each character, from aging king to wood sprite, from Baby Roo to Eeyore. Neary had even staged some scenes from Shakespeare, al fresco, with Johnnine playing Puck in "Midsummer's Night Dream," wearing half an old sheet dyed green and tucked into her panties like a drapey diaper.

"I still want to die," Johnnine said flatly. "Just because a couple of people were nice to me once upon a time isn't enough reason to live—"

"I told you, darling, we'll have to wait and see what The Powers think, they're the ones who issue the tickets..."

Typical, Johnnine thought. You needed a ticket to die but nobody gave a leaping fart about you when you were alive.

"We're skipping ahead several months here, to June of 1953," The Recorder tolled from his corner. "An important moment in the child's soul-life—"

Johnnine suddenly remembered how she'd always felt that her life was really a movie, a very strange and unpredictable flick in which she was as often an on-looker as she was an actress. She told Xofia this thought as Fa, So, and La doused the room lights.

"That's because you spent so much time out of your body," Xofia explained.

"Huh?"

"Your little body was very unhappy most of the time, so your soul hung out outside a lot, looking on. No soul likes being in a body in pain. It's worse than going to a party and getting cornered by a drunk."

"What do you mean—?"

The All Souls' Waiting Room

"Sshh, darling. Lights, camera, action time!"

"Now, class, I want you to copy down the sentence on the board," Miss Laputo was saying to Johnnine's second-grade classroom. She had her thick hair pulled back and wore a pale yellow sweater draped over her thin shoulders. "Vinnie, please stand up and read it out loud." She pointed to the blackboard with a brass-tipped yardstick.

Vinnie stood up nervously and adjusted his new and unwelcome eyeglasses, no longer the cocky little boy he had been the year before. "Yes, Miss Laputo. It says, 'I love my country'."

"And?"

"...and 'I am proud to be an American'."

"Thank you, Vinnie," Miss Laputo nodded. "Does anyone know what today is?"

Several hands waved in the air. "Angela?"

A pudgy, dark-haired girl with a halo of tight braided hair answered. "It's Flag Day, Miss Laputo."

"That's right. At lunch recess, we're going to have a little parade up and down King Street holding our flag unfurled in front of us. Who wants to carry the flag for our class?"

Almost all the hands in the class shot up, including Johnnine's.

"Carrying the flag is a great honor." Miss Laputo cautioned. "It can only be carried by someone who's worthy, a boy or girl who does their homework assignments, listens to their parents, and above all, a boy or girl who never lies—"

Half the hands slowly returned to their owners' sides, also including Johnnine's.

"Arthur, would you like to carry the flag for us today?"

A perky, brown-haired boy with ears that stuck out almost at right angles from his head stood up and beamed at the teacher. "Yeth, Mith Laputo!" Arthur spit as he spoke excitedly.

At her desk, Johnnine fiddled with her pencil and looked downcast as the scene faded out.

"Miss Laputo, I have to tell you something..." Johnnine whispered to her teacher as the class filed down the metal stairs, the clatter of dozens of feet making a tremendous metallic racket in the enclosed stairwell.

"What? Speak up, Johnnine, I can't hear you."

Johnnine waited until the last of her classmates went by them. "I—I lied to you, about my mother having a baby."

Miss Laputo stopped and looked down at her sharply. "Well, I must say I wondered at the time—you can stay after school and write 'I will not tell lies' one hundred times on the blackboard."

Johnnine hung her head in shame.

Miss Laputo smoothed Johnnine's hair back from her face and smiled. "I'm glad you told me, Johnnine. Now it won't weigh on your conscience, will it, dear?"

Johnnine lifted her head and let out a long, relieved breath. "No, Miss Laputo." She beamed up at her teacher, grateful for absolution. "Thank you, Miss Laputo!"

An unmarked government car, a gray Ford sedan, pulled up in front of Daniel Pahlser's apartment building on Grove Street. At the wheel was F.D.A. agent Timothy Wurton, in the passenger seat another man also in a plain dark blue suit and white shirt.

"The red door," Wurton said, nodding at Pahlser's building and mopping his face with a handkerchief. "Remember we're not doing anything yet, we just want to keep track of who comes and goes. And don't worry about being obvious. Some of his patients might be more willing to talk to us once they know he's being watched—"

"Right," the other man said, getting out of the car. He carried a folded-up newspaper. "You'll be over at the Hapgood woman's place?"

"Yeah," Wurton answered. "Let's check back in around 0300, I'll meet you at the coffee shop across the street."

"Right." The subordinate agent touched the brim of his hat as Wurton pulled out into traffic in the nondescript gray vehicle.

Johnnine marched behind a proud, perspiring Arthur Tannenbaum in the hot June sun pouring down onto King Street. The children of P. S. 8 were on the empty street in front of the school, putting their fire-drill training on parade. Yellow New York Police Department sawhorses at either end of the street blocked off automobile traffic.

When Johnnine's class had made it to the corner and orders were given for 'bout-face, Miss Laputo came up from the rear, gently lining up the shoulders of the children in her class. She paused when she got to Johnnine. "How would you like a turn carrying the flag, Johnnine? Telling me what you just did was a brave thing to do..."

Johnnine blanched and looked away. "I, no, I can't, Miss Laputo."

"Why not?"

Johnnine was clearly inventing an excuse to cover her shyness. "I—I might trip or fall or something."

Miss Laputo raised her hand to shield her eyes from the glaring mid-day sun and squinted down the line to where Arthur stood patiently waiting for the start-up whistle to blow.

"All right, I won't force you if you don't want to. But don't forget I asked you. Which means I think you're worthy. Good American boys and girls always tell the truth. That's part of what makes us a great country."

Johnnine blushed uncomfortably, but she looked pleased nonetheless. "Yes, Miss Laputo."

The whistle blew and the class shuffled unevenly ahead, trying to keep its five-rowed, five-abreast square box formation. Johnnine stared intently at her feet to keep in step with her classmates. The scene faded.

Chapter Twenty-five

"Look," Johnnine cried out desperately, "you guys don't understand. I *have* to die. There's something really wrong with me, I'm unloveable the way I am!"

"You are nothing of the sort!" Xofia was adamant.

The Recorder cleared his throat, a low, imposing rumble. "Love takes many strange forms, young woman. Your mother tries to love you, and the world, through the distorted lens of her own childhood..."

This did not cut any ice with Johnnine. "Then that's another reason for not living! I might have children and end up making *them* suffer. It'd be inevitable, right? The sins of the fathers—well, no thanks, better to die than do that to some innocent little kid—"

"Ah, but you are forgetting the Great Paradox," Xofia sighed enigmatically.

"What 'Great Paradox'?" Johnnine asked derisively.

"Out of suffering comes wisdom."

Johnnine blew her nose, crossed her arms over her chest, and hid her sorrow behind a mask of irascibility. "You guys can stuff all the suffering where the sun fails to shine. All I want is a nice and permanent *lights out*—can the flying kewpie-doll in the corner do the honors? The faster this is over, the better."

The next scene opened on an exterior of the farmhouse in winter, at night. A raging blizzard blurred the outlines of the house, which were further obscured by five-foot snowdrifts piled up around doors and windows. A feeble beam of light from one window on the ground floor lit up one small rectangle of whirling snow.

Inside the house, Dinah and Johnnine were huddled in the farmhouse's tiny, cheerless bathroom. Fully dressed and wrapped in Indian-patterned blankets, they sat on the edge of the tub and the toilet seat. The coils of a small gas heater glowed blue-red in between them. On the rim of the washbasin, several candles stuck in jars flickered in lieu of electricity.

"What if he doesn't come?" Johnnine asked anxiously.

Dinah's mouth was set in a grim line. "Briggs will get here somehow, he's not going to let us freeze to death—"

Johnnine looked up worriedly as the wind howled around the house, hurling itself at the window as though intent on breaking in. "But maybe he'll get lost in the snow!"

"Briggs will get the snowplow here by morning come hell or high water."

"But what if—"

"Let's sing some Christmas carols." Dinah's tone was firm.

"Christmas is over."

"Who cares? We can sing carols whenever we feel like it." Dinah's deep and plangent voice filled the utilitarian, off-white bathroom. There were no softening touches such as a rug or curtains. "*O-little-town-of-Bethlehem, how-still-we-see-thee-lie—*"

Johnnine made a face and interrupted her mother. "I don't like that one. Let's do 'Hark the Herald Angels Sing' instead..."

Without acknowledging Johnnine, Dinah switched songs in midstream, putting herself into the singing with studious concentration. "*'Hark-the-herald-angels-sing'...*"

"*'Glory-to-the-newborn-king'*," Johnnine piped in.

"*'Peace-on-earth-and-mercy-mild'*—"

"*'God-and-heaven-reconciled'.*" Johnnine sang the carol enthusiastically, with a clear and tuneful voice. She broke off before the second verse. "Mom, do you believe in God?"

"If you mean an old man with a white beard up in the sky, no. But I do believe there's a certain order to things, a timeliness that's bigger than individual people. Maybe that's God, I don't know."

"What about baby Jesus?"

"I think he was a great teacher and healer. But Christianity's become an ugly distortion of what Jesus stood for. That's why I've kept you away from churches."

"Except we went to that one on Christmas Eve."

"Yah, for the choir singing, not the sermon."

Johnnine frowned, lost in thought. "I believe in Jesus, I think he was a beautiful baby. But how come they always show him dying?"

"Supposedly—" Dinah lit a cigarette and exhaled. "—to remind us that he died for our sins."

Johnnine blew the smoke away from her. "What sins, what's that?"

"Nothing, I don't believe in them." Dinah tapped her ash into the sink.

"But what's sin?" Johnnine frowned.

"Supposedly something someone does God doesn't like."

Johnnine shifted her weight on the closed toilet seat. "I thought God was supposed to love us."

Dinah shrugged. "Yah, well, that's what they say."

"Then how can he hate things we do?"

Dinah took a swig from her flask and laughed approvingly. "Ah, ducklet, out of the mouths of babes—" Her eyes glowed and her wide mouth parted in a smile. "You know how much I wanted you before you were born, don't you? Your father told me to have an abortion, but I wouldn't do it. I wanted you with all my heart. Having you was the most important thing in the world to me, you were a much-wanted, much-loved baby." Dinah looked at her daughter, her ruddy face full of emotion, but did not reach out to touch her.

In the All Souls' Waiting Room, it suddenly occurred to Johnnine that Dinah was making up for her own unwanted infancy. Johnnine remembered Dinah's frequent rounds of sentimentality when she was under the influence, while the rest of the time time her attitude was one of harsh indifference. These confessional bouts made Johnnine miserable. Dinah always said how much she wanted Johnnine when she was a baby. But she never said she loved her or wanted her as a child.

"How about 'Deck the Halls'?" Johnnine said.

Dinah led off with a rousing introduction. The frail wood-frame house was buffeted by gale-force winds, slowly being buried in snow.

"I have been too stunned the last few days to even keep up these entries," Wilhelm Reich dictated as he sat at his Observatory desk. Camera showed the swirling nighttime snowstorm outside the window, though the room was bright with light and a cheering fire burned in the massive fireplace at his back. There was a thick sheaf of documents in front of him on the wide Danish modern desk.

Reich looked haggard, his voice sounded hoarse. "On February 10, the U. S. Attorney for Maine, at the FDA's request, filed a complaint for injunction against me and the Wilhelm Reich Foundation. Paragraph...On the same day, the U. S. Attorney General's office also announced the complaint action for an injunction against the interstate shipment of accumulators. The latter pretends to 'prove' the nonexistence of orgone energy!"

Reich paused in his dictation to run his hand through his unruly shock of silver-white hair. "In other words, I am to be persecuted for being a healer. The most serious charge is that all my books must be recalled, even the ones published in German, if there is so much as a mention of orgone energy. That means *Character Analysis*, *The Sexual Revolution*, even *The Mass Psychology of Fascism* may all comeunder the FDA's 'prayer for relief.' A bitterly ironic term. What is the American public's prayer for relief from the Food and Drug Administration? Paragraph..."

Reich leaned back in his wooden swivel chair, then slumped forward wearily. "I have called a meeting of my most trusted orgonomists, to see how we should handle this latest attack from the emotional plague..."

The film cut to later that evening, to the main hall of the Observatory. Couches and chairs were grouped around a large coffee table under a Western-style wrought-iron chandelier. Daniel Pahlser, Nathan Katzman, and another orgonomist from New York, Edgar Cooke, were seated, watching Reich pace back and forth.

"...and so I am thinking to make my appearance in court, even though I deny the right of a jury made up of laymen to decide matters of scientific fact—"

Pahlser's tone was angry. "And what happens to the truth in all this?"

Katzman said, in a low, dispirited voice, "In legalistic terms, it comes out of the embarrassment each side inflicts on the other."

Reich stopped pacing to stare at Katzman, his eyes wide with consternation and disbelief.

Pahlser seized the opportunity to press his point, addressing Reich heatedly. "Is that what you want, Dr. Reich? To be treated like a quack? 'Have you a license to practice medicine? Yes or no, doctor!'"

Reich winced visibly before flaring up. "I have given my life for science! I will not stand for being publicly humiliated in front of a jury of laymen! NO!!! It is settled, then. I *will not* appear in court—"

Katzman exchanged a troubled glance with the slight, brown-haired Edgar Cooke. The scene faded out on Cooke as he stared at the floor and almost imperceptibly shook his head.

In the All Souls' Waiting Room, Johnnine remembered how vitriolic Dinah's diatribes against Cooke and Katzman had been. Weren't they all on the same side? What was it with grown-ups, anyway? Would she ever understand why they did things? Were they mysterious or just hopelessly fucked-up?

Later that evening, Reich was alone in his office, dictating: "...there are conspirators around whose aim is to destroy human happiness and self-government. Is the right of the conspirator to ravage humanity the same as my right to free, unimpeded scientific inquiry? It obviously is *not the same thing...*"

Camera panned to the window, where the scene went to black.

"...and it is not permissible, either morally, legally, or factually, to force a natural scientist to expose his scientific results and methods of basic research in court..."

In a large, old-fashioned, lofty-ceilinged courtroom, empty except for one reporter, two bailiffs and several men at the prosecutors' table, a bespectacled judge was reading aloud from a typed statement. "To appear in court as a *defendant* in matters of basic natural research would in itself appear, to say the least, extraordinary. It would require disclosure of evidence in support of the position of the discovery of the Life Energy. Such disclosure, however, would involve untold complications and possible *national disaster*, underlined. I therefore submit, in the name of truth and justice, that I shall not appear in Court as the defendant. Dated February 25, 1954. Yours sincerely, Dr. Wilhelm Reich."

The Judge looked up over his bifocals as he put the letter down. "Well, gentlemen, a most unusual response—"

"We think you will find, as we have, your Honor, that all of Dr. Reich's responses can fairly be classified as unusual," the prosecutor said drily. He spoke briskly and professionally. "We recommend the Court find in favor of the injunction. Specifically that interstate commerce be disallowed and all so-called 'orgone energy accumulators' leased to patients be recalled and destroyed. Additionally, we pray that all in-stock copies of Reich's soft-cover publications having to do with orgone energy likewise be destroyed. The prosecution also suggests that Reich's hard-cover books be withheld from further distribution until and unless all statements and representations pertaining to the existence of the so-called orgone energy and allied materials are deleted."

"Very well," the judge assented, sighing. "In lieu of any disputing evidence, the Court hereby finds for the prosecution. We will issue an injunction against interstate shipment as recommended by the U. S. Attorney General's office...a disappointing day for the adversarial system, gentlemen. I wonder if the defendant understands what he's given up."

The men at the prosecutor's table exchanged brief, clipped smiles.

The judge banged his gavel. "Court is now adjourned." The scene went to black.

On an early spring evening two months later, Wilhelm Reich sat at the controls of his cloud-buster in back of the Observatory. The sky was dark with clouds. Reich appeared animated, maneuvering the bank of long pipes in sweeping semi-circles from east to west.

Nathan Katzman came outside and walked quickly over the thinning snow to the cloud-busting platform. "The new lawyer just called, Dr. Reich. I told him you were busy but he has some important ideas for the defense."

Reich did not take his eyes off the sky. "Have you seen the UFO's that are watching over us at Orgonon? I saw one earlier, the driver tipped his ship to let me know he saw me." Reich's face lit up, he beamed at Katzman. "I suddenly realized that they're probably adding to the planetary emergency, with the exhaust from their spaceships. We need to re-double our cloud-busting. Then, with a lot of rain, I can clean out the DOR in the atmosphere and prove the importance of orgone to Washington!"

Katzman looked away from Reich, disappointed. "The lawyer thinks we should fight the injunction on constitutional grounds. The government can't go around ordering the destruction of books, it contravenes the First Amendment, our freedom of speech..."

"Nein, Katzman," Reich said, looking patiently down at his worried assistant. "What is really at issue here is freedom of *science*."

Katzman grew frustrated, his voice had an edge of impatience. "We can't rewrite the rules, Dr. Reich. There are excellent grounds for dismissal. The case reports the FDA used were gross distortions of your experiments, they weren't even trying for accuracy—"

Reich spoke calmly. "The emotional plague always distorts the truth, Katzman. And it is unbeatable at playing legal games."

Katzman's eyes flashed. "So what are you saying? That we should lie down and play dead?" Katzman immediately regretted his outburst. "I'm sorry, Dr. Reich." He continued in a softer voice. "The lawyer said if you'd appeared, he might have been able to reduce the complaint, get the injunction to apply just to the accumulator rather than the literature as well..."

"Katzman," Reich said gently, as if he were speaking to a child. "A man of principle does not compromise. I will not bargain the accumulator for my books. To do so would acknowledge the FDA was right. But they are *wrong* and I will prove it. I have decided to go to Arizona this fall, to make rain in the desert. *Then* let them deny my work, my discoveries!"

Camera panned back to show the twilight sky in swirling motion. The film did a freeze frame on Reich's inspired face. He was an imperious conductor, pointing his hollow batons at a celestial orchestra.

In the All Souls' Waiting Room, Johnnine could not separate out her complicated feelings for the man. Was Reich a madman—or a saint?

Chapter Twenty-six

"Any comments, young woman?"

The Recorder startled Johnnine. Her eyes were glued to the freeze-framed image of Reich's face, his liquid brown eyes full of tormented love for the world. "What do you mean?"

"How do you feel about these scenes with Willie?" Xofia interpreted.

Johnnine looked away from the screen. "They remind me of *Viva Zapata...*"

"What's that?" Xofia probed.

"A movie," Johnnine answered, passing her hand over her forehead. "I saw it about five times one summer...not because I liked it, only because the Waverly didn't change films and I wasn't allowed to go as far as the Loew's Sheridan by myself."

"What was it about, darling?"

Johnnine frowned slightly, remembering her considerable frustration at having to see the same movie every week. Now she wondered if the universe hadn't been trying to tell her something. "Marlon Brando played the part of a Mexican revolutionary, Emiliano Zapata. I hated the story, it was just like my life, depressing grown-ups running around being depressing. But staying home was even worse, and the Waverly was at least air-conditioned, so every Friday when I got my allowance I'd buy a chocolate Italian ice, go sit in the loge, and watch Brando get mowed down by the Federales one more time. At the end he gets lured into a trap, he thinks he's going to meet a bunch of his supporters or something, only he rides into an empty arena and then the soldiers stand up all around the rim of the stadium and shoot him with machine guns. The worst thing was they killed his horse, too, a beautiful white stallion—"

"Hmmm," Xofia murmured. "So you saw political parallels?"

Johnnine rubbed her eyes. "I don't know about politics. All I know is I couldn't take the ending, the way Zapata's eyes looked when he knew he'd been betrayed by his men."

"Emiliano Zapata and Wilhelm Reich both chose a hero's death," The Recorder interjected lightly. "Shall we?"

Johnnine was put off by the Recorder's breezy tone. They were not discussing the weather here. Then she realized that he saw things from a very different perspective from hers, a timeless one. Jesus Christ, she suddenly thought. Did people really choose the way they died? Her head spun at the idea. No, she decided, the concept was too bizarre even for Mondo Bizarro.

The freeze-frame on Reich's face dissolved into a new scene.

"Here's one. A gangster's seafood." Dinah bounced around in the cab of a large, heavy truck with bad shock absorbers.

The All Souls' Waiting Room

It was a steamy summer night in the city. The humid breeze from the open window blew her short hair around her face.

Sy Minnowitz was driving, handling the floor-shift with the ease of a former trucker. "A gangster's seafood?" he repeated.

Johnnine sat with her legs hanging on either side of the large, cumbersome gear box. "That's too easy, Mom," she chirped. "Mobster's lobster."

Dinah laughed. "All right, miss smartypants, you do one."

"Okay..." The truck jolted them up and down and side to side as it lurched over the unevenly-paved streets. "A drunken meany," Johnnine said smugly.

Sy and Dinah looked at each other, mouthing the definition quizzically. Sy slowed the truck down as they passed under the concrete supports of the West Side Highway.

Johnnine looked from Sy to her mother expectantly, sure of stumping them. "Give up yet?"

"Yah, I guess so," Dinah shrugged. "What is it?"

"A-*hem*! A drunken meany is...a plastered bastard!"

Dinah and Sy burst out laughing. Dinah leaned her head out her window to shout. "Daniel!! *Pink-stink*!"

Camera pulled back for an exterior of the two-ton, eight-wheel flatbed truck as it lumbered past the wharves and docks of lower Manhattan. Mounted and bolted down on the back was a slightly smaller duplicate of the Orgonon cloud-buster, Pahlser's portable model. The chains holding the pipes in place clanked and thunked as the truck jounced over cobblestone streets laid down in another era. Daniel Pahlser and Monte Balikovsky rode standing up, holding onto the wooden partition between the cab and the truck bed. Behind them, the cloud-buster looked like an instrument of war.

Pahlser leaned down closer to Dinah's window, his frizzy tonsure of hair blown straight back from his face in the truck's airstream. "What??" he shouted over the truck noise.

Dinah yelled even louder. "A drunken meany!"

"A drunken what?"

"*Meany*! Em-ee-ay-en-wy!"

The cloud-busting truck came to a halt at the entrance to Gansevoort Pier. The noisome grind of gear-changing echoed off the sides of old Port of New York warehouses as Sy turned the unwieldy truck around.

Johnnine stuck her head out the window. Her clear young voice rang out on the deserted pier. "A drunken meany is a plastered bastard!"

Pahlser smiled distractedly, eying the truck's backward progress down the pier. Monte Balikovsky's explosive laugh startled the sleeping seagulls off the moorings and shook pigeons loose from the eaves of nearby dock buildings. "*Ha*! Good one, Johnnine!" Monte jumped off to direct the backing-up operation, gesturing into the side mirror so Sy could see him. The truck's rear tires bumped up against the huge, splintery old ship's timbers at the end of the pier. "*Whoa*!" Monte shouted, shooting his hand out.

The truck came to a stop with a loud mechanical exhalation. Monte hoisted himself back up onto the truck bed where he and Pahlser quickly started uncoiling flexible metal conduit connected to the ends of the cloud-buster's pipes.

Sy stood on the edge of the pier, pulling on thick workmen's gloves, and began feeding the cables from the truck into the inky, oily water of the Hudson River. They worked in the dim light from two small outdoor floods on metal poles at the end of the pier. Across the river, the lights of Jersey City, Hoboken, and Weehawken twinkled on the surface of the thick, black water.

Pahlser took his seat at the controls of the cloud-buster. With a look of proscribed pleasure, he maneuvered the battery of mounted pipes to point at the sky. "This'll do it. I can sense it, the atmosphere's very open to us tonight...no, Johnnine," he said as she started to climb up, "you need to stay off the truck. The energy near the buster's too strong for you to be around. It's almost too strong for us—"

Johnnine let herself off the side with easy, athletic movements and jumped onto the pier pouting.

"Go sit in the cab if you can't stay out of the way," Dinah added.

Sy kept slopping the half-dozen long lengths of cable into the river. They made a metallic slithering sound as they snaked over the edge of the dock. "A lot of DOR in the air tonight."

"As well as being hotter than hell—" Monte added.

"I can feel it on my skin," Dinah said.

"Yah, a clamminess," Monte said. "Almost hard to breathe."

"The buster will break it up." Pahlser was confident. "Once we get the rain it'll clear the air. Someone get the other binocs, they're in the locker under the seat. Dinah, you have the logbook?" The adults busied themselves with pre-assigned duties.

Johnnine stood off to one side of the truck, staring up at the reddish-black sky. It was a moonless night, the city's ambient light made the stars null and void. She gaped at a small pinprick of color as it headed straight for them, looming larger and larger. "UFO! It's a UFO!"

"What?!" Pahlser looked up. "Where??" A pair of binoculars hung from a strap around his neck.

Johnnine pointed excitedly. "There! Twelve o'clock!"

Dinah and Monte rushed to the edge of the truck bed, both holding a pair of binoculars. Sy's mouth dropped open and he let go of the cables.

"Dinah, make a note!" Pahlser said urgently from behind his binocs. "It's blue—no, now it's white—two o'clock, no wait, now eight o'clock. It's doing zigzags! Definitely not a normal flight pattern, couldn't be anything *but* a UFO—"

Johnnine scrambled up onto the back of the prohibited truck. "I want to see!" she whined. "I saw it first—"

Monte handed her his binoculars and showed her how to adjust them. "Move the little dial in the middle until it's in focus."

"Look!" Sy pointed. "It just came to a full stop, now it's just hanging there!"

Johnnine raised the binoculars to her eyes. At first in two distinct circles side by side, camera showed what Johnnine saw: the double image of a distant shimmering ovoid shape, pulsing with pale blue light. "I see it!" Johnnine cried. "It's beautiful, like a Christmas tree light!"

"If they're not giving us a friendly going-over, I'll eat my hat!" Pahlser said excitedly. "Reich says they know the work we're doing, they're trying to encourage us..."

"It's leaving!" Johnnine sounded bereft. "God, it moves so *fast*!"

With her eyes riveted on the sky, Dinah said "Don't say 'God,'" automatically. "I wonder if it's the same kind as the one we saw up country. The one that buzzed the car, remember?"

"I don't believe it!" Monte was bobbing and weaving with excitement. "This is the most fantastic thing I've ever seen in my life!"

"Ditto," Sy murmured, standing as still as a rock.

The throbbing, brilliant diamond-point of light streaked away at an incredible speed, vanishing over the Jersey palisades. Everyone was silent for a moment.

"Probably just the first of many sightings to come." Pahlser broke the spell as he began working the gears, re-positioning the pipes to point at the darkest clot in the night sky. "Good work, Johnnine. I think you should come with me when I go to Arizona to help Reich with the buster."

"But, Daniel," Dinah said pointedly, "she'll be in school."

"I'll talk to her teacher." Pahlser overrode her objection smoothly. "I think a trip to the desert is worth missing a few weeks of fourth grade—we'll talk about it later. We need to finish up here before the police get curious..."

Monte snorted. "Yah, there's probably a law against trying to clean up the atmosphere."

"Or if there isn't," Sy said, "they'll write one just for us..."

Johnnine looked up wonderingly, her expression bemused as she stared up at the sky from the back of the cloud-busting truck. "A UFO," she was saying softly to herself. "I finally saw a UFO—and they saw me!" Johnnine was the only one standing still as the grown-ups bustled around her and the scene faded.

In the All Souls' Waiting Room, Johnnine wondered if what she'd seen had been real or some sort of optical illusion. Then she remembered the other sighting. The LaSalle had been packed with babies and one or two adults on their way to Lake Belvedere for a swim. Dinah was driving, Johnnine sat behind her. They were on a straight stretch of road between two high, bare, treeless hills on either side. Johnnine recalled the landscape as unnaturally barren-looking. Normally there were trees, cows, or fields of crops everywhere up country.

From out of nowhere there was suddenly a huge shadow over the car, even though it was a sunny bright day and there were no clouds in the sky.

Dinah stuck her head out the window. "A UFO," she said in a strained voice. She slowed down but didn't stop the car. There was no other traffic on the road. "There's a UFO over us—dear God, what do I do?"

By the time Johnnine cranked down her window and put her head out, all she could see was the smooth silverish underbelly of what looked like an enormous airplane. It was so close overhead that she couldn't make out its outline. Then it took off down the road ahead of them—without a sound. It vanished completely in the space of time it takes to blink.

In the All Souls' Waiting Room, Johnnine defended her visions of flying saucers even though no one was challenging them. "I knew it was real," she said. "I didn't feel afraid, it was exciting, I felt like it was a sign of favor. I always hoped they'd come and take me away."

"Be careful about wanting deliverance from afar, darling."

"Why?" Johnnine asked belligerently.

"You just might get your wish..."

The next scene opened on Daniel Pahlser and nine-year old Johnnine coming out of a prop-engine passenger plane at Tucson municipal airport. Pahlser wore round, blackish-green sunglasses against the hard glare of the Arizona sun. Johnnine's light cotton dress was blown around by little dust devils that danced in off the surrounding desert.

They crossed the tarmac and entered the small terminal. Johnnine gravitated to a window display of turquoise and silver jewelry. Reluctantly, Pahlser let Johnnine lead him inside the small shop.

Cut to Pahlser and Johnnine in a cab heading down a wide, sun-blasted avenue. In the back seat, Johnnine held up her arm, admiring her shiny new silver thunderbird bracelet, while Pahlser peered out the window. The street was dotted with occasional palm trees, their shadows as wide as upside-down exclamation points. The sidewalks appeared to be moving, covered with runlets of large black beetles.

"What are those insects?" Pahlser asked the cabbie.

"Oh, just a harmless desert beetle. Don't do anything except make a mess when you step on 'em—"

"*EeeYUUWW*!" Johnnine exclaimed.

The cabbie grinned. "Don't usually get 'em this time of year," he continued. He had a leathery sunburned face and wore a greasy blue bandana around his neck. "...guess they're comin' up 'cause of a couple little cloudbursts we had the last few weeks. Water soaks into the ground where they live, forces 'em up outa their little holes."

"Rain isn't normal this time of year, is it?" Pahlser's attention was divided between scanning the scorched landscape and talking to the cabbie.

"Not in my memory. 'Course it's been so long since a good rain, can't nobody almost remember when..."

"What about these cloudbursts? Are they helping the drought any?"

"Nah, they don't count. Sorta like spittin' at a furnace."

The cab pulled up to a Southwest Car Rental lot. Pahlser got out to pay. Johnnine looked at the sidewalk before she put her foot down. Repelled by the three-inch, slow-crawling beetles, she let her legs dangle. "*EeeYUUWW*!" she cried.

Cut to later on the same day. Pahlser drove the rental car down a sandy road, past expensive private residential enclaves interspersed with stretches of unmanicured, low scrub desert. He turned off the car radio and slowed down as they approached a six-foot high, dark green wooden fence.

Pahlser drove through the open gate and parked the car in the driveway facing an ultra-modern, flat-roofed house. Its walls consisted of large sheets of unpaned, uncurtained plate glass. The dried-out fronds of several fifty-foot royal palm trees towering over the house clacked woodenly, disturbingly, in the slight breeze off the desert.

Pahlser got out and slid a shiny aluminum suitcase along the back seat, handling it very carefully. "You've got your comic books?"

Johnnine nodded.

"I want you to wait here while I see Dr. Reich."

"Can I listen to the radio?"

"Not now, I don't want to run the battery down."

Wilhelm Reich came out of the house wearing khaki chino pants under his short white lab coat. His thick white hair looked unbrushed, his demeanor was both hectic and calm, like a man keeping a tight rein on himself.

Ten-year-old Peter Reich, wearing a fancy red cowboy outfit with long white fringe on the shirt, hung back behind his father. Johnnine remained in the car. Peter stared at her.

"The trip was all right?" Reich asked Pahlser.

"Yah, fine, no trouble. I gathered from a cabdriver the people are noticing the unseasonal rains."

Reich frowned. "It's not enough yet. I need the Orur needle to make the cloud-buster more effective, it doesn't have enough of an orgonomic charge for conditions as bad as this—"

"Well, here it is." Pahlser smiled briefly, looking down at the briefcase.

"*Gut*. Come, I'll show you where we set up the buster. And a small lab. I've named this place Little Orgonon..."

Reich and Pahlser went off together around the side of the house. Peter stalked the car, hiding behind the base of one of the huge, fish-scaled palms. Johnnine silently watched him as he rushed the car, sticking his guns through the car's open window. "Bang-bang-bang-bang-BANG!!"

Johnnine flinched at the loud noise and shrank back against the car seat. Then she shouted at him, her fright making her angry. "Go away!" Peter stuck his tongue out at her and left. The scene went black.

Later that day, Johnnine sat in the front seat of the car in the circular asphalt court of the Desert Breeze Motel. She was staring at an hallucinatory Western sunset: layers of vivid chartreuse, orange, and red floated in the sky over the desert like a liqueur parfait of creme de menthe, curaçao, and grenadine. Gogi Grant's voice poured out of the car radio: *"And-the-wayward-wind, Is-a-restless-wind/A-restless-wind, that's-born-to-WAN-der..."*

Cut to that night, Johnnine coming out of the bathroom in her nightgown, her new turquoise bracelet banding her wrist. Pahlser, wearing eyeglasses and pajamas, was sitting up in one of the room's twin beds reading. He did not look up as she padded past.

Johnnine screamed as she pulled back the covers of her bed. "A beetle!!"

"They don't bite, Johnnine, they're harmless. Just brush it off."

Johnnine's arms jerked involuntarily against her chest in horror. "No!! You do it!"

Pahlser sighed as he got out of bed and crossed to Johnnine's side of the room. He brushed the beetle from between the sheets then he stepped on it with his slipper, making a noisy wet crunch.

Her face contorted with disgust. *"EeeYUUWW*! Why'd you kill it?"

"So it wouldn't get back under the covers with you." Pahlser crossed back to his bed. "Good night, Johnnine."

Johnnine jumped over the squashed beetle into her bed. Shuddering, she pulled up the covers. "Night, night. Don't let the bedbugs bite."

Johnnine closed her eyes. Camera panned over and held on Pahlser reading a slim paperbound volume titled "The Oranur Experiment, First Report 1947-1951," published by the Wilhelm Reich Foundation. Scene faded out.

In the All Souls' Waiting Room, Johnnine remembered her sense of overwhelming relief when Pahlser hadn't gotten into bed with her. She still didn't really know why he'd taken her to Arizona. To "make nice," make amends for his earlier sexual violation? Why hadn't he thought to tell her the script had changed half-way through, that he was now intent on making like a father? It didn't show in the Akashic film, but Johnnine remembered feeling enormously anxious around him, never sure if he was going to make her go through another 'session.'

She had never liked Pahlser. He was dour and humorless, condescending and distracted. Still, the film was jogging her memory about him, the time he took her to Macy's to buy her a cowgirl outfit like Peter's when they got back to New York. He was the one who taught her how to swim, how to ride a bike. Why did she feel so ungrateful? Hadn't he tried to win her love? Her mother had revered Pahlser for his therapeutic skills, the parents of the children he delivered practically worshipped him. Why, if he was so wonderful, did Johnnine's insides still shrivel when she thought of him?

Chapter Twenty-seven

"The most frequently-asked question of my childhood—"
"What was that, darling?" Xofia elegantly lit a Dark Star cigarillo.
"'Who are you mad at'?"
"And what did you frequently answer?" The Recorder got up to pour himself a cup of *kaffee* sans *schlag*. The cherubs flew down to polish off the Sachertorte. Seraph A. remained up on his perch, shifting position so he could recline.

Johnnine, uncharacteristically, did not feel like stuffing her face. "Nothing. I wasn't mad at anyone. And even if I were, I sure as hell wouldn't tell *them*—"

"Darling. We need to look at our definitions of the word mad...let's proceed—"

The LaSalle hearse's wipers hissed and smacked back and forth across the windshield. Rainy, dark streets of the Lower East Side showed as wet smudges through the windows. Pahlser was driving, Dinah was snoring gently in the front seat, Johnnine and Sandra Kriegen were in the back.

Sandra smoked a Pall Mall fiercely, tapping ashes into a little beanbag ashtray on her lap. Her hair was clean, her brow was smooth, her face more peaceful than it had been on the way up country. With one arm crooked over the back of the seat, she gently rocked Matthew, asleep in the bassinet just behind her. She didn't seem too "schizzy" anymore, Johnnine thought, whatever schizophrenic meant in the first place.

Johnnine sat next to her, reading with the help of a flashlight. "Finished!" she said triumphantly, closing the book on her lap.

"What'd you think?" Kriegen asked.

"I *loved* it—I love stories about Africa..."

"I'll get you a copy of '*She*'," Kriegen said. "I might even have a copy at home, if The Bastard didn't take it—it's a wonderful story, about an ancient white goddess who lives in this really desolate country in the middle of Africa—"

"There's a place in Africa I know I've been before," Johnnine said. "I can see it real clearly in my head, but it's not like from a book or movie or anything, it's somewhere I know, somewhere I used to live...it's really beautiful, the sky is kind of lavender? And there's this big giant tree, I think it's a baobab, sitting all alone in the middle of the veldt." Johnnine relished using her African nouns.

"Maybe it's a scene from a past life," Kriegen suggested.

"What's that?"

"Some people believe we reincarnate. They think that after we die we're born again in another body, for an entirely new life. In the East, most people don't believe there is such a thing as final, end-of-it-all death—"

"Wishful thinking," Pahlser said, eavesdropping from the front.

Kriegen shrugged. "Only one way to find out, after all—"

"Who else writes about Africa?" Johnnine was not interested in talk about dying.

"Ernest Hemingway, Robert Ruark—" Pahlser threw in.

Kriegen wrinkled her nose. "But they're boring! All they do is stalk animals and shoot at things." Her eyes lit up as she leaned towards Johnnine. "I'll get you somebody really *marvelous—Isak Dinesen...*" She spoke the name as if it had magic powers.

"Who's that?" Johnnine asked, ready to be enchanted. While at first it had been heavy sledding, she was liking Kriegen much more now that they had established the bond of books.

Kriegen's expression suddenly changed from one of animated interest to abject terror. "*Oh, God*!" She snapped to a ramrod-straight sitting position. "I just had a déjà-vu—" She looked around her with unseeing eyes. Her voice got louder. "I feel terrible, like there's something pressing down on me, a boulder pressing down on my chest." She began crying and anxiously biting the back of her hand at the same time. Then she fumbled for another cigarette.

Pahlser slowed down, checking her in the rear-view mirror. "It's all right, Kriegen. Lots of people have the same experience, it doesn't mean anything's wrong—" Even though his words were assuring, there was a crease across his forehead.

He glanced over at Dinah, who had been snoring soundly the whole while, then shook her arm. "Dinah, wake up. Dinah? We're almost at Kriegen's place—"

Groggily, Dinah roused herself and looked out of the car window. "Where are we?" She turned around at the sound of Kriegen's soft moans, then looked quickly at Pahlser.

"She's frightened, another déjà-vu..." Pahlser said in a low voice.

The street lamps on The Bowery could barely be seen through the steamed-up windows of the LaSalle. Winos in front of a bar, their heads ducked down into their collars, looked like a cluster of empty long coats in the foggy drizzle. A man's shape lurched off the curb, materializing in front of the headlights so quickly there was no time to stop. Kriegen screamed. There was a a soft, sickening impact as the man disappeared under the hood. Pahlser slammed on the brakes. Horns wailed around them, tires screeched, a cabbie rolled down his window to curse at them. The sound of Sandra's hysterical keening filled the hearse.

In the All Souls' Waiting Room, Johnnine only now remembered that night, the night the hearse had accidentally hit someone. Why was it in her film? She hadn't been responsible. Nor could she think, though it was a sorry episode, what lasting effect it had had on her.

"I think it's part of the larger picture, darling," Xofia answered uncannily, reading Johnnine's mind. "You did learn something —about the depths of human despair..."

A short while later, they were inside the large, square main room of the Bowery's police precinct. A line of wooden armchairs sat against the walls, which were thickly plastered and swirled. At the far end of the room was a raised platform with several desks behind a wrought-iron railing. Two plainclothes policemen sat behind the desks, a few uniformed patrolmen passed in and out. It was a slow night.

Kriegen clutched her son, who mewled from inside his cocoon of blankets. She looked around the police station with unnaturally bright eyes, dilated with terror. "I made it happen, it's my fault," she whispered repeatedly, shrinking against the back of her chair.

Pahlser squatted in front of her. "No, you didn't, you had nothing to do with it...Look at me, Kriegen—" He tried to maintain eye contact, but hers kept slipping away like wet marbles. Pahlser straightened up. "See if you can keep her focused," he told Dinah, who looked pale and terrified herself. Pahlser went somberly back to the front desk, where the desk sergeant handed him a cup of coffee.

"Don't get too worked up about it, doc," a Detective Mazzoli said matter-of-factly, sitting at a desk with a file folder in front of him. "Happens all the time. The bums get too drunk to see or care. They weave out into traffic and whammo. You got a morgue statistic."

Pahlser's face was ashen. "I couldn't stop until it was too late."

"You were probably doin' him a favor...sorry, but we gotta get you to fill out some forms—"

Dinah got up. "I think I'd rather wait outside—"

"Sorry, lady," the detective explained. "We gotta get statements from you, too. Coroner don't usually run inquests on this kinda case, but you gotta dot the i's and cross all the t's..."

Dinah sank back into the chair. "May I smoke?" Her voice was low and trembling.

"Sure, sure—" Mazzoli said affably. "Have some coffee, it'll help you relax. Dugan," he said to the uniformed sergeant, "where's your manners? Pour the ladies some java—" To Johnnine, he said, "Want a lollipop? We got some somewhere, we keep 'em around for lost kids—"

Johnnine shook her head. "No, thank you. I'm not lost."

Mazzoli smiled, kicking his leg back and forth as he sat on the edge of his desk. He glanced back and forth between Johnnine and Pahlser, the one face fair and blonde, the other Semitic. "Your daughter, doc?"

Johnnine was staring at the scrolled, wrought-iron light fixtures on the walls. They reminded her of Zorro.

The All Souls' Waiting Room

"No. My ward." Pahlser did not look up from the forms he was filling out. He had slipped his black bifocals on.

"Sure is an interesting car you drive." The detective wore a broad necktie, painted with palm trees, loose around an unbuttoned shirt collar. "Don't think I ever seen a body buggy painted green before—"

"No, probably not." Pahlser's did not match Mazzoli's chatty tone.

"Bet you get stopped by a lot of traffic cops, huh?" The detective was half-smiling.

Pahlser looked up, his face grave. "Lieutenant, please show me where to sign so we can leave. My patient urgently needs to get home." He nodded in Kriegen's direction. "This is very hard for her. The accident, being here, she considers herself in some way responsible—"

"Oh, sure, doc. She's a little—" The detective stood up, tilting his hand back and forth from the horizontal to the vertical plane. "—ain't she? Here, bottom line, right here..."

Pahlser and the detective huddled over the desk's blotter. Kriegen, Dinah, and Johnnine sat in a row like clay pigeons. Kriegen was white-faced and withdrawn. Dinah looked frozen, immobile. Johnnine surveyed the two men at the desk, where Pahlser, not the detective, seemed to be the man in charge, Mazzoli deferring to him not as a criminal but as a superior.

"...and humidity readings at Tucson Airport since I arrived have been higher than ever recorded...paragraph..."

Wilhelm Reich sat at his desk in the lab at Little Orgonon outside of Tucson, looking out the enormous plate glass window in front of him. The sun was just coming up, bathing the bare desert in a brilliant wash of orangey-gold. Reich looked intense and tired as he dictated into the Stenograph.

"...agent Wurton paid a visit from Washington. Eva told him I wouldn't see him, though I did later talk to the marshal, who is a very warm person, a genital character like Eisenhower, someone who is not afraid of his own emotions. The FDA is undoubtedly interested in the Orur material Pahlser brought down with him. They must know how close I am to breaking this drought. If I succeed, they would have to revoke the injunction...paragraph...

"The landscape continues to lose some of its more threatening DOR aspects the longer I am here. The cloud-buster is having some impact, but still I feel angry that it is not working faster...the 'expression' of the desert is the same as that of a severely-armored patient, cut off from full life expression. There are important parallels between the shutting down of life in any biological entity. We must, in this planetary emergency, find a way to save ourselves from orgonomically 'dead' rulers who kill everything around them with their own emotional deadness, their plague. These are the same rulers who explode deadly nuclear bombs, putting radioactivity into the atmosphere, and tell the people it's for their own good —while at the same time they persecute researchers into Life Energy, biological vigor, and orgasmic potency. Rulers and politicians do not want the masses to be free and self-governing, they would then be out of power...paragraph...

"...Pahlser is now my closest associate in the cause of orgonomy, doing cloud-busting work in New York City, treating patients, birthing children at home with the Hapgood woman. I feel he has lost the sharp destructive edge he had when I first met him. If he has some of the zealot in him, that is all right, the work channels and focuses it. He is the only one of my orgonomists without the demands of a family and so has made himself very useful...paragraph...

"Peter and Eva are growing closer, which does me much good to see after all the difficulties between me and Eva's mother. Eva is helpful in the lab and is thinking about a medical degree. Peter I take with me almost everywhere, he is the light of my heart. It is important he understand the urgency of my work and the fact that the CORE spaceships may be coming in greater and greater numbers in the near future. They are friendly towards us, probably because they have already harnessed orgone energy for their own purposes...paragraph...

"...I will close now until after the morning's work with the cloud-buster..."

On a brilliantly clear day in early January, alone in the empty LaSalle, Daniel Pahlser drove down a recently-plowed road leading out of Rangeley, Maine, towards Orgonon. Metal chains on the tires of the hearse bit into the heavily-salted, icy road under the chassis. All around him, the boughs of the tall evergreens were heavy with snow.

The hearse turned into Orgonon's sloping driveway, climbing slowly until Pahlser swung to the right and parked in front of the unoccupied student lab building. He took off his jacket and retrieved a pair of pliers and a Phillips screwdriver from the glove department. Then he got out and waded through the snow to the lab's door, packing down a rough path with his enormous black rubber galoshes.

A little while later, Pahlser emerged from the student lab, the sleeves of his flannel plaid shirt rolled up. He was carrying two flat side panels of orgone accumulators, about four by five feet, beige chipboard on the outside and plain wire mesh on the inside. Pahlser slid them into the back of the LaSalle, laying them down on a stack of half a dozen other panels. In the front passenger seat were two large open boxes of books, showing the name and logo of the Wilhelm Reich Foundation.

A blue sedan drove up, spraying snow. Nathan Katzman slammed the door and got out. "What are you doing here?" He looked suspicious as he checked inside the back of the hearse. "And what are you doing with those?"

Pahlser rolled down his sleeves, towering over the shorter, younger Katzman. "I needed a couple of accumulators. With everybody in Arizona, I decided to come up and get them myself. You can bill me later."

Katzman became very agitated, pulling his hands out of the pockets of his heavy overcoat, darting over to the back of the hearse. "You can't do that! What about the injunction?"

"I'm not named," Pahlser said, locking the rear door. "The injunction's against Reich and the Foundation, not Daniel Pahlser."

"But you're clearly defying the intent—"

"Katzman, take a deep breath. It's *two* accumulators. Two. The FDA's not going to bother us. How will they even know? We're not going to tell them, are we?"

Katzman frowned. "This is dangerous, you're courting trouble—"

Pahlser shrugged. "Life is dangerous. You have to be willing to take some risks..."

"Not foolish unnecessary ones!" Katzman's voice lashed out over the snowy yard. "What if Reich finds out?"

An odd smirk came over Pahlser's large features. "Who says he doesn't know about it?"

Katzman was taken aback for a moment. "I don't believe you. He wouldn't take such a chance—"

"Ask him yourself, then. If you don't mind implicating him, that is."

"This is destructive, Pahlser, I can feel it in my gut."

Pahlser's face turned red. "Well, feel this in your gut, too!" he said angrily, keeping his hands by his sides even as he leaned closer towards Katzman. "The government's out to destroy us! To ridicule and disparage Reich and his work and everything he stands for, us along with him! The plague has the upper hand—are you going to stand there and defend it?"

Katzman looked away, scowling.

The two men were at an impasse. "If you call Reich to tell him, that'll just tip them off, the phones are probably all tapped by now—that's why I didn't call," Pahlser added in a lower voice.

Katzman made an effort to calm himself. His voice took on a more placating tone. "Why now? What's the goddamned big rush?"

"I have patients who need them, that's the rush!" Pahlser said forcefully. He looked away and then back at Katzman. "I'm a doctor, Katzman. So are you. Are you going to keep me from healing my patients?"

Katzman jammed his hands back in his pockets without answering.

"Good," Pahlser said, getting into the La Salle. "Happy New Year, Katzman!" He slammed the door.

When Pahlser pulled into the No Parking zone in front of his apartment building late that night, Grove Street was deserted. He unloaded the accumulator panels from the back of the hearse and carried them into the building's hallway. But in a bar across the street, a man in a gray hat sat watching Pahlser's activities. Slowly, he paid for his drink and walked unhurriedly to the pay phone at the back, outside the door marked GENTS.

On a mild and sunny day in early April, the film showed a small hubbub of activity on Carmine Street, just opposite Dinah and Johnnine's apartment. The hearse was parked in front of a dusty storefront with large X's of masking tape across bare, grimy windows. A faded metal sign above the door named the former occupants as the Carmine Street Social Club. Pahlser stacked cartons of books onto a dolly and trundled them inside, where Dinah was organizing books on newly-assembled metal shelves. The entire space was floor-to-ceiling bookshelves, crates and cartons of books were everywhere. Monte Balikovsky and Sy Minnowitz put up the last few shelves on the back wall.

Pahlser edged the last several cartons off the dolly and looked around the jammed little storefront. "That's it," he said tiredly. "Twenty-seven thousand volumes..."

"Do you think there'll be much demand for the German editions?" Dinah asked, filling a shelf with new copies of *The Function of the Orgasm*. Then she laughed. "Assuming I could even read the orders—"

Pahlser smiled and sat down on an unopened crate. "I think we should collect all the accounts payable before we ship any out. Reich's badly strapped, the expenses in Arizona are much higher than he expected—"

"Expenses always are. Briggs' first law of finances, remember?" Dinah recited. "Everything costs twice as much to fix as you think it will and takes three times as long to finish as you expect it to. Missus. As Briggs would say—" She smiled at Pahlser. "Do we know how much money's outstanding?"

"I've got the account books in the front seat—" Pahlser got up and went out to the LaSalle. He came back with two ledgers and a card file and handed them to Dinah.

"*Stinking* of Cooke and the other orgonomists not to send Reich the rent money on the accumulators," Dinah fumed as she leafed through the first ledger, largely written in red ink.

"Cooke's afraid," Pahlser said contemptuously.

"Well thank God we're not!" Dinah said.

"Not I, Gunga Din!" Monte encouraged from the back.

Dinah shot him a scathing look. "Sometimes you have to put yourself out on a limb when you believe in something. How the hell do they think Reich can make it without any income? They know he's not seeing patients in Arizona, the cloud-busting's costly—"

Sy spoke up in his soft voice. "I think Cooke and his group are hoping lack of funds will force Reich to fight the injunction on constitutional grounds...didn't they offer to pay for the defense?"

"Reich won't do it their way!" Pahlser was irate. "It's a moral, scientific principle, not a dry legal issue!"

"We don't believe in the injunction!" Dinah seconded hotly. "Nor will I let the government stop us from distributing Reich's work!"

"Once you give in to the plague, you've lost everything," Pahlser said emphatically.

"Reich really doesn't know about this?" Sy asked, screwing the last two shelves together. "I mean you taking charge of the books and the billing?" He laid down his tools and picked up a dirty paper cup of coffee.

"No," Dinah said. "We saw a need and we decided to fill it."

"I've kept him purposely uninformed, so he couldn't be implicated—" Pahlser said.

Monte shifted a carton of books, lifting it off the dolly and transporting it to the rear of the improvised warehouse. "That's probably not the way the law's going to look at it..."

"What do you mean?" Dinah said testily.

"Technically speaking, I wonder if it even matters that Reich doesn't know. Violation of the injunction is violation of the injunction. I mean, the *intent* is to keep books and accumulators from being distributed. I don't know if they'll care who does the distributing ..."

"Whose side are you on?" Dinah challenged.

"It's not a question of sides, Hapgood, it's a question of not waving a red flag at a herd of bulls—"

Johnnine had been standing in the doorway for a few minutes, absorbing the conversation and staring at the piles of books all around the storeroom. Finally she addressed her mother. "It's Friday, Mom. Can I have my allowance?"

"Yah, but run across to Pops' and get me a pack of cigarettes—here." Dinah handed her some change.

"I gotta go," Monte said, picking up and dusting off his tan corduroy jacket. "Captain Kangaroo waits for no makeup man—"

Dinah watched him leave with narrowed eyes. On the sidewalk outside, he took Johnnine's hand as they crossed the street together. "I think he's getting plaguey," she said to Pahlser in a stagey whisper when he was out of earshot.

"Yah, could be," Pahlser said, opening a carton of books.

Johnnine came running back in a few minutes later. She handed Dinah a pack of Viceroys and unwrapped a cherry Tootsie Roll lollipop for herself. "There was a man at Pop's that looked like an agent," she said quasi-casually, trying to see if she would hit a nerve.

Pahlser looked up. "Why, what did he look like?"

Johnnine put the lollipop in her mouth, talking around it. "He's not Italian, he's got really short hair, he's wearing shiny black shoes and a seersucker suit."

Pahlser and Dinah exchanged a quick look.

Johnnine slurped on her lollipop. "Pop wanted to know what you were doing over here."

"It's none of his business." Dinah's voice was sharp. "What'd you say?"

"I told him you were all really big bookworms..."

Dinah burst into raucous, relieved laughter. "That's my kid!" She turned around to make sure Sy and Pahlser got the joke. "Bookworms!"

"Yeah, come over every hour and make us laugh, Johnnine, we could use it," Sy said.

"How much'll you pay me?" Johnnine quipped.

"I won't charge you for dinner," Dinah said, interrupting. "Now—" She handed Johnnine the two ledger books and card file. "I want you to take these upstairs—they're very important to us and to Dr. Reich, don't drop them."

"I *won't*," Johnnine said, annoyed.

"And keep that tone out of your voice."

Johnnine turned away from her mother, her mouth pressed into a tight line. She crossed the street and went up the shallow steps into their building carrying the books for the Wilhelm Reich Foundation.

Next door, a small, noisy clot of teenage boys pushed and shoved each other around in front of Rossetti's candy store. Pop Rossetti, stoop-shouldered and white-haired, swept the sidewalk while a man in a seersucker suit sat at the counter reading a paper over a Coke. All of them watched the installation of the Wilhelm Reich Foundation's new book depository with varying degrees of interest.

Johnnine trudged up the stairs to her apartment and opened the door to the front room. Lily Neary and Sandra Kriegen had joined hands with several of the older children in a circle. "Ring Around the Rosy," they chanted. Neary's theatrically-trained, resonant voice wafted clearly above the toddlers and pre-schoolers. "*Pocket-full-of-posies/Ashes-ashes-all-fall-DOWN!*"

The children giggled and collapsed on the floor in a happy heap. Johnnine laid the ledgers next to the phone, silently turned away, and went to her room.

In the All Souls' Waiting Room, Xofia got up out of her chair. The room lights came up as she waved her cigarette holder around dramatically. She looked as though she were doing a Bette Davis imitation. Or did Bette Davis imitate her, Johnnine wondered. "What would you say these last few scenes had in common, darling?"

"I don't know," Johnnine said in a low voice. "Except maybe scariness—" The wino's suicide, Reich's crazy talk in the desert, Pahlser breaking the injunction, then the scene in the bookstore, with Pahlser and her mother under government surveillance. "Everything started feeling really wrong, it was creepy...I remember I had a dream I was in a wooden barrel, heading for Niagara Falls." Johnnine looked down at her hands. "I could sort of hear the roar getting closer and closer but even though I didn't want to be there, the current just carried me along with it. When I stuck my head up out of my barrel, I could see everybody else bobbing around in flimsy wooden tubs, too—Reich, and Pahlser, my mother, even Peter Reich." Her expression was bleak as she looked at Xofia. "We all went over the edge together. Separately, but at the same time..."

"And what happened?"

"I don't remember, I guess I woke up."

"But so you felt powerless to affect your future," Xofia said with meaningful emphasis.

Johnnine nodded.

"How else did it make you feel?" The Recorder asked her.

"Mad," Johnnine whispered. "Mad as hell."

"That word again..." Xofia chimed. "It certainly seems to be part of your fate."

"Yeah." Johnnine turned her head away from them. "Like leaky wooden barrels." Her eye caught the figure of a small jade paperweight carved in the shape of a Chinese lion on Freud's desk.

Xofia wafted around The Couch. "The past is not the same thing as a script for the future. Think of yourself as the survivor of a shipwreck, darling. Some of your fellow travelers weren't so lucky."

Johnnine became irate. "What do you mean, survivor? I want to die!"

"Ah, but you're not dead yet—" Xofia tapped the copy of the "Egyptian Book of the Dead" on the table next to The Couch, cocked her head, and smiled brightly. In one awful moment, her looks changed from Bette Davis to Doris Day. "And I wouldn't bet on you getting your ticket."

No, probably not, Johnnine thought morosely. She hadn't grown up miserable enough, she needed to go back, to suck up more suffering.

Chapter Twenty-eight

"Willie," Schlomo said pointedly. He was sitting just behind Willie's large head in the All Souls' Waiting Room version of Demel's coffee shop. His former associate was still lying prone on the three chairs placed next to each other in poor imitation of a couch. "Think, Willie. For what crime did you need to be brought to trial?"

They had just reached the time of Willie's pre-trial hearing, in the summer of 1955. Schlomo had his work cut out for him, getting Willie to take an overview instead of getting tangled up in the literal traces of events. "You must shatter your old perceptions, your old illusions, so you can *think*—"

Willie was resistant. "But I *like* my old illusions!"

"*Ja*? And does the world need more blind men?" Schlomo asked rhetorically.

Willie became petulant and childish. "Why must *I* always be the sacrificial lamb? Why not you once in a while?"

"I have had my time on the chopping block. We each have our own destinies, Willie. At the moment we are dealing with yours."

Willie knew more than enough to recognize his own resistance, in spite of his great need for healing. He felt as though he were a parched plant in the desert, a saguaro cactus, bristling with spines. Hadn't he been one of the first—if not the only—to see the analogies between the aridness of the physical desert and the emotional desert in armored man, the thorns and spikes of the desert plants representing the prickly outer behavior of armored human beings? The desert at first "defied" his cloud-busting treatment, "resisting" his prescription of rain. Many patients reacted to therapy in the same way. Himself included as it turned out. "I seem to be in a state of psychic paralysis," he finally said through clenched teeth.

"Close your eyes and take a deep breath...we will try and see that the pain is minimal," Schlomo said sympathetically.

"You always were a terrible dissembler, Herr Professor." Willie's jaw muscles felt as though they were considering locking up forever.

"When are we going to get there?" Johnnine's tone was peevish. Crammed in the back seat with Dinah and Lily Neary, she looked disheveled and bleary-eyed, as did everyone else. The LaSalle hearse was stuffed with people and travel paraphernalia.

"We're just on the outskirts of Portland," Balikovsky said as they entered a neat New England town and passed a small white-steepled church. There was no humor in his voice.

The grownups were unusually tense and apprehensive, tired from the overnight drive from Manhattan. Even Phil Berman, who had been stretched out in the back, had none of his usual good cheer when he sat up to yawn and stretch. "Christ, I feel like a bag of dirty laundry."

"Where's the courthouse?" Lily Neary asked, rubbing her eyes. "Do we have time to stop for coffee?"

"We're early, and I need something stronger than coffee," Dinah said. "Turn left up here at the light." Her demeanor was grim.

The wide, small-town streets of Portland were almost empty in the early morning as the hearse pulled up in front of the Federal Courthouse. There was no one about. Johnnine and the others stared at the white painted facade. The courthouse's stately Doric columns, made of wood instead of marble, implied that within its walls citizens would find the impartiality of ancient Greek justice tempered with the tolerance of the American backwoods.

Dinah spotted a bar across the street. "Anyone else for an eye-opener?"

"God, yes..." Balikovsky said. "I need some tomato juice with my tomato juice—" It was an old W. C. Fields line, but no one laughed.

The deshabille group piled out of the LaSalle, following Dinah across the street and through the creaking door of the Dew Drop Inn like troops following their platoon leader.

Later, Johnnine and her mother's group filed into the sparsely-occupied, lofty-ceilinged main courtroom. They sat as close as they could behind the defense table, rows of empty, highly-polished oak bench seats stretching out behind them.

Daniel Pahlser and Wilhelm Reich stood in front of the high judge's desk, facing the black-robed judge. Though Reich was shorter and stockier than Pahlser, the two men looked alike from the rear. Both had silvery heads of hair, both wore corduroy jackets with elbow patches, Reich's hunter green, Pahlser's burgundy.

In the All Souls' Waiting Room, Johnnine relived her feeling that this was where all the wooden barrels had ended up, smashed beyond recognition after hurtling over the waterfall. And that there was something terribly, unimaginably wrong about them being there, a waking nightmare.

The judge, white-haired and spectacled, addressed them in a level tone. "Dr. Daniel Pahlser. Dr. Wilhelm Reich. You have both been charged with criminal contempt of court. How do you each plead?"

"Not guilty," Daniel Pahlser said distinctly.

Reich's voice was firm and steady. "Not guilty, your Honor. May I now speak?"

The judge nodded and removed his glasses. Reich turned around to face the courtroom. Pahlser returned to the defense table, his face burning from a smouldering inner fire.

Reich spoke simply and movingly, without notes. He was relaxed and at ease, an excellent and practiced extemporaneous speaker. His small band of supporters looked strained and riveted at the same time. "I wish to make it clear that it is factually impossible to plead either guilt or lack of guilt. The demands of the injunction are impossible to fill. My books on orgone energy, as well as the orgone accumulator, are out in the world. I could not get them back even if I wanted to, my work is in the hands of people all over the world. You cannot order the stop of ideas once they have begun to spread...

"No matter what the court or the FDA does to me, if they put me in jail, or chain me, or fine me, I will never permit them to pass judgment on the validity of orgone energy or the accumulator. The court cannot say whether the universe is empty or full of orgone. When and if that happened, the United States would have become like an Iron Curtain country.

"I want now to propose a 'Board of Social Pathology' to examine my whole case on an educational and medical level. And I would like to take up some of the many lies of the Food and Drug Administration by saying that they—"

The judge interrupted Reich, not unkindly. "Dr. Reich, if you had wanted to refute the evidential findings against you, the time and place to do so was at the original hearing. We can't take up these matters now."

"But I could not appear then!" Reich twisted around to appeal to the judge face-to-face. "I would have felt smothered! I had to collect my evidence, put my case together. I have it now—"

The judge shook his head. "I'm sorry, Dr. Reich. It's too late."

"But the Board of Social Pathology," Reich continued, confused. "It's wrong to label people criminals when that is merely the symptom, not the cause of the problem. People turn to crime for deep emotional and economic reasons, things society can help to change—"

The judge shook his head again, more decisively. "I can't rule on such a proposal. It's out of the court's purview."

Reich's voice took on a pleading tone. "You mean there is no opportunity to talk about the FDA's persecution of me or the discovery of the orgone?"

"There is not," the Judge said clearly. "We are here strictly to decide if you and/or Dr. Pahlser wilfully defied the court order against interstate commerce of the orgone accumulator—I also must rule in favor of the Food and Drug Administration and order the Wilhelm Reich Foundation to turn over its records for examination."

Reich glanced at his lawyer, who remained motionless. Their eyes locked, as if they had discussed this eventuality beforehand. Reich's words sounded rehearsed. "I am not sure I can obey, your Honor. There are issues of conscience involved."

"This is a direct order of the court, Dr. Reich."

"I understand, your Honor," Reich said graciously, nodding and looking back up at the judge. He had fully regained his composure. "But if I comply, I want it noted that I do not take any responsibility for the outcome."

The judge nodded. "I will take full responsibility," he said gently, civilly. He banged his gavel. "The verdict of the court is that Daniel Pahlser and Wilhelm Reich shall stand trial for criminal contempt at a date to be determined. Court is adjourned until 9:00 tomorrow morning."

Reich walked buoyantly back to the defense table. "Never mind," he said cheerfully. "We will find a way of showing how the FDA distorted their facts—no one can suppress the energy of truth. The Red Fascists will not win without a fight!" Reich raised a hand in a rallying gesture. "You will see, the President will come to our aid..." Reich smiled confidently.

Frightened and confused, Johnnine looked sideways at her mother, whose heavy face was full of foreboding. Her mother did not meet her glance. Berman, Balikovsky, Neary and Sandra Kriegen looked depressed, or scared, or both. Reich's supporters seemed to avoid eye contact, as if it were too charged, too painful. The scene faded to black.

Johnnine remembered the doomed atmosphere of that cold courtroom, the chilling way Reich had seemed happy to be in the jaws of the dragon.

"Poor darling," Xofia murmured in the momentary dark between scenes. She sighed sadly. "He sent his mind out to play, things just got too dismal for him..."

"A commonly-used exit," The Recorder agreed. "All souls can become madmen, murderers, or martyrs—as well as saints and saviors—it only requires the appropriate pressure at the inappropriate moment..."

"What are you saying?" Johnnine felt her loyalty challenged. But then, who was she supposed to be loyal to? A crazy Reich or a crazy government?

"Oh, you know us, darling, we're just driveling on. Forgive us our penchant for esoterica...continue!" Xofia snapped her fingers. The film flared up.

On the lawn in front of the farmhouse, Dinah sat on a low stool spooning baby food into the mouths of several toddlers who buzzed around her like baby bees, their mouths open, sagging diapers hanging below their rounded bellies.

Johnnine moped out of the house. She sat on the swing hanging from the huge old maple tree that shaded half the front yard. "My record player's broken, I've read all my books a million times, there's nobody to play with. It's boring up here."

"Only boring people are ever bored," Dinah said automatically, a saying Johnnine had heard before. "I've never been bored, there are too many things I'm interested in—what about my Agatha Christies?"

"I read them. And your Ngaio Marsh, and all the Reader's Digest Condensed books..."

"Where's the Polaroid Berman gave you?"

"No more film." Johnnine flashed a wicked little grin. Her mother hated having her picture taken.

"Well thank God for small favors—"

"I finished the jigsaw puzzle, except there's still two pieces missing out of the mast. Taffy probably ate them."

Dinah scooped baby food from the chin of an inattentive eater. "Then take a walk to town, I'll give you a dime."

"God," Johnnine exhaled wearily, "two miles for a Fudgsicle."

"Gosh, Johnnine, not God—" Dinah wiped a baby's face, not looking at Johnnine as she spoke.

"You say God."

"I do not. Go on, bring me my purse."

Johnnine dragged herself off the swing. "The Brewster kids will chase me again."

"No they won't. I talked to the mother."

"Yah, but maybe Mr. Brewster beat her up again and she's back in the hospital, and then the kids will be even worse—"

"Go get my purse!" Dinah yelled, making the babies around her jump and blink. "And stop whining, for Christ's sake!"

Johnnine ambled idly towards town, picking wild honeysuckle by the side of the hilly dirt road. She stopped to suck the sweet blossoms, holding the stems as though they were lollipops. Above the metallic background chorus of cicadas, the flute-like birdsong of sparrows and red-winged blackbirds punctuated the throbbing summer air.

From over the crest of the hill came the sound of a galloping horse and rider. Johnnine's eyes grew rounder when she saw that it was Peggy Brewster and her horse, Geronimo. Peggy had a pushed-in face and a nasty disposition. Geronimo was Roman-nosed and wall-eyed, his face and eyelashes as white as bone. Mr. Briggs said Peggy and her horse were a match made in Hell.

Peggy cantered Geronimo recklessly down the hill, her long, thick brown braids flying out from the sides of her head like undulating snakes. She let out a war cry and goaded her horse even faster when she saw Johnnine by the side of the road. "AhhEEEahh!" she yelled.

Johnnine stood transfixed as Peggy rode straight at her, Geronimo's white-and-tan hide steaming in the August heat. Johnnine looked around frantically for an escape route. There was none. She started a bolt for home, but was quickly overtaken by the horse's ground-eating gallop. Johnnine jumped into the ditch next to the road. She tumbled down a steep bank, rolling through some brambles, and landed at the bottom in a foot of sludgy ditch water.

She sat up and surveyed her torn shirt and scratched and muddy limbs. Crying with fear, anger and frustration, she stopped sniffling when she looked up at the top of the ditch.

Peggy Brewster leered down at her from Geronimo's back, looking victorious, as well as four stories tall. "I'm taking you prisoner," she said with satisfaction.

Johnnine was close-marched into a decrepit old barn. Three younger children flanked Johnnine while Peggy, the oldest, brought up the rear. Johnnine stopped at the bottom of a narrow, dangerous-looking flight of stairs leading to the barn's second floor. "I'm not going up there."

"Oh, yes, you are," Peggy crowed. "You'll do whatever we want you to do—" Peggy poked her whittled riding crop into Johnnine's back. At the next to last step, Johnnine could see into the dark, cobwebbed recesses of the empty old hay barn. She hesitated. Peggy hit her on the shoulder with her switch.

"OWWW!" Johnnine cried. "Don't hit me, goddamit!"

"Get some baling wire," Peggy commanded her younger siblings. They scurried off and returned a moment later with loops of rusted wire.

"You're goin' in here," Peggy said, shoving Johnnine into a small room with half its floorboards rotted away. "We're goin' to tie you up and leave you while we get the matches and kerosene. Then we're gonna set the barn on fire—"

Johnnine shot Peggy a terrified look, then quickly covered her fear as the others bound her wrists and ankles with baling wire. "You wouldn't dare. Your father would kill you." She pulled at her constraints.

"I'll tell him you did it," Peggy grinned. "He hates all you goddam fancy New Yorkers as much as we do." She smiled crazily, cunningly. "You'll be roasted alive in half an hour—" Peggy turned on her heels and slammed the door behind her so hard it almost fell off its hinges.

Johnnine listened to the Brewster tribe descend the stairs, whooping and shouting, pretending to be Indians on the war path. Haltingly, she dragged herself across the splintery floor to the edge of the broken floorboards and peered down. Under her was the old dairy, unused milking stalls and mounds of mucky straw filling the concrete manure runoff channels. Johnnine began untwisting the wire from around her ankles. Grunting and crying, she soon kicked her legs free, bringing her feet down sharply on the weakened flooring. There was a loud crack as Johnnine fell through the ceiling.

Half an hour later Johnnine ran into her front yard looking like an escaped convict. Her clothes were torn and soiled, her hair was matted with straw, her eyes were wild as she looked back down the road, fearful of pursuers. "The goddam stupid Brewster kids tried to KILL me!"

Dinah lay in a canvas hammock, a highball in one hand, a paperback in the other. She did not look up from her book. "Don't swear, Johnnine, and don't exaggerate, you're like the little boy who cried wolf—and *don't* slam the door when you go in, I just got all the kids down for a nap. Why don't you take one, too?" Dinah yawned. "Afternoons are so peaceful up here..."

In the All Souls' Waiting Room, Johnnine's voice burst out of the darkness. "So far you guys aren't doing a goddamn *thing* to change my mind about dying—"

Paki S. Wright

"We're not trying to change your mind for you. You're the one who has to do that—" Xofia answered tartly.

"What? Are you seeing the same film I am?" Johnnine demanded.

"Yes. And I have to tell you I've seen many worse. What happened to Peggy Brewster?"

Johnnine lost some of her self-righteous ire. She looked away in embarrassment. The last time she'd seen Peggy had been at the A & P in Cherry Valley, a baby in her arms and another one on the way, rumor had it they were her father's. Peggy had put her hand over her mouth to hide the fact that she'd lost most of her teeth. Tears glistened in Johnnine's eyes. "Why are people always so horrible to each other?" she cried softly.

"They're not, and you are not a helpless victim of fate," Xofia admonished.

"Then why does it *feel* that way?"

"Because that's how you're looking at it," The Recorder said maddeningly, refusing to soften Johnnine's despair. "We'd like you to start noticing what doesn't happen to you..."

"What do you mean?" Johnnine asked guardedly.

"You do have a lucky star, darling, you just haven't recognized it yet. For instance, the barn didn't burn down around you, did it?"

"No—" Johnnine admitted. "—but that was just because they couldn't find any matches."

"Johnnine." The Recorder's voice was stern. "Watch the film."

"...and you are willing to be orgonomy's caretaker when I am gone?" Reich looked Edgar Cooke deeply in the eyes as he handed him a sheaf of papers. They were standing in the well-appointed bedroom of a residential hotel. Reich looked strikingly, robustly handsome but also elegiac in a black tuxedo. From the adjoining sitting room came sounds of festive Christmas music and a subdued party.

"With great pleasure and honor, Dr. Reich," Cooke said.

Reich gave a small smile. "Good. I have one other request." He looked towards the door and then back at Cooke. "Will you, would you supervise the construction of my tomb? I have picked the spot I would like to be buried in. There is no one else I want to ask. My family would be too sad."

Cooke looked down for a moment before he swallowed and nodded, raising his pale hazel eyes to Reich's, black and lustrous as coal.

Reich smiled and put his hand on Cooke's shoulder. "Thank you for this, I feel easier. Now let us enjoy what we are fortunate to have—"

Reich crossed the room and opened the door. The tune of "Adeste Fideles" was playing on a radio in the next room, where a small group of people were decorating a Scotch pine. Eleven-year old Peter held up an ornament. "Papa, where should I put the herald angel?"

The All Souls' Waiting Room

"On the top, liebling," Reich smiled warmly.

"That's what I thought. But why?"

"Because angels are supposed to be closest to God..."

Reich poured himself a drink and watched his handsome brown-haired son hang the angel. A young woman in a red chiffon dress turned her head to smile at Reich. Reich's returning smile was full of tenderness and sorrow.

On a blustery West Fourth Street in Greenwich Village, Dinah and Johnnine clutched their coats around them as they descended several steps into a garden-level Chinese restaurant, bereft of other customers. The radio blared a loud and brassy rendition of "O Come All Ye Faithful." Long Low, the proprietor, hurried out from behind the cash register to smile at them. "Melly Clissmis! Suplise to see you today!"

"Merry Christmas to you, Mr. Long," Dinah said formally in her deep voice. "Our usual table, please?"

"Shew ting—no one else today, that for shew."

Dinah and Johnnine moved into the back room, its low ceiling gridded with wooden lattice and hung with colorful paper lanterns. Fake palm fronds added to the room's exotic, unseasonal look. Johnnine and her mother slid into a high-backed wooden booth enameled an eye-popping orangey-red.

"I want egg foo yong—" Johnnine chirped.

Dinah smiled at Long Low as though she were a society hostess ordering for her entourage. "The usual, please, Mr. Long. Egg foo yong, shrimp in lobster sauce, a glass of milk and a double Manhattan—"

"Shew ting," he said, nodding assiduously. To Johnnine, he said, "So, you see Santa Craws yet?"

"I don't believe in Santa Claus," Johnnine said in a stilted, unnatural voice. "Or Christmas, for that matter. It's too commercial."

Dinah smiled proudly at her progeny.

Long Low raised his eyebrows. "Oh!" he said. "So, you want side ordeh spalelibs?"

Chapter Twenty-nine

"So just tell about the trial. In brief," Schlomo directed. He took his unlit cigar out of his mouth.

Willie stared up at the cherubs, who, after a protracted *apfelstrudel* binge in the ethereal Viennese coffee shop, had been dozing through much of his life story. His sigh was a wracked one. "Pahlser and I were arrested the day before and put in jail overnight. We were brought into the courtroom in handcuffs—"

"Why was that?"

Willie scowled. "There was a...a mix-up about the court date."

"What kind of mix-up?"

Willie shrugged. "We weren't there, the judge issued a warrant for our arrest."

"And why weren't you there?"

Willie's black eyes caught fire. "I received a notification of the date from the court clerk and I wrote back that I expected it to be signed by the judge, not a clerk."

"Wasn't that a matter for your lawyers?"

"*Nein*! It was a direct slap in my face!"

"What happened?"

"I didn't receive an answer from the court, so I assumed the date had been postponed. Except that they came to arrest me in Washington, at the hotel where I was staying. Pahlser they got in New York."

"So whose mix-up was it?"

"Theirs. Well, no, perhaps it was ours—*ach was*, what does it matter? My prediction about being brought to trial in chains came true!"

Schlomo arched an eyebrow as he made a note: 'Exactly as he himself predicted, i.e., self-fulfilling prophecy.' "And then what happened?"

Willie closed his eyes, as if remembering things too painful to be borne. "The prosecution and the FDA painted me as a criminal, implying I was a racketeer siphoning money from deluded patients." His eyes flew open. "This, when I spent $350,000 of my own money to fund orgone research!"

"That must have made you very angry," Schlomo said deliberately.

Willie tossed and turned on the improvised couch but did not rise to the bait. Instead he sighed heavily, lacing his hands together on his barrel-shaped chest. "They would have come after me on some phony charge or other. I do not click my heels and salute the prevailing political order. Therefore I was someone they needed to annihilate..."

Schlomo decided not to take issue with Willie's raging paranoia for the moment. "And the verdict?"

Air whooshed out of Willie's mouth, filling out his round, ruddy cheeks. "Our licenses to practice medicine were revoked. I was sentenced to two years in a Federal penitentiary. Pahlser got one year."

Schlomo was shocked. "Prison?! *Mein Gott*, Willie!"

Willie's face became animated as he struggled with his emotions. "They ordered my books destroyed—all the books of the Wilhelm Reich Foundation that were in stock."

Schlomo recalled hearing how the Nazis burned *his* books in Vienna, after he'd made his escape to London. "But you were in America!"

Willie was impatient, almost scornful. "Don't be naive, Herr Professor. Authoritarianism exists in every country, only in different degrees," he said darkly. "I discovered what fosters it—patriarchal family structures, devaluing of women, repression of childhood sexuality. Now what the world must learn is how to unlearn. I did what I could to show them the way."

Schlomo felt sympathy for him, this was one area in which there was no need for debate. "*Ja*. So, enough *mit die* politics," Schlomo said genially. He relit his cigar, exhaling a small cloud of ethereal smoke. "Here we can cut through the rigmarole and go straight to the heart of the matter." He cleared his throat. "Willie. Why did you provoke this trial, this verdict?"

"I did not provoke it!" Willie argued.

"Of course you did," Schlomo said heatedly. Wonderful, he thought, to forego the pretense of detachment. "You violated their laws, you gave them no choice but to lock you up, make you a martyr. So I am asking: for what crime did you really want to be punished?"

"I don't understand—" Willie sounded desperate.

Schlomo took the cigar out of his mouth. "Pretend this is not your case, Willie, but that we are talking about a patient of yours."

Willie was quiet for a moment. "Oh, I see," he said slowly. "*Zu dumm*, too stupid. Of course—" He turned his head away. "There must be a stiff penalty for murder..." His voice was almost inaudible.

"Whose murder, Willie?" Schlomo asked gently.

Willie's eyes fell on the cherubs Ti and Do, who were sitting up and fully attentive, as they always were when a soul faced itself squarely.

"The murder of my parents."

"And how do you believe you murdered them?"

"I—I told my father about Mama's affair with my tutor. She killed herself. Papa could not stand his grief—" His tone was full of feeling, but not morbid.

"And what did your Papa do?" Schlomo prompted. Now they were getting somewhere.

"He stood in a pond up to his knees in water, fishing all night in a rainstorm..." One of Willie's hands fingered a button on his lab coat. "He caught what he wanted, a cold that turned into pneumonia."

There was a momentary pause.

"*Gut*, Willie. Let us finish with this sad business." Schlomo took his handkerchief out of his pocket and dabbed at his brow. Then he set about mopping up the remains of Willie's guilt and remorse. It had been a belatedly successful, ethereal analysis.

"Thank you for your time." The tow-headed young prison psychiatrist, William Meadowbrook, was deferential to the famous older psychoanalyst. "Is there anything you need, Dr. Reich?" he asked politely.

A subdued Wilhelm Reich sat on the other side of Meadowbrook's desk in prison dungarees and a blue chambray shirt. "Some Vaseline, please, for my skin, an old eczema problem has erupted again." Reich touched his inflamed cheek. "You see, my mind almost accepts my situation, but my body rebels..."

Bill Meadowbrook made a note and stood up. "I'll see to it right away." He extended his hand. "It's been a pleasure, Dr. Reich. And an honor to meet you—"

Reich's smile was one of sad amusement as he firmly returned Meadowbrook's handshake. "Maybe we could talk sometime, in my cell? I am writing an important new book, but a little honest, intelligent conversation would be a welcome diversion occasionally. There is really no one here for me to talk to."

A frown crossed Meadowbrook's smooth face. "I'm afraid the regulations wouldn't permit it."

"Oh." Reich looked disappointed.

"But perhaps if you wouldn't mind coming here, to my office—"

Reich smiled brightly. "I will check my engagement calendar."

Meadowbrook smiled back and pressed a buzzer on his desk. A guard stepped into the office. "You can take Dr. Reich back to his cell now."

The guard nodded. Reich passed out of the room. Meadowbrook tore several pieces of lined yellow paper from a pad and stuffed them in a file folder. He pressed the intercom. "Sarah, please tell the warden I'm on my way."

Meadowbrook left his office and walked down the hall, knocking on a door at the very end.

"Come in, Bill!" Warden Manning Keaters sat behind a large old-fashioned desk with a well-used leather blotter on top. He was going through files, crumpling letters and throwing them in the wastepaper basket. He had a powerful, rectangular face which contrasted with thick, owlish eyeglasses and dry, thinning sandy hair. "A little housecleaning. Sit, sit."

Meadowbrook took one of the two leather chairs facing the warden's desk. "I just finished with Dr. Reich."

"Good! Type anything up yet?"

"No, you said you wanted to see me first."

The All Souls' Waiting Room

Keaters arched an eyebrow and shot a glance at him. "What conclusion you come to?"

Meadowbrook gave a wry, puzzled smile, as if being asked a simplistic question. He crossed his legs and looked down at his shoes for a moment. "He has a very complex, extremely multi-faceted personality. I felt a little over my head, to tell the truth. Doing a psychiatric examination of Wilhelm Reich—" He shook his head.

Keaters looked at him intently. "You read his books in college?"

"Several. I thought they were brilliant."

"Yeah? Strikes me as a class A loony—all this orgone business."

Meadowbrook fingered the arm of his chair. "I don't think you can dismiss him that easily. He's incredibly insightful, a societal observer who happens to be fifty years ahead of his time—"

"Yeah, I've heard that one before," Keaters said, continuing to clean out his desk. He gave Meadowbrook a dazzling smile. "So what were your findings? What are you going to say in your report?"

"My diagnosis is fairly straightforward." Meadowbrook opened his file and read from his notes. "Paranoia manifested by delusions of grandiosity and persecution. Personality largely intact but enough psychotic thinking to warrant hospital observation. In my view he is clearly, both from a legal and from a psychiatric standpoint, mentally ill. I don't believe Dr. Reich should stand convicted of a criminal charge. Personally, I think a lot of his bizarre ideation is due to the vilification he's gotten, not uncommon with pioneers, in any field."

"Now, Bill, don't let's get carried away." The warden held a manila file folder in his hands. "Just because you studied him in school doesn't mean he's some kind of sacrosanct institution or anything. The guy's a menace to society. And the government doesn't want the case reopened on any grounds, insanity or otherwise. He's where we want him, we don't want to go messing around—"

"What do you mean?" Meadowbrook sat up straight in his chair and uncrossed his legs. "Who exactly in the government?"

Keaters leaned back and smiled. "Never you mind," he said knowingly, tapping the desk with the edge of his folder. "Certain interested parties high up just think it would be demeaning to his reputation—"

"Demeaning?" Meadowbrook blurted out. "After he's been imprisoned? How much more demeaned can he be? Or are they thinking about the embarrassment of criminally convicting a man who's legally insane?"

Keaters' face quickly became hard and stony as he stared across his desk at the idealistic young doctor. He turned the file folder he was holding sideways and slowly tore it in half. "What I'm saying, Dr. Meadowbrook, is that as far as the government's concerned, this case is *closed*. And I wouldn't go rocking any boats if I were you."

Bill Meadowbrook's features flushed with anger as he got up from his chair. "I'll keep it under advisement." The scene faded.

In the All Souls' Waiting Room, Johnnine felt confused. Had Reich been crazy with his Red Fascist conspiracies—or were there in fact grounds for his wild contentions? She realized she would probably never know. Then she thought of the old joke, Just because I'm paranoid doesn't mean there isn't somebody out to get me.

In her sixth-grade P. S. 8 classroom, eleven-year old Johnnine took her seat with the other children, settling in for the morning's lessons. Mrs. Muldoon, her stout middle-aged teacher, wore an ankle-grazing blue flowered silk dress with a tatted lace collar and matronly black leather shoes, her shape roughly that of a pouter pigeon. She was stern and imposing but not always successful at hiding her fierce affection for the children.

"Please hurry, class," Mrs. Muldoon said in a high but raspy voice, as she stood in front of the blackboard. Her hands rested on her hips, but they tapped impatiently. Her lips compressed like a coin purse as latecomers opened and shut their desk tops. "We have good news this morning! One of us has won a prize!"

The children looked around at each other. Johnnine put a newly-sharpened pencil in the carved-out slot on her small wooden desk.

Mrs. Muldoon shook a letter she was holding importantly, making the paper crackle. "This is a letter from the Managing Editor of the *New York Herald Tribune*." She puffed out her rounded chest and looked inordinately pleased, her small blue eyes twinkling behind her steel-frame glasses as she read. "'Dear Mrs. Muldoon: Please offer our congratulations to your student, Johnnine Hapgood, for her essay on Current Events, which has won First Prize among sixth-graders in our city-wide contest. She, along with the other winners in the four other categories, World History, U. S. Government, Civic Pride, and Poetry, will read their prize-winning essays on a special broadcast of WNYC radio this summer. We are enclosing, in a special cardboard binding, an advance typeset copy of Johnnine's essay on last fall's invasion of Hungary. This piece, along with the other winners, will be printed in this Friday's edition of the *Tribune*, which believes in helping children understand the world they live in. Yours very sincerely,' *et cetera*."

Mrs. Muldoon beamed at Johnnine, whose cheeks had turned the color of cooked beets. "Isn't it lovely?" she said, holding up a brown speckled folder with a gold star on it, opening it to show the small newspaper article pasted inside. "Congratulations, Johnnine! Say congratulations, class. Just imagine, some time this summer we'll all be listening to our classmate on the radio!"

Johnnine looked at her proud and well-meaning teacher with abject terror. She seemed to be trying to hide as she swung her head and plastered long strands of dark blonde hair against the sides of her face, like blinkers on a horse.

In the All Souls' Waiting Room, Johnnine could practically feel the tingling nervous sensations again, her keen pleasure at winning the prize, followed by paralyzing stage-fright at the thought of talking on the radio. "Another perfect example of how things work on Earth," Johnnine said out loud. "No good stuff without something totally terrifying thrown in."

A large dump truck backed down the Gansevoort Pier in lower Manhattan, its open rear bed piled high with cartons of books published by the Wilhelm Reich Foundation. His light summer shirt blowing in the hot, humid breeze, Phil Berman rode shotgun, hanging onto the sides. Inside the cab, Seymour Minnowitz was driving. Next to him sat Dinah and Monte Balikovsky, their faces blank, sick-looking, and damp with perspiration.

At the end of the pier, Doctors Katzman and Tripp stood over a small hillock of books that had been unloaded earlier as the truck backed down the pier towards them for the second time that day. Next to them stood two business-suited Federal agents and two New York City sanitary engineers in dirty white overalls. One of the agents spoke to Dinah as she got out of the truck. "Is that all of them?"

Dinah nodded miserably, not looking at him. "The storeroom is empty."

"Okay!" the agent shouted. "Let 'er go!"

Inside the cab, Balikovsky angrily pulled a lever which slowly raised one end of the truck bed. The truckload of books slid in a disorderly rush onto the pier.

"Let's get going," the second agent said, nodding at the sanitary men. They moved off towards the huge open steel doors of a concrete-encased incinerator on the side of the pier. "Human chain, come on."

Nathan Katzman, William Tripp, Phil Berman, Sy Minnowitz, and Monte Balikovsky formed a grim-faced line between the mound of books and the mouth of the roaring incinerator, passing the cartons of books from one to the next. Dinah and the agents watched as one of the city garbage men dumped the cartons upside down while the other shoveled the loose books that fell onto the pier into the flames.

Two hours later, the last carton of books was sent along the line of Reich's analysts and followers. They were sooty and soaked with sweat, physically and psychically exhausted, especially Nathan Katzman, who spoke angrily to the agents as he turned to leave. "Do you have any idea of the importance of the six tons of books we just destroyed?"

One of the agents took a toothpick out of his mouth to answer. "Look, we're just doing our jobs..."

"Oh, for Christ's *sake*," Balikovsky said disgustedly as he walked off toward the truck. "That's what the German soldiers said, too, you know that?"

Dinah pushed him ahead of her, moving slowly through the thick August heat of the city. "Monte, stop. The damage is done. What we need is a very dark, very cold, very air-conditioned bar," she said in a wan voice.

Sy came up behind them looking gray with weariness. "I feel too nauseous to drink."

"Good," Berman snapped, "then you can drive. Because I intend to get absolutely shit-faced."

Soot-covered and blotchy from the heat, the disheveled, disheartened group clambered back into the empty truck. The scene faded out.

In the All Soul's Waiting Room, Johnnine felt sorry for them. She had forgotten her mother's role in the destruction of Reich's books. Knowing how strongly Dinah felt about Reich's work, she reflected that having to help burn his books must have been like asking someone to dig their own grave before they were executed. "What the hell was the government so afraid of?" she demanded angrily.

"What they're always afraid of," The Recorder toned. "Loss of power."

Johnnine laughed in disbelief. "But that's ridiculous! Reich wasn't a serious threat, he wasn't interested in taking over or anything!"

"Ah, but he was a threat, darling," Xofia corrected her. "In the deepest sense, to the entrenched status quo..."

"Are you saying there was a conspiracy against him?"

"Not exactly. But—just because you're paranoid, darling—" Xofia dangled her sentence and left it unfinished.

Yeah, but who was *really* paranoid, Johnnine wondered. Wilhelm Reich? Or the U. S. government?

"Now, kids, there's absolutely nothing to be nervous about." A black-haired, deep-voiced man spoke to Johnnine and four other children seated around a rectangular table. In front of each of them was a large microphone bearing the call letters WNYC. "You just speak slowly and clearly into the mike and everything'll be fine. Don't be afraid of it, it won't bite. Ha ha." The announcer's red polka dot bow tie bobbed up and down over his prominent Adam's apple as he pretended to laugh.

Johnnine's eyes were glazed and she was swallowing rapidly as she glanced around at the other kids, a red-headed boy wearing thick glasses and a *yarmulke*, an overdressed blond girl with long pigtails and satin ribbons, a pudgy Chinese boy, and a thin pretty black girl who was shivering even with a sweater on.

"The main thing to remember is not to talk too close to the mikes, or too far back. They're very sensitive. Absolutely no talking to each other once you see that light go on." He pointed to a red lightbulb over the door of the studio, under which a sign read ON THE AIR. "Oh—and absolutely no chewing gum. It creates havoc in the sound booth." He gave them another fake smile.

The All Souls' Waiting Room

The blond girl took a wad of bubble gum out of her mouth. "Where should I put this?"

"Don't you have a piece of paper?"

She shook her head. Distastefully, the announcer put out his hand.

"Anyone else?"

Johnnine and the others shook their heads.

"Good. You all have your essays," he said, running his eyes around the table, seeing them all laid out in front of the children, checking his watch against the large clock on the studio wall. An engineer on the other side of a plate glass window raised his hand.

"Okay, now, absolutely SHUSH." The announcer pulled back his lips in grotesque imitation of a smile. "I'm going to announce you so do not, repeat, do NOT speak until I tell you to..." He kept his eyes on the red lightbulb, which lit up suddenly.

Speaking into the microphone as though he were making love to it, his voice turned into syrupy dark molasses. "Good morning, New York! This is Dennis Holmes, host of WNYC's special broadcast honoring the winners of this spring's *Herald Tribune* essay contest..."

A faint jangling sound from under the table made the announcer's face pucker into a fleeting frown as he spoke. The noise stopped, his face returned to normal. "First I'd like to introduce the first-place winner of the Current Events category. Tell us your name, please, young lady, and what school you're from."

The announcer nodded abruptly at Johnnine, silently but violently shooting his arm out at her. The jangling sound grew a lot louder. "My name..." She licked her dry lips. "...is Johnnine Hapgood...and I go to P. S. 8 on King Street. That's in the Village," she added, red-faced but smooth-tongued, leaning in closer to the microphone and causing a small explosion of sound. The metallic tumbling noise became more insistent.

"Good, Johnni, now could you please read your—" The announcer's voice sounded warm and welcoming, but his face was contorted with annoyance. "Excuse us, listeners, we seem to be having a slight noise disturbance—"

"It's John-NEEN," she said emphatically, bringing a set of keys she had been nervously fingering up from her lap and banging them on the table in front of the microphone.

The engineer in the recording booth shot up from his chair and ripped off his headphone. At the same instant the announcer's back arched as though he were doing a reverse eject from a burning plane while he kept his mouth six inches from the mike. "Please read your essay—" he said fervently, then dashed around the table to grab the keys out of her hand.

"*Now?*" Johnnine stalled.

The announcer leaned over her shoulder to speak into Johnnine's microphone. "Yes, please. NOW!" He pulled her head back about six inches from the mike. She glared up at him before she began to read: "Last October, the Russian Army invaded a tiny country in Eastern Europe called Hungary. They sent in tanks and soldiers with guns to frighten the people, make them do what they did not want to do." She gulped audibly. "I think it is wrong for the Russians to take over Hungary. They have their own country, why don't they stay there? Why do they need to make Hungary afraid of them? Don't they have enough things to do? The people of Hungary want to be free. I think they should be free to think and do what they want to do. I hope the whole world will help the Hungarians get rid of the Russians, who should go back to Russia."

There was tremendous relief in the announcer's voice as he spoke. "Thank you, Johnni Hapgood."

"John-NEEN."

The announcer glowered at her. "And now, moving on to our next winner in the Poetry category, who I believe has a little ditty about the joys of skipping rope."

Johnnine slumped back in her chair.

"And what's your name, little lady? My, that's a pretty bow in your hair!" The announcer poured his voice into the microphone as though he was pouring motor oil into an engine.

The scene did a slow fade-out.

Chapter Thirty

In the All Souls' Waiting Room, the film appeared to be consumed by a large black spot that grew cancerously in the middle of the screen. The room lights came on as the cherubs rushed to cut and splice. Johnnine found herself staring at fragments of Egyptian mummy bandages Schlomo Freud had framed on the wall, two strips of yellowed linen with fine ink drawings of one-dimensional gods and hieroglyphics. Appropriate, she thought. She'd felt like a mummiform on the radio show, a little spark of sentience swaddled in constricting bandages. She'd never understood why she had been so terrified, only that it felt more like dying than simple stage-fright.

"Maybe because you were so desperate," Xofia purred.

"Desperate?" Johnnine returned, not unused to her mind-reading by now.

"For attention, darling—"

Xofia poured herself more bubbly and picked up the "Book of the Dead." The Recorder fingered a faience amulet of the Sphinx, continuing his intermittent catalogue of Schlomo's desk ornaments. Fa, So, and La, performed film repair.

Johnnine reflected. Was that it? Or was it a reluctance to project herself out into the world, the same world that had an unhealthy tendency to turn people into targets. Maybe her terror on the radio show had been a form of prescience about what was ahead. Because that same summer of 1957, she left girlhood firmly behind and swam for the rocky shoals of adolescence. In quick succession, she graduated from P. S. 8, got her first brassiere, then her period. Her passionate interest in dogs was replaced by the same in boys. Alan Freed's rock 'n roll show on WMCA became her clock-radio wake-up call, American Bandstand her reason for living.

Johnnine remembered it as a bleak period. Dinah's New York Reichian circle dissolved, patients and analysts went underground after Reich's imprisonment. Dinah went back to lab tech work, though all she could find at first was a part-time job in a doctor's office. She and Johnnine moved from the apartment on Carmine to a five-flight walkup on the Lower East Side. Dinah began her day with a cup of coffee and a shot of vodka, though Johnnine only rarely saw her mother drunk. She just drank and ate, anesthetizing her deep wounds. Johnnine's own wounds, she now realized, were not so obvious.

Greenwich Village and Avenue D were like different worlds. The only thing the two neighborhoods had in common for Johnnine was that she was a bizarre outsider in both. A bohemian WASP among her Italian-Catholic schoolmates, on the Lower East Side she was a blonde shiksa from Little Italy.

The best thing about the move was that Johnnine liked her smart new classmates and encouraging teachers. She was in a Special Progress class—ninety-five percent Jewish, five percent Other—designed to get bright kids through junior high school in two years instead of three. Surrounded by irreverent, quick wits, being at school became fun. No one explained the advantages of the "SP" program, nor was she asked if she wanted to be out of high school two years early (she had already skipped a grade). Johnnine's consent was taken for granted, as if anyone in their right mind would jump at the chance to be in college when they were sixteen.

"So." Xofia's voice brought Johnnine's attention back to the All Souls' Waiting Room. "Your first sign of favor—"

"What?" Johnnine asked, disoriented for a moment at having her memories interrupted.

"The essay prize, darling!" Xofia punctuated the air with her long-handled cigarette holder, which she proceeded to fill with another Dark Star cigarillo. "And don't you find the sequence of events interesting?" she went on blithely. "Poor Willie gets thrown in the clunker and you write a winning protest letter."

"I think the word you want is clinker, Xofia," The Recorder corrected somberly.

"Thank you, darling." Xofia smiled benignantly in his direction, *á la* the bewitching English actress, Joan Greenwood. "I depend on you."

Johnnine was practically salivating for a cigarette and a swig of champagne but she knew what they tasted like in the All Souls' Waiting Room so she shook her head to clear her thoughts. "What does protesting the invasion of Hungary have to do with Reich going to prison?" she demanded impatiently.

Xofia clamped the cigarette holder between her teeth. "Think *broadly*, darling," she said, her long, graceful hands describing circles in the air. "Think bigger than you are. Think about *theme*. Terribly important for writers to understand."

"Who said I was going to be a writer?"

Xofia batted her eyes ingenuously. "Why, you did, darling. You met your destiny when you won the essay contest..."

"Destiny?" Johnnine hooted. What the hell was Xofia talking about? To have a destiny you had to have a future.

Xofia turned to The Recorder, taking her cigarette holder out of her mouth. "We have here a tough nut."

"I've seen tougher," he shrugged. "Let's move on—"

The ancient, faded green moving truck of the Flying Ferragamo Brothers shimmied down a busy, two-way Avenue D. On the east side of the avenue were the high-rise brick towers of the Lillian Waldman Housing Project. The cheerless rows of tall buildings looked as though they were being force-marched toward the East River. Across the street sat squat, unlovely tenement buildings, aged small shops, and grimy stores.

The three hirsute Ferragamos sweated freely through their dingy white nylon tank-tops. Salvatore was driving. Across the mountainous, mute Luigi,

Salvatore addressed his older brother. "What's she doin' movin' in with the kikes?"

"I dunno," Giuseppe said, mopping his face with a blue bandana. "It's cheap here, maybe that's why. Turn the truck around so we can pull up by the curb—" Salvatore made a traffic-stopping, gear-crashing, mid-block U turn.

A Rubenesque Dinah, dabbing her upper lip and throat with a handkerchief, stood chatting with a portly man wearing a faded *yarmulke* and denim overalls. He was holding onto a pushcart filled with barrels of pickles. Everyone dripped perspiration in the wet heat of late August.

Moishe Cohen eyed the spavined old Ferragamo truck warily as it pulled up to the sidewalk. "You couldn't find some nice Jewish movers?" he asked Dinah with a thick Eastern European accent.

Giuseppe strutted over, hoisting up his pants. "Hey, lady!"

Dinah smiled. "The Ferragamos have been moving me around New York for years—Mr. Cohen is my new landlord," Dinah said by way of introduction.

"Yeah," Giuseppe said, "we wish all our customers moved as much as her. Okay, where to this time?"

Dinah nodded at the building behind them. "Fifth floor, Mr. Ferragamo, apartment C."

Giuseppe manufactured a heavy groan. "*Madon*! Jesus, lady, whaddya wanna do, kill us? Maybe you betta stay put this time—"

Dinah enjoyed the repartee, turning flirtatious. "I don't know, Mr. Ferragamo, it depends on whether or not I find a man."

"You still unmarried? Whatsa matta, you can't cook?"

"I know how to do more than cook, Mr. Ferragamo," Dinah said saucily.

Giuseppe laughed boisterously and swaggered back to the truck, hoisting up his pants again.

Johnnine was sitting near her mother on the broad, shallow steps of the shabby apartment building, her curvy shape outlined in short shorts and a halter top, her dark blonde hair in a ponytail. She blushed and slid the piece of newspaper she was sitting on to the other side of the stoop, pretending she didn't know any of them.

Moishe Cohen looked embarrassed. He nodded at Dinah and shoved off around the corner with his heavy wooden pushcart.

Giuseppe noisily and officiously supervised the unloading. Mighty Luigi got a blonde wood television console strapped to his back while Giuseppe and Salvatore carried an empty dresser inside the building.

A family of Hasidic Jews passed by, the men wearing long, curled *paises* and flat, wide-brimmed black hats even in the punishing heat. Johnnine and Dinah looked after them and made brief eye contact.

Dinah nodded after the Hasidim. "I've heard the men have to make love to their wives through a hole in the sheet."

"Why??" Johnnine asked, turning to stare at their receding backs. The women wore old-fashioned dresses and walked demurely behind the men.

"Because they're not allowed to see each other naked."

Johnnine shot her mother a quick, incredulous look. She turned back to watch the mysterious family recede down Avenue D. "Why are the women in back?"

Dinah shrugged. "They think men are superior to women. Otherwise, I quite like Jewish people, they're very warm and vital. And don't let me hear you call them Jews or kikes," Dinah added.

"Why not?"

"It's an insult, like wop to the Italians."

"What's the insult for us?"

"Us? I don't know...limey, maybe—"

"Doesn't sound so bad to me," Johnnine leaned back against the open moving truck and blew a large pink bubble with her chewing gum. A gaggle of black and Puerto Rican teenage girls jostled past, eying Johnnine with unfriendly suspicion. Johnnine ignored them. "Are we poor now, Mom?"

Dinah said brightly, full of bravado, "I don't feel poor, do you?"

Johnnine looked across the street at the city housing project. The few scraggly trees had garbage for mulch around their trunks. "Do we still have the house up country?"

Dinah frowned for a moment. "No, I had to put it on the market. Daniel will need the money when he gets out of prison next spring."

Johnnine looked thoughtful. "You mean we don't have any assets anymore?"

Dinah laughed ruefully as she dipped into a pocket of her sleeveless tent dress and fished out a flask. "I guess you could say that—but at least we have each other!" Dinah raised the flask to Johnnine before she lifted it to her lips.

Johnnine's almond-shaped green eyes clouded over as she turned away from her mother. She was quite pretty but her expression was troubled as she stared down poverty-blasted Avenue D.

Wilhelm Reich sat hunched over the table in the corner of his cell. He looked old and care-worn as he wrote a letter under the single lightbulb:

"Dearest Peter:

Only a few more days until we are together again! How I've missed you, your laughing eyes, your warm hands and hugs. Yes, please find us a nice place to stay in Poughkeepsie, maybe a Howard Johnson's, so we can try more of the 31 flavors! Anyplace is fine, as long as they don't have chlorinated water. I've told you how bad it is for the body.

"I hope you are remembering how to cry, with sound. Even here, for me it is a deep release, a good way to keep my belly soft.

"I am working on a new book. It's called 'Creation'. I carry most of the equations on space and negative gravity in my head, so that they can't be stolen. I know what they will do to me if they have the chance. All my thoughts lately convince me that God and orgone energy are the same thing, that we need to let our lives be governed by the laws we discover, align ourselves with the natural forces in and around us...

"I am feeling a little tired now. Will rest until morning and then send this off. All my love, my sweet boy, and Papa will see you soon!"

Reich got up from the table and crossed to the cot. Sitting on the edge, he exhaled heavily, wearily. He removed his shoes, lay down, and turned his face to the wall as his cell door opened quietly from the outside.

When the feeble light of morning came through the high window bars, Reich lay inert on his bed as a guard unlocked the door and entered the cell. Another uniformed guard stood outside. "Come on, doc, you missed roll call, what's the—"

The first guard scanned Reich's unmoving body. Quickly, he moved to the bed, leaned down, and put his ear to Reich's chest. Straightening up, he felt for a pulse. "He's gone. Just in time, too. Up for parole tomorrow..."

The guard laid Reich's arm down alongside his body. The film did a freeze-frame on Reich's fleshy face, drained of color and life.

There was a pregnant pause in the All Souls' Waiting Room. The lights came up slowly, as if out of respect. Johnnine sat up and swung her legs off The Couch. "I want a drink and a cigarette and I don't want any shit about it," she said decisively.

"Done, darling." Xofia snapped her fingers. A cherub appeared instantly on either side of Johnnine. One held a glass of Dom Elysee and the other a filter-tipped Bright Spark. "Abusing yourself won't help," Xofia muttered, "but I know that's for me to know and you to find out—"

Johnnine coughed on the cigarette and spluttered after sipping the champagne. "Shit. How the hell do you get out of it up here?"

"There is no getting out of it," Xofia said softly.

Johnnine's face grew red. "Reich got out of it!" She shouted irately, jumping to her feet. "He got to die!"

"Aren't you forgetting what happened after he died?" The Recorder put in. "He's been holed up with Schlomo Freud—hardly the road to oblivion."

Johnnine snorted harshly. "You mean there's no escape from analysis? Neither sleet nor snow nor even death shall stay the dedicated head-shrinker?" She sat down again, clearly distraught. "Christ!"

Xofia took a soothing tone. "It might help if you told us what you're feeling, darling."

"Shit, I don't know." Johnnine shifted to the other side of The Couch. "It's too complicated, I don't even want to think about it..." She took a deep breath, then appeared to calm down a bit. "Reich didn't deserve to die in prison! He wasn't a murderer. He didn't go around hurting anybody, he wanted to help people...and—" Johnnine looked anxiously up at Xofia. "—and if he could end up like that just for saying what he thought, anybody could, even me."

Xofia and The Recorder exchanged a meaningful glance.

"Let's press on," Xofia said. "There's a place I want to show you when we've done with your life review—"

"So, *nu*, Johnnine, about that sweater—" A boy said breezily as he brushed past her, ogling her new green fuzzy top.

"Watch your mouth, Marty," she answered in a bantering tone. "I don't see you setting any fashion trends."

They were outside the Isidore Fish Junior High School on East Houston Street, part of a colorful mixture of pubescent students. With bright orange, Tangeed lips and badly-set hair, Johnnine hugged a conspicuous pile of books to her budding chest. Under a light jacket, she wore an amazingly furry, bile-green sweater.

"No, no," the gangly boy with heavy spectacles said. "I was only going to ask—whaddya feed it?" He guffawed and disappeared in the crowd.

Johnnine suppressed a smile.

A very tall girl with a corkscrew-curled ponytail bent down to hiss in her ear. "Just ignore him, Johnnine. Marty Mandelbaum's a total jerk, just so immaCHER—" Marilyn Leibowitz's New York accent was as thick as chopped liver. She swung her head from side to side, her ponytail swinging back and forth like a wagging, disapproving finger.

"At least Marty's funny sometimes," Johnnine said as they walked alongside the chain link fence enclosing the school grounds. "Not like the other SP boys. They're just plain jerks."

Marilyn rolled her eyes as they walked towards Avenue D. "Do I know or do I KNOW? Little *boys*, sometimes I feel like their *mothah* or something already."

Johnnine and Marilyn sighed deeply, despairingly, in unison. The autumn weather was mild. They strolled leisurely, knowing they had a full fifteen minutes before Dick Clark claimed their afternoon.

"I wish they'd put some of the non-honors boys in our classes," Johnnine sighed again. "Some of the cute ones. We just see the same boring smart-mouths all day..."

The All Souls' Waiting Room

"Yeah. *Short* boring smart-mouths...ooh, look, the Dragons!" Marilyn pointed.

Johnnine followed Marilyn's rapt gaze down the street. A group of young black men wearing narrow-brimmed black hats and short black capes took up the sidewalk with unflustered arrogance. The Dragons walked in a lope-strutting, flying wedge formation behind a handsome, pale-skinned boy, heading north on Avenue D.

Johnnine's eyes went wide. "Who's THAT?"

"Who, the leader? Ronny Coleman. His nickname's Sir Galahad."

"How come? He's not Jewish, is he?"

"Oy, Johnnine, do me a favor already! Ronny's a dumb mick, the only white kid in the gang. The Dragons used to be all *shvartzers* but Ronny beat up everybody else that wanted to be the leader, so now *he's* the leader. But he's real polite to all the teachers, so they call him Sir Galahad."

Johnnine had not taken her eyes off him. "Does he go to our school?"

Marilyn shrugged. "When he feels like it..."

The gang cut an impressive group figure on the dirty slum street. They looked like a precision drill team, their bop-walk carefully choreographed, identical black capes flashing red satin linings. People crossed to the other side of the street to let them pass.

Johnnine was agog. "Is everybody afraid of them?"

"Well, you don't want to make them *mad* at you, that's for sure. But they're a lot better than the Forsythe Boys—those scumbags! The Dragons just protect their territory. Any time a Forsythe Boy tries to come up here or messes with a girl who lives in Dragon turf, there's a rumble."

"They *protect* us? All the girls in their territory?" Johnnine looked starry-eyed.

"Sort of. But don't let Paula Kozlowski catch you looking at Ronny like that. She's his girlfriend and she's tougher than he is, she'll tear your eyes out. I gotta go. See you tomorrow." Marilyn peeled off into the ugly brick housing project, turning around to wave at Johnnine, who smiled and waved back.

Waiting for the light at the corner of Avenue D, Johnnine saw her mother in front of the kosher deli across the street. Dinah looked terrible. She was crying and holding a handkerchief to her face.

Johnnine looked around furtively as she went up to her. "Mom, what's the matter?"

Dinah grabbed onto Johnnine's arm. "Reich's dead..." She burst into tears. "He died last night, in his cell."

Johnnine's face went blank, she seemed not to have any reaction. She looked more concerned about having a sobbing mother clinging to her arm than about Reich's death. "Oh," she said.

Dinah was oblivious to everything but her grief. "The guards found him this morning. He wasn't feeling good but he didn't tell anyone, probably so they wouldn't delay his parole—"

Johnnine's eyes were drawn to a little pizza parlor on the other side of the street. A song poured out of the jukebox: "...*wa-alks, with PERSONALITY, talks-with-PERSONALITY, and-plus-she's-got-a-great-big-HEAR-AR-ART*!"

The nattily-dressed Dragons milled around in front of the pizza place. Johnnine glanced at their blue-eyed, black-haired leader with awe and longing. The song continued: "...*so-ovah, and-ovah-ah, I'll-be-a-fool-for-you, 'cause-ovah, and-ovah-ah, what-more-can-I-do?*"

Half-weeping, half-speaking, Dinah continued, holding the handkerchief to her face. "He was a great man, Johnnine. We're lucky to have had him in our lives. The world crucified him but his work will make things better for your generation. Better than they were for mine..."

Johnnine stared across the street, ogling the dashing young princeling surrounded by his subordinates. She spoke to her mother off-handedly, without taking her eyes off Sir Galahad. "Yah, Mom..."

"Come in, Dr. Pahlser—"

Stooping slightly as he went through the doorway, Daniel Pahlser entered the office of Lewisburg Penitentiary's medical director. Dr. Mark Hirschfeld sat behind his desk in a long white lab coat looking crisply professional.

Pahlser was resentful and uneasy, covering up his discomfort with a set jaw and a defiant look in his eyes. "You sent for me," he said.

"I have something to tell you. First, how're you feeling? Any more arrhythmia?"

"No," Pahlser said sourly. "But I am very angry at not getting the conjugal visits I'm entitled to—"

Hirschfeld looked surprised. "But, Dr. Pahlser, you're not married!"

"That doesn't matter!" Pahlser was angry. "I know several women who would be more than willing to relieve my sexual tension!"

"How fortunate for you," Hirschfeld said coolly, raising an eyebrow. "However, I doubt if the prison authorities subscribe to your doctrine of so-called sexual freedom. In any case, such a stream of women might not be good for your heart condition—"

"Being denied my sexual rights isn't, either!"

Hirschfeld raised a hand phlegmatically. "I will take it up with the Medical Board, but I wouldn't count on anything if I were you." He paused for a moment. "The reason I called you in was to give you some news that I thought, as a fellow physician, whatever our differences, you deserved to hear in private."

"What is it?" Pahlser looked wary.

The All Souls' Waiting Room

"Wilhelm Reich died last night..." Hirschfeld put on a pair of glasses and read from a note on his desk. "Myocardial insufficiency with sudden heart failure, associated with generalized arteriosclerosis and sclerosis of the coronary vessels."

Pahlser looked as though he had been struck.

"I'm sorry," Hirschfeld added.

"No, you're not." Pahlser got to his feet, gray and shaky. "This is exactly what you all wanted." His voice rose with his anger. "Reich was too big for this world, he made everyone else look small—and he was hated for it." A light seemed to flash in his eyes and then go out. He made his way to the door. "I'd like to be alone now."

"Certainly," Hirschfeld said drily. He picked up the intercom on his desk. "Dr. Pahlser to be returned to his cell," he said into the phone. "Although technically, you're not a doctor anymore, are you?" Hirschfeld added as he put it down. "What are you going to do when you get out—I mean, since you can't practice medicine?" Pahlser did not turn around from the door.

"Bell captain..."

Daniel Pahlser stood in a hotel lobby six months later wearing a maroon uniform with tasseled epaulets, calmly and competently dispatching bellboys to waiting guests. His oversized, brooding features looked resigned as he answered the telephone on his standing desk.

"Oh, Dr. Grossman..." He looked quickly around. "No, I have a minute, I'd like to know—" He riffled through some papers on his desk as he spoke. "Yes, I see, I thought so, the pain's gotten quite intense. I felt contaminated with DOR in prison, it couldn't have helped...I'll call back later, it's getting busy again." Pahlser hung up looking pensive. The hotel manager, a chubby young man with a carnation in his lapel, beckoned him with his index finger from the registration desk.

Late that night, Pahlser drove through a wooded area of Van Cortlandt Park. He parked the rented car and turned off the headlights. From inside his breast pocket, he removed a white envelope and propped it up on the dashboard. Then he took a small vial out of the glove compartment and stared at it a moment. Unstopping the tiny cork, he put the clear liquid to his lips and swallowed. Half a minute later, his body went into racking convulsions and slumped sideways.

Early the next morning, Johnnine got out of bed as the phone rang in the hallway of the Avenue D apartment. A fire escape was visible through pale-gray Venetian blinds. The walls of her room were papered with leafless trees in alternating rows of pale blue, green, and gray, the floor painted a matching shade of gray enamel. The room's overall effect was one of stately sadness.

Johnnine heard her mother answer the telephone. She crossed the room in a few steps when she heard her mother scream.

Dinah looked stunned. She stood in the hall with the phone dangling from her hand, her eyes blurry with bewilderment and grief. "Daniel...Pahlser..."

Johnnine stared at her mother, whose round, highly-colored face looked like it was sliding off its bony foundation. "He—he committed suicide last night. Some boys found him this morning, in a car." Dinah broke into sobs.

Johnnine kept staring at her mother. Her adolescent features were as hard as marble. "Don't expect me to be sorry," Johnnine said, her voice stiff with strain.

Dinah was horrified. "Johnnine! He loved you—us!"

Mother and daughter looked at each other across the two feet of cracked linoleum as though it were a seven-league chasm. Silently, Johnnine closed her door. She recrossed the room and went to her desk. Sitting down, she stared blankly at the denuded trees on her wallpaper before writing a few lines on a piece of paper.

> "He's dead.
> My first thought is: he won't ever be able
> To touch me again.
> I feel no tears,
> I feel relief.
> Words are like stones
> Thrown down an empty well."

Johnnine put down her pencil and picked up a hand mirror. Her reflection showed a lovely young girl with glittering dry eyes.

Chapter Thirty-one

As if to shed light on the murky state of her feelings about Daniel Pahlser, the room lights in Freud's office came on unbidden. Naturally, Johnnine thought. When I want them on, I have to raise hell. When I don't, they come on by themselves. "I suppose now you're going to ask me how I'm feeling—again?" Johnnine said defensively. "See if I feel sorry he killed himself."

Xofia merely looked at Johnnine with large, all-suffering eyes.

Johnnine hardened her defenses. "Well, I don't," she said abruptly. "I was glad when he died. I felt like a huge weight was lifted out of my life. That makes me a monster, right? That's what Mom said, she never understood anything about how I felt..."

"Darling," Xofia said very softly. "It has nothing to do with you being a monster. It has everything to do with the price you paid for mortaring up your heart—"

"You think I had a choice?" Johnnine cried. "I was evil, there was something wrong with me for not mourning the man who fucked up my life—"

"You did what you had to do. Then. But now perhaps you need to tear down the walls you built."

"I DON'T WANT TO! I'd rather die!" Johnnine shouted. "The walls are the only thing that protect me!" There was a wild quaver in her voice.

"Johnnine." Xofia looked at her with grave sympathy. "Darling. You don't have a choice this time, either."

"Yes, I do! I'll find a way of dying where I won't run into you two!"

The Recorder spoke smoothly, unperturbed by Johnnine's histrionics. "You don't have to do the work on your soul all at once," he intoned. "Or all by yourself. The Powers don't expect you to jump tall complexes in a single bound—"

Johnnine was crying openly now, wringing her hands. "I don't want to see Pahlser again!" She looked frightened and woebegone at the same time.

"You won't have to," The Recorder said reassuringly. "Like all successful but unticketed suicides, he was sent right back."

"What?? Swear to God?"

There was the hint of a smile in The Recorder's voice as he held up a hand. "I swear to The Powers."

"Of course you won't be able to avoid seeing him in your dreams," Xofia added calmly, sitting down beside Johnnine. "Probably quite often. That's how you'll know..."

"Know what?" Johnnine sniffed.

"When you've reached forgiveness." Xofia patted her hand.

"What are you talking about, forgiveness?" Johnnine pulled her hand away. "I'm not running for sainthood."

"Things change..." Xofia said patiently.

"You mean I will run for sainthood?" Johnnine quipped.

"Shall we?" The Recorder cut in. "Not much more to go—"

"Why do we have to?" Johnnine felt irritable. "I lived through this stuff! I already know what's coming."

"There are always fresh perspectives, darling, new angles, even surprises." Xofia sounded vomitously perky and enthusiastic, sort of like Judy Garland suggesting to Mickey Rooney that all the kids get together to put on a show.

"Surprises." Johnnine's voice was flat as a board. "Great. I hate surprises."

"Less than ten minutes to go to the New Year...!" The announcer's voice boomed out of the blond wood television console. On a chenille-covered daybed-cum-couch in the living room, Dinah and Johnnine wore heavy robes and shared a leopard-spotted throw. The large room was only sparsely furnished. Dinah's mirrors, on three of the walls, made it seem even larger, reflecting the lonely scene into infinity. An old steam radiator in the corner clanked, hissed, and sputtered. Dinah drank and smoked. Thirteen-year old Johnnine sulked.

Guy Lombardo and His Royal Canadians strained "Auld Lang Syne" through saccharine saxophones. The picture switched from the white-tuxedoed orchestra to the giant ball of lightbulbs on top of the New York Times Building, then panned over the anti-freeze-filled multitudes thronging Times Square below. Roving searchlights lit up home-made signs in the crowd: "University of North Carolina—Go Tarheels!" "From Kalamazoo and Darn Proud of It!" "New York, New York, One Hell of a Town!"

The phone rang as the crowd on the TV roared. Johnnine got up to answer it though her words could not be heard by the audience in the All Souls' Waiting Room. A minute later, looking no less pouty, she padded back to the couch. Without turning to look at Dinah, she pulled the lap robe over her legs and spoke in a toneless voice. "Berman says Happy New Year..."

"That was nice of him to call."

"How come we don't see anybody from Carmine Street anymore?"

Dinah took a sip of her drink. "I think everyone's still raw. Things came too close together, first Reich, then Pahlser—people don't recover overnight..." Her voice had a catch in it. She put her cigarette in the beanbag ashtray and poured more rye into her highball glass.

Johnnine watched her mother drink and smoke. "Can I have one of your cigarettes? I bought some of my own, but I ran out."

Dinah gave Johnnine a questioning look. She hesitated, then handed her the pack of Viceroys. "I guess if you're going to do it anyway—"

Johnnine shook a cigarette loose out of the pack and put it to her lips. It looked obscene in the middle of her young face.

Guy Lombardo's background swell of "Auld Lang Syne" was relentless. Dinah raised her resonant voice in a chorus of one: "*Should-old-acquaintance-be-forgot, And-never-brought-to-mind, Should-old-acquaintance-be-forgot, And-days-of-auld-lang-syne? And-days-of-auld-lang-syne, my-dear, And-days-of-auld-lang-syne/We'll-take-a-cup-of-kindness-yet, For-auld-lang-syne.*" She sang with all the maudlin sentiment the song demanded, then burst into tears.

Johnnine glanced at her mother out of the corner of her eye and then looked away, the martyred teenaged companion of an unsought parent. "God, I wish I had a date," she said under her breath.

Dinah stopped crying abruptly. Adept at emotional quick changes, she wiped her eyes and put on her cheery voice, the one with the Jewish accent. "So, *nu*, why don't you, already yet vonce?"

Johnnine wrinkled her nose disdainfully. "The boys in my classes are all BA-bies."

Dinah briskly patted Johnnine's hand. "Wait'll next year, ducklet. By the time you start high school, we'll be beating them off with sticks."

Johnnine's mouth pulled back in a mirthless smile.

"Which reminds me," Dinah said. "Let me know before you want to have intercourse, so we can get you fitted for a diaphragm—"

Johnnine looked embarrassed. "God, Mom, you've only told me a million times..."

Dinah continued as if Johnnine hadn't spoken. "No unwanted pregnancies, for God's sake! That's the last thing we need—"

Johnnine frowned silently. Emotions played over her expressive face but she kept them to herself. "Can I have a drink?"

The clamorous roars from Times Square via the TV filled the room. The announcer sounded breathlessly excited, as if he had never been present at a changing of the year before. "It's a new year, folks! Let's ring in 1959! Happy New Year, New York! Happy New Year, America!"

Dinah looked uncertain but handed Johnnine her drink. "I guess you're old enough for everything now—let's drink to the New Year! And please God let it be better than the old one!" Dinah's mouth smiled uncertainly while her eyes brimmed with tears.

Johnnine took the highball glass from her mother and downed half of it in one long swallow. She made a hideous, puckered face, shaking her head and shrugging her shoulders as Guy Lombardo bleated his last and the frenetically cheering, horn-tooting crowd on 42nd Street went wild.

"Hot enough to fry your kishkas here—"

That summer, at a down-at-the-heels family resort in the Catskills, a dozen inert vacationers broiled themselves under a flaming sun around a very small, kidney-shaped pool. No one ventured near the water. In a one-piece swimsuit, Johnnine lay on a webbed recliner next to Marilyn, who lay next to her mother, Sadie Leibowitz. Mrs. Leibowitz had tightly-curled, peroxide blonde hair that peeped out from under a red hair turban. She wore black plastic eye-protectors that looked like goggles for blind dwarfs and she had propped up her chaise so she could hold an aluminum tanning reflector under her chin.

From a pole at one corner of the pool's chain-link fence, a nerve-jarring squawking and clicking burst out of the PA loudspeaker. A sign under the speaker box announced pool rules and hours: Parents 10AM - 1PM, Children 2PM - 5PM. "Mrs. Sadie Leibowitz, Mrs. Sadie Leibowitz, please come to the camp counselor's office right away."

"Oy!" Sadie said, taking off her black eye cups. "If that's Howie getting into trouble again, I swear I'll murder him, so help me!"

Johnnine and Marilyn lifted their heads to watch the buxom Mrs. Leibowitz slip her tanned, pedicured feet into a pair of red mules and clack off towards the office. The girls looked at each other and smiled, their faces blotchy with heat and dripping with sweat.

"Wanna take a swim?" Johnnine asked.

"No, I don't want to get my hair wet."

"Me neither."

They put their heads back down on their towels and readjusted their sunglasses, passing the Coppertone back and forth.

Early that evening, Johnnine and Marilyn rushed out of a tired-looking wooden bungalow, one of a line of twenty others. The ripped screen door slammed shut as a man's voice bellowed after them. "Just remember, you two! Marilyn, you hear me?! I brought you up here as virgins and that's how I'm taking you home—eleven o'clock curfew or you'll both get a hairbrush on the toosh!"

Marilyn shouted over her shoulder. "Yes, papa!" She squinted at Johnnine. "He means it, too—"

"I'd kick him where it hurts if he tried to lay a hand on me," Johnnine bragged. "Besides, spanking's bad for kids."

"Why?"

"It makes them constipated—"

Marilyn laughed and shoved Johnnine. "Ooh, what you said!"

"What, constipated?"

Marilyn looked around. "You don't have to yell—"

"I'm not yelling," Johnnine argued. Then an impish look came over her face. "Unless of course I feel like saying DIARRHEA, that's when I really feel like yelling. Something about the word DIARRHEA, makes me want to sing it out loud—"

A car went by and Johnnine turned fuchsia. She and Marilyn collapsed against each other in a fit of giggling.

They left the confines of the Loch Sheldrake Family Resort and walked up the peaceful, tree-lined country road. They wore long white men's shirts over dungarees and had their hair elaborately curled into up-turned flips. Marilyn's tall, elongated body moved with the hesitant grace of a young giraffe. Shorter and more compact, Johnnine's figure had turned into well-proportioned curves. She walked with a proud, almost belligerent air, uneasy with herself, uncertain how to wear her body.

They passed a pocket mirror back and forth and applied makeup as they walked. They were not going for a natural look: raccoon-like rings of black pencil around their eyes, and greasy, iridescent white lipstick looked startling against their bright-red, freshly-burnt faces. They laughed and nudged each other until a teenage boy went by on a bicycle. Immediately banishing all traces of amusement, they appeared coldly disinterested as he slowed down to check them out.

When he was out of sight, Marilyn pretended to swoon. "Did you see that? Are we talking gorgeous or are we talking *GORGEOUS*!! I'm dying already."

Johnnine stared at the bike's dust as though at the trail of a minor deity. "GOD!!!"

"Just think, a whole hotel of them, starving for the company of women," Marilyn said greedily, quickening her pace.

Johnnine and Marilyn exchanged looks of pubescent female lust as they walked into the large compound of Wasserman's Hotel. Avoiding the main paths, they dodged guests and darted around trees, making a clandestine game of getting to their goal: the rear door of the main dining hall. Behind a flat-topped, clipped bush which gave them cover but afforded a good view, they kneeled like watchful pilgrims, never taking their heavily-blackened eyes off the back door. Every few minutes, good-looking young men in black pants and white shirts spilled out. Sharing quick cigarettes, they made jokes and spit into the grass before returning to the dining room.

Marilyn and Johnnine leered lasciviously at each other. They had found their quarry.

A well-built, clear-skinned, brown-haired boy with a see-through-to-the-scalp crew cut came outside. Johnnine's eyes lit up. "Ooh, look at that one!" she whispered urgently.

"Which—oh, him?" Marilyn sounded uninterested. "That's Timmy Brown, the goy from Ohio. I think he goes to Kenyon College..."

"He's a goy? GOD!!! Don't you think he's fantastic?" Johnnine's whisper was heated, reverent.

"He's awright, but I like Izzy Fishbaum better. See the one over there with the shiny black hair? N. Y. U.," Marilyn sighed. "Something about a Brylcreem man, they really send me—"

"Yeah, a little dab'll do ya!" Johnnine hissed.

They both began to giggle. Then they clapped muffling hands over the other's mouth as they sank to the ground. Nervously, they peered through the bush to make sure they were undetected.

"When do we make our move?" Johnnine looked suddenly stage-struck. "God, my legs feel like silly putty—"

"After dark, when they change shifts," Marilyn instructed. "Then they can't see our zits. So how old are we?"

"Eighteen," Johnnine answered solemnly.

"Yeah. So what year were you born?"

"Nineteen-forty..." Johnnine paused, doing mental calculations.

Marilyn was stern. "You gotta say it *fast*—nineteen-forty-ONE! They won't want us unless we lie about our age. Remember these are college boys!"

Johnnine was duly imbued with awe at this reminder. "Yah. GOD!"

The girls returned to their scrutiny behind the box hedge.

A late-forties model Chevy sedan, parked on a deserted country lane under an extravagantly full moon, appeared empty but nonetheless rocked and rolled on its motionless wheels. Steamed-up windows and occasional moans and groans added to the impression that the car was alive. A back door burst open.

Johnnine half-staggered out, her blouse undone, her hair in disarray, her face flushed, mascara streaking her cheek. She began to put herself together as a boy's voice from inside the car pleaded.

"Johnnine, come on, come back in here—"

"No, Timmy."

"Why not? Jeez," he groaned loudly. "I told you, I have a rubber!"

"I don't want to do it here, like this—"

Timmy spilled out of the car, which continued to bounce on its shocks. His clothes in deshabille, his wholesomely handsome face was distraught, almost desperate. "Well *where* then? *When*?? Jesus, I can't wait forever!" He pinned Johnnine up against the car with hot, coercive kisses.

"Timmy—" Johnnine muttered in between frantic tonguing and lip-sucking, "this is only our first date..."

Timmy tried to change her mind by slowly grinding his pelvis into hers, as if screwing her to the car door. Johnnine was not immune to his single-minded passion but managed to push him a few inches away from her body. She panted for air. "Timmy—I have to go to the bathroom—"

The rhythmic rocking of the car suddenly stopped. "Wait!" Marilyn shouted from inside. "I gotta go, too!"

Cautiously the girls tripped away down the moonlit road, looking for a discreet spot. Marilyn looked back over her shoulder. "God, I didn't know college men were so, so—"

Johnnine exhaled and fanned her face with her hand. "Hot to trot, my mother would say."

Back at the car, Izzy Fishbaum crawled out of the front seat. Leaning against the fender, he lit a cigarette, inhaled deeply, and grabbed his crotch. "Jesus, my balls ache."

Timmy reached for Izzy's cigarette. "Same here, man," he said, taking a drag.

Izzy combed his thick, greasy hair back into a pompadour. "Are we gonna beat the meat again tonight or we gonna get some real poon for a change?"

"Mine says she doesn't want it with a rubber..."

"What? How else is there?" Izzy was indignant. He narrowed his already-narrow eyes. "You think they're cock-teasers?"

"Nah," Timmy said dismissively. "All the C.T.'s in the world live in my home town. We got ourselves some fast women up from the city looking for action!"

"Yeah!" Izzy said, a willing believer. He and Timmy slapped hands.

"Now, you have your diaphragm in?"

Johnnine nodded.

"And you used the spermicidal jelly the way the doctor showed you?"

Johnnine rolled her eyes and looked mortified. "Mo-om—"

Dinah and Johnnine stood in the front hall of the Avenue D apartment. Johnnine held the door open as Dinah prepared to leave. Daughter looked guarded, mother looked teary-eyed.

"I hope your first time's as wonderful as mine was," Dinah said nostalgically. "Roy was such an exciting lover, I didn't know where I ended and he began. Did I ever tell you about the way he used to suck my toes when he—"

Johnnine cut her off. "Mom, Timmy'll be here soon..."

Large tears sprang to Dinah's eyes as she looked at her beautiful, tense, coolly self-contained young daughter. "Oh, God, you're not my baby anymore, are you?" Dinah turned away and hastened down the stairs, still in her large white summer duty uniform and thick-soled white shoes from work.

Johnnine closed the door and walked down the hall to stand in front of a cheap mirrored armoire. She looked strikingly pretty in a green shirt-waist dress that matched her eyes, preening and posing for herself. She was adding more liquid eye liner to the thick streak already on her eyelids when there was a loud knock on the door. Johnnine jumped and drew a black line up through her eyebrow. "Just a minute!" she yelled, grabbing a Kleenex to scrub at her eye. She walked quickly down the hall and opened the door.

Timmy was neatly-dressed in chinos and a short-sleeved Madras shirt. He grinned and held up a manila envelope. "I brought a Peter Gunn album. You *sure* this is okay with your mother?"

Johnnine was too nervous to smile. "Yes, I told you. She'll stay out until eleven."

"Where'd she go?"

Johnnine shrugged. "A bar..."

Timmy shook his head and stepped inside the apartment. "This beats anything I ever heard about New Yorkers."

Johnnine closed the door. Timmy turned to her. "You know you're very pretty."

Johnnine flushed and looked pleased. Timmy kissed her heatedly, dropping the album on the floor. Johnnine responded awkwardly but willingly.

An hour later, with the driving sax solo of the Peter Gunn theme wailing from the record player in the living room, Timmy blew a smoke ring at the ceiling of Johnnine's room. They lay next to each other in bed, not looking at each other. An ashtray rested on Timmy's hairless, bare chest. "Jesus, if I'd known you were a virgin...it didn't hurt, did it?"

Johnnine lay on her back and addressed the ceiling. She looked a little dazed. "It doesn't matter, I didn't want to be a virgin anymore. All I've ever heard about growing up was sex this, intercourse that. I had to find out what it was like—"

"Jeez," Timmy said enviously. "All I ever heard about was the crops and the weather. So, you coming up to Loch Sheldrake again?"

Johnnine watched him blow another smoke ring. "I don't think so. Marilyn's family's back here now."

"What else you gonna do all summer, get a job or anything?"

"No, I can't get a work permit yet, I'm too—" Johnnine blanched, horror-stricken at her slip. "I mean, Mom doesn't want me to—"

Timmy sat up abruptly. "What do you mean, you can't get a work permit? You only have to be fourteen, for Christ's sake!"

Johnnine turned her head away but Timmy grabbed her chin and forced her to look at him. Her eyes welled with tears.

"Holy goddam Toledo, you're under-age! Aren't you!?! You know what kind of trouble I could get in? How the hell old are you??? No, *shit*, don't tell me, at least I could plead ignorance—"

Timmy jumped out of bed, stubbed out his cigarette, and yanked on his jockey shorts, keeping his back turned to her. "Christ, what I had to do to get a day off, too—just so I could sleep with jail-bait! Goddamit, Johnnine, you shouldn't lie about your age! You could be somebody's baby sister!"

Johnnine held the sheet up to her chin. "Where are you going?" Her eyes looked miserable.

Timmy shoved his sockless feet into brown penny loafers. "Back to the hotel, where I should've stayed. Look, you just forget me, forget my name, forget what happened. No hard feelings, okay? I shoulda known it was too good to be true..."

He bent down to kiss her on the cheek. Johnnine moved her head so that their lips met. Timmy began kissing her in earnest but quickly wrenched himself away. "*Damn*!!!" He tore out of the room.

Johnnine froze until she heard the front door slam. Then she turned over and buried her face in her pillow.

Chapter Thirty-two

In the All Souls' Waiting Room, Johnnine felt a sharp tug of physical desire. Intercourse with Timmy hadn't been all that hot, but she loved being close to him, having him hold her. That was a decided downer about dying, she realized. No more guys.

"And that was your first time?" Xofia asked sympathetically. "Poor darling."

Johnnine was so unused to this tone that she shrugged it off. With a glum face, she said, "The way it is. You want someone, they don't want you back. Someone likes you, you can't stand them. A loser's game."

"There are other games, games of love at which the odds are much better, more in your favor."

Johnnine's mouth pulled back inadvertently. "Don't tell me—the only hitch is you have to be born in Monte Carlo."

Xofia smiled sardonically. "Not necessarily. But you do have to leave the casinos where they use marked decks."

Johnnine frowned. "We're talking metaphor here, right? Can you use plain English for a change? I'm a college drop-out, remember—"

"Darling." Xofia changed her appearance to Greer Garson. She looked at Johnnine's gloomy countenance tenderly. "Would you believe me if I told you you've been through the worst, that nothing in your life will be more painful than being a child?" Xofia shot a glance at The Recorder. "It's all right to tell her that, isn't it? Surely we have to give her hope?"

The Recorder shrugged. "She won't remember any of this. You can say whatever you want—"

Xofia turned back to Johnnine. "I've scanned your soul scroll. You're due for some very good fortune, darling. The only *hitch* is you have to be there to get it—"

Johnnine would have liked to believe her. Then she recalled an episode brought about by Lily Neary. "That's weird you should say that. Some *ferkockteh* astrologer told me the same thing, only I thought he was out of his mind. I mean, if he thought my life was lucky, he'd have to be—" She looked thoughtful for a moment. Without seeing it, her eyes took in Schlomo's collection of small terra-cotta figures of Eros. "But isn't astrology just a bunch of bullshit?" Part of her desperately wanted to make a leap of faith, but the cynical sophisticate in her kept her from springing.

Xofia shrugged and stretched luxuriously. "No more than a lot of the beliefs on Earth...there will even be a President of the United States who will use the stars to his political advantage. He will of course be ridiculed for it, even at the same time he is called the most mysteriously successful politician of the century—"

Johnnine narrowed her eyes, uninterested in the political fortunes of future presidents. Xofia could just be handing her a line, some kind of pre-manufactured pep talk they gave everybody in the Waiting Room. "Yeah, so what kind of good fortune will I have?" She was no hick from Passaic, plus she had read her fairy tales. "Like inheriting a million dollars—or having a runaway bus miss me by a few inches?"

"I can't tell you exactly, darling. That would be cheating. You make your own particulars. But in general, the signs are very favorable."

Johnnine grunted. "Then something's really screwed up. Up to now they've been, like, Go Back, You Are Entering A One-Way Street."

There was a low chuckle from The Recorder. He put down the figurine of Artemis he was handling. "That's because you've been on the boulevard of self-destruction rather than the one of self-knowledge...things change once you get onto the right thoroughfare."

"I'm not self-destructive," she argued, in a breath-taking example of denial. "I don't act any differently than the people I grew up with!"

"My point," The Recorder nodded his cowled hood, "is made."

Whoa! Johnnine thought. Shit, could it be Old Faceless had her?

"Lights, camera, action!" Xofia commanded. The cherubs flew to comply.

The film skipped ahead to Johnnine's senior year at Seward Park High School. Johnnine sat opposite a middle-aged teacher in a glass-paneled cubbyhole, one among many in a humming warren of guidance counselors. At fifteen, Johnnine wore her long blondish hair in a French twist, with enough black eye liner to give her green eyes a startlingly theatrical, almost Oriental look. Her facade was city-slick but her words did not follow suit.

"...so it's clear from your classes what direction you should be heading in for college, Johnnine. Outstanding grades in English, French, History, and Drama, Honor Society Secretary, prize-winning contributor to the school paper...You'd make an excellent English teacher." Mrs. Traynor, the senior class guidance counselor, studied a file on her desk. She was well-intentioned, overworked, and evoked the silent-movie era with thick black bangs, vermilion lipstick on a Cupid's bow mouth, and plucked and penciled eyebrows.

Johnnine looked uninterested, almost bored, until Traynor's last remark. "But I don't want to teach. I want to be a vet!"

Mrs. Traynor's eyebrows disappeared under her bangs. "A vet? You mean a veterinarian?"

"Yes!" Johnnine insisted. "I've always wanted to be a vet, that's all I've ever wanted to be, since I was five or six. I love dogs more than anything, more than people—"

Her counselor's face went from disbelief to disapproval. "But Johnnine, science isn't your strongest subject. Your SAT's are much higher in English than in math—and you'd have to take a pre-med course, a very difficult undertaking for a woman, especially a pretty one. Do you know how much attention you'll get? How few women actually graduate? Most drop out to get married, they simply can't take the pressure—"

"I get A's in all my classes," Johnnine said defensively. "Including math and science..."

"Yes, dear, but this is high school, not college. You'll be a sixteen-year-old freshman, you should make it easy on yourself. College is a big adjustment after all, you'll be completely on your own. Now let's put our heads together. Your Regents scholarship pays your way to any college in New York State. Have you thought about which ones you'd like to apply to?"

"Cornell has the only vet school—" Johnnine said sulkily.

"Ye-es, but I can't really advise you to take that course. From what I've heard, vet school is the same as med school as far as women are concerned. The men make it almost impossible—"

"I'll DIE if I don't go to vet school." Johnnine picked up the edge of the pile of books in her lap and let them fall back down, making a soft plop against her thighs. "I'll just die..."

Mrs. Traynor pursed her carmined lips together. "Don't exaggerate, dear. You can certainly apply to Cornell, no harm in that, but why don't I put down a few others as well, just to be safe, like C. C. N. Y., all right? It's a first-rate college, I went there myself. You could live at home and take the subway, just like I did. It would be very economical, the Regents' award pays for books as well as tuition. You're a very lucky girl. Not many students get all their expenses paid for college."

Mrs. Traynor wrote down her recommendations in Johnnine's file. The scene faded out on a close-up of Johnnine's unhappy, unenthusiastic face, flashes of anger and rebellion in her heavily made-up eyes.

"I don't know exactly. Neary just said he wanted to meet you," Dinah said testily, "that you had a very unusual astrological chart."

Dinah and Johnnine stood outside Ratner's Jewish Delicatessen on Second Avenue, obviously waiting for someone as they looked up the street. Dinah wore her white duty uniform under a light spring jacket, Johnnine had on her usual sulky expression.

"When did she get so interested in astrology?" Johnnine studiedly ignored two passing men who turned their heads together to give her openly appreciative looks. She was inured to double-takes, especially on the Lower East Side, where she was stared at like a princess in a pawn shop.

"A year or two ago, I think," Dinah said, smoking as she eyed the men eying her daughter. "Maybe we better wait inside—"

"Is that her?" Johnnine nodded incredulously at a transformed Lily Neary coming down the street. There was an older man by her side.

The All Souls' Waiting Room

Neary waved. "Yoo hoo!" She called out in a voice trained to project into the top balcony, in the unlikely event they couldn't see her coming. While the man with her looked fairly ordinary—middle-aged, overweight, frizzy-haired, in a well-rumpled herringbone suit—Neary was dressed in a long bright red skirt and clashing orange blouse with bat-wing sleeves and had hidden her graying blond hair under a screamingly vivid scarf. She had turned herself into a fortune-telling gypsy.

Johnnine's stare was almost rude. "Good God, Neary! Where's your crystal ball?" she said bluntly.

Neary looked deflated for a moment. Then she laughed her wonderful, throaty laugh. "I guess I do rather like to dress for my roles—Johnnine, Dinah, this is my astrology teacher, Benjamin Starr..."

Starr offered his hand, limply, and they all moved inside Ratner's and took a table. An old waiter carrying a huge tray piled with steaming dishes of food glided by. "You want the strawberry shortcake," he said authoritatively, laying out greasy menus with his free hand. "I'll be right back—"

"SO—" Neary made her soulful, heavily mascaraed eyes big and wide, smiling at her teacher who was blinking owlishly at the noisy, bustling restaurant scene around them. "I used your chart, Johnnine, as one of my early attempts at interpretation. When I showed it to Benjamin—" She paused, waiting to see if he would speak. He didn't. He looked distracted, as though he had not been out in public for some time. "—he said he wanted to meet you in person..."

The waiter buzzed back to their table. He was a short, gnarled little old man, surprisingly forceful and energetic. "So what else besides the shortcake? Glass tea, cream soda?" He whipped out a dog-eared order book and looked over his shoulder, to check on his many other customers.

"I'd like coffee, too, please," Dinah said, not disputing the imposition of Ratner's famous strawberry shortcake.

"Me, too," Neary seconded.

"Tea," was Starr's first word so far.

"Cream soda," Johnnine said in a muted voice, her withdrawn looks making it clear she did not relish being where she was.

The ancient waiter shot her a smile. "Good goyl, that's how you grow up strong and even more beeyootiful." He disappeared.

"What in particular interested you in Johnnine, Mr. Starr?" Dinah's question drew Starr's pale hazel eyes away from their wanderings around the crowded restaurant.

"What? Oh." He pulled a folded piece of paper out of his breast pocket. "Well, her natal chart's got several unusual aspects. For instance, her moon squares Uranus and Mercury—difficulties to be overcome—but then it has a direct trine to her sun, as well as Venus—opportunities to be realized. There's a very interesting T-square grand trine, a number of air trines and even some fire trines—" He was animated and engaged for the first time.

Dinah and Johnnine looked at him with blank expressions.

Neary interposed. "What I found, and what Benjamin corroborated, was that Johnnine has a very powerful communications chart. The stars are on her side in the field of writing. With Jupiter and Venus in her tenth house..."

Dinah looked at Johnnine, who was silent. She avoided looking directly at any of the adults, preferring to fix on the delivery of her cream soda. The waiter was already back with their drinks, setting them rapidly down before speeding away. Johnnine applied herself to tearing the paper off two straws and languidly inserting them into her glass.

"Well," Dinah said, "that doesn't surprise me. But she's not interested in writing. Are you, ducklet?"

Johnnine shrugged. "I like to write," she said, taking a pull on her soda.

"She needs a way to support herself. I told her to get something practical under her belt, like typing." Dinah laughed. "That's writing, isn't it?"

"Not in the sense we're looking at," Neary said. She looked out of place sitting in Ratner's sipping coffee, as though she had misplaced her gypsy wagon. "Johnnine has very favorable aspects in her house of careers and, AND," Neary added with a dazzling smile, "most importantly, in her house of LOVE—" Neary said the last word in an exaggeratedly deep voice.

Johnnine colored. She lowered her head over her Dr. Brown's. Starr was preoccupied with drinking his glass of hot tea in the Old World way, through a sugar cube between his teeth. Around them were tables of garrulous Jewish men, the noise of their discussion overridden by the barks of the post-retirement waiters. The restaurant was over-heated and the huge plate glass window facing the street was fogged up and sweating.

"What career, that's the question," Dinah said sharply. "She's planning on vet school, though I don't see how I can do it financially—"

Benjamin Starr set down his 'glass tea.' "I see a pronounced inclination for some sort of detective work," he said crisply. "Not necessarily literal detective work, she could dig into essential philosophical or esoteric truths, or even family history, for example. That and a passionate interest in the occult, which hasn't manifested yet. If the two things combine, it could be a very powerful direction for her."

"Yah?" Dinah asked skeptically. "How would she make a living?"

"The occult?" Johnnine asked. When her interest was peaked, the clouds parted from in front of her face and she became lovely-looking. "What's that?"

The waiter slammed down their three plates of shortcake, buried under quivering hillocks of whipped cream. "We got people waiting for your table," he said. "Just so you know. Enjoy your food, you should wear it in good health." He ripped off a check and slapped it down on the table.

"...It's an interest in the supernatural, things beyond the five senses," Neary answered. "With your sun in Scorpio, metaphysics is bound to be very important to you—"

"Shades of her grandmother...What else did you see?" Dinah asked.

Starr squinted at his notes. "She will marry twice, have one child, if any. The first marriage will be rocky, the second will be to an older man and it will be stable. There will always be men in her life. Money won't be a problem."

"I knew it!" Dinah snorted and removed a flask from her purse. Very covertly but unapologetically she poured straight vodka into her coffee. "I always said my kid was a lucky little bitch." Her smile at Johnnine was a mix of pride and jealousy.

Johnnine winced and looked away from her mother's strained smile.

"While her mother, on the other hand, was born to be a workhorse." She drank deeply from her coffee cup and set it down. "Nothing I didn't already know..."

"Books, film, theatre seem to play a big part in your later life, Johnnine," Neary said. "Have you decided about college yet?"

Johnnine frowned at her shortcake. "Everybody keeps telling me I can't be a vet, but I can't think of anything else I want to do—"

"The well-beaten path is not for you," Starr said around a piece of cake, a large fleck of whipped cream on the side of his mouth. He swallowed and blinked. "Yours is a very capable, very old, very individualistic soul. You were born into great difficulty but you have the will and enough favorable aspects to undergo a profound spiritual transformation. You require an intensity of life experience out of which you create a wealth of meaning. You have not yet begun to tap into your natal powers, your true nature. You do not yet know who you are." Starr delivered his speech in a monotone, as if he were reading off an internal teleprompter.

Johnnine shifted in her seat, looking uncomfortable under his scrying gaze.

Dinah laughed. "So who does, already yet vonce?"

Neary looked at the large clock on the wall and downed her cup of coffee. "We have to get back, we only snuck out for a few minutes between readings—can you—?" She gestured at the table. "Usually clients pay for a consultation like this."

Dinah finished her coffee. "What else is new?"

"Benjamin?" Neary spoke to Starr as if he were a child. "Call us if you have any questions, Johnnine—" The would-be gypsy swept her moony mentor outside. The old Jewish deli would probably not see their like again for some time.

Johnnine looked unimpressed, even slightly disgusted as they made their way to the front cash register. "The only question I have," she said to her mother, "is whose chart they were reading. It didn't sound like me at all...are you sure you gave Neary the right time of birth?"

"You think I don't remember when you came out?" Dinah asked indignantly. "In any case, it's on your birth certificate—" They stood in line for the busy cashier. Dinah was snitty. "An actress down to her bones. Neary has to dramatize everything, everything has to be a big deal. And that teacher of hers! I don't believe a word he said, he had a handshake like a dead fish. Wouldn't you know it, they want to see you and I end up with the check?"

Johnnine rolled her eyes, pulled one side of her mouth back, and looked around as if seeking escape. There was none.

Two months later, a cab pulled up in front of a well-preserved brownstone off upper Madison Avenue. Johnnine got out between Monte Balikovsky and Phil Berman. She wore a simple straight sleeveless dress of green linen—a thrift shop find—that showed off her figure and showed up her eyes. Her face was professionally made up, her long hair curled up at the ends. She brushed herself off as Berman rang the doorbell, looking like a young actress with two agents, or a very young call girl with two pimps.

"Just relax, be yourself," Monte advised, fixing a strand of her hair.

"Yah." Berman touched up her face with a few hurried pats from a pressed powder compact. "Nothing to be nervous about, meeting one of the biggest fashion photographers in the world—"

Johnnine flashed Berman a sickly-grateful grin. The door opened to a sexless, black-clad assistant who peered at them through tortoise-shell glasses.

"Hi! We have an appointment," Berman said breezily, already over the doorsill.

"With Henry?" the assistant asked.

"You got another photographer here?" Monte parried.

They were led towards the back of the brownstone, to a high-ceilinged room containing an aluminum forest of photographic lights. Huge rolls of colored paper tumbled from the ceiling like fake waterfalls. In front of one salmon-colored cascade, Henry Yardley was posing a group of three fashion models, thin as clothes hangers, wearing winter coats. A fan blew their hair around while they struck dramatic poses and sucked in their hollow cheeks even more.

A man spoke from behind the slender cover of a tripod. "Give me cold outside, but toasty warm inside your gorgeous new winter coat." The models made love to their coats while Yardley clicked away for several minutes. "Good, gooder, goodest! Stacye, next batch—"

Yardley's assistant materialized with a rack of coats. "Some people to see you..."

Yardley turned around to face the arrivals with the air of a potentate scanning a group of humble supplicants. His smile at Berman was perfunctory, Monte and

Johnnine barely got a glance. Johnnine colored and looked uncomfortable, her eyes flitting up and down the models' Vogue-thin figures.

Yardley checked his watch. "Okay, two minutes." He stepped away from his tripod.

Berman moved smoothly into his field of vision, his hand extended. "Henry!" he said, confident and friendly. "Nice to see you! Phil Berman, from 'What's My Line'—remember, you said you'd take a look at my niece?"

"Oh, right, right, right. Comp sheet?"

Monte was instantly at Yardley's side, unzipping a legal-size leather portfolio. "I took these myself, Henry. Monte Balikovsky's my name. Of course I'm still an amateur, nowhere near your league, but I sort of think they do her justice—"

Yardley pulled up a small magnifying glass hanging around his neck. Johnnine stood still as a statue while he scanned her photographs, her face turning pale, a trace of panic in her eyes. "Hmmm—" Yardley said under his breath, not taken, but not turning up his nose.

While Yardley scanned the glossy sheet of small black-and-whites, Monte moved in beside him. "Her cousin's Suzee Steele," he said in good toady fashion, dropping a name. "You know, the model? She's in that hit TV series, 'The World of Goldie Billings'."

Yardley looked up for the first time, giving Johnnine a brief, professional once-over. "I know Suzee, I did a shoot with her a few years ago." He glanced back down at the photos. "I can see a bit of a resemblance. They have some of the same spoiled bitch quality around the mouth. Yours has good bones, but she'd have to drop twenty pounds for the camera—"

Johnnine reddened and dropped her eyes. She clutched her patent leather clutch purse convulsively.

"What about for TV commercials?" Berman pressed.

"Same thing. And I don't know how much call there is for pouty little sexpots. Her cousin Suzee may have cornered the market..."

There was a hand flutter from Yardley's assistant. "Back to work. I'm on a hellishly tight schedule—" Yardley handed the proof sheets back to Monte.

"Thanks for your time, Henry," Berman said, leading the threesome over the black electrical cords that littered the floor like jungle vines.

Johnnine hit the street first. Her cheeks were burning. "That was the *pits*!"

"What are you talking?" Monte said aggravatedly. "He liked you! All you have to do is lose some weight—"

Johnnine glared at him. There were volcanic sparks in her eyes. "Twenty pounds is not *some* weight, Monte. The only way I could lose that much weight is to cut off both my legs."

"So how do you feel?" Berman asked.

"HUNGRY," Johnnine declared.

"I had a feeling you were going to say that." Berman sighed. "Well, okay, so be it, me, too—there's a Hamburger Heaven over on Lexington."

Flanked by her two ersatz uncles, Johnnine turned east, setting a quick march pace. Inside the hamburger emporium she slid into the booth closest to the door. The lunch-hour crowd had not yet peaked and the place was only half full. She ordered a club sandwich, a chocolate shake, and a side order of deep-fried onion rings.

"This is not the best way to shed unwanted pounds, Johnnine," Balikovsky pointed out. He had ordered a BLT and black coffee.

Johnnine stuck her tongue out at him.

Berman sighed as he diligently applied himself to his chocolate ice cream soda. "Some things are more important than being thin and famous."

"So, okay," Monte counseled. "Maybe you're not a model. Even though you are one gorgeous dish, stick-thin you are not. What are you, then?"

"A veterinarian," Johnnine hissed. She hunched down on her side of the booth and squeezed her eyes into slits.

"Oy." Monte shook his head. "You still stuck on that? What about your other talents? You're verbal, I've even known you to be witty on occasion. When you're not stuffing your face, that is. Why don't you do something with those parts of yourself?"

"What am I supposed to write about?" Johnnine challenged sarcastically.

Berman happily spooned ice cream into his waiting mouth. "They say you're supposed to start with what you know—"

"Well, that's a problem, then, because according to the world at large I'm too young to know anything." Johnnine spoke as if victoriously proving a point. "Besides, writing's too easy for me, I need something hard—"

"Life's hard enough!" Monte warned. "Don't go looking to make it harder. Find your God-given talent and use it, for Christ's sake!"

Johnnine fed herself with large, undainty bites of sandwich followed by angry snaps at a kosher dill. Her cheeks bulged defiantly with food. She looked like a squirrel storing up nuts for the winter.

"Look, Johnnine. Honeypie," Berman began in a placating tone. "You graduate high school next month. Monte and me—I?" He shrugged. "We feel like Dutch uncles, we want to help you. What'll you do if—just if—the vet thing doesn't work out?"

"Die!" Johnnine said emphatically.

"How are you going to pay for vet school, assuming you get that far?" Monte asked. "Be practical—"

"I'll rob a bank! Okay?" Johnnine was being loud as well as wildly facetious. Other diners stared at them.

"Johnnine honey," Berman pleaded, pushing his glasses, which habitually slid down his nose, back up. "We know you haven't had an easy time of it growing up. We just don't want to see you do something neurotic." His voice was caring but his words angered Johnnine.

"I *won't*!! All right?" She had eaten her way through their advice. "I'm still hungry," she said, pushing away her empty plate and lighting an unfiltered cigarette with all the insouciance of a practiced young jade.

Monte and Phil looked at each other sadly.

Chapter Thirty-three

In the All Souls' Waiting Room, the film did a freeze-frame on Berman's and Balikovsky's avuncular despair over their rebellious 'niece.' Then the film broke again, rattling and snapping in the projector like a pair of chattering teeth. The lights came on as Fa got out his little splicing machine.

Johnnine saw herself, in the film, as petulant, ungrateful, and wrong-headed. She would never have made it as a veterinarian, though not for the reasons everyone gave her. Assisting in a small animal vet's office, she'd passed out during a hysterectomy on a basset hound. Squeamishly watching the animal's convulsive recovery after surgery had been even worse. The semi-conscious dog twitched, slobbered, and moaned until Johnnine thought she'd go out of her mind. She'd quit that afternoon. The simple truth was that she loved dogs, but that didn't mean that veterinary medicine was her calling.

Johnnine casually picked up Xofia's copy of the Egyptian "Book of the Dead." "Is this good?" she asked.

"Well, I think so, darling, but then I have rather unusual tastes."

Johnnine looked around Schlomo's packed bookshelves. "Are there are any Victorian novels?"

The Recorder was continuing his cataloguing of Schlomo's artifacts, working now on the next-to-last row of objects in the bookcase behind the desk. "Those are your favorite sort of books, are they not?" he asked her.

The cherubs So and La added to their whittled stockpile of love darts while Fa continued to splice the film.

"Yah," she admitted. "Austen, Eliot, the Bronte sisters!" She sighed with ardent admiration. "Meredith, Trollope, Dickens, Goldfield, Hardy, I love them all, their use of language alone was phenomenal—" Johnnine studied Schlomo's shelves.

"You won't find them here," The Recorder added. "Not because Freud didn't read them, but because they are your favorites."

"Excuse me?" Johnnine wasn't sure she had heard correctly.

"This is not a facsimile of Heaven, wherein you would have whatever you most loved at your fingertips. Nor is it one of Hell, where you would be surrounded by whatever you most hated."

Johnnine blinked as his meaning sunk in. "You mean it's like with the food—I can eat, but it won't taste good?"

The Recorder nodded his head. "Precisely. You can peruse anything that's here, but you won't find your favorite reading matter. And as for the other things you're fond of, as you can see, the only animals are inanimate—" his robed arm pointed towards Schlomo's little forest of figurines "—and the only males are infant cherubs or aged analysts."

Johnnine shuddered. The thought of her present surroundings being all there was, for all Eternity, was daunting. A new and disturbing conclusion was becoming unavoidable. Maybe Berman and Monte and Mrs. Traynor had been right, maybe she needed to go with what whatever gifts she'd been given. Maybe, she thought, picking up a small Roman bronze of the goddess Athena from Schlomo's desk, maybe she should even get back to the novel she'd started. She held the four-inch tall, powerful womanly figure absent-mindedly, remembering the fun she'd had plotting and planning the story, which she'd called "Paradise Farm." She still sort of liked her first page, which of course she knew by heart:

"Karl Fredericks gazed out the window without seeing the busy scene before him. The Nairobi street was crowded with people walking, running, and riding to get their little jobs done before the heat of mid-day made movement of any kind impractical. Tall, blond, and weathered, he got up out of his chair and looked around his new, modern office. With all its conveniences, Karl preferred his old quarters. They had been somewhat shabby, not always clean, and certainly not modern, but there had been an atmosphere of familiar comfort that was completely lacking in this plush new office. Maybe he would get used to it; in any case, Karl had other things on his mind. He had promised Dr. Whitehead he would run over to his old friend's improbably-named Paradise Farm for lunch before the new veterinarian arrived from England.

"'The damnedest thing,' kindly but old-fashioned Edward Whitehead had said over the phone, 'the bloody government's gone and hired a woman vet.'

"Karl knew this would rile his friend's Victorian sensibilities. He, Karl, wanted to be there when she—undoubtedly homely, middle-aged, and dressed in a tweed suit and sensible shoes—made her first appearance."

The only trouble was, Johnnine needed to get to Nairobi to do background research. She couldn't write a novel about a ruggedly handsome white hunter, who eventually falls in love with a beautiful young female English veterinarian on a Kenyan game preserve, without actually ever having set foot in Africa. The unlikelihood of a trip to Kenya in her future set off Johnnine's despair again. She put the bronze Athena back on Schlomo's desk.

"There are many things that get in the way of using one's gifts," Xofia said, reading Johnnine's mind again. "That's partly why humans are so resourceful, to figure out ways around themselves."

Johnnine's usually mobile face was blank and vacant. "Huh?"

Xofia smiled gently. "It doesn't matter. What does matter is that you're seeing things a little differently. Grow or wither, those are the two only real choices on Earth. Both are painful, but one's a little more rewarding than the other..."

"I personally have always been into withering," Johnnine said flippantly, hiking up one shoulder as she sat back down on The Couch.

"Darling," Xofia replied coolly, dispassionately. "This much is obvious."

Johnnine smarted silently as Fa at last joined the ends of the film together and doused the room lights.

In the large auditorium of Seward Park High School on Manhattan's Lower East Side, students in dark blue gowns and mortar boards sat in rows of folding chairs on the stage behind a speaker's podium. Johnnine sat at the end of the first row on stage. Red-faced from the heat and self-consciousness, beads of sweat trickled from her hairline. She stared over the heads of the audience at a large, roman-numeraled clock on the back wall of the auditorium. The clock was set in the middle of a mural depicting Industry and Virtue as two men in flowing white robes heading for the gates of a factory.

Johnnine unhappily watched her mother making her way down the aisle in a large, loud turquoise dress and matching low-heeled pumps, fanning and mopping herself with a handkerchief. Following haltingly behind her was an old man in a short-sleeved white nylon shirt. He had a fringe of white hair around a largely-bald dome. Johnnine did not recognize him.

Dinah took an aisle seat and waved gaily with her handkerchief. Johnnine shrank back against her chair and looked quickly away as her mother sneaked a swig from the flask in her purse. Dinah distinguished herself from the sweltering throng around her by appearing to enjoy herself excessively, laughing and chatting with parents in front, in back, and to the sides of her. The man who took a seat next to her looked around uncertainly, by contrast a great deal more tentative in his pleasure in the occasion.

Two hours later, in the school's front lobby, Johnnine stood holding her high school diploma. She looked morose under Dinah's voluble domination of the conversation.

Her mother was relentlessly energetic, dauntingly perky, proud of her role as parent of a graduate. "—so I says to myself, I says, Self, what would you like for graduation if you were Johnnine? A father! I says." Dinah was doing her Popeye the sailor man imitation. "So I called him. You know the phone number is still the same? and wa-la, here he is."

A brief embarrassed look passed between Duncan Cameron Kirk and his daughter. "I was glad Dine reminded me," Duncan said in a soft voice. Johnnine's features and build were markedly like her father's, except for his washed-out blue eyes. "Otherwise I might've forgotten. I'm very busy writing up synopses of my work, getting the patent applications ready—"

Dinah spoke sharply. "Not now, Duncan. We agreed we wouldn't talk about your invention."

"Oh, right, right." He seemed easily confused, readily acquiescing to Dinah's ground rules. "Here, Johnnine, say something—" He held out a small microphone from a portable tape-recorder slung over his shoulder.

Johnnine recoiled, her eyes widening. "What am I supposed to say?"

"Oh, anything brilliant will do." Her father laughed, a small but genuine bubble of amusement. He looked very boyish when he smiled. "I'll just keep the tape running. It's a way of documenting the event."

"For posterity, you mean?" Johnnine mocked.

"Of course!" her father shot back. "You don't have any doubts about posterity being interested, do you?" His eyes twinkled. "After all, you are the daughter of soon-to-be world-famous D. C. Kirk..."

"In sperm only," Dinah muttered under her breath.

"You know what I'd really like for graduation?"

Dinah broke in abruptly. Duncan swung the microphone over to her. "I was quite pleased when he said he'd try and come," Dinah said. "We had a nice talk, didn't we, Duncan, until he started talking about his invention. I couldn't care less, I said, I just called to ask you to come to Johnnine's graduation. A special suss-prise for Johnnine, your daughter's graduating from high school, did you realize? Mit honors and a college scholarship, already yet vonce. Can you make it or not? I said. I can, he said—"

Johnnine repeated herself, more forcefully. Duncan directed the mike back to his daughter, as if he were covering a verbal ping-pong match. "Mother, I said, I know what I want for graduation."

Dinah looked startled at the interruption of her soliloquy. Her brown eyes grew large. "Oh!?! What is it?" She gave a wily smile, regaining her arch self-amusement. "Whatever it is, the answer's no."

"I want my own apartment," Johnnine said flatly. Her face reddened with her own boldness but there was a firm refusal to be put off in her look.

Dinah groaned. Duncan dutifully moved the microphone. Dinah brushed it aside as though it were a bothersome insect. "How much?"

"I found a really cheap little place in the Village, on Leroy Street."

"Leroy Street?" Dinah asked, distracted into another solo stroll down Memory Lane. "I remember Leroy Street, don't tell me I don't. Remember when we lived on Carmine? We used to go to the Leroy Bar and Grill, you'd have a Shirley Temple and play the jukebox, I'd have a—"

"*Mom*," Johnnine persisted. "I need three hundred dollars key money."

Duncan broke in in a horrified voice, automatically putting the microphone in front of his own mouth. "Three hundred dollars!"

"Shut up, Duncan!" Dinah was highly annoyed. "This has nothing to do with you. You've never helped financially and you never will." She looked back at Johnnine. "I might be able to finagle a loan, but what about the rent?"

"I can pay you back from my summer job..."

"You have a *job*?" her father asked, as if amazed at her enterprise.

"Yah, at N.Y.U," Dinah said stiffly. "A friend of ours got her in."

"And I'll be working part-time while I go to school, so I can cover the rent, it's rent-controlled, only $50 a month—"

"Fifty dollars a month! That's a lot of money!" Duncan seemed dismayed.

"I can afford it," Johnnine said with a defensive edge in her voice.

"Well!" Dinah boomed. "Your own apartment! This calls for a drink. I'm buying!"

Duncan fumbled in his tape-recorder carrying case. "Oh, Johnnine, here. I almost forgot." He handed her a small wooden music box. The rectangular lid had a picture from a magazine carefully pasted over it, the image of a prehistoric stag. "The photo's from the Lascaux caves, in France," he said, leaning close. "They just discovered some amazing cave paintings there. You knew I was born in France, in Étaples, didn't you? My father, your grandfather, had his painting studio there before World War I—"

"You weren't born in Étaples, Duncan," Dinah corrected. "You were born in Aix. It's on your birth certificate."

Duncan straightened up and stared at his ex-wife. "Good Lord, Dinah, I ought to know where I was born."

Dinah flushed, her eyes flashed. "You ought to know a lot of things you don't!"

Johnnine turned the box over and bemusedly wound the key underneath. A feeble but unmistakable version of Lohengrin's Wedding March tinkled out. Johnnine looked up at her father in utter mystification.

"This is getting boring." Dinah turned away from Duncan and threaded her arm through Johnnine's. "Let's go, I'm thirsty—did I ever tell you about the time Duncan and I were on our way to City Hall to get married?" She bustled them towards the double front doors.

"Yes, you did. Wait a minute—" Johnnine stopped to take off her cap and gown. She smiled somewhat wanly at the attendant who was hanging up the rented gowns on a pipe rack set up in the school's lobby, ready to be returned to the clothes rental store.

"I'll take the cap," Dinah said with forced merriment, putting the black mortarboard on her head at a rakish angle. "I used to look good in hats—"

"No, mother," Johnnine said, unamused, taking it off.

"No?" Dinah repeated in a childish voice.

"No." Johnnine handed it to the attendant.

They emerged onto a hot, profoundly-unswept Broome Street. Seward Park High School took up an entire city block, dominating the area with its huge five stories and its B-movie prison architecture. Half the small stores around the school were boarded up, the rest displayed arrays of cheap merchandise. The streets were empty of car traffic. Most of the other graduates had melted away or were congregated inside the corner deli. Dinah clung tightly, possessively, to Johnnine's left arm. Duncan stood on her right. Johnnine's drooping look was that of a captive audience. She stared at the bleak street scene around them with forlorn eyes, wanting nothing so much as her freedom.

"We-ell," Dinah ignored Johnnine's lack of interest and warmed into her story. "I was sitting on one side of the cab, your father was on the other. Remember, Duncan? And mother was in the middle—"

Duncan held the microphone across Johnnine to catch Dinah's words before he spoke into it. "Of course I remember. Esther was wearing a navy-blue dress and a hat with a little white feather in it."

Dinah's eyes narrowed with hostility. "Do you remember what I was wearing?"

Duncan frowned.

"No, I didn't think so," Dinah said bitterly. "Never mind. *I* remember, that's what's important." Leaning towards Johnnine, she said, "Anyhoo, mother leaned over and whispered in my ear—remember I was more than slightly pregnant with you by then—and she said, 'You know you don't have to go through with this, Dinah'."

Duncan looked clearly agitated for the first time. "Esther didn't say that to you, she said it to me!" His former wife had finally drawn blood.

"What are you talking about?" Dinah shouted. "Esther was my mother, she said it to me!"

"You know Esther loved me, too. We adored each other."

"So what, she never said any such thing to you! Don't try and usurp my mother just because yours died young—"

Johnnine pried her mother's hand from her arm and tried to change the subject. "Anyone want to hear about me and C.C.N.Y.?"

"Not now, Johnnine!" Dinah bristled. She spoke to Duncan with a tight jaw. "I think you better leave—"

Duncan packed his microphone away. "Just as contentious as ever."

Dinah's rage, always on the simmer, boiled over. "Don't you dare criticize me! I'm the one who raised Johnnine, *and* all alone! Not a shred of help from you or anyone else!"

Duncan protested. "You wouldn't take any! You *wanted* to raise her by yourself, you chased me away—"

Johnnine stared at her father. "What??"

"He's lying through his teeth," Dinah hissed furiously. "Making things up for his own convenience. Same as always." She jerked Johnnine away. "I should never have called him, but believe me I won't make that mistake again. Come on, ducklet, I need a *drink*!"

Johnnine looked back over her shoulder at her father as her mother dragged her away. Duncan stood in place with a closed, unreadable expression on his face before he turned and walked off in the opposite direction.

"To think how much I used to love that man! And now he's completely, completely...what's that marvelous Yiddish word? *meshugge*." Dinah's laugh was a pained bark. "Yah, *meshugge*!"

Johnnine looked down at the dirty sidewalk. She walked woodenly, silently, alongside her mother as they turned towards Grand Street.

"So where was I before I was so rudely interrupted? Oh, yes—your grandmother and me and your father who wasn't so crazy then, on our way to City Hall to get married, me in the middle more than slightly pregnant with you..."

Dinah stepped off the curb to hail a passing cab. She turned to Johnnine as it stopped. "Remember when you were four years old and you ran to the edge of the sidewalk and raised your tiny hand and yelled 'Tapsi! Oh, tapsi-cab'?"

Dinah's laugh was hollow and slightly manic. "Uptown, driver! Uptown!"

Johnnine looked withdrawn as they climbed into the back of the yellow Checker. Staring straight ahead of her, she put her purse on her lap as Dinah slammed the cab door.

In the All Souls' Waiting Room, Johnnine felt as though she were being sloshed around in a washing machine with some very old, very dirty clothes. She couldn't sort out her feelings, she simply felt overwhelmed with unhappiness. More than anything else she wanted to go to sleep. Forever.

Xofia's voice came to her out of the darkness. "You'll find it really helps to put words to your thoughts, darling."

Johnnine gave a little mew of angst. "My parents, they're both clinical cases, aren't they? So where does that leave me—except in the snake pit?"

"No, actually, it leaves you in Schlomo Freud's consulting room," Xofia said reportorially. "Or others of its ilk," she added with dry humor. "But tell me—how did it feel to see your father again?"

Johnnine swallowed and watched her hands grip The Couch convulsively. "It was awful. I didn't recognize him. I thought he was just some old man Mom'd picked up in a bar somewhere—" She began to cry. "I wanted to die standing next to them. Or else hold up a sign that said, I Am a Hospital Changeling."

Xofia smiled sympathetically. "What was that invention he talked about?"

The room lights came on.

"Oh, God." From a slumped position, Johnnine sat up straight for a moment, then slumped again. "It's a mathematical formula he says can save the world. My father thinks we're destroying ourselves with overpopulation. He made up some kind of dial thing so women can figure out when they're safe and when they aren't. He says it's a recalculation of the rhythm birth control method, that the original mathematics were wrong, but I don't understand it and I don't even want to. I always felt jealous, he gave it all his attention, his whole life. I don't know how it works or even if it does—"

"Oh, yes, it works," The Recorder threw in blandly. "The father Duncan is of the visionary class, but because of previous karma—"

"Let's not get too esoteric on her," Xofia interrupted. Turning back to Johnnine, she said, "So you were jealous of your father's work—"

"Who wouldn't be?" Johnnine huffed. She balked at being labeled. "I used to call him every few years, when I got desperate for a father, and all he could talk about was his invention. It was more important to him than anything, much more than me." She shrugged mightily, in an attempt to make light of it. "I usually ended up telling myself I was better off without him. You can't miss what you never had, right?" Johnnine put on a false smile.

"You most certainly can," Xofia corrected.

Johnnine's eyes danced away from Xofia's penetrating glance. She changed the subject. "What was the music box all about? I could never figure out why he put that picture of the prehistoric stag on it. I mean, it must mean something."

"Perhaps it was a reference to your father's damaged masculinity. Put it together with the Wedding March and you have a pointed, though symbolic, statement about your parents' marriage. By the way, there's one thing you have in common with him..."

"What?" Johnnine challenged.

"You both use intellect to hide from your emotions."

Johnnine didn't have a clue what Xofia was talking about, but she was too proud to admit it. She changed subjects again. "What did my father mean, that my mother didn't want any help raising me?"

Xofia's smile was cagey. "The only way you'll find out is to live your life, Johnnine. There are lots of mysteries that can't be solved from the All Souls' Waiting Room—"

In other words, Johnnine thought to herself, Xofia hadn't the foggiest.

Chapter Thirty-four

The cherub Fa flew to the light switch on the wall. At the same time, Seraph A., who had been lying dormant on his cornice, let fly with a musical decrescendo.

Xofia interpreted. "Aloysius is reminding us that we're coming up on the last episodes in your life review film. After which, darling, we're taking you on a little tour of the Waiting Room—"

Johnnine gave a small sneer: as if that was the answer to her problems. "Peachy keeno," is what she said as the room went black and the film bloomed back up.

In an immense, medieval-looking stone hall hung with banners and thronged with students, Johnnine stood in front of a table bearing a hand-lettered sign, "Senior Student Advisers." Anxiously scanning a list of classes, she consulted with a good-looking male senior. Johnnine appeared nearly undone by the task facing her. Her youthful adviser smoothed back his thick brown hair, dressed for the part of wise upperclassman in a very tweedy sports jacket. He took an unlit briar pipe out of his breast pocket and sucked donnishly on its stem.

"And calculus? I'm really scared of calculus—" Johnnine said.

"It's okay if you get the right teacher," advised her adviser. "You sure you need it?"

"According to the office I do, they said I need the same math and science classes as pre-med." She laughed ruefully. "Actually, I want to be a veterinarian, though when I said 'vet' they weren't sure what I meant, so I guess I'm a first at C.C.N.Y.—"

The senior adviser smiled noncommittally but looked her up and down with heightened interest. "Well, for pre-med you definitely need calculus." He withdrew a folded piece of paper from his inside pocket. "I just happen to know who's teaching what this term," he said as he ran his finger down a list of names. "Hey, you're in luck. Faddington's out of mothballs. Old as Methuselah but he's the one you want, best brain in the math department. He could teach numbers to a duck."

"Thanks a lot." Johnnine's smile was wry. "Which class?"

"Looks like North Campus, eight o'clock."

"Oh, God," Johnnine groaned softly. "My brain doesn't punch in until ten."

"Old Fad's the only way to get through freshman calc," her adviser pressed her, looking up briefly as he was jostled by the crowd of surging registrants around them. "Unless you're a math genius."

"*Pas moi.* Unfortunately."

"No, you couldn't be, way too pretty." He smiled at her, clearly intending his remark as a compliment.

Johnnine looked equally flattered and perturbed, but she let it go. "Where do I go for tutoring, in case?"

"Just so happens I do a little private tutoring on the side, but only for very special cases." He scribbled something on Johnnine's list. "Here's my home number. Name's Jerry."

"Thanks," Johnnine smiled. "I hope I won't need it, but I probably will. Um, where do I go now?"

"Get your calc class, and don't settle for anyone but Faddington, get it?"

"Got it."

"Good." Jerry smiled. "And call me anyway! We'll go for coffee—dutch."

Johnnine's smile was ambiguous as she vanished into the crowd.

In the All Souls' Waiting Room, Johnnine vividly remembered her feelings of being dismissed intellectually because she happened to be pretty, as if a brain couldn't handle its housing looking good. Not that she was a *real* brain, she thought to herself, but neither was she a complete drooling idiot. She had to learn to cut herself some slack.

"Good going, darling—" Xofia encouraged from the sidelines, reading Johnnine's mind again.

"Why couldn't you be one of my teachers?" Johnnine wished out loud.

"But I am," Xofia responded eerily.

One week later, Johnnine groggily stumbled out of bed as her alarm clock went off at 6:00 in the morning. She left her miniscule bedroom and walked several steps into the miniature kitchen. Beyond her was an eight-by-ten living room, barely big enough for a dresser, a home-made desk, an upholstered chair and a small jade green sofa.

Johnnine switched on the overhead kitchen light. The splash wall behind the sink turned into a brown mosaic of cockroaches. Johnnine did not appear to notice her co-habitants. She took her toothbrush and toothpaste out of a hip-high refrigerator and began brushing her teeth, spitting a thin stream of rinse water at the slower-moving roaches on the back of the sink.

Half an hour later, Johnnine sat swaying groggily, still half-asleep, in an express subway as it roared uptown. The number of other riders dwindled until Johnnine was almost the last person in the car when it stopped at 140th Street and Morningside Drive. She left the station and began a long vertical hike through Morningside Park, which encompassed a steep, lightly-wooded hillside. Old-fashioned, wrought-iron street lamps were still on in the misty half-light of the early morning, menacing shapes seemed to move about behind the trees. Johnnine hurried up the remaining flight of steps, checked her watch, and broke into a run.

A short while later, she was catching her breath in a dark and dingy North Campus classroom. A young man in shirtsleeves and argyle vest stood in front of a much-washed blackboard on which was written, Calculus 101, Instructor

"I'm not 'most chicks'!" Johnnine said angrily. "And I hate that phrase. Why can't you say 'have intercourse'?"

"You're *weird*, you know that?" Jerry said, getting up and zipping up his fly. "If you're saying you won't give head without me muff-diving, let's forget it, okay? Plenty of other dummies who want tutoring—"

Johnnine's face grew very red. "Go stick it in a textbook! And then try slamming it shut!"

Jerry stood over her and wagged his finger. "You are going to fail calculus without me." He grabbed his coat and stormed out of the apartment. The door crashed shut behind him.

Johnnine picked up Moppie and buried her face in the dog's soft white fur. "*Bastard*," she said, and began to cry.

In the All Souls' Waiting Room, Johnnine found these scenes of defeat and failure bitter pills to swallow—again. She'd felt soiled after Jerry left, used, abused, and rejected. He'd completely misunderstood her as well. It wasn't that she wanted him to "go down" on her—the idea frankly made her a little sick—it was the unfairness, the one-sidedness. Me, man with cock, me get sucked. You, woman with hole, you get fucked. Wasn't she ever going to find a man to love her body *and* soul?

"Your second husband, darling, remember your astrology reading?" Xofia said over her umpteenth glass of Dom Elysee. "You'll find your man when you find your true path—"

"But that's a long way away!" Johnnine half-wailed.

Xofia shrugged. "Good things take time."

The following week Johnnine sat in her abnormally-quiet calculus classroom. The other students were hunched industriously over their desks, busily scribbling. Johnnine merely stared at the paper in front of her. Finally she got up, collected her things, and deposited her unfinished test sheet on the teacher's desk. Some of the other students looked up briefly but quickly returned to their work.

"I'm sorry, I really tried, but I just can't seem do it," Johnnine whispered.

Kessler's hard young face did not soften. "I'll have to fail you if you don't finish the final."

Johnnine nodded disconsolately and left the classroom.

When she emerged from the subway at Sheridan Square, the December weather was cold and raw, the sky a depressing steel-gray. She crossed Seventh Avenue, making a stop at the Smiler's deli, and re-emerged with a bag of groceries.

Inside her apartment, Johnnine lay on the couch, watching TV and eating. An assortment of half-consumed food lay spread out next to her on the coffee table: the remains of a meatball hero sandwich, a double bag of potato chips, a quart of chocolate milk. Johnnine groaned as she ate her way through a pint of pistachio ice cream. Putting it down, she looked slightly green, vaguely bilious, until she stuck her finger down her throat and began to retch. Then she dashed into the kitchen and bent over the sink. Moppie gave up chewing on her little rubber ball to run after her, wagging her tail and barking, thinking Johnnine was playing a new game.

Somewhat later, Johnnine had recomposed herself. The television was off, all traces of her eating binge had been cleared away. The tiny living room looked neat and tidy. Moppie was in frog position, her hind legs spread flat on the floor, contentedly gnawing on a fresh stick of rolled rawhide. In the mirror over the dresser, Johnnine was applying thick black eye liner and brushing her hair. An envelope lay propped up on the coffee table, addressed to To Whom It May Concern, next to a bottle of Ballantine's scotch.

Johnnine sat down on her couch and opened a vial of prescription pills and a bottle of Nembutal. She poured them both into her lap and began scooping up handsful of pills, chasing them down with a tumbler of the scotch Jerry had left behind. She groaned and shuddered after each swallow.

Moppie jumped up on the couch and began licking her hand. When Johnnine had taken all the pills, she looked sick for a minute, as though she was going to throw up. She lit a Pall Mall and inhaled deeply, which stopped the gag reflex though she went into a coughing fit. Then she stubbed out the cigarette and lay down full-length on the jade green couch and pulled her black corduroy jumper down to her knees, smoothing it over her legs so it lay flat and neat. She looked down at her feet, encased in her favorite black fake lizard high heels. Then she put Moppie on her stomach. "Don't you worry, you'll be okay," she said, stroking the dog's small domed head.

Crossing her arms over her chest like an Egyptian mummy princess and closing her eyes, Johnnine waited. On the radio next door, Barbra Streisand began singing "Happy Days Are Here Again." The phone rang. A moment later Johnnine's soul-form peeled away from her unhappy body. First it hovered just below the ceiling. Then it moseyed out through the closed window and past the rusty fire escape. The screen went black.

There was a moment's pause in the All Souls' Waiting Room before the cherubs went into a kazoo-like version of "The Funeral March."

"Now you know that that's just the beginning," said The Recorder.

"I can see how you might have gotten discouraged, darling," Xofia said. "But you did have other options."

"Like what?" Johnnine defended herself. "When there's nothing left, when you're a complete failure at everything you do, when everything you try turns to shit?"

"Why don't you do what everyone else does? Blame your parents instead of yourself for a change?" Xofia purred.

Johnnine was utterly taken aback. She couldn't even respond at first, it was such an outrageous—but utterly irresistible—proposition. She got up off The

Couch. Could Xofia have a point here? Maybe she wasn't a hopeless case. Maybe if she figured out what was wrong with her mother and father she would understand what was wrong with her.

Xofia's smile was tender. "That, my dear, could be your life's work—come, it's time for our tour." Xofia stood up. "Aloysius, are we ready?"

Seraph A. flew down from the cornice and blew whistle commands at Fa, So, and La, who bustled about rewinding the film and closing up the projector.

"It's been an informative viewing, young woman," The Recorder said to Johnnine. "You'll be seeing me again shortly, so this is only *au revoir*." He glided out of the room, his dun-colored robe trailing after him.

"What did he mean by that?" Johnnine asked nervously. She still hadn't gotten a glimpse of his facial features. If he had any, she reminded herself, getting goose bumps again.

"You'll see. Ready, darlings?" Xofia chirped at the cherubs. They chirped back. "Then let's went."

Johnnine wondered if Xofia used some of the same expressions as her mother on purpose or if it was merely coincidence.

"There really is no such thing as coincidence," Xofia said over her shoulder as the entourage left Schlomo's office. "Things happen the way they need to happen—"

This was too arcane for Johnnine. "You mean I *needed* to try and kill myself?"

"In a sense, darling."

"Why?"

"So you could be introduced to your spiritual side..."

They left the flat, took the single flight of wide, well-worn marble stairs down to the lobby and emerged onto downward-sloping Berggasse. There was an old-fashioned black wooden *fiaker* at the edge of the curb. The cherubs placed the can of film and the bulky, old-fashioned Akashic film projector on the front seat.

"What's this?" Johnnine could not hide her amazement.

"Oh, just an old horseless carriage," Xofia said as she climbed in. "Get in, darling, we're going for a little ride."

Johnnine took the springy little metal step into the open carriage. She sat bemusedly next to Xofia. "But how?"

"Aloysius!" Xofia said in a rather imperious tone.

The little seraph and his three cherub colleagues picked up the cab's wooden shafts. Instanter, they were airborne.

"Holy shit!" Johnnine exclaimed breathlessly.

"Such a curious phrase," Xofia said. They rose rapidly into swirling white clouds, edged with just a hint of pink and gold. "Is it an oxymoron, a paradox, or a sublime truth?"

Johnnine ignored Xofia's rhetorical whimsies and looked upward. "You're not going to tell me we're going to heaven now?"

Xofia laughed. "No, of course not, darling. Primarily because there is no such place, except in excessively religious imaginations. Though one could say that heaven and hell are on Earth, depending on what humans make of their lives. No, things don't change all that much after death—people get what they expect they'll get, at least for a while..."

"But what exactly does happen after you die? I mean, people do die sometime or other."

"You mean when the corporeal body dies? We'll show you."

The antique, cherub-powered cab floated effortlessly down through a large building apparently made of ethereal pastry dough. They landed silently and unobtrusively in the back of a large classroom. Johnnine was surprised to see The Recorder sitting behind the desk at the front of the room. On the blackboard behind him was written Akashic Returns 101. His sonorous voice broke the attentive silence. "Juan Cardinal Carlos, please rise—"

A man in the front row in a rich red satin robe got to his feet.

The Recorder addressed him directly. "For the advancement of your spiritual understanding, to experience the other side of the coin, it would be advisable for you to return as a devout Catholic female and to bear and raise sixteen children in the slums of Rio de Janeiro."

There was an audible groan from the former cardinal.

"A good call," Xofia whispered.

Johnnine soberly took in the sight of the All Souls' classroom, where all sorts of souls waited patiently for their Akashic assessments. Was that really what life was, she wondered, lesson after spiritual lesson? "Does he have to do it?" she asked Xofia.

"Not necessarily." Xofia still whispered. "Humans have free will, after all, darling. And thank The Powers, otherwise things would get very boring, the cherubs would have nothing to bet on—"

"*Will* he do it?" Johnnine kept her eyes on the forlorn former cardinal as he dragsouled out of the classroom, looking a bit like she felt about returning to life.

"Probably not. He seems hooked on Pride. Thus ensuring many, many more lifetimes of edifying toil and strife...Aloysius!"

The cherubs rose into the air and whisked the cab back into the clouds. Johnnine was lost in deep and painful thoughts. "You mean the deal is, a shitty life now or an even shittier one next time?"

"That's about it, darling," Xofia said equably. She was looking like smug Glenda the good witch again. "Make the best of what you get because it could get worse—"

The magical horseless cab flew through the glory-tinted clouds, the adorable cherubs' lustrous wings beat double-time, and yet in spite of her wondrous surroundings Johnnine felt sorely cheated. "That means there's no way out," she said despondently.

"Well, no, technically speaking, there is one," Xofia hinted. "After one has plumbed all the depths of one's soul, learned all the lessons life has to teach—"

The *fiaker* descended dizzily through the pallid All Souls' air and landed in the Prater amusement park, next to the huge ferris wheel. As they watched, a long line of disembodied souls—more or less featureless, more or less sexless—handed tickets to a bewinged wheel attendant.

"These are highly-evolved souls," Xofia pointed out.

"How can you tell?" Johnnine asked.

"Notice how they don't push or shove?"

The enormous, gaily-painted ferris wheel made one full revolution. When it stopped, the soul at the very top opened the bar across its bucket seat. Leaping off the wheel, the disembodied soul gave out an ethereal, spine-tingling yell, and then disappeared into the ether in a blaze of transmogrifying light.

"The Wheel of Enlightenment, darling." Xofia's tone was reverent. "That particular soul has earned the right not to re-incarnate."

Johnnine watched another soul getting off at the bottom. It headed straight for the outdoor beer garden opposite the ferris wheel, over which hung a banner that read, For the Best of Beers, Try Eternal Return.

"Why didn't that one jump off?" Johnnine asked.

"Some souls choose to go back and help others."

"Why??"

"Oh," Xofia smiled. She looked like Greer Garson again. "It's kind of an in thing to do."

Johnnine couldn't picture herself going back if she didn't have to. Life hurt too much. "I'm not going to get my ticket, am I?" she said resignedly. Her eyes followed the souls filing into the beer garden. Tanking up, she thought, at the thought of going back to Earth.

"Your ticket to die, darling?" Xofia shrugged. "Only The Powers know for sure. Aloysius!"

Johnnine felt a regressive state coming on, suddenly overwhelmed with self-pity. "If I'm supposed to live and be fruitful, why'd I get such a shitola start? How am I supposed to get anywhere with parents like mine?"

"Darling," Xofia said sympathetically. "Parents are both the road and the potholes in the road. Your spiritual task is to get past the potholes without falling in."

Great, Johnnine thought, just what I need. Another goddamned conundrum. She had a momentary longing for an Earthly conversation, where people said dull, mundane, understandable things to each other like 'hot enough for you?' and 'pass the salt.'

Xofia, however, was not finished. "You chose the pay-first, fly-later childhood plan. You've paid, now perhaps it's time to fly—"

Chapter Thirty-five

Xofia was not speaking figuratively. The *fiaker* zoomed up into the clouds again, coming quickly but gently back down to the ground in front of the All Souls' Bibliothek, in the palatial Heldenplatz.

"What's this?" Johnnine asked, looking around.

"This—" Xofia waved airily at the large open square around them, bordered by two wings of the stony grandeur of the Hofburg Palace and graced with two bronze statues on horseback. "This is the Square of the Heroes, darling. Come, we're returning your film to the Akashic archives."

Johnnine followed Xofia as she glided up towards the imposing Hofburg Library, her cherry-red kimono wafting behind her, her high Wedgie heels clacking on the stone steps. Seraph A. flew ahead of them while Fa, So, and La chittered at each other, struggling with the cumbersome projector and the can of Johnnine's life review film. When they passed through the portals, over which Johnnine noticed the inscription, Abandon All Ignorance All Ye Who Enter Here, the cherubs flew off through the frescoed lobby to return the film to its proper shelf.

Johnnine saw miles and miles of shelves on which sat rows and rows of tightly-rolled scrolls under endless cans of film, stretching from the lobby to the back of the Bibliothek, into what looked like infinity. She also saw Willie Reich and Schlomo Freud standing by one of the nearest stacks, presumably those of the most recently-departed. They were snorting with undisguised glee over one of the unrolled scrolls and smoking, Schlomo a cigar, Willie a cigarette, under a clearly-legible NO SMOKING sign.

Johnnine felt immediately tongue-tied in front of the dynamic duo, but Xofia was undaunted. "May I ask what two such illustrious modern heroes find so amusing?" Xofia's tone was cordial, ready to be amused.

Willie and Schlomo advanced towards them. Willie's arm rested casually on the shorter Schlomo's shoulder, suggesting an unusual degree of camaraderie. Something must have really changed, Johnnine thought.

"Jung's scroll," Schlomo said, wiping tears of laughter from the corners of his eyes. "He died recently, you know," he added, without a hint of grief.

Willie smiled warmly at Johnnine. "I hope you're feeling a little better?"

Johnnine nodded and blushed. Everything she had ever wanted to say to him was wiped from her head, as though someone had scrubbed a formerly-filled blackboard clean. But she was very glad he had asked.

"I never thought there could be such engaging entertainment after death!" Schlomo laughed, shaking his head. "First, I complete a long-overdue analysis of my first protégé." He glanced fondly at Willie, who looked enormously pleased. "And then I get to read up on the antics of my second..."

The All Souls' Waiting Room

"But what's so funny about Jung's scroll?" Xofia smiled.

"Oh, some of his *meshugge* theories." Schlomo puffed on his cigar indignantly. "All that alchemical business," he added. "The three stages of individuation, he calls them. Nigredo, albedo, and rubedo, if you can credit such nonsense. *Meshuggas!*"

"Jung always did get on your nerves," Willie pointed out.

"Perhaps because you started out as a neurologist?" Xofia quipped.

Schlomo chortled. "Very good, very good..."

"The man was a raving mystic, not a scientist." Willie was disdainful.

"One must be careful of one's judgments of others, lest they come home to roost," Xofia said portentously.

Willie guffawed, catching her drift. "What? No, never! Impossible—with my scientific credentials?"

Ti and Do flew into the lobby from the nether reaches of the Akashic Records, where they had been napping on an out-of-the-way shelf. Their enthusiastic reunion with their confreres resulted in a joyous mid-air huddle. Amid much fluttering of wings, they broke into a wordless barbershop sextet version of "Me and My Shadow," circling over the heads of Johnnnine, Xofia, Schlomo and Willie like an angelic chandelier.

Xofia looked up and smiled. "Charming, darlings." Then she addressed the group on her own level. "Shall we go? I promised the child a special treat before her audience with The Powers. What do you suppose it is?"

Schlomo, as always, was the first to answer. "Since we are in Vienna, or a facsimile thereof, what else could it be but *Sachertorte*?"

"Exactly," Xofia beamed at him. "Would you care to join us?"

"Delighted," Schlomo said graciously.

"Willie?" Xofia queried.

"It won't be as good as mama's," Willie muttered under his breath but followed the group out of the Bibliothek anyway.

Johnnnine was miffed that Xofia hadn't consulted her about asking Willie and Schlomo along. Couldn't she have her free time away from the two old intruding psychoanalysts? Johnnnine was thinking about how she could protest this new trial when they emerged onto the wide stone landing at the top of the Bibliothek's stairs. The group's attention was immediately drawn below. In the empty Heldenplatz, a white-haired man in a rumpled white linen suit stood next to the *fiaker* parked at the curb. He had small beady black eyes and wore round, steel-framed glasses.

Willie and Schlomo both let out an unrepressed howl of dismay. "Gus!"

Xofia grasped the situation at once and glided vampishly down the stairs to greet him, graciously extending her hand. "Dr. Jung, I presume—"

"Oh, thank God I've found you," were his first words, in a clipped Swiss accent. "I saw you at the Prater and was praying I'd see you again." He ceremoniously clasped one of Xofia's elegant hands. "Now I know I need look no further. I've found the woman of my dreams—"

Schlomo and Willie exchanged an incredulous look and charged down the steps.

"Just a moment! We saw her first!" Schlomo said heatedly.

"Yah! You can't just barge in and take over here—" Willie added, indignant.

"Ah, but gentlemen," Xofia turned to smile beatifically at Willie and Schlomo. Gus still had hold of her hand. "You did not court me."

Johnnine wondered what in the hell was going on. She joined them at the bottom of the steps. "What's he doing here?" she hissed at Xofia through her teeth. Two old farts were bad enough, but three! "I mean, why'd he show up now?"

"Well, you might call it synchronicity," Xofia said lightly. "Then again, you might not. He's here, darling, because he just recently died and all former psychoanalysts have to make at least a brief return, pay homage if you will, to the Viennese section of the All Souls' Waiting Room. But also because he will play an important part in your later life."

"How can he, if he's dead?"

"Don't be obtuse, darling. I mean his work—"

Jung looked like just another boring grown-up to her. Johnnine was infinitely more interested in the *Sachertorte*. "What about my cake?"

"I didn't forget, darling—" Xofia disengaged her hand from Jung's gently proprietary clasp. "Gentlemen, we have a sublime oral experience in store—"

The three former psychoanalysts raised their eyebrows at each other, following close behind Xofia as she took off at a brisk pace on foot. "It's only a few blocks—"

The men began to bicker almost immediately on leaving the Square of the Heroes. As they passed under the Hofburg's ancient stone archway, they complained that the sidewalk was not wide enough for all three of them and began trying to edge each other into the street.

In the middle of the cobblestone intersection, Gus made as if to turn to the left. "But Demel's is this way—" he said.

"But we're not going to Demel's, darling," Xofia said smoothly, continuing on her way past the Spanish Riding School. "We're going straight to the source. The Hotel Sacher."

Johnnine could not quite believe she was destined to spend her near-death time in some sort of celestial bakeoff contest. What about the dignity of life? Or death? Or whatever the hell state she was supposed to be in? Jesus, she thought, nothing on Earth had been more absurd than what she was being subjected to in Mondo Bizarro. And at least there had been people her own age.

The cherubs dashed ahead of the procession, vanishing out of sight down the narrow, crooked old street. A few minutes later, Johnnine's group walked under a gilt-edged, maroon canopy and passed through the hotel's elegant lobby into the Sacher's dining room.

In the jewel-toned, paisley-wallpapered room, under a sparkling crystal chandelier, a single round table was laid with pink linen, heavy silverware, crystal goblets, and fine china. Five places were set with name cards indicating who should sit where, Johnnine on Xofia's right, Gus on her left. This caused disgruntlement among Schlomo and Willie, which erupted in a miniature battle over who should hold Xofia's chair. Willie won. Schlomo sat down in a pout.

The cherubs flew in from the kitchen to serve steaming cups of *kaffee mit schlag*. "And so—let the great cake debate begin," Xofia prompted.

Schlomo took his cigar out of his mouth and substituted a forkful of the famous torte. "Dreamy," he pronounced. "*Wunderbar*! The original recipe, still by far the best!"

Gus took a small bite. "Not bad, but I like Demel's version better—it's lighter, not so heavy."

Willie picked up his piece of cake and took several big bites. Washing it down with a large swallow of coffee, he at once cried, "But it gives me a belly-ache!"

"*Mein Gott*, Willie," Schlomo said, "you still have your oral fixation!"

Willie's pockmarked face grew red. "And you, Herr Professor, do you still have your anal complex?"

Gus clapped his hands together delightedly. "*Déjà-vu*!" he exclaimed.

"Gentlemen, gentlemen," Xofia soothed. "Let us respect each other's opinions without theory-baiting, please! Everyone's palate is different, after all. One man's favorite torte is another's perfect torment..."

The men grumbled and returned their attention to the cake and coffee.

"I have a very special surprise for the three of you in a minute," Xofia said with a sparkle in her eye. "But tell us, Johnnine, how do you like the cake?"

"I'd rather have a Devil Dog," she said flatly, putting down her fork.

"Devil Dog? *Was ist das*?" Gus asked.

"And I would like to know why you insist on infantilizing us," Schlomo said to Xofia, a challenging edge to his voice.

"I wasn't aware of behaving inappropriately—" Xofia answered innocently.

"Aha!" Schlomo pounced. "Is that supposed to mean it's appropriate for you to infantilize us?" His gray eyes glittered. "That we are, in your eyes, only helpless infants?"

"Schlomo, your hostility towards women is showing," Willie pointed out, lighting a Bright Spark.

"Don't be ridiculous—and don't try to analyze me!" Schlomo said vehemently. "I have no hostility towards women! It is simply extremely aggravating when they give themselves superior airs—"

"And why is it aggravating, Herr Professor?" Gus asked closely.

"Because they are not superior, they are inferior to men!"

"Why must one sex be better than the other? Why can't they be co-equals?" Xofia asked.

"Classic masculine over-compensation," Gus said, shaking his head. Jung removed a cheroot from his breast pocket and rolled it between his fingers, reminding Johnnine of a smooth-talking riverboat gambler. Reich looked like an angry guerrilla scientist in his plaid work shirt and short white lab coat, Freud an uptight tenured professor of archaeology in his three-piece gray.

"It is an extremely aggravating fact that there is nothing more important than mothers," Willie said. "—without whose love and caring no one would survive."

"And yet it is the 'bond that must be broken,' is it not?" Xofia's smile at Schlomo was a forgiving one. Then she looked up at the cherubs. "Aloysius—you may bring them in now."

The cherubs pulled back a curtain at the back of the room to reveal three women in late nineteenth-century garb.

"Cecilia!" Willie gasped.

"*Mutter*!" Gus exclaimed.

"Mama!" Schlomo cried.

"And now if you will excuse us, please," Xofia said to her amazed and preoccupied guests. "Johnnine and I have an audience with The Powers, after which I will return."

Xofia led Johnnine, who was suddenly prey to a sinking heart, out of the room as the three mothers rushed toward their famous sons.

"Liebling!" said Willie's plump, dark, and attractive young mother.

"Shooshoo!" Schlomo's mother was sophisticated and coquettish in a wasp-waisted black dress edged with bugle beads.

"Gussiegussiegander!" Gus cringed at his large, plainly-dressed mother's use of a childhood nickname.

Johnnine watched the mothers smothering their sons, enveloping them in their arms and clutching them to their respective bosoms, with a strange sensation. Something like envy mixed with nausea.

Outside the hotel, Xofia smiled ruefully as they took their seats in another empty *fiaker*. "Let us hope they have an enlightening visit together."

Johnnine looked in through the Sacher's dining room windows. Gus, Willie, and Schlomo appeared to be doing their best to disentangle themselves from their mothers' grasps. "Why does it matter?"

"The fate of the Earth may depend on it," Xofia said enigmatically.

"But they're all dead—"

"Ah, but only temporarily."

Seraph A. and the cherubs flew to pick up the shafts and carry them into the All Souls' air. "The Palace of the Powers, please, Aloysius."

The All Souls' Waiting Room

Johnnine's mind was whirring. She was getting tired of all the grown-up guessing games. Her head ached trying to figure out what was going on. There were no cute guys, no books, no Devil Dogs. Mostly all there were were analysts and mother figures. In other words, Mondo Bizarro was a lot like Earth but without the pleasurable Earthly sensations. Was this what she had tried to kill herself for—to end up here?

The cab whisked them up through a thick layer of clouds and bore them into a magnificent throne-room with vast floors of polished green marble. Off in the distance, Johnnine could just see a sumptuous gilded throne chair mounted on a high, round dais. A dimly-visible male deity faced forward into rays of dazzling light that pierced the surrounding clouds. It looked like a stage set designed to impress people.

"Mr. Powers," Xofia whispered.

The *fiaker* took them around to the back of the dais, where a female deity sat facing backward into the dark.

"Mrs. Powers," Xofia added.

"Mrs. Powers?" Johnnine was incredulous. "You mean there's a woman God?"

"Of course, darling! How could it be otherwise? We don't come from one gender, do we? Aren't they magnificent?" Xofia gazed at The Powers reverently.

Johnnine's sense of fair play was offended. She shifted impatiently on the cab seat, unable to share Xofia's awe. "But why don't they share the throne?"

"Very perceptive of you, darling. Just what the Committee for a Better Universe is working on. Things get into an horrific mess without the right balance of masculine and feminine—anyway, just stand up and raise your hand while you look in their general direction. They know what you've come to ask. They know everything—I find them a little daunting, actually..."

Feeling more than slightly timid and a little bit foolish, Johnnine stood up and raised her hand. The open cab shook slightly—or was it her knees?

The Powers slowly turned their heads in her direction. For some reason, Johnnine could only seem to see their outlines, but what she could see was clear enough: first the mute Missus, then the dazzling Mister Powers raised their right fists, turned their hands over, and pointed a thumb at the ground. Then—did she imagine it?—Johnnine thought she saw Mrs. Powers wink at her.

"Well, there you have it, darling," Xofia sighed with relief. "Ticket denied. I must say I'm glad. Back to Earth for you—"

Johnnine sat back down heavily, causing the old-fashioned cab, whose ethereal essence was probably horse pucky, to bounce on its springs. She wasn't all that surprised at The Powers' verdict, but she felt called upon to assert herself. "What about my free will?"

Xofia laughed. "Oh, you don't get *that* much free will, darling. Just enough to get you into trouble and out again. Your time is up when your time is up. And yours isn't yet, you've got too much to learn."

Johnnine looked apprehensively around the enormous throne room, expecting bouncers to rush out at her from behind the fluted columns. Eighty-sixed from Mondo Bizarro, she thought. And returned to my old messed-up, all-there-is life.

"The cherubs will escort you to the edge of the Waiting Room. I shall rejoin the reunion of the three wise men and their mothers—as referee."

Johnnine's eyes filled with tears as she turned to Xofia. "That means I won't see you again." About this she felt truly bereft.

Xofia held Johnnine's chin with her hand. Once again, it felt like being brushed with the warm tips of feathery wings. She smiled deeply into Johnnine's eyes, though for one brief, jolting moment she looked like Dinah Hapgood before she returned to the sultry siren looks of Tallulah Bankhead. "Not literally, perhaps, at least until you've finished this life. But I live through you, darling, through all women, for that matter, never forget that. Oh, here, I meant to give you these—" Xofia reached under her seat and took out a bundle of rags.

"What are they?"

"Your unowned feelings, darling. You have to take them back with you, you can't leave them here."

"What do I do with them?" Johnnine asked, accepting the sorry little bundle.

"Put them on, wear them. A lot of them are feelings about your mother. Don't banish them just because they're painful. They are some of the better parts of your soul. *Adieux*—"

And then it seemed that in the blink of an eye, Johnnine was being borne through the air to the edge of the cloud that marked the farthermost boundary of the All Souls' Waiting Room. Gently, the cherubs put her down in front of the celestial telescope. Johnnine peered through it down towards Earth. She vaguely remembered having done this same thing, performed this same rite many times before, but even so, she hesitated.

"All that *sturm*, all that *drang*," she pleaded to the little seraph hovering above her. Past lifetimes of lessons flooded over her, as well as a vision of all the giant holes in her spiritual understanding. She knew she *needed* to go back but that was a far cry from desperately *wanting* to. Would she be able to do any better this time? Wasn't there any way of stalling? "Come on, you guys, have a heart. You could just let me hang out here, couldn't you? I won't tell if you won't."

Fa, So, and La were lined up in the air. They did an imitation of Monkey See No Evil, Monkey Hear No Evil, Monkey Speak No Evil. Ti and Do flew to either end of Johnnine's soul form. On a whistle command from Seraph A., which sounded particularly harsh to Johnnine's ears, they picked her up and

The All Souls' Waiting Room

began swinging her back and forth by her arms and legs. Once, twice, then a third and last time they swung her out over the edge of the fleecy clouds and let her go. As she was released, she thought she heard a celestial chorus humming Brahms' Lullaby: *Rock-a-bye-baby, in-the-treetops, when-the-bough-breaks, the-cradle-will-DROP.*

Seraph A. followed her progress back down towards Earth through the Waiting Room's old-fashioned, ornate brass telescope. Her soul no longer looked quite so bruised and pummeled, there was a promising pinkish glow around it. In a way it was too bad. Her chances now no longer in question, at least for a while, Aloysius would not be able to get good odds on her survival.

Johnnine came to in her apartment, on her couch. Moppie was whimpering and yipping at her and the phone was ringing. Her first olfactory input told her she was in the vicinity of vomit. Turning her head, she saw a small, smelly puddle on the rug below her head. Christ, she thought, I must have done that in my sleep. Maybe that's why I'm alive, I threw up half the pills. Instead of being depressed, she felt strangely elated. She looked around the room with new eyes. At the nice red upholstered chair and walnut dresser the Bermans had given her, the simple little desk Monte had made of a white formica top and black wrought-iron legs. It felt good to be back in her body, her healthy, young body. Surely someday someone would love the lonely, longing soul inside.

She sat up, dizzy at first as she reached for the phone. But there was no one there. They must have given up, she thought. Then she shuddered, rubbing her arms. Like I almost did.

Her watch read four o'clock. It was daylight, which meant she had been out for almost twenty-four hours. She couldn't remember anything since she lay down on the couch, no dreams, no—wait, hadn't there been something about a bunch of angels? And hadn't she seen scenes from her life, like they said drowning people saw? She wasn't sure, her mind was still cloudy. The radio next door was still playing, only now it was Mongo Santamaria's "Watermelon Man."

Johnnine was still numb with pain and shame at failing calculus. She didn't know what she would do now. She supposed she was through with veterinary medicine, or rather, that it was through with her. She didn't think she could take going back to C. C. N. Y., it was too big, too impersonal. There were other courses she'd like to take, psych, maybe, and English lit, and film, she could always transfer schools, change majors. But first she had to get a handle on her life. A little woozily, she cleaned up the rug, brushed her teeth, and changed her clothes. Then she called her mother and told her she needed to see her.

"Why, of course, ducklet, I've been hoping you'd call—" Dinah said.

Johnnine didn't hold out much hope for their interview, but she had to let her mother know where she was at. Moppie's leash and collar jangled musically as she took them off their nail by the door. "Wanna go out?"

Moppie barked and danced around her feet.

Johnnine's head ached. "Oy," she said. She put on her fake camel's hair coat and turned off the lights.

She was almost to the stairs when she stopped in her tracks, scooped up Moppie, and ran quickly back to the apartment. Without turning the lights back on, she grabbed her suicide note off the bureau. At first she stuffed the number ten envelope in her coat pocket, but on her way out through the kitchen she took it out, tore it in half, and threw it in the garbage can.

She hustled herself and Moppie down the four flights of worn stairs. The physical activity cleared her head because out of the blue, three fully-formed sentences arrived unbidden in her mind, like the news flashes on The New York Times building: "Johnnine had chosen the pay-first, fly-later plan of childhood. She had paid. Now all she had to do was learn to fly."

What the hell? she wondered, bolting out of her decrepit building and onto dark and dirty little Leroy Street, which today looked quaint and grimly picturesque, like a scene out of Dickens. Sounded like the last line of a novel or something, she thought, as she ran to catch a passing cab.

About the Author

Wright's reviews and literary humor have appeared in magazines and newspapers, including The New York Times Book Review. Her dramatic work has been produced on Bay Area radio stations and she is the 2001 recipient of a Marin Arts Council playwriting grant. This is her first novel. Born and raised in New York City, Wright now lives in Northern California and considers herself biographically bi-coastal.

CPSIA information can be obtained at www.ICGtesting.com
Printed in the USA
LVOW12*0314050314

376075LV00001B/22/A